By the same author

RING A-ROSES
MAGGIE CRAIG
A LEAF IN THE WIND
EMMA SPARROW
GEMINI GIRLS
THE LISTENING SILENCE
LISA LOGAN
THE CLOGGER'S CHILD
POLLY PILGRIM

A BETTER WORLD THAN THIS

Marie Joseph

GUILD PUBLISHING
LONDON

Copyright © Marie Joseph 1986

All rights reserved

This edition published 1986 by
Book Club Associates
by arrangement with
Century Hutchinson Ltd

Typeset by Avocet Ltd
Printed and bound in Great Britain by
Mackays, Chatham, Kent

For Mary, Norrie and Jamie

PART ONE

Chapter One

'Have a look through the window, Daisy! You've got Clark Gable out there queueing up for a spud pie and a basin o' peas!'

The girl holding out her hand for change from half-a-crown turned round to the crowded shop and winked. 'Dimples 'n all. Wouldn't mind finding one like him in me Christmas cracker!'

The cotton mill across the street from the pie shop had closed its gates for the day, and the weavers were clattering in to buy a two-pound loaf or a bag of barm-cakes to spread with margarine and jam for their tea, if money wouldn't run to fish and chips again that week.

Behind the wide counter Daisy Bell passed over the crusty loaves, standing them first on a layer of tissue paper which she twisted swiftly into little points.

'I'm glad I put me curlers in last night,' she confided, jerking her head towards the window. 'D'you reckon it really is Clark Gable? Do you suppose he saw me beauty when he was passing and wants me for his next film?'

She stood first on one foot, then the other. It had been a long day, starting for Daisy at half-past four that morning, and once the rush was over she was looking forward to having her tea, then going to the second-house pictures. Sliding three Eccles cakes into a paper bag, she considered carefully. Evelyn Laye was on at the Olympia. 'Music, Comedy, and Charm' the advertisement in the *Weekly Times* had said.

'Four barm-cakes, Mrs Margerison.' She smiled, slipping them floury and soft into a bag. She quite liked Evelyn Laye. Possessing hair as fair as Daisy's was dark, the musical-comedy star had a look of appealing fragility about her. Evelyn Laye looked like a fainter, and fainters always came off best. Daisy often considered fainting when her legs were aching and her feet killing her. She'd be good at it too after watching so many glamorous stars of so many Hollywood films slide gracefully to the floor with soft little moans.

Daisy spent a lot of time dwelling on glamour, there not being much of it about in the north-east Lancashire cotton towns during the depressed middle thirties.

The shop was slowly emptying, and 'Clark Gable' was coming closer by the minute. Daisy reached for a slab of parkin, leaning sideways for a better look at him. He really did bear more than a passing resemblance to the handsome star who, in a recent film, had startled audiences by revealing that beneath his shirt he was vestless. How *manly*, Daisy had decided dreamily. She stole another look at the man now approaching the counter.

Yes, he had the star's broad shoulders, and the black hair springing away from a crumpled forehead. Plus the same air of cheerful impudence as he grinned at her, and jingled a handful of coins in his hand. He wore a chauffeur's pale grey uniform, buttoned down the side of the jacket, with epaulet shoulder pieces. A peaked cap was pushed cheekily to the back of his head. Not from hereabouts, definitely not from round here, Daisy told herself, flashing him her open friendly smile.

'And what can I get for you, sir?' His eyes were dark blue, his eyelashes as long as a girl's. Oh, yes, she was right. They certainly didn't grow men like this vision up here. The men in this town all looked as if they'd been grown in the dark, like mushrooms.

'I'll have two of those, please.' The voice was low, with a caress in it.

Daisy poshed up her accent as she spoke to him. 'They're

called Eccles cakes, sir. Me mother's speciality. The kids call them flies' coffins. They're luvly spread with a bit of butter and warmed up in the oven.'

'Are they now?' He handed over the money, and was she imagining it or did his hand close over hers for a second as she gave him change from a shilling?

The shop was empty now, and he stood there, smiling, swinging the paper bag from his hand.

'I'm afraid these will have to be eaten as they are. In my boss's car. And without making crumbs.' He leaned forward. 'It's a Rolls-Royce. A Phantom. It goes at over seventy miles an hour.' His eyes narrowed into mischievous slits. 'I once saw my boss whip out a gun and shoot a bird stone dead for doing its whatsit on the bonnet.'

'You never!' Daisy was enchanted. He talked as if he was wobbling a hot potato round his mouth. A bit like Ronald Colman. 'You're having me on.'

'Nope.' He began to back away, his broad forehead crinkling into mock anxiety. 'I've left it parked outside the mill. Do many cars get pinched round here?'

'Well, they wouldn't get far with it, would they?' Daisy's eyes twinkled. 'Aw, mister. Folks round here are still using hand-carts for flitting. A lad with his wits about him can make a penny a bucket from horse droppings.'

As she laughed out loud, Sam Barnet stopped in his tracks. He'd never heard a woman sound quite like that before. It was a child's laugh, throaty and uninhibited. Warm, filled with gaiety as though it could obliterate all the sorrows of the world. Motherly too, and yet she couldn't be more than in her middle twenties. He glanced at her hand as she lifted it to push a wayward strand of dark brown hair into place. No ring. . . .

On an impulse he stepped forward, oblivious to the fact that an elderly woman was watching him intently from a crack in a door to his left.

'I know this sounds a bit of a cheek, but would you let me take you to the pictures tonight? I'm free when I've driven

5

my boss to his hotel.' His smile was now that of a little boy lost. 'I'm a complete stranger to these parts. You'd do me a favour if you came with me.' He held out his hand. 'Sam Barnet. Chauffeur to a London businessman who hopes to bring a deal of work to this town.' He grinned, the dimples flashing. 'Well, what do you say, Daisy? See, I know your name, so that's a beginning.'

Daisy could see her mother standing motionless behind the door leading into the back living room. Listening so intently it was a wonder her ears weren't flapping. *Spying*, if you decided to call a spade a spade, which Daisy always did. She could almost smell the disapproval emanating from every pore of the squat little figure with its pouter-pigeon bosom encased in the old-fashioned black marocain blouse.

Daisy's dark brown gaze flickered from her mother's set face to the handsome one smiling at her across the width of the counter. Marking time, she picked up a cloth and gave the mahogany surface an unnecessary wipe. A tiny frisson of excitement inside her told her she was being picked up. That she had clicked. She, Daisy Bell, spinster of this parish, good-for-a-laugh Daisy from the pie shop. Liked by just about everybody, but loved, alas, by no one in particular.

Her mother's shadow shifted slightly and Daisy's mind was made up.

'Well . . .' she said, pretending to consider. 'All right, then. I can cancel the engagement I already had. No problem. Call for me about half-past seven at the door round the corner by the bakehouse. Ta-ra, then. Enjoy your cakes.'

Smiling as she turned away, hearing the shop door ping closed, then widening her eyes as she pretended to see her mother for the first time.

'Well!' Martha Bell had never minced her words and she wasn't going to start now. 'I hope you know what you're doing. What about that girl up Oswald Street who went out with that commercial traveller and was never seen again?'

'What about her?' Daisy could feel the euphoria of the past minutes fading away.

'White Slave Traffic,' Martha said, going over to lock the shop door. 'An Arab's plaything that poor girl will be now. Doped and drugged into a life of shame.'

She marched through into the living room, muttering to herself, knowing she had wiped the look of happiness from her daughter's face, and not sorry, neither. Accepting too that she still saw her only daughter as a clumsy little girl with ribbons in her hair that never stayed tied, an apple-cheeked child with straight hair and round horn-rimmed glasses always slipping down her nose.

'I'll go and get the tea.' Daisy walked quickly through into the kitchen and opened the pantry door. She stared at the basin of potted meat on the cold slate slab, but made no attempt to reach in and get it. Through the gauze over the tiny window she could see the bakehouse wall, the bricks running damp, the recent pointing standing out like fretwork.

On her fourteenth birthday ten years ago she had left school and started working in the bakehouse, with flour in her hair and murder in her heart. She had told herself then that this was the way it was going to be for the rest of her life. And she'd been right. Daisy gloomed at the thick white basin. Pricking pies round their edges and knifing them to let out the steam, it seemed at times as if she was driving the blade into her own heart. Education could have opened the doors to a wider world than this. With education you could have a face like the back of a frying pan and it wouldn't matter. Schooling opened doors to the world of dreams Daisy was sure lay far beyond the confines of the Lancashire market town. Think about the Brontës. They would never have been discovered by a Hollywood talent scout, not according to Branwell's portrait of them, but think of the passions concealed in those flat maidenly bosoms!

'I've mashed the tea, Daisy!' Martha's voice seemed to be coming from far away.

Daisy took no notice.... *Passion*. That was a word Daisy often pondered on; a word she had never said aloud.

7

Carrying the basin of potted meat into the living room, she set it down on the table. What would happen if she were suddenly to turn to her mother and say:

'There is a need in me for passion, Mother. I am twenty-four years old, and all I know of passion is one kiss on the way home from a chapel hot-pot supper when I was seventeen. It was a French kiss, and for three weeks I thought I was going to have a baby, but now I'm willing to give passion another try.'

'What are you going to put on if you're set on going?'

Daisy blinked at the sound of her mother's voice. 'Me mink, of course,' she said dreamily.

'I told you that bottle-green coat did nothing for you when you got it.' Martha upended the potted meat neatly like a blancmange on to a plate and began to slice it to have with the tomatoes arranged in a blue dish. 'And your edge-to-edge will be too draughty. Unless, of course, he's coming for you in the Rolls.'

'You heard that too?' Daisy decided, not for the first time, that she didn't like her mother. *Loved* her, but didn't *like* her. Was that possible?

'He won't turn up.' Martha was sprinkling sugar on her tomato to bring out the flavour. 'He'll be like a commercial traveller, with a girl in every town he visits.'

'But I'm not a girl, am I?' Daisy got up and stared at her reflection in the fluted mirror over the fireplace. 'And *he's* not a boy, is he?'

'Fancies himself in that uniform. With them gaiters.' Martha's eyes skinned over with spite. 'Ivor Novello would have him in the chorus quick if he clapped eyes on him.'

'Mother?' Daisy turned round, her eyes willing Martha, just this once, to be *glad* for her. Even to laugh with her and agree that no harm could come of a visit to the pictures with a man who would be gone tomorrow. But Martha had her martyr's face on her. So Daisy sat down again at the table and sprinkled salt on *her* tomato. Just to be different. 'You're right, he won't turn up,' she said, reaching for a slice of bread

8

and butter, relenting and choosing one with rounded edges because she knew her mother only liked the square.

'Your father wouldn't like it.' Martha was making a sandwich from a slice of the jellied meat. 'Revolving in his grave at this very moment, more than likely.'

Daisy stared down at her plate.... When I was a girl, her mind screamed silently, no more than a girl, my father left the bakehouse one day to help repair the engine at the mill across the street. Because he was a wizard with engines he helped out, then lay trapped beneath a mass of machinery. And since that day, ten long years ago, I've tried to take his place....

'Don't worry. He won't come,' she said. 'Me father can lie undisturbed.'

'Till the trumpets shall sound,' said Martha, starting on a slice of date and walnut loaf spread thickly with butter.

Sam came promptly at half-past seven, giving them plenty of time to queue for the second house. Daisy was upstairs getting ready, just in case, trying on a hat in several different ways. Best like a push-back beret, she decided, with her hair rolled up into a sausage anchored by Kirby grips.

She heard her mother let him in, and the murmur of voices. After a last despairing glance at her reflection in the tripled mirror on her dressing-table she ran quickly downstairs, pulling on a pair of black leather gloves with fluted gauntlets.

'Hello there!' Sam came forward with outstretched hands to greet her.

Just as though he had never expected to see her again, Daisy thought, wondering what had happened to the handsome man in the smart grey uniform, hating the shabby brown suit and the way he was carrying a raincoat over his shoulder instead of his arm. The very gesture made him seem alien somehow.

Sam smiled at her, wondering what she had done to the glorious mop of curly hair, telling himself that surely she couldn't have cut it off since he saw her a couple of hours ago.

9

'Well, you'd best be off then.' Martha jerked her head towards the mantelpiece. 'You've forgotten your glasses,' she said with spite, pointing at a shabby, peeling case. 'She won't be able to tell the News from the big picture without them,' she informed Sam sweetly. 'See she puts them on, won't you, Mr Barnet.'

'Your mother's a card.' Outside in the street Sam did a twiddling step to get to the polite side of the pavement. When he put his trilby on, the wide curving brim shadowed his face.

He isn't a bit like Clark Gable now, Daisy thought. More like George Raft in *Scarface*, in fact. He stopped to put the raincoat on, then tucked her left hand into the crook of his elbow so that they walked along together, welded like lovers.

Daisy gave a little gurgling laugh, just to show she was used to that kind of thing; she hoped they would meet someone she knew, but it was so cold and wet, people hurried past with heads bowed against the driving wind. He said something to her, but the freezing wind tossed his words away, so they walked the rest of the way in silence.

In the pictures it was better. To Daisy's delight Sam bought two tickets for the circle, and for the first time in her life Daisy walked up the wide shallow stairs with their rubber nosings to seats exactly in the middle of the back row.

She touched the bulge in the front of her handbag and decided against wearing the glasses. What did it matter if the figures on the silver screen were a blur? And what if she couldn't read the adverts, or make sense of the trailers for next week's performance? At least if Sam kissed her he could do so without bumping his nose on the despised tortoiseshell frames.

Adolescence had been and gone without touching Daisy. She had never dreamed long hours away in sulky idleness; never danced in the Public Hall till two o'clock in the morning; never gone to late-night parties, or even stayed up late listening to the big bands on the wireless – Jack Hylton,

Ray Noble and Ambrose. Since her father's accident her life had been ruled by the great fire-oven in the bakehouse. The gaping black hole that gobbled up coal with a never-flagging appetite.

Now, in the warm gloom of the cinema, she had the feeling she was sitting in the middle of a cloud. When Sam reached for her hand she curled her fingers into his. A sensation like pain shivered through her. When the big picture came on the music swelled as if it was coming from somewhere deep inside her. Sam's arm was round her shoulder now, his fingers in her hair as he loosened the Kirby grips from the carefully rolled sausage. Obligingly Daisy removed her hat, placing it on top of her handbag and the bulge concealing the hated spectacles.

He kissed her as the music soared three beats to a bar. He struggled with the buttons on her coat, and when his hand slid inside and cupped her breast she trembled, partly with happiness but mostly with shame.

'No!' When his fingers began to move gently round and round, Daisy sat bolt upright and pushed his hand away.

To stare unseeing at the silver screen, where a dog – or it could have been a cat – lolloped across a lawn dappled in sunshine.

When she got home she crept upstairs to undress in the dark, but light or no light her mother appeared, standing by the bedroom door in her long flannel nightdress.

'Well?' Without her teeth Martha's plump face looked as if it had been squashed in a nut-cracker. 'You've not come straight home, have you?'

'We were talking.' Getting into bed, Daisy pulled the sheet up to her chin. 'I have to be up in less than five hours, Mother. I'll tell you about it tomorrow.'

'You've not washed your face, neither. You'll have spots the size of ping-pong balls leaving that powder muck on. Sets like biscuits on your cheeks when you sweat in the night.' Taking a step forward into the room Martha clasped the brass knob on the bed-end with both hands. 'That man is no good.'

'Oh, Mother, you don't know him.' Daisy's feet had found the comfort of a stone hot-water bottle. She closed her eyes in a kind of shame. 'He's a kind man. And he's in work. He's got a good job.'

'He's a southerner.' Martha's hands tightened on the brass knob. 'He's a here-today, gone-tomorrow sort of man. Smarmy. Unstable. Too good-looking for his own good. Men like him prey on a girl's feelings, then leave her with her heart broke into little pieces.' She polished the knob with the sleeve of her nightgown. 'Why did he pick on *you*, when the shop was full of girls from the mill? Why ask *you*, and not one of them?'

'I wonder?' Daisy's voice was rough with the hurt of her mother's words. 'You can ask him yourself tomorrow. He's taking his boss to Burnley and Padiham, but they should be back here by late afternoon. I've asked him to his tea.'

'So it's serious between you, then?' Martha sniffed. 'Talk about not letting the grass grow underneath your feet . . . you've not even given yours a chance to seed!'

In the soft plushed cinema he had kissed her. Daisy traced the contour of her lips. He had tried to touch her, but when she said he mustn't he hadn't persisted. His hands had been cool and hard, and now and again she had stolen a glance at his profile, stern and somehow beautiful in repose. Like a head on a coin.

Daisy closed her eyes, willing a sleep that would not come. On the way home they had talked and talked.

'Why have you never married, Daisy?'

'Because I'm an unclaimed blessing.'

He had stopped then and laughed out loud before suddenly lifting her off her feet and whirling her round and round. And she'd felt just like Ginger Rogers or Anna Neagle, dancing in the street with a man who turned out to be a millionaire, ready to whisk her off to a life spent lying on white fur rugs, wearing backless satin gowns, listening to the popping of champagne corks.

Sam came at half-past five, and because it was a Thursday and half-day closing, the shop had been shut since one.

To Daisy's surprise her mother had said nothing when she emerged from her lie-down to see the table set with the rose-sprigged cups with gold fluted rims, and the cloth embroidered with blue forget-me-nots. There was ham off the bone, Canary tomatoes in the blue dish, four small pots of shrimps with the butter softening nicely on the tops, a plate of thinly-cut bread, and a three-tiered cake-stand. Scones on the bottom plate, risen high and brown, fatty-cake on the middle tier, short with best lard and stiff with currants. And on the topmost layer a feather-light sponge sprinkled with caster sugar and split with home-made raspberry jam.

Sam apologized for not having had the time to change out of his uniform, but Daisy was glad. She told him to make himself at home and take off his jacket, and when she saw that instead of braces he was wearing a brown leather belt which nipped in his narrow waist she couldn't look away from him. If a man could be described as beautiful, she decided, then Sam Barnet was beautiful. She was so aware of herself she blushed each time she spoke. She prayed she looked all right; sure she did not.

'Your Auntie Edna's coming.' Martha made the announcement without looking at Daisy. 'So we'd best not tuck in till she arrives.'

A headache of despair settled on Daisy. Her mother's sister lived two doors up the street by the bakehouse, and the two were welded together with an affection compounded of envy and spite. Edna was one up at the moment, for although her husband Arnold had been out of work for two years, her daughter Betty was married and pregnant at the age of nineteen.

'My sister's daughter's husband works at the Town Hall.' A malicious expression drooped the lines of Martha's round face. 'With a pension to come when he's sixty-five.'

Daisy sat next to Sam on the two-seater hide settee with its velvet cushions, feeling sorry for him and sorrier for

13

herself. She tried hard to think of something interesting to say, and wondered if her mother knew that the bones of her corsets were outlined through the tightness of her brown dress.

'Did you know, Mr Barnet,' Martha said into the silence, 'that through the wireless the chimes of Big Ben can be heard up here before a man walking down Whitehall can hear them?'

'No, I didn't.' Sam grinned. 'That's marvellous.'

'Do they have the Means Test in London?' Martha's answering smile was evil. 'It would do a lot of them snobs good to come up here and see what goes on. Folks up here are starving while they line their pockets.'

'Yoo-hoo!'

At the sound of her auntie's voice Daisy gave a huge sigh of relief. Once her mother got into this mood there was no knowing what she would say next.

'Well, then!' Edna came into the room, a sparse little woman with a neat monkey face and grey hair permed to an immovable frizz. She was wearing a green dress fastened for modesty's sake with a large gilt brooch in the shape of an anchor. 'So this is Daisy's new beau?' She held out a hand and as she came closer Daisy saw the layer of talcum powder dusting her nose. 'Pleased to meet you, I must say. I've heard a lot about you!'

It was worse at the table. Sam ate with head lowered, answering personal questions with a quiet dignity, although Daisy could sense his irritation. She wished she could take his hand and lead him away, out of the house, into the rain-swept street outside, and never mind if it took the curl out of her hair.

'Our Betty's expecting a happy event, bless her,' Edna said into the lull between the ham and the cakes. 'I think nineteen's just the right age to start a family so you can enjoy them when you're young.' She accepted a scone. 'Do you like children, Mr Barnet?'

There was a slight hesitation. 'Excuse me, ladies.' Sam

pushed back his chair, leaned across and picked up his jacket from the back of the settee. Taking a wallet from the inside pocket, he took out a photograph.

'My children,' he said, offering it to Edna first. 'The boy is six and the girl is five.'

'So you're a widower, then, Mr Barnet?' Edna's features sharpened visibly.

'No.' Sam shook his head, smiling. 'No, I'm not a widower. My wife is very much alive.'

Daisy saw the glitter of triumph in Edna's button eyes; saw her almost hug herself in delight as she helped herself to a second scone and a further dollop of raspberry jam.

'You know, you could be an announcer on the wireless, Mr Barnet,' she said, rooting for a raspberry seed in a back tooth. 'Your accent would be just right. You must have a most interesting job driving a limousine all over the country. I suppose your wife has got used to you always being away?'

Martha seemed to have been struck dumb. Not daring to meet her eyes, Daisy pretended they needed a fresh pot of tea. Taking it through into the kitchen she set the kettle to boil on the gas stove and leaned against the sink, listening to her auntie's voice going on and on, interspersed with refined little bursts of laughter.

Why hadn't he told her he was married? Last night they'd talked and talked and he had never said a word about a wife. Squeezing her eyes tight shut Daisy willed the threat of tears back. She would never have asked him to his tea had she known he was married. And her mother would never have asked Auntie Edna in if she hadn't wanted to show off – show her sister that *her* daughter could get a man too.

For a moment Daisy saw her cousin Betty's husband in her mind's eye. Middle-aged at twenty-three, living with his mother-in-law and going off to work with his red hair smarmed back, and forty-two years to serve before he got his pension.

No wonder Martha had wanted to swank with a man who resembled Clark Gable and dressed in his chauffeur's

15

uniform looked like Maurice Chevalier in *The Merry Widow*.

Now it would be all over that Daisy Bell from the pie shop was knocking about with a married man. Angrily she brushed back an escaping tear with the back of her hand.

'I'm off now, Daisy.'

When Sam appeared, buttoning himself into his jacket, she could sense the irritation held tightly inside him. He was smiling at her, but his blue eyes stayed cold

'That woman. . . .' He jerked his head towards the living room. 'If she was thrown to the lions they'd spit her out.'

Surprising Daisy, he took the teapot from her, then held her firmly, forcing her to meet his eyes.

'I'm sorry, love. Believe me, I had no intention of starting a family bust-up when I took you to the pictures last night.' He shook her gently. 'And I never dreamed that accepting an invitation to tea today cast me in the role of your suitor.'

'Oh, how can you say that?' Humiliation brought the tears to Daisy's eyes. She trembled with the shame of it. With self-disgust she remembered how he had touched her breast in the pictures and how she had only knocked his hand away because she was scared. Her lack of sophistication was total. Her experience of men less than nothing. 'Yes, go,' she said loudly. 'I'm sorry you've been embarrassed. Please . . . just go.'

'I never knew that such narrow-mindedness existed.' This time his smile was genuine as he trailed a finger down Daisy's cheek. 'But you're okay, love. You're a lot more than okay. I've enjoyed meeting you.' Pulling her to him, he kissed the tear-stained cheek she tried to twist away from him, then opened the door and stepped outside, leaving her alone with a terrible all-enveloping shame.

'Daisy?' Edna's voice was wobbly with a vibrant satisfaction. 'He's gone then, has he?' She advanced towards the teapot. 'Your mother and me's spittin' feathers waiting for another cup of tea. Aw, come on, love. He's not the only fish in the sea, and you weren't to know he was married.' Licking a finger she smoothed an eyebrow. 'Good riddance to bad rubbish, and a good job I was here to rumble him. There's no flies on your Auntie Edna.'

'I'm going to my room.'

Daisy's face was wrenched out of shape with the force of her emotions, but Edna noticed nothing. 'You'll be frozen stiff up there, love. It's chucking it down in buckets outside.'

'I'll go down the yard first.' Pulling the door open so violently it was in danger of coming adrift from its hinges, Daisy escaped. Hardly feeling the torrential rain beating down on her head she lifted the latch of the yard door and stepped out into the street.

And miraculously, round the corner by the shop front, Sam was there. He had put his raincoat on and he was standing at the kerb pulling the collar up round his throat. In the darkness, in his peaked cap, he looked, she thought, like Lew Ayres in *All Quiet on the Western Front*.

When she clutched his arm he was startled at first, then concerned.

'For God's sake, Daisy! You're wet through. Here, come back here.' He pulled her backwards into the doorway of a greengrocer's shop, into a pungent smell of rotting cabbages and bruised apples. 'Now then. What's all this about?'

'I want to talk to you.' Daisy heard her voice, hoarse with uncontrollable emotion, and yet a part of her was so calm, so determined, it was as though she was in a film reading from a script. A wild woman, drenched with rain, pleading with the man she loved not to leave her. 'Not here.' Taking Sam by the hand she led him round the corner and into her own backyard. 'Shush,' she said, although he hadn't uttered a sound. 'In here,' she whispered, opening a door and pulling him inside. 'It's nice and warm in here.'

'Where the hell are we?' Sam waved a hand in front of his face. 'I can't see a thing.'

'I can't put the light on.' Daisy reached up and took a large torch from a high shelf. 'They would see it from the house.' She shone the torch on a pile of coal, the overflow from a wooden bunker. 'See. That over there is the fire-oven, and here . . . this is where I shovel the coal. Into the firebox, you can see the ashbox below it. And the heat of the oven is controlled by that damper up on the wall.'

She was like a tour guide explaining things to a group of schoolchildren. She was close to hysteria; she could feel it like a spreading lump in her throat. She did not need to shine the torch into Sam's face to know that he was staring at her with a look of mild astonishment. All she knew was that she had stopped him walking down the street, out of her life, for ever.

She had to keep him, just for a little while. For long enough to explain that asking him to tea had been a terrible mistake. That a worse mistake had been her mother jumping the gun and asking Edna along. Only to show off, of course, to make it plain that Daisy could get a man if she wanted, that she wasn't well on her way to being an old maid.

And most important of all, Sam had to be told to forget the whole thing. To remember her, if at all, with some kind of respect. No, that wasn't true. She didn't want him *remembering* her. She wanted to keep him, to never have to say goodbye, to love him, to have him make love to her. . . .

There was no pride in her thinking, no way she could explain, even to herself, how she felt. She was in an alien world she had never entered before. In this world she was young, she was beautiful, and he was there, the man she loved. . . . Daisy shivered. It was like all the films she had ever seen, only better. Or worse.

'Let's sit down, shall we? Then you can tell me what all this is about.' Sam's eyes were used to the darkness now, and taking her hand he led her over to a pile of sacks in a corner.

He was behaving, he knew, in a way he hadn't behaved since he was fifteen years old. All spots and incipient moustache, and kissing a girl on the top deck of the tram on the way home from school. Daisy's hair had come out of curl with the rain. She sighed when he put his arm round her, snuggling close to him like a child, with her hair tickling his chin and her arm lying loosely round his waist.

There was a sweet vanilla smell, and Sam could see cobwebs festooning the corners of the whitewashed walls. There were baking tins piled high on shelves, and two long tables at the far end of the large room with open-tread stairs leading to an upper floor. In the light from a street lamp directly outside Sam saw the gleam of a piece of machinery clamped to the wall and guessed it was some kind of mixer for the dough. From somewhere deep inside Sam's bank of memories he saw himself as a small boy helping the village baker with his round. Hanging the baskets on door knockers, baskets filled with orders of rock cakes, doughnuts, crusty loaves of bread and Atora beef suet wrapped in greaseproof paper. The crust of that bread, he remembered, had crackled and flaked in his mouth.

'Now then....' He tightened his hold on Daisy, whispering into her hair. 'What's all this about. We're too *old* for this kind of thing. We're not a couple of kids snidging in corners. Are we?' he said, giving her a little shake.

'It's nice in here, isn't it?'

Her voice was soft, light and dream-tinged. Like a woman's when the act of love is over and she needs to be held for a while, Sam told himself.

'I like it in here very early in the mornings, before the men come in, and the mad rush starts.' Daisy's breath was close to his ear. 'I tried to tell you about this place last night, how I like being in here on my own, well, *love* being in here on my own really.'

She could hear herself speaking in what her mother would undoubtedly have called her 'poetry' voice, but it wasn't intentional. It was just the way she felt, all dreamy and far away. Her upturned face was gentled with love.

'I come in here long before the knocker-up comes down the street with his long stick tapping on the windows to get folk up for the mill. I come in here before the chill has gone from the streets, but it's warm and cosy quiet, with no sound but the cinders clinking down into the ashpan over there. And sometimes, where there's a moon, it makes the oven

19

door shiny and black as treacle. Like a Pontefract cake. And sometimes the policeman on his beat stops and knocks on the window. He comes in if it's wet and shakes the rain from his cape. "Nasty neet, Daisy," he says. "You mean nasty morning," I say, and I make him a pot of tea. And when he goes I climb on that stool and look through the window to watch him go up the street, with the light from the lamp silvering the drizzle.' She sighed. 'Mornings can be very beautiful, Sam.'

'You're a funny one.' Sam shifted his position slightly. Her voice . . . like warmed honey poured over silk, he decided. A voice to come home to, he told himself. 'You're a lonely girl, aren't you, Daisy?'

Her head came up so quickly it butted him on the chin. 'Me? Lonely? What a daft idea! It's like bedlam when the men come in, and goodness, you saw me in the shop, run off me feet. And I make enough noise for a dozen. I'm always being told that.'

'*I'm* lonely.' Sam gently pushed her head down again. 'Most people are, if they admit it. It's only the very lucky ones who find someone to share their loneliness. A friend. Or a lover.'

Daisy shivered. His whole manner, his very way of speaking was new to her. No man from round here would have said the word 'lover', not in that way. Words like that were left to books or films, and yet Sam had just said it in ordinary conversation. She didn't *know* him at all, and yet strangely she had no desire to know him as a friend. All she wanted was to love him. For him to be her lover. . . . She closed her eyes.

'I wish we could stay here for ever.'

Above her head Sam Barnet pursed his lips in a soundless whistle. He felt suddenly totally dispirited. What in God's name was he doing? What in God's name was he getting himself into? This wasn't the kind of girl he was used to. Not a cheeky uncomplicated lass from the mill who would have gone out with him, said yes, or no, and that would have been

20

that. No recriminations. Nothing. 'Ta-ra then,' as they said up here.

Daisy spoke to him with the candour of a child. No guile, no flirtatious manner. All at once he thought of her coming into this dark hole of a place, early in the mornings, shovelling coal into that black firebox. Every day since she was fourteen, she had said. And seeing the lamp-light silvering the drizzle....

'I'll be back in London by the weekend.' He shook her gently. 'Wake up, Daisy, love. Stop making something out of nothing. You'll have forgotten me in less than a month.'

She ignored him. What kind of talk was that, anyroad? Forget him? She had managed to forget that he had a wife, hadn't she? From that first mention of her she had blotted her out completely. She didn't want to know what she looked like or what her name was, and she certainly wasn't going to let go of this dream. Not yet... oh no, not yet.

Sam got to his feet, pulling her with him. Cupping her face in his hands he kissed her mouth, his fingers absent-minded in her hair as he tried to think of a way of letting her go, of saying goodbye without making her cry. But the sweetness of the kiss caught him unawares, and he strained her to him, feeling the stirrings of desire.

If he had been a lesser man, he told himself, putting her resolutely from him; if she had been a different sort of girl – the pompous phrases inside his head caught him unawares. He would lie down with her on the pile of sacks and make love to her. And she would let him. Her thinking had gone beyond reason; with a girl like Daisy it was all or nothing. And if he made love to her she would be committed, and a commitment was the last indulgence he could afford.

'I'm married,' he told her cruelly. 'Why look at me like that? I can't give you anything. I can't make you happy. Why have you gone all serious on me?'

'I'm not going to cry,' Daisy said.

'Well of course you're not going to bloody well cry!' Sam's exasperation spilled out into his voice. 'Look, I can't

21

face that harridan coming looking for you and finding us in here together. And she will once she realizes you're not in the house. And God knows why, but I can't say goodbye to you like this, because tears or no tears you're upset.'

'Stop shouting at me.'

'Tomorrow then. Down the town.' Sam began to button his raincoat. 'Outside Woolworth's. I suppose you've got a Woolworth's?'

'Not far from the Boulevard.'

'The Boulevard?'

'Where the trams and buses start off from.'

'At half-past seven. We'll go to the pictures again.'

'I'll wait till you come.'

Moving quietly, Daisy opened the bakehouse door and walked across the yard to the back gate. Lifting the sneck she opened it just wide enough for Sam to slip through.

The rain had stopped. Thin clouds veiled a drifting moon. When Sam got to the top of the street he turned round to look down over the town. Twinkling lights were spiked with the tall outlines of mill chimneys, and the air was so sharp and clean he fancied he could taste the tang of the sea.

What on earth had made him suggest seeing her again? His life was complex enough, without any further complications. He walked on, ashamed of his weakness. But so help him, it was a long time since a woman had looked at him like that. With her soul in her eyes. As if he were God. And yet... and yet, Daisy was no mealy-mouthed nothing. She had guts; must have plenty to get up each morning before dawn, stoking that great gaping hole with coal, then working with the men, one of them, an equal he suspected. Integrity – she had that, too. Living with that mother who had had the sweetness soured from her soul a long time ago, he guessed. And that other one, Edna, with the spite-filled laugh and the anchor clipping her non-existent bosoms together.

Daisy Bell had done something for him he wouldn't have believed possible. She'd put the fire back in his belly, that's what she'd done.

Sam snatched off his hat and walked along swinging it by his hand. The digs he'd found were the other side of the Corporation Park and as he entered by a side gate he saw the dark shadow of a family of ducks, huddled into the shelter of an overhanging tree. The gravel crunched beneath his feet, and a man walking a thin wet dog called out a greeting.

'Nasty neet,' he said, and Sam nodded.

'Pity them at sea,' he said.

'Aye, the poor buggers,' the man called over a disappearing shoulder.

'So you've come in, then?'

Martha was clearing the cups and saucers from the table, clattering them together as if they were her everyday thick Willow and not her Royal Albert from the china department at the Co-op Emporium. She had switched off the ceiling light, and in the softer glow from the standard lamp the veins stood out on her cheeks like a contour map drawn in red ink.

'You've not been upstairs. Not you, madam. You've been in the bakehouse getting up to God knows what with that . . . that dago.' She slid a lace doyley from beneath a couple of scones and shook it, ready to go in the drawer for next time.

'It isn't like that, Mother. You don't understand.' Daisy picked up the milk jug, just to show willing. 'Don't humiliate me. Please?'

Martha gave a snort half-way between a sneer and a Victorian pshaw. 'Not understand? Aw, my goodness! *You* might have been born yesterday, but I wasn't. Not by a long chalk *I* wasn't!'

'You'd no right to invite Auntie Edna.' Daisy's voice shook. 'You only asked her just to show off. To show Sam off. Like he was a trophy, a silver cup I'd won at tennis.'

'You was never any good at tennis.' Martha was already losing control of the argument. 'All that money I laid out for your subscription and those two white dresses from Lewis's at Manchester. Good as new, hanging in the wardrobe for the moths to get at.'

'It's my life,' Daisy shouted emotionally, 'to do with as I please!'

'And me having to be mother and father to you all these years, and our Edna doing sweet Fanny Adam to help, and coming to the funeral in a pink hat. After me going up the street day after day with her husband's dinner between two plates while Madam Muck went off to her Ladies' Guild and the Inner Wheel, not to mention the Mothers' Union even though she's chapel.'

'There has to be *something* for me!' Daisy fell into the rhythm of the row. 'You stopped me being Eliza in *Pygmalion* at the Dramatics because you heard there was a swear word in it! You said Bernard Shaw must be a dirty old man!'

'You're a silly, stupid girl!' Globules of spit were frilling Martha's mouth. 'It said on your last report from school that you lacked self-control, and you do. The first man that beckons and you're like a bitch on heat!'

'Mother!'

'Our Edna will have told half a dozen already. She saw that torch flashing in the bakehouse. "And I bet that's not all he's flashing," she said.'

'It's not like that!'

Daisy's voice tailed away as she saw her mother clutch her heart, saw her blink her eyelashes up and down as if in surprise, and her lips turn blue as if she'd been sucking an indelible pencil. Groping behind her for the comforting feel of an armchair, Martha lowered herself down slowly into it.

'Leave me be,' she whispered through terrible blue-mauve lips when Daisy knelt down beside her and began to try to loosen her blouse. 'It's only me palpitations. I'll be all right when I get me breath back.' She tried to sit up, but fell back, beads of sweat standing out on her forehead.

'I'm going for the doctor.' Daisy, with a last despairing glance at her mother, made for the door, only to turn round in time to see her mother pushing herself up by the chair arms, her face grey with determination.

'You'll fetch no doctor. I'm not paying him seven and

sixpence for nowt. It's passing. Stop fussing. I'll be right as rain when I've had a lie-down.'

Leaning heavily on Daisy, she managed to climb the steep narrow stairs, but in her bedroom she stood like a child and allowed Daisy to undress her.

'Leave me vest on! Roll me corsets up! And hide me knickers under that cushion.'

Lying quiet and still for once, beneath her green silk eiderdown in the icy room, Martha's panting breath seemed to ease a little.

'I'm going for the doctor. I don't care what you say, I'm going.'

Daisy ran down the stairs with the sound of the protesting voice spiralling after her. Stopping only to grab a coat from the nail behind the kitchen door, she ran out into the yard, past the bakehouse and into the street.

If her mother died, then it was all her fault. She would carry that burden of guilt with her for the rest of her life. She would have killed her own mother as surely as if she'd stuck a knife in her heart.

The little waiting room in the surgery across the street was empty, its horsehair stand-chairs lined against the walls, and its NO SPITTING notice peeling from the wall. For a moment Daisy stood irresolute, wringing her hands together, praying that the doctor hadn't been called out.

'I was just about to lock up.' The doctor's wife came out of the tiny dispensary, a bottle of cherry-red medicine in one hand. When she saw Daisy's face she went to fetch her husband.

Doctor Marsden was past retiring age. He had been on the go since seven o'clock that morning and his exhaustion showed in his red-rimmed eyes. He had brought Daisy into the world, and he had tried in vain to put together what was left of her father after the accident at the mill. He knew Daisy's mother for what she was – a stubborn Lancashire woman who would die on her feet rather than rest. He knew that her dominance over her daughter was total, that Daisy was her insurance for life, that even if Daisy married she would merely move in next door or in the next street, never *really* leaving home. It was a repeating pattern he had seen over and over again among the working classes of this town he loved so much.

In Doctor Marsden's opinion it was an abomination, but the pattern had been forged, he guessed, before the Industrial Revolution, when whole families had looms set up in their front rooms, and travel, even to the nearest town, was an adventure.

'Your mother?' The question was more of a statement. 'I'll be with you in a minute, Daisy.'

Already his wife was helping him into his coat and winding a long woollen scarf round his neck. 'You're wearing your carpet slippers!' she shouted after them, but it was too late. Without a spare inch of fat on his large frame, Doctor Marsden was as nimble as a mountain goat.

'In bed, is she?' Inside the house he made straight for the stairs. 'What did you do to get her there? Pole-axe her?'

'She had a bad turn, Doctor.' Stumbling after him Daisy stopped dead in the doorway of Martha's bedroom, her eyes wide with shock:

Sitting bolt upright against her pillows, two spots of bright colour on her cheeks, Martha twinkled roguishly at the doctor.

'So she fetched you, then?' With normal-coloured lips she smiled, showing the bright pink gums of her dentures. 'There's nowt wrong with me but a bit of heartburn, and that's gone. But you can syringe me ears out as you're here, if you like. Our Daisy'll bring a bowl of water and a towel up from the kitchen, won't you, love?'

Doctor Marsden sat down on the side of the bed and opened his little black bag to take out his stethoscope. He knew his patient's history without having to take down his boxes and consult her record card. He had nursed Martha through the Spanish 'flu after the war; he had personally wiped away the black mucus streaming from her nostrils; he had ordered her warm milk and brandy at that terrible time when up in the cemetery people were being buried in their hundreds by torchlight.

He had watched Martha sponge her little daughter all over with eucalyptus oil when Daisy seemed to be choking her life away with diphtheria, and when Martha's husband had been brought from the mill, carried across the street on a door with his blood seeping down into the cobblestones, he had sewn up his wounds, pulling the great gaping holes together, even as he knew that all hope was gone.

'Go downstairs and make your mother a cup of tea.' He motioned to Martha to undo the top buttons on her nightdress. 'I'll just have a listen to your chest, Mrs Bell.'

'You'll 'ear nowt.'

Daisy could hear her mother's voice chuntering away as she set the kettle to boil. Surely her mother hadn't been shamming? Best use the rose-sprigged cups, or she'd be in bother. Surely she hadn't imagined the pallor of her mother's face, the rapid gasping for breath, the frantic fluttering of the eyelashes? Hadn't she herself tucked her mother up into bed and left her lying there like a corpse waiting to be boxed in its coffin? Best put two cups out and the apostle spoons, and a crochet-edged cloth on the tin tray. Martha was a stickler for wanting people to know they knew what was what. But she *never* drank tea in bed. Since almost dying of the 'flu Martha had never had a single day in bed, despising women who, as she put it, enjoyed bad health.

'I'll go out till the day I die!' she was fond of saying, even if going out most days meant no further than across the yard to the bakehouse.

'I don't think there's too much to worry about at the moment.'

Doctor Marsden's sudden reappearance startled Daisy so much she set the cups and saucers rattling as she put the tray back on the table.

The doctor waved the tray away. 'Put the cosy on the teapot and have it when I've gone.' His eyes were very shrewd as he shrugged himself back into his coat, then stared down ruefully at his mud-stained slippers. 'There's some enlargement of the heart,' he went on, 'and her pulse is too rapid, but then she's no chicken. You were a menopausal baby, weren't you?'

He wasn't surprised to see a blush stain Daisy's cheeks. It was a prim, puritanical working-class mentality; he came across it all the time. Why, the women would have their babies with their legs crossed, some of them, if they could. He rubbed the stubble on his chin reflectively, remembering for the first time that he hadn't shaved that day.

'Your mother is no chicken, Daisy. A woman of her age should be resting up a bit, not working every hour God sends.' His sidelong glance took in the half-filled plates of cakes on the dresser, the butter in its blue dish and the large glass sugar-bowl. 'Too many starches are bad for her. She's carrying too much weight for her height. Far too much.' He had seen in the upstairs room the corsets pinkly furled, standing to attention on the basket chair. He decided to be blunt. 'Eating a meal like that...' he nodded towards the dresser, 'with her stomach tightly bound is enough to give anyone palpitations. One proper meal a day is enough at your mother's age.'

'We had a bit of a row.' Daisy's head drooped forward. 'I said things that got her worked up. If she'd had a heart attack and died it would've been all my fault.'

'That's utter nonsense.'

Doctor Marsden was so hungry he could almost taste the liver and bacon casserole simmering in the oven in the house across the street. He'd been going to eat it listening to a carol service on the wireless. But he could smell despair as if it were a piece of ripe gorgonzola, and this young woman was, he would swear, in some kind of emotional frenzy.

'What was the row about, Daisy?' He put his bag down on the table with a little thump. 'You can tell me all about it if you think it would help. It won't go any further, I can promise you that.'

28

Daisy picked up a teacloth and began to twist it as if she was wringing water from it. Suppose she said to him: 'Doctor, I met a man just yesterday, and something has happened to my mind. I can't stop thinking about him, not for a minute, and if he asked me to go away with him I would, even though I know he's married. I'd leave me mother and the shop, and though it would hurt me to do that, nothing could compare to the hurt I'll feel when he goes away. He's so handsome it makes my heart ache just to look at him, and he's kind; no one can tell me that he isn't kind. I love him, Doctor. It was love at first sight, just like on the pictures, but a million times better than the pictures because it's real.'

'Daisy?' The doctor's voice seemed to be coming from a long way away.

'Sam listens to me, really listens when I talk to him, and I don't have to make jokes all the time just because I'm Daisy Bell, good for a laugh. But he isn't serious with me; half the time he can't make me out.'

For a moment Daisy wondered if she had been speaking aloud, but the patient waiting expression on Doctor Marsden's face told her she had not.

'There's nothing wrong I can't sort out for myself,' she said firmly. 'Will you be coming to see me mother again?'

'I'll keep an eye on her.' The doctor picked up his bag. 'Remember, Daisy, if ever you do want a chat you know where to find me.'

'A hop, jump and a spit away.' Daisy's joky response was automatic, she knew it was expected of her.

'Your mother will be all right. *If* she rests.' Doctor Marsden turned at the door. 'You can't expect her to go on for ever, working like a cart-horse.' His thin face was crumpled into a genuine anxiety. 'Does she still help with the baking early in the bakehouse, then stand all day in the shop?'

'The pies,' Daisy said. 'Only she knows the right consistency for the fillings. She won't let nobody else touch the mixing. Just now she's on with the Christmas cakes, an' that's her secret recipe too. She puts marmalade in them, an'

29

she'd slit me throat if she heard me telling you.'

'I will put up a notice in my surgery.' The doctor opened the back door. 'Mrs Bell from the pie shop puts marmalade in her Christmas cakes.' He touched a hand to the brim of a non-existent hat. 'Remember what I said, now. Keep her in bed for a few days, then get someone to replace her in the shop.' Again he turned, frowning. 'You mustn't take it so hard, lass. We all have to grow old, and most women of your mother's age have put their feet up years ago.'

An umbilical cord, he told himself, that had never been cut. Devotion that turned a girl like Daisy into an old maid before she'd had time to be a lass. Me mother this, me mother that. Middle-aged women helping their mothers along the pavement, settling them into their chairs by the fire. Bound hand and foot by a love that was self-destructive in its loyalty.

'Will she be all right if I leave her by herself tomorrow night?'

The doctor's eyebrows shot up at the question, so unexpected, so contrary to what he had been expecting her to say. 'You mean *all* night, Daisy?'

'No. Just from about seven o'clock till eleven.' Her chin was up as she faced him with a defiance he couldn't see the reason for. 'I could ask someone to sit with her if you think it's necessary.'

Assuring her that it wouldn't be necessary, the doctor smiled, nodded and stepped out into the rain-swept yard, a man as bewildered as he looked. So much for imagining he could read his patients like a book, he muttered, heading off across the cobbles in his carpet slippers, with the rain beating down on his uncovered head.

Daisy went upstairs and found her mother sleeping. She stood in the doorway, noticing the whiteness of the puff of hair teased up from Martha's forehead. There were whiskers sprouting from the small determined chin, black whiskers at variance with the bleached white of her hair.

And it came to her that if her mother *had* died she would

have left her covered with a sheet and still gone out to meet Sam.

No one had warned her that falling in love was like this. In films there were coy glances, there were dewy-eyed faces staring into mirrors, fingers touching lips that had been kissed. There were melting glances exchanged across candle-lit tables, and love letters pressed to quivering lips before being hidden beneath silk stockings and lace-edged handker-chiefs in top dressing-table drawers.

Love, she had thought, would be a gentle sort of glow suffusing the heart, not a low grinding actual pain in her lower belly, as if she'd eaten plums from a tin that had blown.

Back downstairs she stood recklessly on the raised tile hearth to see herself clearly in the fluted mirror.

'Oh, God, don't let anything stop me going to meet him tomorrow,' she whispered to the reflection of a wild-eyed woman she hardly recognized. 'Don't let me mother work herself up again, 'cos I'm going, even if she rolls on the floor and froths at the mouth.'

Her half-closed eyes held an expression she was hard put to identify. They were the eyes of a woman desperate for the touch of a man; they were slumbrous with desire.

Passion.... For the first time in her life Daisy knew the meaning of the word as she stepped back, pressed both hands to her breasts, and with a conscious effort shook the shocking thoughts away.

'Oh, God, help me....'

It was not a blasphemy, it was a prayer. Whipping the embroidered tablecloth from the table, she shook the crumbs in the hearth, then went to put it in soak when she saw the tea stain ringing a wreath of blue forget-me-nots.

Chapter Two

Martha was up and doing the next morning when the first batch of loaves had been set in rows in the proving oven. Fifty bags of flour were due to arrive from a mill at Liverpool and she wanted to be there on the spot to count them as they were carried into the bakehouse. The pork steak from the butcher's was late, and she was all for going down the town to give somebody a piece of her mind.

'Folks *die* in their beds,' she told Daisy, getting her spoke in before Daisy had a chance to say a word. 'Doctors know nowt, but he'll send his man round just the same on Friday night to collect his shilling. I bet that bottle of tonic you've to go for this dinner time'll be nowt but coloured water. Cochineal in tap water, that's all it is. No wonder his wife has a new outfit summer and winter.'

Martha's gaze was lynx-like as she stared at her daughter. Oh, aye, she told herself, it was all there, written on Daisy's sloppy face. The red-rimmed eyes telling of a sleepless night, the haunted expression, and the naked anguish in the large brown eyes, all telling their tale, revealing that Daisy was in love. Or thought she was, the silly faggot.

Martha had seen it all before. Their Edna had been in just the same state during the years coming up to the war, when she'd been courting Arnold, swooning about all over the place and reading poetry in bed. The same as that daft 'aporth of a girl they'd taken on as errand girl when young Bill had gone to his death in France. Martha could bring her to mind right this minute, riding the shop tricycle with her garters showing, till her stomach got too swollen for her to cock her leg over the cross-bar.

Romance. The whole stupid business made her feel sick. Men! Walking around with their brains in their trousers; there wasn't one among them worth a twopenny bun. Fourteen years Martha had courted before she got married, and then only because her mother had died and didn't need her any more. Working day and night to get the business going hadn't left time or the energy for jumping around in bed.

Whoever had invented that carry-on needed their brains seeing to! Clever-clogs Edna had sworn that Martha falling with Daisy must have been the second immaculate conception! Then laughed her silly head off. But then, Edna had always laughed at nowt.

'He's not worth it, you know.' She speared a slice of bread on the toasting-fork and held it to the fire. 'His eyes are too close together for one thing.'

'I'm seeing him tonight.' Daisy's voice came out in a croak. 'For the last time. To say goodbye.'

'You're what?' Martha felt sympathy slide away from her like butter from a dish tilted too close to the fire.

'He's going back to London on Saturday.'

'To his wife?'

Daisy watched her mother spread about half a pound of butter on her toast. 'The doctor says you have to cut down.'

'Well, he would, wouldn't he, with a wife with a bottom like two eggs in a handkerchief. Have you thought what you'll do when that dago's wife comes up here and smacks your face? Bit of the tar-brush in him, if you ask me.'

'Stop talking like that!' Daisy laid a hand dramatically over her heart. 'And I don't want no toast. Thank you.'

'You were such a good little girl.' All at once Martha reached for a corner of her flowered pinafore and dabbed her eyes. 'Do you remember that white silk dress I made for you, the one with three tiers in the skirt, all picot-edged from the button stall in the market-house? You never used to answer me back in them days.'

'I should have!' Daisy's voice rose to a wail. 'I should have stood on me own two feet a long time ago. I'm not a child, Mother! Have you forgotten how old I am?'

'Standing there with mucky thoughts in your head.' Martha pushed her chair back and stood up. 'Telling me you're going out with a married man. Bold as brass and twice as cheeky. You'll kill me before you've finished.' With her feet set at their ten-to-two angle she marched through into the kitchen, to appear almost at once with the long brush held out in front of her as if she was on a bayonet charge. 'All I can say is I'm right glad your father isn't here to see the day!'

All day long Daisy kept stealing glances at her mother's face. It was as smooth and bland as the barm-cakes she slid into paper bags before handing them over to the customers standing three deep in the little shop. No sign of the drama of the day before.

'I have to go,' she kept muttering to herself. 'Dear God, help me, but I have to go and meet him. I'll die if I don't see him again,' she told herself, dashing from the bakehouse with trays of hot meat-and-potato pies, covered with a cloth because it was flamin' raining again.

By seven o'clock she was dead on her feet as usual, feeling sick on account of picking at her tea, but ready to meet Sam wearing her green coat and hat and a pair of shoes that killed her even when she was sitting down.

'I'm off then.' She put her head round the door of the living room and saw her mother knitting feverishly at a mauve wool jumper in a raspberry stitch with a deep welt.

'I'm trying to get this finished for you in time for Christmas.' Martha sighed deeply. 'It was meant to be a surprise, but you're too old now for surprises I suppose.' She held the knitting up to her eyes as if her sight was failing. 'Pass wool over needle and knit three times into next stitch, then wool round needle three times. I've been working on it on your picture nights. On me own.'

'You'll be all right, Mother?'

'I'll have to be, won't I?' Martha paused with one finger crooked over the knitting needles. 'It's got puffed sleeves and a Peter Pan collar above a ribbed yoke.'

'It'll be lovely.' For a moment Daisy hesitated, then knowing her mother wasn't going to make it easy for her to go, nodded twice before closing the door behind her.

Half-way down Victoria Street she stopped, sure she could smell rain in the wind. To go back for her umbrella was out of the question, so she walked on, taking tiny steps to accommodate the pain of the too-tight shoes bought in a weak moment from a newly-opened shop in King William Street. Mock crocodile, they came to a point, gripping her toes as if in a vice, making each step a burning agony. But by the time she had reached the town her excitement spilled over so that she forgot the pain. On a corner, by the school clinic, the green hat blew up from her head, waving like a sail, tethered only by a pearl-headed pin. She stepped into the wide doorway of the Home and Colonial grocers to fix it back, hoping her hair hadn't come out of the small sausage curls she'd made by curling tiny strands over her finger back in the icy chill of her bedroom.

It was dead on half-past seven, but he wasn't there where he had said he would be, outside Woolworth's. Daisy ran quickly round the corner, ashamed of being first. Suppose they'd said seven and not half-past? Suppose he'd been and gone? Yesterday had been so awful, he couldn't be blamed if he never wanted to set eyes on her again. For a frantic moment she couldn't remember his face.

The pavements shone like black glass after the day's rain. The short side street was as deserted as if a curfew bell had sounded, but soon they would be queueing for the second house, and the first house would be coming out of the picture palace nearby.

Naughty Marietta with Jeanette MacDonald and Nelson Eddy. Daisy had been to see it on the Monday, before Sam had walked into the shop, and the bit at the beginning where

Jeanette MacDonald as a young French princess had yearned for a man to love had answered an echo in her own heart.

With her curls neatly arranged round her heart-shaped face, the princess had cried out something like: 'Oh, how I would love to meet him, standing so tall and noble in the rays of the sun.' Then she had run away to America to avoid an arranged marriage to an old and ugly man. Feeling a spot of rain on her nose, Daisy stepped backwards into a doorway. And the ending... oh yes, the ending where Jeanette MacDonald had sung 'Ah, Sweet Mystery of Life', and Nelson Eddy as a dashing Yankee officer had listened to her with a dazed expression on his face, then joined in, gazing into her eyes.

The sentiments were lovely, but Daisy wasn't too sure about the appeal of a couple of lovers singing up each other's nostrils. Perhaps they would be better going to see *The Thin Man* with Myrna Loy and William Powell. The newspaper had said it was all about a sophisticated marriage. Daisy peered out from her shelter, holding firmly to her hat. Or maybe *The Count of Monte Cristo* with Robert Donat? But that was a bit of a walk, and she didn't want to arrive looking like a drowned rat.

A man walked by, pausing to light a cigarette. Thinking she was a street woman, Daisy decided, and making up his mind to ask her how much she charged. Turning her head away she walked quickly past him, the too-high heels making little staccato noises on the shiny pavement.

When she rounded the corner and saw Sam coming towards her, her instinct was to rush into his arms and have him lift her up and swing her round, but he merely raised his trilby a few inches from his head so that the lamp-light shone on his Brylcreemed hair.

'Good timing,' he grinned, the elongated dimples coming and going.

'I was delayed,' she lied. 'I'm glad I didn't keep you waiting.'

He seemed preoccupied, almost embarrassed. Daisy felt a

36

sudden sinking of the heart. 'Where shall we go?' She took hold of his arm. 'I can tell you everything that's on so you can choose.'

'Look, love. . . .' Sam shot out a wrist and glanced at his watch. 'There isn't time for us to go to the pictures. My boss has decided he wants to go back tonight, leaving about ten o'clock. He's a family man and doesn't like being away from home too long. So that doesn't give us much time. We can go to the pictures if you like, and come out before the end.'

'No!' Daisy knew she couldn't bear it. Not to sit on the back row with him in a double seat and have to come out long before the ballroom scene with Nelson Eddy with his cloak swirling round him as he sang 'Ah, Sweet Mystery of Life' to Jeanette MacDonald's upturned face. Life wasn't a mystery; it was predictable, at least as far as she was concerned. Already Sam seemed to have gone from her, borne on the freezing wind whipping a torn newspaper across the road.

There were things she had to say to him, things that would make him remember her for ever. He was so good-looking, just to be with him was an ache inside her. His handsome face was so noble in the lamp-light and she could feel his arm strong and powerful through her fingers on the sleeve of his raincoat. She had bitten off her Tangee lipstick and she didn't care. The pain of his going was already hurting. If a lorry or a bus had mounted the pavement at that moment and killed them both, she felt it would have been right and proper.

'Where *can* we go if we don't go to the pictures?' He seemed uncaring, totally impervious to her distress. 'I don't suppose there are any cafés open at this time of night?'

'This isn't London,' she reminded him, strident in her misery. 'People stop in up here and listen to the wireless or go to the pictures, or to concerts in King George's Hall. It's *The Messiah* in two weeks' time, with a chorus of two hundred and fifty,' she added wildly. 'Or they go to school prize-givings, or to roller-skating at the Overlookers' Hall. There's *always* something going on.'

Sam suddenly presented his face to the sky. 'It's raining.'

He spoke with a kind of satisfaction. 'Suppose I walk you home, love? I really do have a lot of things to do before we leave. Suppose we just nip round the corner to the pub and have a drink?'

Daisy opened her mouth to tell him that nice girls never went in pubs, only tarts and women who should have known better, but at that very moment a tram blundered round the corner, sparks whooshing from the arm clamped to the overhead wires.

'I know! Let's go for a tram ride!' She ran across the street, pulling Sam with her. 'Come on! It's better than standing about not knowing what to do.' She was behaving badly, she knew, but it was as though she'd been taken over by a woman who did strange and unpredictable things. Her heart was beating so madly she could hear it in her head, pounding away like a drum. 'You'll have plenty of time,' she told him, climbing the stairs and swaying in front of him to a seat further along. 'I'll show you the town.'

The tram heaved its way round a sharp corner, a lumbering clanging ship in a rough sea. The window on Daisy's left side was half-way open and a stinging wind made Sam turn up his collar and curse.

'You have some funny ideas,' he told her, but she wasn't listening.

'That's where we have the market. Wednesdays and Saturdays, and in a minute you'll see the shops all dressed fancy for Christmas!' She bounced round in her seat. 'Those are the posh shops. Ten shillings and sixpence for a shirt! That's two shillings more than they pay round us for rent!' Happiness was making her light-headed. The tram swooped up the Preston Road, past the park gates on the right, and the High School further up on the left. 'That's the school I won a scholarship to. I would have gone there if me father had had his way, but me mother said it would be a waste when I'd be going in the shop anyway.'

Obligingly Sam looked at the dark building set back from the road, amused and irritated at one and the same time.

Settled back in the slatted seat, he let his body sway with the movements of the tram. He had thought he knew women, but this one had him beat. She was different, so very, very different; young beyond belief for her years, and yet somehow as mature as a woman twice her age.

Last night she had told him she could see beauty through the high window of a dismal bakehouse at five o'clock in the morning, and now she was exhilarating in this ride along a road of dimmed lights, with dark silhouettes of houses now on either side.

In this, his first visit to the industrial north, he had been appalled at the drabness of the mean streets. Yesterday he had seen groups of the unemployed, standing idly on corners, hands in pockets, as if waiting for a bus they knew would never arrive. Waiting outside the Town Hall for his boss, he had left the Rolls for a moment and seen men in flat caps shuffling into the reading room at the Public Library, to spend the the day, he guessed, sitting or standing in a fug of damp clothes, turning newspaper pages over and over to read the hours away.

He had followed his boss into the cotton mill across the street from Daisy's shop and seen the weavers standing at their looms, cotton dust in their hair. Over the clanging clatter of the machines, they communicated with each other with exaggerated lip movements, stretching their mouths and pointing at their chests. And laughing, always laughing. What, he had wondered, had they found to laugh at in an atmosphere which surely should have sapped their spirits long ago?

'Up here is where the nobs live,' Daisy told him, as they climbed down from the tram at the terminus. 'Doctors and solicitors and the like. If you live up here folks know you're *it*.'

The felt hat had slipped back from her forehead, and her upturned face was luminous in the darkness. 'It's stopped raining, thanks be to goodness,' she said. 'I'm going to show you now where I go for a walk on Sunday afternoons in

summer. With my friend Florence. She works as an usherette
at the Rialto cinema, so I only see her on Sundays. It isn't far,'
she told him when he hesitated. 'You can get back in plenty
of time. It isn't right what I know you're thinking about
Blackburn. You've only seen the part down by the mills.' She
urged him forward. 'There are fields not far away, Sam.
Miles and miles of meadows, and rolling hills and trees, and
little sparkling rivers.' She tucked a hand into his arm.
'Pretend it's summer. Go on. It's easy if you try. I'm wearing
a blue dress, pleated all round, and you're wearing a pair of
grey flannels and a yellow-spotted cravat tucked into the
neck of your shirt.'

They were walking up an incline now, away from the
terminus. Set back from the road on either side were tall dark
houses, solidly Victorian, fronted by tiny gardens fringed by
brick-built walls.

'Nearly there!' Suddenly Daisy let go of his arm and strode
up an unmade road to the left. 'Up here, Sam! Come on,
you'll soon see what I mean.'

'Where the hell are we now?' Sam wished he wasn't so
good-natured. His wife would never have called him that,
but he knew he was. Why else would he be God knew where,
trudging up a muddy lane and climbing into what seemed to
be a large stone boxers' ring, instead of behaving like the
sultan his wife thought him to be, and putting paid to this
ridiculous escapade with an imperious wave of a hand.

'You've no imagination!' his wife had often screamed at
him. 'That's what comes of being a glorified car mechanic.
You've got gear oil instead of blood in your veins, Samuel
bloody Barnet!'

A car mechanic. . . . Sam winced as if the words had come
at him out of the darkness. He'd show her, when he'd finished
with his engineering exams and got certificates to prove he
was qualified. A late starter he might be, but he was catching
up fast. And as for having no imagination. . . . He bounded up
the stone steps after Daisy, feeling the sun warm on the top of
his head, spruce in his grey flannels with a yellow-spotted

40

cravat tucked into his open-necked shirt.

What was she doing to him, this strange young-old girl with the dark-brown voice, running ahead of him now to lean over a railing as if she was on the deck of a ship watching the moon shining on the sea? Why did he feel so protective towards her? As if she needed shielding from all the hurts of the world. No one could do that. When it came to it we were all alone, like animals, fending for ourselves, and making the best of things. Working out our salvations and knowing that the paths we trod were the paths we chose. Of our own volition, God dammit.

Almost as an extension of his own thoughts he went over to the railings and put his arms round Daisy, straining her to him, just as a fierce gust of wind, seemingly from Siberia, tore the ugly felt hat from her head, bowling it along in the darkness like a leaf before swooping it up and casting it into the darkness below.

'I *hated* that hat,' she shouted over the sighing moaning wind. 'I didn't suit it, and never have. I only bought it because it matched me coat, and because the lady in the Hat Market said it was just me.' Spreading her arms wide she let the wind take her hair and whip it round her head like a nimbus. 'How did she know what was just me when I don't know meself?'

'I think you *do* know.' Sam pulled her to him again. 'I think you know exactly what you are and who you are.'

'Well, whoever I am didn't suit that hat.' Her laugh was the laugh he remembered from first seeing her, as unselfconscious as a child's. 'On a real summer's day you can see Blackpool Tower.' She pointed away from the town. 'It looks a bit like a mill chimney, and when the sun shines, *really* shines, you can sometimes fancy you see the sea flashing like a silver needle.' She lifted her face. 'Sniff up, Sam, then lick your lips and tell me you can taste the sea. Oh, I *love* the sea. One day when I'm old I will live by the sea, an' I'll go to sleep at night with the sound of the waves in me ears.' Turning suddenly completely round, she pulled him with her. 'And that is the Corporation Park down there, and beyond that the town. If only it was light you could see the tall chimneys waving little banners of smoke.' Again he was whirled round. 'Back to the sea now, Sam. But before you arrive there are more than thirty miles of green fields and woods.'

'With your hat whipping through them.'

'Fetching up on the sands at Blackpool.'

He hugged her close. He couldn't help himself. She put her mouth to his and as the kiss deepened, he tasted the sweetness of her.

'I'm getting better at kissing, aren't I?'

Even as she spoke the rain came swiftly, a cloud-burst directly above them, it seemed. Before they reached the road her hair was soaking wet, flattened to her head, a black rubber bathing cap. Sam offered her his own hat, his coat, anything, but it was obvious to him she didn't care.

The misery of his going had hit her with the force of the deluge of water cascading down from an unseen sky. Already the grids were overflowing, and the gutters ran like rivers. It was Hollywood rain, Joan Crawford in an oiled perm, with lipstick intact on her wide-gashed mouth, with a man beside her in a riding macintosh, wide-brimmed trilby lowered over his face, a strong arm round her as he urged her along so quickly it seemed as if her feet would leave the ground. 'How beautiful you look in the rain,' he would say. 'All woman.'

'You must have a hot bath as soon as you get inside,' said Sam.

'I won't melt,' Daisy told him, wondering if he knew that taking a bath meant bringing in the zinc bath from its nail on the backyard wall, heating the water up in the kitchen copper, then carrying it in pails through to the fire.

As they reached the bottom of the slope and turned the corner, a tram was there, with the conductor standing on his platform, his finger on the bell.

'Nice weather for ducks,' he grinned. 'Chucking it down in buckets,' he added from his shelter. 'Been for a swim in the park lake, have you, love?'

Ignoring him, Daisy made for the front of the tram, swayed almost off her feet as it jerked into motion.

'Does it ever do anything else but rain up here?' Taking off his hat Sam shook the raindrops from it, scattering them like beads on the corrugated floor. 'Here, take my hankie and wipe your hair with it.'

'I suppose it never rains in London?' Daisy scrubbed away at her wet face. 'I suppose you have to crawl about on dusty roads with your tongue hanging out wailing for water?'

All at once the mock-crocodile shoes were giving her gyp, and looking down she saw her lisle stockings hanging over them in muddy creases. She discovered that she was chilled to the bone; there was a cold wetness trickling down her neck. Her mother would act as if she had caught her death, and make her a pot of cocoa with the steam coming through the froth on the top. And what for? What, in the name of God, was it all for? So she would be well enough and able enough to crawl out of bed in the morning and stoke the fire-oven for the massive Saturday bake? For the one-pound and two-pound loaves, the soft-centred barm-cakes, the scones, the iced Bath buns, the sultana sponges?

'You are not walking me home.' Her voice was ragged with misery. 'You have a lot to do before you go back to the Sahara. What do you do when you're nearly there? Swap your chauffeur's fancy hat for a pith helmet?'

Sam leaned across her to breathe on the steamed-up window. As removed from her as if they had already parted, she guessed. The back of his coat was black-wet, and she hoped it had gone right through to his vest. If he *wore* a vest, she wondered, remembering that Clark Gable never did.

'If you're sure.' Sam wrinkled his nose against the smell of wet raincoats as the tram filled up at the park gates with a crowd of parents on their way home from a grammar school prize-giving. 'If it freezes on top of this the roads will be like glass.'

All at once Daisy saw the Rolls-Royce limousine skidding from the road, overturning in a ditch with its wheels spinning. With Sam slumped lifeless over the wheel, and his boss dead as a door-nail on the back seat with his eyes wide open and blood trickling from a gash on his forehead.

'Then you'll have to drive a bit slower than seventy miles an hour, won't you?' Daisy turned a despairing face towards him, remembering, as she was to remember for a long time to come, every single word he had ever said.

'She holds the road like a dream,' Sam told her, recognizing they had come to the end of the journey, standing up as if he couldn't wait to be off and away.

On the Boulevard, heedless of passers-by, he kissed her gently, a fleeting on the mouth kiss with lips that tasted of rain. 'Thank you for being so nice to me, Daisy. Thank you for being my friend these past two days.'

Friend? The emphasis on the word stabbed like a finger jabbed into Daisy's heart. She felt the tears prick behind her eyes and blinked them angrily away. She knew that he was trying not to look at his watch, glad that his back was turned away from the station clock.

Sam was controlling the urge badly. There were a thousand and one things he had to do before they started on the long drive south. Already he was feeling a pleasurable anticipation at the thought of sitting behind the wheel of the car he knew to be the best in the world, the Spirit of Ecstasy statuette poised on the bonnet. The Flying Lady, as some preferred to call it. Speeding down arterial roads through the dark night, listening to the rhythmic purr of the engine.

To Sam a car engine was a thing of beauty – to be kept so spotless a man could eat his dinner off it – the Rolls, as *he* drove it, was an extension of his own body. As a surgeon's fingers would probe the innards of his patient on the operating table, so Sam could detect the slightest fault in the engine of a car. Every throb told its own story and he knew he could have dismantled and rebuilt it from instinct.

And one day, when he held his paper qualifications in his hand, he would find a better job, and possess his own car. Giving in to temptation, he glanced at his watch. And winced.

44

'Be happy, love.' He needed to leave this Lancashire lass with his conscience unruffled. He wanted to be kind. He didn't see himself as a cruel man, even though 'cruel bastard' was his wife's pet name for him. No, what he saw himself as was a sort of sentimental softie, a world-weary man with a puzzling attraction for women. And this one was crying. She was trying hard to disguise it and not succeeding very well. Sam came to a sudden decision. Putting her from him he smiled down into her anguished face.

'We'll be up this way again,' he told her. 'In the spring – when the daffodils are blooming in that park of yours. So this isn't goodbye.' He touched the tip of her damp nose with a finger. 'My boss has a lot of unfinished work to do up here.'

Before he turned away he doffed his hat, just a small doff because he hated getting his hair wet. He walked swiftly away, leaving Daisy staring after him, teetering on the kerb in the too-tight shoes, like a suicide deciding to make the final jump into oblivion.

'Daisy!'

When she turned round she saw her Auntie Edna's daughter, her cousin Betty, with husband Cyril, sharing an umbrella as big as a marquee. They were wearing identical fawn gaberdine raincoats, buttoned to the throat, with Betty's straining a little over her stomach where the baby had begun to show.

Considerately, Cyril positioned the massive umbrella over Daisy, so that the three of them stood beneath it in an uneasy lengthening silence.

'You're wet through, our Daisy.' Betty exchanged a wifely conspiratorial glance with her young husband. 'Are you all right?'

'Perfectly all right, thank you.'

Their presence irritated Daisy so much she could hardly bear to look at them. They hadn't even given her time to work out which month the daffodils bloomed in the Corporation Park. Was it before Easter, or after? Late March, or early April? She supposed a lot depended on the weather.

'We've just come off the train.' Betty nodded her head in the direction of the station. Her headscarf, Daisy noted, printed with horses' heads, was pinned at the front with a row of Kirby grips to stop it slipping back from her fair slippery hair. She gave off a smell of Pears soap, and in that moment Daisy knew exactly the kind of baby she would have. Clean and shiny, with round blue eyes and soft sparse hair. Summoning all her will-power, she took her mind off the daffodils and smiled at them through chattering teeth.

'I'm glad about the baby,' she said sincerely. 'You always said you would have one before your twenty-first, didn't you?'

'I don't remember no such thing.' Betty gave her mother's trilling laugh. 'What a thing to say!'

'We've been to me mother's.' Cyril's eyes beneath the neb of his tweed flat cap were kind. He'd always felt sorry for Daisy ever since the wedding when she'd looked awful in a mauve sprigged dress, made to match the younger bridesmaid's with a frill standing out from her neck like Punch, or was it Judy, wore? Picture mad, his mother-in-law had said. Thinks nothing of going night after night on her own and sitting next to God knows who. 'A born spinster,' she'd added maliciously, eyeing her daughter resplendent in wreath and veil. 'Run a mile as soon as look at a man, that one.'

'We go of a Friday, straight from work,' he explained. 'For our tea.' The nudge his wife gave him almost knocked him off balance. 'Well, yes.' He gave a little cough. 'We'd best be going.'

'Yes,' Daisy said. 'Ta-ra, then.'

Again the furtive exchange of glances.

'Look, our Daisy.' Betty's features sharpened into her mother's monkey expression. 'I know it's none of our business, but it's not right you standing here on your own, getting soaked to the bone. If you're waiting for somebody then he's not coming. Not at going on for ten o'clock. Best come on with us, eh, Cyril?'

'Right.' Cyril relinquished his hold on the umbrella. 'You two girls share that, I won't melt.'

'Off you go, then.' Daisy knew she was being rude, but the idea of sharing the umbrella with cousin Betty was unthinkable. She had to be alone. She guessed that they knew about Sam and anticipated the questions that would surely come on the walk home. 'I'm not keeping you,' she said.

'Well!' Taking her husband's arm, Betty wedged him closer to her side. 'Suit yourself, Daisy Bell.'

Daisy watched them walk away, Cyril's baggy trousers flapping wetly round his ankles, Betty's rubber overshoes making little smacking noises on the wet pavement. Their steps matched as if they were in a three-legged race, and even their backs looked affronted.

Bursting to get home and tell Auntie Edna they've seen me standing on the Boulevard at ten o'clock at night, like a potty woman with no hat on, Daisy told herself, waiting until they were well out of sight round the corner by the White Bull.

When she was sure they'd gone she set off herself, the mock-crocodile shoes clenching her toes like viciously held pincers, across the road past Woolworth's with a window dressed with a fan of gramophone records at one and threepence each. Going the long way round to avoid catching up with Betty and Cyril, past the shops and up a side street with a square-faced chapel at the top. Past terraced houses with aspidistra plants in never-used front parlours, with soft lights behind yellow paper blinds at the upper windows.

The shoes were by now a burning agony, so she took them off and ran the rest of the way, tossing the wet fringe from her eyes, Claudette Colbert running through a field of daffodils, with a blue sky above and the sun warm on her head. Running to meet her lover, a tall man with black wavy hair and a profile to match that of Frederic March in *The Sign of the Cross*.

The lights were on in the house as Daisy slopped her way

through the kitchen, making dirty footmarks on the nice clean linoleum. And rising from her mother's rocking-chair, Auntie Edna, stern and forbidding in a cross-over pinafore with safety-pins pinned to the front, her perm trapped in an invisible hairnet.

She wasn't in the mood to pull punches, so she came straight out with it:

'The doctor went an hour back,' she said, 'and she's asleep now, so there's nowt for you to do, madam.' She closed her eyes as if she couldn't bear the sight of her sopping-wet niece. 'Arnold found her in the bakehouse seeing to the fire. Leaning on the shovel with her face as white as a piece of bleached fent. Trying to do your job while you were out breaking her heart!'

'The fire didn't need seeing to!' Daisy was already half-way to the stairs. 'I left it damped down, and she knew it. There was no call for her to be in there lifting that heavy shovel.'

At the door of her mother's room she stopped, her hand going to her throat at the sight of Martha neatly parcelled into bed, her face grey, but her eyes wide open and glittering, as if they were the only thing about her alive.

Down on her knees by the bed Daisy stretched out a hand and gently patted her mother's face. 'You had no call, Mammy,' she said, using the childish word she hadn't used since she was very small. 'You've never lifted that big shovel before.' Her voice caught on a sob. 'Why do it tonight? You knew I'd be back to see to it. Why? Listen to me! Why?'

'Because I just felt like it, that's why.' Martha pushed Daisy's hand away. 'Fat lot you care, anyroad.'

'Yoo-hoo!'

Cousin Betty's voice spiralled up the stairs and, hovering in the doorway, Edna turned with obvious reluctance.

'It's our Betty, bless her. Come to see what she can do.'

Daisy sighed with relief as she heard the slip-slop of her auntie's down-at-heel bedroom slippers receding. Betty bless her, she told herself, eager to tell her mother about seeing me standing on the Boulevard with no hat on and crying like a potty woman.

'What did the doctor say?' she whispered. 'He told you you had to rest. Did you tell him you'd been stoking the fire-oven when there was no need?'

'You never said what time you were coming back.' Martha's small beady eyes were slits of accusation. 'You might have been stopping out all night for all I knew.'

'Oh, Mother. . . .' Daisy's wet hair drooped over the shiny green eiderdown. 'Why do you say such things when you know they aren't true? You know I'd never do a thing like that.'

'Is he getting a divorce, then?' Martha spat out the word as if it were an obscenity. 'Bringing a divorce into our family? Shaming us in front of your Auntie Edna?' Her head turned wearily towards the wall. 'The BBC won't have no truck with divorce. They sack them if they're the guilty party. Give them their marching orders, that's what they do.'

'He doesn't *work* for the BBC!' Getting up from her knees Daisy caught sight of herself tripled in the swing mirrors on her mother's dressing-table. Green coat black-wet, hair dangling round her face like wet snails. 'He's gone, Mother, and I doubt if he'll be back.'

Deliberately she put behind her the scene where Sam came to meet her, striding through a field of yellow nodding daffodils. The singing in her heart had gone too, fading as if it had never been. That had been the dream. This was reality.

'You have to rest.' She found she was wringing her hands, when she had thought people only did that in books. 'We can afford to get someone in for serving in the shop, and I can manage the rest. I'm strong, Mother. Hard work doesn't bother me. I can supervise them in the bakehouse and see to the shop, and look after you.' Her voice rose. 'But you have to let me take care of you!'

Peeling off her sodden coat, she found the rain had soaked through the lining, staining her blouse in bottle-green patches. In the chill of the unheated room she was shivering as though she'd been for a dip in the sea at Blackpool when it wasn't fit.

'We can pick and choose with half the town on the dole,' she said through chattering teeth. 'A nice girl to give the shop a bit of tone. Florence,' she added on impulse. 'She hates her job at the Rialto. You know how nicely she speaks. You've always said so. Remember when she read the Lesson at chapel last May on Anniversary Sunday? You'd've thought she'd had elocution lessons.'

'Her father's nowt but a butter-slapper at the Maypole,' Martha said, perking up a bit. 'And he's living over the brush with that woman out of Tontine Street.'

'You can *retire*.' Daisy hugged the damp coat to her chest to hide the stains on her blouse. 'You can stop in bed till dinner time reading and knitting. We'll have *Woman's Weekly* delivered with the papers. There's nice knitting patterns in there. And nice stories. You like stories and reading. I know that.'

'About daft woman who fall in love with stupid men swishing riding crops and being masterful?' For the first time Martha seemed to notice the state her daughter was in. 'Best get them wet things off,' she said. 'Before you get pneumonia. The double kind by the look of you,' she added, closing her eyes again.

Daisy hesitated by the door. Downstairs she could hear the rise and fall of Auntie Edna's voice, interspersed by Betty's clear childlike treble. She would have to face them when she had changed out of her wet things, but there was a terrible longing inside her to go back to the bed, take her mother's hand, and tell her how much she loved her. Tell her that even if she never got out of bed again she would care for her and keep her clean. Send for a commode out of the Sunday paper, and repaint the basket chair for visitors to sit on when they came to call.

But she knew exactly what her mother would do and say if she did just that.

'Stop being dramatic,' Martha would say. 'Who do you

think you are? Barbara Stanwyck?'

So Daisy left the room, taking the square landing at the top of the stairs in one stride before going into her bedroom to peel off her wet things.

Missing entirely the sight of her mother, holding a hand to her chest where the pain had raged and left her drained. Peering over the top of the dark green taffeta billowing eiderdown, like a terrified animal staring panic-stricken from its cage.

Chapter Three

'You look,' said Florence, 'a bit like Anna May Wong with your fringe uncurled like that.'

Daisy didn't mind the personal remark. She was used to her friend Florence Livesey being critical. Perhaps one day she would flash out and ask her friend why she always wore *her* hair scragged back and up into a French pleat, making her look at least ten years older than her twenty-five years. And why she wore net gloves when anyone knew they were common, and why she crooked her little finger when she drank a cup of tea. But she knew she wouldn't. Florence's good opinion of herself mattered a lot. Daisy knew that instinctively. The woman her father was living with was two years younger than Florence herself, and it was said he drank more than was good for him, so Florence had plenty of crosses to bear.

It was the week coming up to Christmas, and they had been as usual to Sunday School at the chapel set back behind railings not five minutes' walk away from the shop. They had sat with the Ladies' Class and sung 'We Three Kings from Orient are' before going out of the big hall into the side vestry for a talk by the Superintendent, a man with thin grey hair and an Adam's apple that moved up and down out of his white starched collar like a yo-yo.

Now they were sitting drinking tea in Daisy's living room because their Sunday walk had been sacrificed so that Martha wouldn't be left too long on her own.

'How is she?' Florence jerked her neat head in the direction of the stairs. 'Does she always have as long as this for her lie-down?'

Daisy nodded. 'It worries me. One time she couldn't sit still; now she sleeps all the time. It can't be natural.'

'Nature's remedy,' said Florence who was very well versed in all things medical. 'Her body is healing itself.' She passed over her cup for a refill. 'Sleep that knits up the ravell'd sleave of care,' she said. 'Shakespeare.'

'I wish you could have come to work in the shop.' Daisy fingered her hair. 'I don't have time to put me curlers in,' she explained, not wishing to look like Anna May Wong. 'I'm that tired when I go to bed. Mother insisted on Auntie Edna taking her place in the shop, but she does more gossiping than serving, then she goes home, leaving me with all the clearing up to do. I'm whacked by the time I get me mother her tea, then see her back to bed. And with Christmas coming there's all the extra. Last night I was icing cakes till midnight.'

'Sometimes I think I'll do away with myself. Throw myself into Potter's Pond,' Florence said, startling Daisy so much she almost dropped her cup and saucer. 'We don't speak now, that . . . that woman and me. And the noise they make in bed. It makes me feel sick.'

Daisy felt the blush spread up from her throat. She wouldn't have believed her friend could have said a thing like that. Not right out on a Sunday afternoon, sitting sipping tea with her little finger crooked.

'You must get away,' she said through the blush. 'I don't suppose they want you there if the truth were told.'

'The truth *is* told!' Florence put her cup down on the tiled hearth, took a clean folded handkerchief from her handbag and began to weep tidily into it. 'I objected to her wiping the gas oven down with the dishcloth the other day and she yelled at me, and my father came in and said the best thing would be for me to get out. "Get out," he shouted.'

'He wouldn't mean it, love.' Daisy glanced anxiously at the door. It would be just like her mother to come downstairs now to be struck almost paralytic with such talk. And calling Florence 'Florrie' when she knew she hated it. She frowned and bit her lip. 'Your father always was a . . .' she sought for the right word '. . . a virile sort of man.'

'He sleeps with nothing on. And walks along the landing stark naked.' Florence was obviously determined to have her say. 'I never liked him,' she added. 'Neither did my mother. He was descended from fair folk, you know.'

A terrible picture came into Daisy's mind – of Mr Livesey with his red bull neck and mutton-chop whiskers trotting along the landing in the altogether. She suppressed a shudder.

'Where would I *go*?' Florence was beside herself. 'My wages wouldn't pay the rent of a single room, let alone keep me in food and clothes. I'm a suffragette in here.' She stabbed at her chest. 'I believe in the emancipation of women. Passionately.' Her lip curled. 'I do not regard a man as a meal ticket, and yet I am beholden to my father, because he pays the rent. I want to scream at him that I will go, that I will manage, but emancipation takes money, Daisy! Think about those women who fought tooth and nail for the vote for us. The Pankhursts, Annie Kenny. They were financially independent *before* they became suffragettes. They submitted to being force-fed because they knew their dinner would be waiting for them if they *chose* to go home. They sang as they were marched into prison, and when they were let out they went back to the bosoms of their families, to be cosseted back to health. But they had made their gestures! Don't you see?'

Daisy was losing the thread of the argument, but she nodded vaguely. Florence always sounded as if she knew exactly what she was talking about.

'We should have been teachers.' Florence was weeping again. 'Both of us top of the class and what good did that do? You went straight into that bakehouse at fourteen, and I went to work as an usherette so I could mind my mother during the day.' She lifted her head, her expression bleak. 'Don't you ever look at the rows of pies and loaves of bread and tell yourself there should be something more to life than

that? Do you ever want to open that door and just walk
away?'

Now Daisy was on firm ground. 'Every single day.'
Leaning forward she took the cup and saucer from Florence's
trembling hands and set them back on the table. 'But we can't
always turn our backs on a life that doesn't turn out to the
pattern we dreamed up for it. Sometimes the gesture we
make if we stay is braver than the one we would make if we
ran away.'

Something had stopped her telling Florence about Sam,
but she was pretending, she knew, that he had asked her to go
away with him. That she was staying to nurse her mother
because of duty. That even if he had gone down on his bended
knees she would have refused him gently, pointing out where
her duty lay. It was the only way she could go on. And on and
on and on.

'It's all right for you,' Florence was saying. 'You *belong*.
You may get bored, or frustrated, but you *belong*. You're
needed. I'm not needed any more.'

'But you won't do . . . do what you said?' Daisy watched as
her friend pulled on the lacy gloves with their tiny frilled
gauntlets. 'You would never do away with yourself?'

Big-boned and desolate, Florence stood up and adjusted
the flaps of her hat which was modelled on Amy Johnson's
flying helmet. It lent an air of gauntness to her long face, and
at once Daisy was struck by the thought of how noble her
friend would have looked chained to a row of iron railings,
and wished she'd been given the chance.

'I am not brave enough, alas,' Florence said, and held up a
netted finger. 'Don't get up, Daisy. You look as if you might
be coming down with a cold.'

But Daisy followed her through the kitchen and out into
the yard, surprised to find that the fog which had threatened
as they walked back from Sunday School was now a blanket
of sulphur-smelling thickness, so all-enveloping it was
almost tangible.

Florence lifted the sneck on the back gate. 'Even if I had

decided to throw myself into Potter's Pond,' she said, 'I'd never find it in this lot, would I?'

'See you next week.' Daisy closed her eyes in relief. Her friend's wit might be as dry as a ship's biscuit, but at least she still retained it. And that was all that mattered. Florence would survive.

Peering up the street she tried to see her walking with her loping stride, large feet encased in nurse's lace-up shoes because standing so long at work had dropped Florence's arches. For a moment Daisy thought she saw her, wreathed in yellow fog, a shadowy figure in a spy thriller, Mata Hari going to her doom.

'They never do it when they say they're going to,' Daisy reassured herself, rubbing the tops of her arms as she walked back up the yard. 'It's the ones who suffer in silence and say nothing who do it.'

She imagined Florence walking past her own house, up Earl Street fields, past allotments with their hen-pens and pigeon cotes. Tall and long-necked with a felt hat like a flying helmet hiding the scragged-up hair. On across fields to the local pond, a sheer drop into a murky splash of water into which it was said a man, three years on the dole, had hurled himself one wintry day, sinking like a stone to his death.

'Why is life so . . . so awful?' she asked herself, setting the table for a boiled ham tea, turning an anguished face towards her mother appearing droop-eyed from her long sleep.

'They never do it when they say they're going to,' Martha said, when Daisy voiced her fears. 'I only dozed,' she went on. 'I've been reading the paper. It says that the people living on the dole are existing far below the threshold of adequate nutrition. And *they* don't go jumping into mucky water. Neither will Florrie Livesey. Her mother was a grand little woman, God rest her soul.' She pulled her chair up to the table. 'Fourpence a quarter for that ham,' she grumbled. 'It's cut that thin I can see the pattern on the plate through it. I'll have to double it up if I'm going to make it into a sandwich.'

*

It snowed that Christmas, and on mill lodges ice formed. On Christmas Day nearly thirty thousand followers of the Rovers watched them play football at Ewood Park. A very much alive Florence came to tea and advised an exhausted Daisy to use Knights Castile soap for tired skin to revive her sallow complexion. Or to use rouge, just a touch on the cheek-bones, to brighten her tired eyes.

'You're doing too much,' she told her friend kindly, and went on to describe the current film at the Rialto: *I Was a Spy* with Conrad Veidt, Herbert Marshall and Madeleine Carroll. 'Her humanity impelled her to serve in a German hospital,' she informed Daisy and her mother. 'And they trapped her so she was forced to work as a spy. But they wouldn't have forced *me*,' she added, pale eyes glistening. 'Put me against a wall and shoot me, but never expect me to betray my heritage.'

'A fat chance,' said Martha, eyeing her malevolently.

The biting winds of a spring coming too late for comfort flattened the daffodils in the park as if an army had trampled them. Still there was no word from Sam.

In May the Broad Walk in the park was lined with mauve and pink rhododendrons and Daisy, to cheer herself up, bought a new straw hat from the Hat Market. She wore it for the Anniversary Sunday at chapel, its spray of scarlet cherries bobbing as she walked up the street with Martha who was breathing hard and leaning heavily on her arm. Daisy had taken in the seams of her mother's good linen coat, and beneath the veil on a hat that made her look like a consumptive bee-keeper, Martha's once round face was drawn and pale.

Like the spring daffodils, Martha had drooped and flattened as each month went by, her once towering cottage-loaf hair-style sunk to the thickness of an oatmeal biscuit. A fierce lady from Spirella had visited the house and fitted her with a new pink corset more in keeping with her shrinking frame, and her old ones had gone for fourpence each at a chapel jumble sale.

Daisy had long since lost her battle to have Florence working behind the counter in the little shop. Edna was firmly ensconced and would take some shifting now.

'They need the money with Arnold being out of work and the baby coming,' Martha had argued.

'It's Betty's and Cyril's baby!' Daisy's objections were loud and forceful, but her mother was adamant.

'It's her first grandchild and I know how she feels. I would go out and scrub floors for a grandchild of mine,' she added, shooting a baleful glance at Daisy. 'But then I won't be here to see one of *mine*.'

She sat constantly over the fire, needles clicking as she worked on a matinée jacket in yellow with an intricate scalloped edging. In yellow, because that would do for either.

'Your Daisy's seen the back of that Londoner,' Edna said one day.

'He's spoilt her for other men,' Martha agreed at once. 'She's started going to the pictures again once she's got me to bed, but she won't meet the right sort that way. She'll never meet a man if she doesn't mix up.'

'It isn't natural a girl of her age going to the pictures on her own.' Edna smiled complacently. 'You never know who she's sitting next to. Our Betty, bless her, and Cyril, never go out except to his mother's of a Friday. They've got more to do with their money.'

Neither of them could see or understand that the cinema was a lifeline to sanity for Daisy. Her sixpenny ticket to a world where glossy-lipped beautiful women, wearing satin dressing-gowns and smoking cigarettes in long ebony holders, drove men mad. Exhaling the smoke into their lovers' eyes, they lowered spider's legs eyelashes over pancake make-up, not a hair on their heads out of place, even in force ten gales.

Where Sam's handsome features became superimposed on the rugged countenance of Clark Gable; where the suave John Gilbert's tight smile reminded her of the way Sam had looked the night he went away. The lanky stride of Gary Cooper brought his walk to mind, but on the evening Daisy identified him with Paul Muni escaping from the chain gang, she accepted the fact that she had almost forgotten Sam's face.

Sitting alone, huddled in a tip-up chair in the back stalls, Daisy gave herself up to the Hollywood dream. She was a thick-lidded Garbo in *Grand Hotel*, an anguished Helen Hayes in *A Farewell to Arms* and a husky-voiced Claudette Colbert in *The Sign of the Cross*.

In the cinema she knew that Sam would come to her again.

In the bakehouse in the cold pre-dawn mornings she knew that he would not.

Wakes Week came as usual in the middle of July.

Evolved originally from village religious festivals, the Wakes holidays had weathered the Industrial Revolution, and the whole of the cotton and engineering industries still closed down completely for at least a week.

'If the world was to end with them,' Josiah Wedgwood down in the Potteries had complained a long time ago, 'Wakes *must* be observed.'

The holiday savings clubs were the salvation of the working people. Sixpence a week for a year meant twenty-five shillings plus interest to be collected just before the Wakes, and the amount of money saved was often the deciding factor as to the length of the holiday. Every train carried crowds of holidaymakers away from the smoke and the grime, and the rows of closed shops gave towns the appearance of Hollywood sets shuttered away when filming finished.

In the middle of Wakes Week Edna came excitedly into the living room of the pie shop to announce that she was the grandmother of a seven-and-a-half-pound boy. With her nose and Betty's, bless her, hair.

'We've had a bit of bother with the afterbirth,' she said, sitting down and fanning her hot face with the corner of her

59

apron. 'It wouldn't come away,' she mouthed to Martha, who pursed her lips and jerked her chin in Daisy's direction.

'It's all right. I know where babies come from.' Daisy went back to her library book, an Agatha Christie where the characters were all gathered in the drawing room to be told who had done it. By cheating and looking at the last few pages she already knew, so the book had lost its interest.

'I'm going to put the baby on the bottle before long,' Edna confided to her sister. 'I'm not having our Betty's strength drained, bless her. The baby thriving, and her being pulled down.'

'It's not for you to say, surely?' Daisy could feel herself being nasty. She accepted she was jealous about the baby and admitted that she could just be turning into a sour old maid with bitter and twisted thoughts and a tongue to match. It wouldn't be long, she told herself, before she ran true to form and took to wearing white ankle socks over her stockings, and never ventured out without a safety pin fastening the front of her knickers in case the elastic went.

'The midwife had the cheek to send me out of the room.' Edna was above taking any notice of her niece. 'I'd sent Cyril off to the Town Hall as usual. Men only get in the way at a time like this. He's a proper ditherer, that lad. You'd think he had the St Vitus's Dance even when he's just sat there having his tea.'

Oh, Sam . . . Daisy thought suddenly. Where are you? Did I dream you up?

'His mother's just the same.' Edna wondered when Daisy was going to go through and put the kettle on. 'First time I met her I thought she'd got a wasp in her corsets.'

'After I've made you a pot of tea, will it be all right if I pop round to see Betty and the baby?' Daisy asked Edna in some desperation. 'I won't stop long.'

'Your Daisy must feel a bit put down,' she distinctly heard Edna say as she stood by the stove waiting for the kettle to boil. 'Our Betty, bless her, having a baby before her twenty-first. She'd make a lovely mother would your Daisy, and I hope I don't speak out of turn, Martha, but it was a crying shame she had to go and meet a man who already had a wife and family.'

'There's time enough yet for her to have children of her own,' Martha said in a scolding tone. 'One swallow doesn't make a summer, you know, our Edna.'

Leaving them sipping their tea, Daisy went out the back way and up the street to Edna's house. What she expected to see she didn't quite know, but new mothers in films always seemed to be lying flat in bed with sweat-sticky hair, and eyes still dazed with pain after what they'd been through. Betty, however, was pinkly clean, her fair slippery hair held back with a wide tortoiseshell slide.

'I've brought you a pair of white turkish towels for the baby.' Daisy handed over a large paper bag. 'Boring but practical. Your mother says you have enough matinée jackets and bootees to set up a shop.' She lowered her voice in deference to the snuffling noises coming from a muslin-draped treasure cot. 'I'm really happy for you, Betty. Your mother's as chuffed as if she'd had him herself.'

'It's all been a great strain for her,' Betty said seriously. 'She told me she felt every pain.' Raising both arms high above her head she lowered them quickly. 'Me mam says I mustn't do that till everything's gone back.' She examined a creeping stain on the front of her nightdress. 'See that? Me milk's coming through already.'

Daisy averted her eyes, then immediately felt old-maidish and prudish. 'Your mother's talking about putting him on the bottle, but I expect she was just, you know, giving her own opinion.'

'Oh, no. Me mam says she's seen too many girls go to nothing with struggling to breast-feed. You know, the baby getting all the nourishment while they go to shadows.'

Meeting her cousin's limpid gaze Daisy had the uneasy feeling that there was nothing but an empty void behind the round blue eyes; that Betty was merely an echo, receiving her mother's ideas and repeating them parrot fashion.

Questioning nothing, accepting all. She was prepared to believe that Betty hadn't a wrong thought in her head; the problem was were there any original thoughts there at all? Florence dismissed Betty as a *sponge*. Could she be right? The heat of the day and her own sense of frustration were curdling her tongue:

'But what do *you* want to do, Betty? Breast-feeding's certainly cheaper, and there aren't any bottles to boil up. What does Cyril want you to do?'

'Him?' Betty dismissed her husband with a shrug. 'Men know nowt about that kind of thing. Whatever me and me mam decide to do will be all right with Cyril.'

The baby was crying now, a thin spluttery wail. Betty checked the time on a round alarm clock on the bedside table. 'You can pick him up if you want. The midwife's due any time now. She won't mind.'

Daisy looked down at a small red angry face surrounded by a cocoon of blankets. The eyes were kitten's eyes, blind slits above cheeks so roundly fat they could have been blown up by a bicycle pump.

'Support his head,' Betty said from the bed, but Daisy needed no telling.

With instinctive and age-old tenderness she lifted the baby, holding him in her arms as if her whole life had been a long preparation for just this moment. He fitted the crook of her elbow as if he'd been fashioned for it; when she rocked him to and fro he opened his eyes a fraction; when she held him closer his mouth champed on nothing with little sucking noises.

'Oh, you precious darling. You little love. . . .' Daisy's bad mood vanished. 'What are you going to call him?'

'Me mam likes John.' Betty held out her arms for her son. 'Or Edwin, our grandpa's name. She quite likes Edwin. That's the midwife at the door. You'd best go, Daisy. Thank you for the towels.'

'Daisy feels she's missed the boat,' Betty told herself, smiling at the squat little figure in hot navy-blue serge

62

bustling through the door. 'I saw it on her face when she held the baby.'

'That was me cousin,' she explained. 'She's fetched me some white towels, though me mam says we've enough to set up a shop. Still, the thought was there, wasn't it?'

Arnold was in the lobby when Daisy reached the foot of the stairs.

'He's beautiful.' On a sudden impulse Daisy kissed her uncle's cheek. 'Congratulations, Grandpa. I think he has a look of you. I mean it. I really do.'

'Well, he's bald enough.' Arnold rubbed the top of his head, pleased as punch. 'You're looking a bit off, chuck. It's all wrong you should be cooped up with your mother on a day like this. It's not like you to be so pale.'

'Pale, but interesting, I hope,' Daisy said, quick as a lick, running off down the street and going in through the back way into her own house.

'There aren't many people live in this town, Dad. Are there, Dad?'

Sam Barnet looked down at his son. At six and a half Jimmy was much too old to hold his father's hand, but on Sam's other side a small girl clung tightly, treading pigeon-toed in a scuffed pair of brown sandals.

'It's what they call Wakes Week up here,' Sam explained, crossing the road by Woolworth's with the feeling he had wandered into a ghost town. 'That means holiday time, when people go away. If they can afford to.'

'I don't like it, Dad.' Jimmy's tiredness showed in the hoarseness of his voice. 'It's a horrible place.'

'My feet hurt, Dad.' The small girl stopped suddenly and lifted up her arms. 'Carry me, Dad.'

Bare arms wound themselves round Sam's neck as he swung his daughter on to his back for a piggy ride.

'Hitler's fight is for the peace of the world,' Jimmy read out loud from a torn and wire-meshed placard outside a newsagent's shop, pronouncing each word laboriously. 'Who is Hitler, Dad?'

'A man in charge of a country called Germany.' The child was heavy and Sam wondered how he was going to buy new sandals when it seemed that every single shop had closed down.

'Like the King, Dad?'

'Not quite, son.' Sam broke into a trot, jigging the little girl up and down. 'Nearly there, love. Nearly there.'

'Like a prime minister, then?' Jimmy stared up into his father's face. 'You look hot, Dad, and your nose is sweating.' The neb of his school cap hid the expression in his eyes. 'Why are we knocking at this door when the shop's closed and there's nothing in the window? They'll have gone on holiday. I bet they'll have gone on holiday, Dad.'

'Possibly,' Sam said, setting the child down and knocking again. 'Now remember your manners,' he whispered, hearing footsteps approaching from behind the door and the sound of a bolt being drawn. 'Not too many questions, mind.'

Waiting on the pavement for the door to be opened, they stood close together in the early evening of that hot July day: two children, the boy as dark as the girl was fair, both bearing a marked resemblance to their father, a handsome man in grey flannels, with the collar of his sports shirt laid neatly over his jacket.

'Look what the wind's blown in!'

Edna took them through the shop into the back room, the wrinkled cheeks of her monkey face pushed up into little cushions of triumph with the force of her delighted smile. To think she might have gone and missed *this*, her expression said, her beady eyes noticing the way the colour drained away from Daisy's face as she jumped up from her chair, scattering book and bookmark across the cut rug.

'Sam! Oh, Sam....'

For one startled moment Sam thought Daisy was going to kiss him, but she recovered quickly, crouching down to smile into the children's faces.

'Jimmy and Dorothy.' Sam made the introductions with fatherly pride. 'My boss let me bring them along for the ride. School holidays,' he explained.

'Our mother has gone to France. On business with her boss.' Jimmy's face went red with importance. 'France is too far for children.'

'Of course it is,' Daisy said at once, holding out a hand to Dorothy who hung her head and stuck her thumb in her mouth.

'She's shy,' Jimmy explained. 'Just at first.'

'Well, you'd best all sit down.' Martha was on her dignity, determined not to let her sister sense her agitation. 'My word, but you're two little grand'uns.' Her warm and natural love for children brought a brightness to her eyes. 'Do you know, I've just remembered. I've got a tin of gingerbread men in the kitchen. With currants for eyes. And some lemonade.' Pushing herself up from her chair with difficulty, she stood up. 'Want to come with me and see if I've remembered right?'

'We've got a new baby at our house. New born. This very morning.' Edna's beady eyes had softened. 'I bet you've never seen one as new as that.'

'Is it a white one or a black one?' Colour-conscious since discovering *Little Black Sambo*, Dorothy forgot her shyness enough to ask.

'You have to be born in *Africa* to be black.' Jimmy's voice dripped scorn as they followed Martha and Edna out of the room. Remembering his cap, he snatched it off, holding it to his chest as they disappeared through the door.

'How beautiful they are.' Daisy stared at Sam. Her lips moved as if she was going to say something, then she fell silent again, pleating and repleating the folds of her striped cotton skirt.

'Well, Daisy?' Sam seemed equally at a loss for words. The shock of seeing Martha so changed was still with him. Six months ago she had been full-busted, with high-piled vigorous hair, and now the shadow of sickness had fallen on her like a grey mantle. Daisy too had lost weight, and there was a bruised look about her eyes as if she was sleeping badly. 'This is the first chance I've had to come up here.' He spoke stiffly, hating the necessity for explanation, regretting the impulse that had brought him straight from the uncomfortable sparseness of his digs to the little shop. The very atmosphere was choking him. Outside the street was still warm, golden-tinted from the summer sun. But in here a high-banked fire threw out an overpowering heat, the coals glowing like lava, washing the stippled walls to apricot and bringing the sweat out on his forehead.

'I'm in the district for two days,' he said too heartily. 'The boss knew I was in a spot and said I could bring the children if I kept them out of his way. He knows how I'm placed,' he added stiffly. As if he had said too much, he put up a hand to shield his face from the fire. 'He's not a bad sort. He has four children of his own.'

'He sounds nice.'

'Jewish. Family-minded.'

'I see.'

'We can go and see the baby!' Jimmy's head appeared round the door, black hair almost standing on end in his excitement. 'It's only that big.' Two hands were spread to demonstrate, one holding a sticky gingerbread man. He bit off a leg. 'It's only just born!'

'We won't be long, Mr Barnet.' Martha was animated almost out of recognition. 'I haven't seen it myself.'

'Your mother is ill.' Sam waited until he heard the back door bang to. He leaned forward, his face serious and intent. 'Couldn't you have gone away? The whole town seems to have disappeared.'

'She won't go.' Daisy stared down at her feet, then pushed them underneath her chair as she realized she was wearing her bedroom slippers. 'She just sits.' Her head lifted and he thought he saw the glisten of tears in her eyes. 'You saw how she was before. The doctor stopped her working and that seems to have done for her. Florence says that now her motivation for living has gone she's just given up.'

'Florence?'

'My friend.'

Sam got up and moved to a stand-chair by the table. Away from the fire. The sadness was getting to him. It seemed to be coming at him from the stippled walls. He had decided that he would bring the children, say hello, and go away. He didn't like unfinished business and there had been something definitely unfinished about his last visit. For a moment he saw Daisy as he had left her, on the Boulevard in the rain, wet hair dripping round her face. She had spoiled his lonely Christmas lunch, dammit, appearing before him in his mind, holding out her hands, as if he belonged to her. And he wasn't a cruel man. His wife said he was, but he knew he wasn't.

'I have a job to keep!' he had shouted, when she handed the children over to him. 'If I lose my job, then we're both in the cart.'

'My heart bleeds,' she had said, but she'd turned back and kissed them, before she walked away.

He glared at Daisy. As if it was her fault. Then he smiled. Why not? Why not, indeed?

'The boss is going up to Scotland tomorrow, staying the night in Glasgow, with Mr Bleasdale from the mill. Using his car and his driver.' The grin widened. 'So . . . ? He's said I can take the kids with me for a ride in the Rolls, so why don't you come with us? To the seaside. To that Blackpool you told me about. Why not, Daisy?'

'Because I can't leave me mother.' Daisy's reaction was immediate. 'I can't expect Auntie Edna to stay with her, not with the baby just born. And she certainly can't be left on her own.'

'Why not, for God's sake?' Sam realized they were both shouting. He lowered his voice. 'You can leave her for just one day, surely?'

Daisy shook her head. 'She scalded her hand the other week trying to make herself a cup of tea. She's lost her balance, Sam. She would fall over putting coal on the fire.'

'She doesn't *need* a fire!' Sam's voice rose again. 'Not in the middle of a bloody heatwave.' He fingered his nose and found it was sweating, just as Jimmy had said. 'Are you telling me you're tied to this house? That you never go out? Never?'

'To the pictures. Only when she's safely in bed.'

'Then we'll take her with us. That suit you?' He was laughing, not irritated. Surprising himself.

'She won't come,' Daisy said. 'You can ask her, but I know what she'll say.'

Martha was ready a good hour before the time. She was brighter than she had been for months, pale and resolute in her beige linen coat, with the veil on her hat hanging down over her eyes. Beneath the coat she wore a brown and white flowered dress, with a lace modesty vest pinned into the V with two small gold safety-pins. Already her ankles were flowing over the tops of her patent bar-strap shoes, bulging at the sides where they had spread to accommodate her bunions.

'Dressed up like a dog's dinner,' Edna said, coming in to see them off. 'You're not making sandwiches, are you? There'll be a hamper in the boot with silver goblets, and damask napkins big as tablecloths. Chicken legs and caviar.' The novelty of it all was making her skittish. 'I go to the pictures as well as you, Daisy Bell.'

'Shrimp paste and cucumber.' Daisy looked flustered and pretty. 'She doesn't trust café food.'

'Cucumber repeats on her,' Edna said with satisfaction. She lowered her voice. 'Is it on again with you and him?' She popped a sliver of cress into her mouth. 'You'll be taking a lot on bringing up somebody else's children. Especially the boy. He's too sharp for his age.' A piece of cress dangled from the corner of her mouth. 'We've never had a divorce in the family. It's bound to upset your mother, chuck. What *have* you got in there?' Her sharp features hardened into irritation as Martha came into the kitchen leaning sideways from the weight of a massive brown handbag looped over her arm.

'Your last will and testament?'

'As a matter of fact, yes.' Martha tottered crab-wise to the gas oven. 'And the deeds of the shop, and our birth certificates. You won't catch me leaving this lot behind for the burglars.'

'You look very nice, dear,' Edna said, with deep insincerity.

The children were fascinated by Martha's veil.

'What if you want to blow your nose? I mean, if you forget it's there when you blow your nose?' Jimmy asked.

Martha lifted the veil and tucked it over her hat. 'Like this.' Taking a handkerchief from her pocket she demonstrated. 'All in a day's work.'

She sat on the wide seat at the back of the Rolls between the two of them, unnaturally straight from lacing her corset too tight.

Watching them from the pavement Edna thought her sister looked shocking; hoped Martha knew what she was doing. She waved and smiled before going back to her own house two doors up. 'Thinks she's Queen Mary,' she told Betty, who was having trouble with sore nipples now. 'Sometimes I think your auntie is going round the bend.'

As the big car drew away from the kerb Daisy, sitting in the passenger seat next to Sam, closed her eyes in ecstasy. So as they turned the corner by the front of the shop she failed to see Florence weaving her way down the street like a drunken woman, wild of eye, with her duster coat flying open, and her hair hanging any old how round an ashen face.

It was like sitting on a moving cloud, Daisy thought, opening her eyes to watch Sam's hands at the correct position on the wheel. To make it all perfect the weather was *marvellous*. Blue skies and little puffs of white clouds, just as the man on the wireless had predicted.

Sam drove very fast, so that soon they had left the drab streets behind and were bowling along wide roads, with semi-detached houses set back from green verges, on to a main road lined with trees, and now and then a row of cottages with women hanging washing out to dry.

'All right, love?' Sam put his hand on her knee for a fleeting moment. 'All right there in the back?' he called out.

A little way from Preston he followed a large white sign with an arrow pointing left. 'Blackpool!' he called out, swinging the car smoothly on to the by-pass.

On the wide motor-road he put his foot down hard on the accelerator. With Jimmy urging him on from behind to go faster, faster, they were soon overtaking a stream of holiday traffic. Motorbikes and sidecars, small saloons and lumbering charabancs. Rummaging in the enormous bag Martha produced a pink chiffon scarf and tied it round her throat, in case she felt a draught. 'Can't be too careful,' she told Jimmy.

He nodded. 'You're very old, aren't you?' he whispered, and Martha agreed that indeed she was.

Dorothy was already fast asleep with her head lolling against Martha's arm.

Turning round for a moment Daisy thought her mother looked more peaceful than she had for a long time. There was a serenity in the pinched face as she gently shifted her position to make the child more comfortable. She really loves children, Daisy told herself, turning back again. She would have made the most wonderful grandma. I have let her down, she told herself, by not marrying at eighteen like cousin Betty. She frowned and bit her lip. And was silent for the next few miles.

When Sam was driving, he drove with complete concentration. The car was coasting along, and when Daisy saw on the clock the speed they were going she couldn't believe the evidence of her eyes. Sixty miles an hour, and yet it felt as if they were hardly moving. As fast as the Royal Scot, she marvelled.

She was the first to see Blackpool Tower. Standing like a sentinel, it rose proudly into the bright blue sky. She remembered as a child rushing to the right side of the train to

70

let the window down, craning her head out to see it before anyone else in the compartment.

'If another train is coming the other way you'll have your head whipped off,' Martha had warned without fail every single year, but nothing could spoil that first glimpse of the famous landmark.

Happiness, light as a bubble, gurgled inside her. It was all so unbelievable. There she was, Daisy Bell from the pie shop, sitting like Lady Muck in the passenger seat of a Rolls-Royce limousine, next to a man so handsome he would make Ronald Colman look like something dropped from a flitting. Bowling along a suburban road now, en route to the sea. It was like being in a film, only a million times better. She was Madeleine Carroll, she was Marlene Dietrich, wearing not a blue cotton dress sprigged with flowers but a white satin suit with a big shawl collar, and a silver fox tippet slung casually round her shoulders.

'There's the sea''!' Daisy twisted round in her seat as the car turned on to the promenade by Central Pier. She laughed out loud from the sheer joy of it all, the deep-throated laugh that Sam remembered, waking Dorothy up from her sleep.

Out to sea they could see the curls of crashing foam rising and falling against the black pier-head. On the promenade the wind flapped the trousers of gaily-coloured beach pyjamas on girls with faces burned brick-red by the sun and wind. Small boys dragged iron spades along the concrete, and a panama hat was torn from an elderly man's head, to disappear behind the hooves of a horse drawing a Victorian landeau.

'Woolworth's!' Martha's voice breathed satisfaction. 'Bigger than the one we've got at home.' She craned her head to see better. 'Nay, but it's many a long day since I had a traipse round Woolworth's.'

Behind the store the Tower climbed majestically into the sky. From close up they could see the lift ascending, and the iron lace network of galleries. A crowd of children with clinking buckets and spades charged in front of the car,

71

causing Sam to brake sharply.

Dorothy leaned across Martha to watch a little girl with dress tucked into her knickers walk bare-footed over to the steps by the railings, holding fast to the hand of a boy carrying a shrimping net.

'Donkeys!' Jimmy shouted. 'Can I go on a donkey, Dad? Can I have some ice-cream? Can I, Dad?'

Meshed into the web of holiday traffic, Sam pulled into the side and told them to get out of the car and wait for him, just over there, by the man with the deckchairs.

'He's gone to park the car in a safe place.' Jimmy passed on this information with an air of importance. 'Mr Evison would kill him if it got scratched.'

Holding on to the massive handbag, Martha teetered sideways to the deckchair man in his peaked cap with his leather bag swathed across his chest. She wasn't going to say anything, definitely not going to spoil anybody's pleasure, but the car ride had made her feel distinctly funny. Now the wind was getting at her through her coat, giving her a prickly sensation when she caught her breath. The sun might be shining, oh aye, she'd grant you that, but the wind had an edge to it like a bread-knife. In spite of all the silly beggars walking about with next to nowt on. Women with angry Vs of sunburn at the necks of their print dresses, and men with bald heads who would suffer for it tomorrow.

There was a tight feeling in her chest as if a hand was scrunching it up. She should have stopped at home instead of gallivanting when she wasn't fit. She shot a baleful glance at Daisy leaning over the railing as if she was on the deck of an ocean liner, lifting her face and getting her hair blown about any old how. Happy as Larry, the silly girl, thinking that man was going to marry her, when her mother knew he'd never leave his wife.

What did Daisy know about men? If one hung his trousers on the bedpost she'd think he was just going for a swim. Flinging her hat over the windmill for a man with less life in him than a tramp's vest. Martha had Mr Samuel Barnet

72

weighed up all right. Polite he may be – she'd grant him that – and kind to a point, but he was only out to feather his nest, like the rest of them.

He was going to hurt Daisy and hurt her bad. Martha knew that for sure. And there was nothing she could do about it. Look at those children, down on the sands when their father had told them to stay put. She narrowed her eyes at the sight of Jimmy down on his stomach like a mole, scrabbling in the sand with his fingernails. And his sister shoving her frock into her knickers and whipping her sandals off. Now Daisy was down there with them, on her knees, laughing. At that moment, a child herself.

She would make such a grand mother.... Martha, who never cried, felt the prick of tears behind her eyelids. Why had her daughter got missed when there were married women with faces like rock buns and natures to match? The bag was dragging at her arm, but she wasn't going to put it down, not with that shifty-eyed weasel of a deckchair man giving her funny looks. Men? She'd shoot the lot of them, given the chance.

'Why don't you sit down, Mother?' There was an expression of genuine concern on the deckchair man's face as he pointed to a chair by the railings. 'I won't charge you if you're just waiting for someone.'

To his astonishment, Martha clutched the portmanteau-sized bag to her chest, wrapping both arms round it, glaring fiercely at him through the handles.

'That's me daughter,' she hissed. 'Down there, and her friend's here, coming along the front. You thought I was on me own, didn't you?'

Bewildered, the man went back to his post, shaking his head and hitching at the leather straps criss-crossed over his chest, one bag for the money and the other for the tickets. He was well aware of the fact that you met all sorts, but there were some that should be locked up. Definitely.

By the time Martha was ensconced in a deckchair on the

73

sands with the bag safely between her feet she felt a bit better. Sam had reappeared bearing spades and buckets and two sets of paper flags for the sandpies.

'Would you like a drink of tea out of the flask, Mother?' Daisy knelt by the deckchair, flushed and excited because *he* had come back.

Martha said no, even though her mouth felt parched and dry. She hadn't seen any Conveniences as she stood on the prom, so where on earth would she *go*? They were whispering together, her Daisy and that man. She could see them, even though she couldn't hear what they were saying, and Daisy was smiling and nodding her head, the silly faggot.

Martha closed her eyes. What was wrong with her? For a moment the sea and sky had dipped and swayed together, merging in shiny blue and green ripples, all too much for her.

'Are you all right, Mother?'

She opened her eyes to see Daisy smiling at her. With too much lipstick on, Martha thought. Oh, the silly, silly girl.

'Sam and I are going for a little walk. You won't mind keeping an eye on the children, will you?'

'As long as they don't go near the sea.' Martha nodded through the veil at the row of sandpies and the castle coming on nicely under Jimmy's expert efforts.

'It's Windsor Castle. I'm going to put the Union Jack on top. Watch me!'

Martha smiled and nodded before closing her eyes again, folding her hands over her stomach and settling down into one of her jerky twitchy sleeps.

Up on the promenade Sam took Daisy's hand in his. He glanced back at the sands. 'They like your ma, there's no doubt about that. Kids are funny the way they take to some people straight away. And they like you too, but that's not surprising.'

As they walked away they could see the South Pier in the distance, its Moorish cupolas glistening in the bright sparkling sunshine. Sam was very quiet, but Daisy was so happy she hardly noticed his preoccupation. A trio of girls in floppy hats and beach pyjamas walked past them, licking ice-cream cornets. Mill girls, Daisy guessed, intent on having a good time away from their looms in some vast and noisy weaving shed.

'They used to say that if folks had any money left over at the end of their holiday week they would fling it out of the train window on the journey home. Just to show they'd had a marvellous time and spent the lot. Then start saving again for next year.'

Daisy pointed out a man with a handkerchief knotted over his bald head trotting along in his wife's shadow, a fat short woman in a wallpaper-patterned dress, her plump bare arms mottled red by the sun.

'They're like a couple on one of those rude postcards, aren't they?' She watched the couple with delight. 'Oh, Sam. Thank you for bringing us. I do love you for it.'

At once Sam dropped her hand, striding along more quickly, but Daisy merely tucked the hand into the crook of his arm.

'Just look at the Pleasure Beach! Isn't it wonderful? I once went on the Big Dipper. If I'd coughed I'm sure I would have spat me stomach out. It was in me mouth, that's for sure.' With the habit she had of suddenly turning serious, her eyes clouded. 'When you're here you can forget that behind all this glitter there are thousands of people on the dole who can't afford to come, even for a day.' She squeezed his arm. 'Do you read a lot, Sam?'

There were so many things about this man she didn't know. He had told her very little, she realized; almost nothing about his home. Or his wife. She looked up at the sky, as if surprised to find that the sun was not covered by a cloud. But today the sky and the sea were as one, merging into the far distance with a lone seagull wheeling and dipping its wings in graceful flight. Well, if he didn't want to talk about it, then that was okay by her. And nothing, *nothing* was going to mar this one perfect day.

'Technical books,' he was saying, answering her question.

'Never fiction. I used to be told that sticking your nose in a story-book was a waste of time.'

'In a book I've just read,' she went on, 'a young man called Harry wins on the horses. Twenty-two pounds for a threepenny bet! He gives half of it away, but with the rest he takes his girl Helen away to the seaside. Away from the terrible slum they live in to a place where they can lie in the bracken and watch little boats sailing out to sea. It's called *Love on the Dole.*'

At the memory of what the two young lovers did in the bracken besides watching little boats sailing out to sea, Daisy blushed. She glanced at Sam to see if he had noticed, but he was walking along by her side with his head bent. As if looking for a coin he had dropped and lost. And was determined to find.

Florence had walked for what seemed to be miles, staring down at the cracks in the pavement, putting one foot in front of the other, because something told her that was the way you walked. She had been surprised to find that Daisy was not at home, but not amazed. To be amazed would have indicated feeling of some sort or other, and Florence felt nothing. The only thing she was certain of was that she was never going back to the house again. Never. Ever. Ever.

Being Wakes Week, there were few people about in the streets. The few she met stared at her strangely. She couldn't think why. After all, she had remembered to put on her long coat over her nightdress, and her lace-up shoes over her bare feet, and if her long pale hair was hanging loose down her back instead of rolled up into its neat pleat, what did that signify?

The worrying thing was, where could she go? The neighbours on either side had gone on their holidays, Southport and Cleveleys respectively. Daisy was out, and the one friend she had at work had gone further afield, to Scarborough. Florence saw the park side gates looming in front of her, and with her nightdress trailing, crossed over the road. The sun was so hot that a series of gas-tar bubbles had erupted on the newly-laid macadam surface. She remembered the satisfaction of bursting them as a child, leaving flattened blisters and greasy black marks on her clean white dress when she'd wiped her fingers down it.

There was a bench inside the park, not far from the gates. It was set back from the path, fronting rhododendron bushes, overlooking the duck-pond. As Florence sat down and arranged the nightgown neatly round her ankles, she saw that the hem was all smeared with dust.

'Sorry, Mother,' she whispered, then pulled herself up sharply. 'That way madness lies,' she told herself firmly. 'Shakespeare.'

Oh, but her mother had been such a lovely little woman. Neat as a new pin, with a clean blouse on every day, never missing. She had always arranged the clothes-rack so carefully after she'd finished the ironing. Underclothes first, then laid over them her lace-edged pillow-cases and embroidered mats, starched stiff as planks and ironed first on the front then the back, to bring the French knots into prominence. Fastidious wasn't the word for her mother. Spotless was more like it, from the top of her shining hair to the soles of her polished boots. Not clogs, never, even though her mother had, as a young woman, stood at three looms in a weaving shed. No shawls, neither. She had gone to work wearing a coat and hat, and never stood gossiping on the step like the other women in the street. When she sent Florence out for chips she had always given her a white teacloth to lay over the basket, hiding the basin. When she mopped the front step she had got up early and done it in the dark with a piece of sacking protecting her clean flowered apron.

'Oh, Mother. . . .' Two fat tears rolled down Florence's thin pale cheeks. What would she think about what was going on now? How could she stomach that terrible common woman living in her house, dab-washing in the slopstone and never boiling her whites in the copper?

Florence wasn't going to think about what had been said

that morning. What her father had shouted, standing on the cut-rug in front of the fire, wearing a vest that had gone a bad colour with that woman's slap-dash methods, with his braces dangling, and a love-bite showing up clearly on his thick red neck.

It was terrible ... terrible. Unforgivable. Awful. Getting up from the bench, Florence trailed wearily back along the gravel path. Daisy was bound to be back now from wherever she had been when Florence knocked at the door.

Daisy, with her matter-of-fact ways and her solid common sense. She'd probably gone down to the dairy for the milk, with the roundsman being on his holidays. Leaving her mother in bed, making her promise not to answer the door. Florence walked back up a short road hung with trees like a cathedral cloister, ignoring the rude remarks made by two boys with tennis rackets under their arms. Telling herself they were old enough to know better.

Yes, Daisy would tell her what to do. Kindness personified, that was her friend. Florence could see her filling the kettle, setting it to boil. She could almost hear the gas jet plop into life as Daisy applied a match to it. Feet on the ground, unflappable Daisy, never moody, always the same.

A rock in a storm-tossed sea, thought Florence, wondering if she had read that somewhere. Or just made it up.

In all her wild imaginings Daisy could never have believed that she would be strolling along the prom at Blackpool with the wind and the sun stinging her cheeks and Sam looking so nautical in his single-breasted flannel jacket with brass buttons.

'I have to talk to you,' he said suddenly, drawing her towards two deckchairs set side by side by the sea wall.

'You have to pay even if you only stop for ...'

'It doesn't *matter*.'

He seemed on edge, *irritated*, as he reached into his inside pocket for his silver cigarette case. For a few seconds he busied himself, taking a cigarette, tapping it against the polished surface, then struggling with his lighter, shielding the flame with his hand.

A faint niggle furrowed Daisy's forehead. She stared down at the sands, at the pools left by the morning tide. Surely there were no sands as clean or as satisfying as those at Blackpool? It came from the children's buckets with a decent plop, unsullied by stones or pebbles. There was a family playing cricket by the sea's edge and even as she watched the father hit the ball for a glorious six, while the smallest boy hurled himself face-downwards on the sands because he felt his turn was well overdue.

'I may not be coming this way again.' Sam drew on the cigarette. He looked up at the sky as if searching for the right words. 'I don't want you to read more than there is into our . . .' he hesitated, 'our friendship.'

A drove of donkeys galloped along the beach, girls screaming in mock terror as they clung on for dear life. Quite dispassionately Daisy turned her head to watch them go by. She had the strangest notion that if she ignored what Sam was trying to tell her, the words would float away over the horizon.

'I don't live with my wife.' Sam studied the glowing tip of his cigarette. 'For the past year I've been living alone over the garage at my boss's house.' He cleared his throat. 'Mr Evison understands the situation. It suits him, and it suits me. In return for being at his beck and call, driving the other car to take his wife shopping and picking his children up from school. From three different private schools. As well as doing the garden and acting as general dogsbody. He pays me a decent wage and lets me live rent-free.'

'I see,' Daisy said in a small voice.

Sam flicked the remains of the cigarette over the railings. 'I have one more year to go with my studies – I'm doing a correspondence course in motor engineering – then I will have the certificates to show that I am a qualified engineer. I served my time as an apprentice just after the war, then instead of going any further I got married. My wife's father

79

had a small printing business, and he gave me a job in the front office, being nice to customers and helping them to choose letter-headings and wedding invitation cards. Nicer than wearing overalls and lying underneath cars, you see.'

He reached for another cigarette. 'But he went bust, then he died, and for a while I did anything I could find: door-to-door selling, an attendant at a swimming baths – oh, don't you believe that there's no unemployment down south. And I got the sack – I forget from which job – and my wife got part-time work.' He sighed. 'That was when the rot set in.'

'So you looked after the children?'

Daisy was busy adjusting the white buckle on the belt of the flower-sprigged dress. Straightening it so that the thin material threaded through evenly. Sam suddenly wanted to slap her hand away. Yet what had he expected? That she would burst into tears, and tell him she would die if he meant what he'd said about not coming north again?

'Her mother looked after the kids.' He kept his voice as even as hers. 'So where did that leave me?' He turned to face Daisy and she flinched at the bitterness in his expression. 'After a hell of a dust-up I packed my things and cleared off.'

'Leaving your wife with her mother?'

'Oh, God, no. Now that my wife's working she pays a woman to have them, to pick them up from school at lunch time. Oh, God, no, her mother isn't the clinging type. She has a life of her own, has Queenie.'

'You mean she doesn't live her life through her daughter and grandchildren.'

'Hell, no.'

'It's a working-class thing that, isn't it?'

'I never said that.'

'But it's true.' Daisy seemed to have settled the buckle to her satisfaction. 'Especially up here. It's a trap, really. Florence would have been just the same if her mother hadn't died.'

'Florence?'

'My friend.'

'Oh, yes, you told me.'

'But you are quite wrong in thinking that I read more than I ought into *our* friendship.' Daisy's voice was very high, very clear. 'Florence would laugh if I told her, not that I *will* tell her. I've never mentioned you, as a matter of fact. She doesn't have a very high opinion of men.' She jumped up suddenly. 'I really think we should be getting back. Those children will be hungry, and my mother likes her meals at regular times, even picnics. That's a northern trait, too.'

'Daisy?' Catching hold of her hand, Sam pulled her back to her chair. 'Please listen to me.'

'Is there something else you want to tell me?' Daisy's chin lifted. 'It helps to talk to a friend, I know.'

'Daisy!' Jerking her towards him, Sam held her fast by the wrists. 'Stop being so . . .'

'So what?'

'So un-Daisyish.'

'And what does that mean?'

He missed entirely the break of near hysteria in her voice. 'Pretending not to mind when you do.' His beautiful eyes were liquid with tenderness and she couldn't bear to look at him. '*I* care,' he told her. 'Meeting you has been a revelation to me. You're the kind of person who makes the best of things, love. There isn't a martyred bone in your body. You don't rail against what fate throws up for you. You just get on with living.' His voice was soft, almost soporific. 'You're not for ever thinking the grass could be greener over the other side of the fence. You accept the inevitable, and cooperate with it.'

'And what you really mean is that for me the inevitable is accepting that I will never see you again?'

'That too.' A smile lifted the corner of his mobile mouth. 'You are all right, Daisy. A lot more than all right. No, don't pull away.' Bending his head he kissed her lips in a tender-sweet caress. 'There will always be a special corner in my heart. Just for you, Daisybell. I wish I could have got to know you better.'

81

'Shall we go back?'

Breaking free, Daisy began to walk back along the promenade. There was so much anger inside her she could feel it drumming her heartbearts and flushing her face. How dare he patronize her like that? He wasn't worth one of the shop's twopenny buns, not even one without cream in it. She was sorry for his wife, heart-sorry for her, and it was no wonder she'd chucked him out, in spite of what he'd said about walking away himself. Lies? He could tell them to music. He was as much like Clark Gable as she was like Shirley Temple. His eyes were too close together, just as her mother said. She couldn't bear it. His assumption that she would break her heart. . . .

She began to run, dodging round a woman in a pink floppy hat licking an ice-cream cornet, almost knocking over a toddler with a livid boiled face, staggering bandy-legged beside his pushchair. People were staring at her, and she didn't care. All she wanted to do was to put as much distance between them as she could. Why, she wouldn't touch him with a barge pole, not even a mile-long barge pole. If he lay dying of thirst with a cup of water just out of reach, she would kick it over rather than give him a sip. All this she told herself without believing a word of it.

She could see her mother now on the sands, sitting with her deckchair positioned away from the sun, because Martha didn't believe in the sun. The two children were running backwards and forwards from a pool with buckets of sea to pour into the moat encircling Windsor Castle. Intent on what they were doing.

The beach was very crowded now. Daisy had to step over a fully-clothed man with a newspaper over his face lying prone on a striped towel before she could reach her mother.

Martha's right hand trailed listlessly in the sand. Her head had fallen sideways as she slept, knocking her hat askew. Her mouth was wide open. And behind the veil so were her eyes.

A group of children ran screaming past the chair, dragging a long senna-coloured trail of seaweed; not a yard away a woman, fresh from her swim, struggled out of a wet bathing suit beneath a tent-like towelling robe. A beach ball, red and shiny, bounced almost into Daisy's face and she knocked it away with an automatic swipe of a hand.

Stunned and disbelieving, she looked up at Sam picking his way towards her. Knowing that although the sun was still shining from a clear blue sky, although children played, balls bounced and the raucous voices of Punch and Judy clamoured for attention not yards away, her mother would hear and see nothing ever again.

Trying to take in the indisputable fact that her mother was dead.

Chapter Four

Edna missed nothing that went on in the street. Let a neighbourly row erupt on the flagstones, or the milkman's horse do the unforgivable outside her house, and she would be out there, giving advice in her tinny chirrupy voice.

So it wasn't surprising that she just happened to be standing on her doorstep for a breath of air when Daisy's friend swanned past on the other side.

Edna blinked, trying to believe the evidence of her eyes. Florrie Livesey was wearing her nightie – there was no doubt about it. It was one of those stockinette jobs off the material man on the market, that trebled in length when you washed it. The one Edna had made for their Betty, bless her, had dropped that far she'd got two good rubbing cloths with the pieces cut from the bottom. And there was Florrie Livesey in one, walking down the street with it sticking out like a fish-tail exhaust from beneath her winter coat. Edna stepped on to the pavement for a better view. Come to that, what was Florrie Livesey doing wearing her winter coat on a day when the sweat stood out on you like gob-stoppers? Her hair was hanging loose too, rats' tails over the musquash collar. Edna watched her cross over the street and start to rattle the sneck on the bakehouse door. Saw her rattle it and keep on rattling. Enough to break it if she wasn't careful. Edna went into battle.

'It's no good carrying on like that, Florrie. They've gone to Blackpool for the day. With Daisy's friend.'

'*I* am Daisy's friend!' Florence began beating on the door with clenched fists, crying now, with great glycerine tears oozing from beneath swollen pink eyelids, then staring at Edna with eyes that were dazed and dead in the green-tinged whiteness of her face. 'I want a drink!' Her voice came rusted from the desperation of her need, and her tangled hair fell forward, as knotted as a bead curtain. 'I have to have a drink.'

Edna flared her nostrils. So that was it. *Drink*. She couldn't smell it on her, but it was in the family all right. That randy father of hers would spit whisky if he as much as coughed. Martha had told her he had recently lost his job.

'Florrie!' Edna was determined to show this unlovely apparition what was what.

'My name is *Florence*!' A purplish bruise swelled one cheek and lifted the corner of her mouth from which a cut ran, congealed with dried blood. Florence touched it gingerly. '*He* did this, you know. Because I dared to tell him what I thought of him.'

Normally Edna would have been all agog to hear the details, but she was tired to the point of exhaustion. All that day the sun had beat down from a sky unpolluted by smoke from mill chimneys that normally faded the blue even from a summer sky. Now, with the sun gone and long shadows edging like gloved fingers across the street, Edna was more than a bit worried. They should have been back from Blackpool ages ago. Martha would be fit for nothing. Edna had seen her more than once so tired she could barely climb the stairs to bed, so weary she'd sleep in her corsets but for a helping hand.

'Now come on, Florrie.' Her tone was even brisker this time, standing no nonsense. 'Best get yourself home to sleep it off.'

The last thing Martha needed to come home to was a drunken woman in a dirty nightie, carrying on crying and wailing on the doorstep, Let this Florrie Livesey see who was boss, then she might pull herself together and see sense. That was the only way to deal with drunks. Not that Edna had any first-hand dealings with them.

'Off you *go*, love!' She wagged a tolerant finger now, deciding that the gentle approach would be best. 'I know what these holidays at home can be like. All your club money saved and the shops closed so you can't spend it. Come on, love. Your mother would turn in her grave if she saw you out in the street like this.'

It was the mention of Florence's mother that did it.

The glazed look disappeared from her eyes, to be replaced by a shining, blazing anger. 'My mother! Oh, if my mother saw what he'd done to me it would break her heart.' Again she touched the swelling bruise on her cheek-bone. 'That's what he did to me! And that terrible woman living in my mother's house – he hits her too. But she eggs him on, and do you know why? Because she enjoys it!'

'You mean she likes him hitting her?' Edna was fascinated in spite of herself.

'It is beyond your understanding.' Florence lowered her voice. 'Men and women sometimes do terrible things to one another. For sexual gratification.'

'Oh, my goodness!' Edna stopped her own mouth with her hand, as if she had said such a dreadful thing herself.

'He hits her. She whimpers a bit. He hits her again, then her temper explodes and she hits him back. She throws anything she can get her hands on, but he knocks it all away as easily as if he was brushing a fly from his nose. So she grows madder and madder and claws at his face, but he holds her wrists, and she struggles and struggles. Then, when they are both panting, and have most of their clothes torn off, they.... Well, I was so upset the first time I saw them fighting I tried to help her and she swore at me.'

'You mean they...?' Edna's eyes stood out like chapel hat-pegs.

'Oh, they go upstairs. If I'm there. But if I'm out, I don't suppose it matters where. Some men are worse than animals.' Florence seemed to have recovered a little of her composure. 'I am never going back to that house,' she told Edna in a strange ringing voice. 'I came down this morning and confronted them in the middle of their filthy antics. I called them both perverts – my father a sex-crazed maniac and her a whore.'

'They wouldn't like that, Florrie.'

'No. That was when he landed out at me, but I stood my ground. I asked him did he know it was my mother's birthday anniversary, and he told me to get out and never come back. I got my coat down from its peg at the stair bottom and walked out.'

'First thing this morning?'

'I have been walking all day long, Mrs Bell.'

Edna didn't correct her. What was a wrong name at a time like this?

'Without a drink of water or a bite to eat. I tried to drink from the fountain in the park, but a keeper mistook me for a tramp and shooed me away. Did you know my mother, Mrs Bell?'

Edna nodded. Martha had described her more than once. 'You could eat your dinner off her lavatory seat, she's that clean,' she had said. 'She even takes her oilcloth up from the floor every spring to scrub underneath, going down on her knees to prise every bit of muck from the nicks in her floorboards. Makes her husband leave his shoes outside the back door before he comes in from work. She even irons the cord in his pyjamas, then threads it back again, she's that pernickety.'

Edna was at a loss what to do. She wasn't an unkind person. Not many folks in need were ever turned away from her door. Even though Arnold had been out of work for a long time she never shirked her turn to make the scones for the Ladies' Thursday Afternoon Bright Hour. She could invite this Florrie Livesey into her house, make her a cup of tea and let her wait there comfortable till they got back from Blackpool. But what about Arnold and Cyril having to listen to mucky talk about whores and sex when they'd just finished a nice tea of potato cakes and beetroot? And what about their

87

Betty, bless her, sitting up in bed suffering with her nipples, wondering what was going on downstairs?

'If you'll come with me I'll get you a cup of water,' she said at last. 'Then I really do think you will have to go home.' She patted the sleeve of Florence's winter coat. 'All families have squabbles, love. It's part of life's pattern. Those who say they never have a cross word don't tell the truth. . . .'

Her voice tailed away. Florrie Livesey was off like a cannon shot, half-way up the street already, muttering to herself with her head down, then suddenly beginning to run. Hitching the nightdress up with one hand and disappearing round the corner in the direction of the allotments with their pigeon cotes and hen-pens.

'Potty,' Edna said aloud. 'Maybe not drunk, but definitely potty.'

She didn't go into her house straight away. Instead she stood on the doorstep, arms folded across her flat chest. The glory of the bright day had almost faded, and somehow a great weight of unease had settled on her.

It was the unnatural heat, she told herself, going inside at last and closing the door. Folks weren't used to it up here. It overheated the blood.

Sam had seen to everything. He couldn't get over the kindness of the Lancashire crowd on that sun-drenched beach. A man in a flat cap ran to find a telephone to summon an ambulance. A stout woman with three children grouped round her on a plaid rug found places for Jimmy and Dorothy, holding out two sticky buns with the icing peppered with sand.

'I'm here for the rest of the day,' she told Sam. 'You come back when you can, love. They'll come to no harm. I promise you that. They're better not seeing more than they have to.'

She had a square face, red like a scald, arms like ham shanks, and eyes sunk deep into puffy cushions of flesh. She was clean and kind, as wholesome as a baked apple, and Sam knew he could trust her; knew he had no choice but to trust her. He glanced over to the deckchair. A small but respectful crowd had circled it, offering advice, murmuring sympathy. Someone had put Martha's hand back on her lap; a girl in a one-piece bathing costume was saying that maybe a towel over the old lady's face? Children, wide-eyed with morbid curiosity, were led away. Daisy knelt in the sand stroking her mother's arm.

The ambulance came. Two men wearing navy-blue peaked caps trod splay-footed across the sand, dispensed with the stretcher and carried Martha away, first letting the deckchair down and covering her with a brown blanket.

From the foot of the iron steps Sam looked back at his children. Dorothy was being read to and Jimmy was busy once again on Windsor Castle, with two of the boys from the plaid rug burrowing like moles beside him to deepen the moat.

Daisy was a stone. 'I'm sorry,' she said, as they waited in a corridor of a hospital with wide echoing passageways leading off it in all directions. 'What would I do without you?' she asked, when Sam took over the awful formalities, answering questions for her, even pointing to the place on the form she had to sign.

'She never did get her traipse round Woolworth's, did she?' Her eyes were bright with unshed tears. 'Did you see how small she was? And her mouth seemed to be smiling. Or does that happen sometimes when people die? I think I read somewhere that it did.'

It had all turned out to be so simple really. The body – it was impossible to think of her mother as that – would be taken back home to the Chapel of Rest. They had given Sam a card with the name of an undertaker printed on it in decent black lettering.

'By tomorrow afternoon,' they told Sam, professional, efficient, as if they dealt with people dying in deckchairs every single day. 'Mr Taylor will call.'

'Is that what you want?' Sam asked Daisy. 'You say exactly what you want.'

'There isn't the room,' she said, explaining without saying the words.

'No.' Sam closed his eyes, trying to see Martha in that small overheated room at the back of the shop, lying in a coffin with a white frill round her neck, her hands crossed over that spade-flat chest. He had an overwhelming urge to get back to the children. 'I think we can go now,' he said with gentleness. 'There isn't anything left for us to do here.'

'We must get back to the children,' Daisy said, reading his mind. 'I hope they didn't see. What are we going to tell them, Sam?'

She really was the most incredible girl. Outside the hospital Sam hailed a passing taxi. But that was the way she was; somehow he knew that for sure. The shock had made her seem somehow older and plainer than she had before. It was the liveliness of her normal expression that made her attractive, he realized. In the taxi she turned her head away from him to stare through the window on her side.

'Honeymoon Couple Starves for Love.' Daisy's mind registered the words spelt out on a billboard as the taxi drew near to Central Pier. Only that morning she had thought how colourful the holidaymakers were. How happy they were, like vivid postcards. Now, somehow, they appeared to have changed. The men grim-faced, wearing ill-fitting jackets and trousers, looking bent and ill as though on a hunger march. The women in frocks of dark prints, dragging whining children past a peep-show. 'The Rector of Stiffkey,' the notice shouted. 'Come and see him starving in a barrel.'

It was all there. The pole-squatting, the sixpenny sheet-music bazaars, the stalls with shocking-pink rock layered in tiers. 'Lettered all through.' Girls walking arm in arm wearing KISSMEQUICK hats, laughing at gangs of youths with hair cut close to their heads like convicts.

'Undignified,' Martha would have said. 'Well, let's talk straight, then. Common.'

'In her own way, my mother was a little lady,' Daisy told Sam. 'She was very well respected. She didn't have many friends, but she won't have left any enemies. She was a *dignified* sort of person in her own way.'

'She *died* with dignity,' Sam said soothingly. He helped Daisy down from the taxi, and spotted the children as soon as they were across the tramlines. Tactfully, he curbed the enthusiasm of his wave.

'I'm starving hungry,' Jimmy grumbled, morose and disagreeable, kicking at a pebble. 'Dorothy's wet her knickers. The lady told her to "go" in the sea, but she wouldn't.'

'I've not!' Dorothy jumped up from the plaid rug, a half-moon swathe of wet knicker, sand encrusted, hanging down below the hem of her pink cotton dress. 'What did those men do with that old lady?'

'I've *told* you and *told* you. She's died,' Jimmy said. 'But she had white hair, so it was *time*.'

'That's enough, son.' Sam stared down anxiously at Dorothy, but cocooned in her own important misery she accepted a square of sweating chocolate and crammed it in her mouth, chewing with it wide open so that brown saliva trickled down her chin.

'They don't bother.' The stout woman, her face by now looking as if it had been boiled in a bag, handed over the carrier bag with its string handles. 'It goes over their heads at that age. Callous little buggers, really.' She jerked her chins sideways. 'But *he's* sharp. Knows how many beans make five, that one does.' From behind her back she produced Martha's portmanteau-like handbag. 'I knew you'd never given this a thought, and no wonder, but I brought it over to be on the safe side.'

She knew by the way Daisy's face crumpled that something about the bulky handbag had touched her to the quick. She knew the feeling. It was the kindness in folks that undermined you just when you thought you had yourself under control. She adjusted the hankie tucked into the V of her dress. Best pretend to be doing something to give the lass a chance to sort her face out before she burst into tears. Fussing with the hankie, she knew that in spite of its protection the blisters would come up. But with only the one day at the seaside to get brown in, there wasn't time to hang about. How nicely spoken the two children were. From London, the boy had said. This lass wasn't their mother, though *he* was the father. There were some funny set-ups in this world. Not that it was any business of hers.

'Don't mention it,' she told Sam when he tried to thank her. 'Poor soul,' she whispered, glancing over to where the sand still held the deeply scored marks of Martha's deckchair. 'Has she been badly for long? Or was she took sudden?'

'Both.' Sam held out his hand and felt it smothered up in a warm moist clasp. 'I really can't thank you enough for what you did. It was a kindness I will remember for a long time.' Emotion, held in check for the past few hours, suddenly flooded through him. He bent down and held the sweaty hand for a long moment.

'We only pass this way but once,' the woman said, bemused by Sam's nearness.

'The children must eat, Sam.'

For their sakes Daisy was keeping a tight hold on herself. There was a strange calmness about her, so that she could be quite brisk and sensible, giving the impression that she was being brave, when in reality the awful thing that had happened hadn't touched her yet. She accepted that it wasn't in her nature to roll on the ground and scream, or even have mild hysterics. Play-acting, her mother would have called it. Showing herself up, especially outside the house, was perhaps the greatest sin of all. Emotions and hysterics were for the likes of Joan Crawford and Greta Garbo, and even they looked a bit daft at times. After one of her rare visits to the pictures, Martha had said: 'All that carrying on, when a clip round the ear-hole would have settled it in one minute flat.'

'I couldn't bring myself to touch the sandwiches.' Daisy

looked at the carrier-bag and shuddered. 'They'll be horrible by now, anyway.'

Immediately Sam left her side to tip the whole lot into a waste-bin. It gave him something constructive to do. He had never dealt with someone so recently bereaved before and he wasn't at all sure how to behave. If Daisy had sobbed and cried he could have put his arms round her and comforted her, but although all the vivacity had been wiped from her face she didn't have the haunted expression you sometimes glimpsed through a car window in a funeral cortège on its way to the cemetery.

'I parked the Rolls outside the Savoy.' Best stick to practicalities, he decided. 'You can make a telephone call from there.'

'Who to? Auntie Edna?' Daisy shook her head. 'There's only one man with a telephone round our way, and he's gone on his holidays. Doctor Marsden is away too, and the doctor standing in for him wouldn't know who I was.' She glanced back over her shoulder at Jimmy plodding along with his head bent. 'It's kinder if I tell them myself. It's going to be a terrible shock.'

Dorothy was crying now, a low monotonous wail all on one note. She walked pigeon-toed in the tight sandals; her eyes ran, her nose dripped, and no one had thought to pull her drooping knickers up properly. She looked, Sam thought irritably, like a slum child's picture taken especially for a Sunday newspaper by a photographer showing how the other half lived.

To show his disgust, Jimmy walked a few paces behind, to pretend he was with someone else. Dorothy had no right to be making that noise. It wasn't real crying anyway – just a habit she had got into nowadays. He dropped even further behind, whistling to show his contempt, stuffing his hands in the pockets of his shorts. He had quite liked the lady with the plaid rug, even though he bet she was fat enough to go in a peep-show on the fairground. She had kept them going with food all afternoon, but he wasn't going to mention that. The ice-cream cornet and the wedge of pork pie with the pink meat encased in a salty jelly. Fist time he'd eaten a pie like that. And the crisps with the little blue bag of salt had been good, too. The lady had showed Dorothy how to distribute the salt without spilling any of the crisps when she shook the bag. If Dorothy kept quiet they might get something else to eat, like a cone with candy-floss busting out of the top, or a stick of rock, or a bag of fish and chips with vinegar trapped in the corners so that when you'd finished you could upend it and drink the dregs. Anything would do. Watching these delicacies passing, clutched in sandy hands, he felt the juices fill his mouth and dribble down his chin.

He wasn't going to think about the old lady dying, though, or where they had taken her. How did they know she was dead, anyway? There hadn't been any blood about as far as he could see. She hadn't been shot or stabbed or anything. Nurtured on comics like *The Wizard*, with Lionheart Logan of the Royal Mounties chasing villains through the snow, death for Jimmy was a violence, to be met bravely, murmuring a few well-chosen words of farewell, if possible. Preferably with a bullet hole in the victim's forehead.

He slouched along, the whistling silenced now.... His mother's hair was almost white, especially at the front. The *back* was darker, he consoled himself, but the big front wave was as white as the old lady's hair. His mother did it herself with a brush dipped in a bottle. 'Jean Harlow. The original platinum blonde!' she'd say, and they would laugh as if it was funny. No, his mother wasn't ready to die. White hair didn't count when it was brushed on. She was strong, his mother was. Probably live to about a hundred and ninety, he bet. The whistling began again.

There was a crowd in the hall of the Savoy restaurant, massed in front of the staircase.

'High teas first floor,' Sam said, lifting Dorothy and motioning the other two to follow.

Daisy put a hand over her mouth in a small gesture of

comfort. It was impossible. She couldn't do it. Not walk into a restaurant as if nothing had happened. But she had to. For the sake of the children. They were Sam's children, not hers, and her mother dying in her deckchair like that when she was supposed to have been looking after them could scar their little minds for ever if they didn't play this next bit right. Suppose Jimmy had asked Martha for something; suppose he had touched her and she had slowly toppled over, like bodies did in films? Or even if he hadn't touched her, but merely tried to speak to her, thinking she was listening because her eyes were open?

Daisy followed Sam down the long brown-panelled room overlooking the sea-front to an empty table. 'Thank you,' she said when he pulled her chair out for her to sit down.

I hope someone closed her eyes, a voice inside her head said clearly.

Surely Sam could have got the children a bag of chips? A toffee apple? *Anything*. They could have eaten them in the car. Daisy sighed. But they couldn't do that, could they? Not sitting in the back of the Rolls on that pale beige upholstery, making crumbs, or touching the splendour of it all with sticky fingers. Sam would never have allowed that. She watched him take a menu card from an elderly waitress and study it carefully.

Things mattered more than people to Sam. He was kind and he was caring. But only so far. Daisy found she could think quite logically. You had to have imagination to *feel*, and imagination was lacking in Sam. She tried to be fair. Her mother was nothing to Sam. How could she be when he hardly knew her? But his children meant a great deal to him. You needed no imagination to understand that.

'Sausage and chips for the children, I think, and Welsh rarebit for me. Daisy?' His hand came out to cover her own. 'We haven't eaten a thing since breakfast time. I told my landlady we wouldn't need anything when we got back, so there won't be anything for the children there. I *know* how you feel, but *try*, love. Just a scone or a cake maybe?'

'Afternoon teas downstairs, high teas up here,' the waitress said, but her disapproval was more maternal than unfriendly.

'All right then, but I know I can't.'

Daisy turned her head sharply to hide the glisten of tears. Out there on the sea-front crowds of people still walked about in the wilting sunshine. The light was fading in the restaurant now, the colour seeping from the walls, though darkness was hours away. Daisy wondered what Auntie Edna would do when she heard about it. She wouldn't have anyone to score off now, or boast to, or openly envy. Except me, Daisy thought bleakly... except me.

'Your mother was *very* old, you know.' At once Daisy turned, and saw the widening of Jimmy's troubled eyes, the fear in the self-conscious tilt of his head. His forehead furrowed with the weight of his anxiety. 'People only die when they get old, you know. *You're* not ready yet, Daisy, and my mum isn't ready.' There was a terrible earnestness in his expression. 'She's coming back from France, you know. The boat won't sink or anything. I expect she'll be waiting when we get back home. Won't she, Dad?'

'She'll be back, son.' Sam's mouth tightened. She had better be back. Mr Evison had been more than understanding about the children turning up unexpectedly like that, but he wasn't running a crêche, for Pete's sake. He could fill Sam's job without thinking twice. There would be hundreds of men who would give their back teeth for a job with living accommodation, even if it was only a room over a garage. Where else would he have such a chance to study, way into the night if he wanted, without a wife nagging him to come to bed and telling him for the umpteenth time he was wasting his time when there were B.Sc.s sweeping the streets?

Jimmy was examining Daisy's face closely for any sign that mirrored his own uncertainty. But her face was smooth, much smoother than his mother's face when she'd been rowing with his dad. He touched her dress. Not so she would notice, but touching it all the same.

96

When the meal came he fell on it as if he hadn't seen food for the past three days.

'You understand that I have to go now? That I would stay with you if it were humanly possible?'

By the back door leading into the bakehouse Sam cupped Daisy's face in his hands, gazing deeply into her eyes. The children were fast asleep on the back seat of the car, and he would carry Dorothy straight up to the camp bed in the back bedroom of his digs and tell Jimmy he could go to bed without washing for once. Mr Evison would be back from his trip to Scotland before ten, could even be back now, and he would expect to see the Rolls shining brightly, topped up with petrol, ready for the drive back early the following morning.

'*Of course* you have to go. You've done more than enough already.' Daisy's voice was slightly brisk, her manner forcibly cheerful.

Which was as it should be, Sam thought on a great rush of relief. There had been enough drama for one day, and if that sounded callous he could not help it. He had fetched Edna and tactfully suggested that her husband came with her as the news wasn't good, and now there they were in the living room, Edna crying her eyes out and saying she couldn't and wouldn't believe it, and Arnold standing helplessly on the rug, looking totally superfluous, his hands straigh down by his sides as if he were on parade.

'I don't *want* to go.' Sam stepped back a pace. 'I feel awful. Will you be staying with your aunt and uncle tonight?'

'There isn't the room. Besides, the minute you've gone I'm going to ask Uncle Arnold to go for Florence.'

'Your friend?'

'Yes.'

'That's all right, then.' Still he hesitated, the sight of the dry-eyed Daisy unnerving him. 'I'll be in touch.'

'There's no need.'

Remembering every word of the speech he'd made that

morning on the promenade before . . . before they had found her mother. . . . Daisy knew the cotton-wool head on her shoulders wasn't going to let her down now. Through its weightlessness she could absorb everything going on around her. She could take part, or she could not take part. Even Edna's genuine grief left her unmoved. Well, not unmoved, *pitying*, that was all.

It was funny, she reflected, as she watched the big car draw away from the kerb, that films were so often very far from realistic, even when they were supposed to show life 'right down to the grain'. People didn't always wail in anguish when someone close to them died and have to be led by the arm, even from one chair to another. Prostrate with grief. Was that what she should be at that very moment? Instead of which she was going inside to talk to Uncle Arnold, glad that Sam had at last got over the embarrassment of saying goodbye, and driven away.

'We never had a cross word,' Edna was saying when Daisy went back into the living room.

'Except the time you didn't speak to each other for six months.' Arnold wasn't going to allow his wife to get away with a statement like that. Even under the circumstances.

'She didn't suffer,' Daisy told them for the third time. 'The doctor at the hospital said her heart just stopped beating. She died in her sleep.'

'But in a deckchair!' Edna began to cry again. 'It's a good job we're not RCs and can die without some Father O'Malley or Father O'Reilly telling a great string of beads over us. But it would have been nice if the new minister up at the chapel had been with her. Just to ease her passing.'

'She was *happy*.' Daisy spoke in desperation. 'She was out for the day, in the sunshine, and she was with the children. You *know* how she loved children.'

'She's right, Edna.'

Edna ignored her husband. She had been ignoring him for thirty-two years so it came easy. 'I'm not having you stopping here all on your own tonight, love. You can come to our house and sleep with me. Your uncle can sleep on the settee.'

'No!' The thought of lying side by side with Edna in the double bed in the front room with its mahogany headboards and quilted spread filled Daisy with horror. 'Florence will come.'

All at once Florence Livesey was the one person in the whole world she needed to see. Florence wisping into the house, net gloves and all, shoulders drooping, baby-fine hair scragged back into what she called her French pleat. Florence dispensing advice, her accent at times at variance to her upbringing. The friend who would understand what losing a mother meant. Because I'm damned if I do, Daisy thought, trying once again to grope her way through the billowing wool in her head that seemed to have mopped up all feeling.

'Florence will come,' she said again, appealing to Arnold. 'You know where the Liveseys live. If you say what has happened she will come straight away.'

'Florrie Livesey?' Daisy had expected opposition, but what she wasn't prepared for was the way Edna clapped a hand over her mouth stifling a shriek. As if she'd suddenly remembered something she'd left on the gas stove. 'The last I saw of your friend,' she managed to say at last in a sepulchral voice, 'she was running up the street with her nightie sticking out from under her good winter coat. The one with the musquash collar,' she explained, making the movements of fastening it at the front under her chin. 'Gone to do away with herself by the look on her face, though she's always had a nervous streak in her, and no wonder with a father who belts her round the face and blacks both her eyes.'

'She wouldn't do a thing like that, love.' Arnold caught up with Daisy outside the back door. 'They never do it when they threaten.'

But Daisy was half-way up the street, and Arnold knew there was nothing else he could do but lumber after her.

*

99

Florence sat on the grassy bank, her body curled over her bony knees. The grass was dirty; she had taken a blade and run it through her finger and thumb and the soot was there all right. It didn't even *smell* like grass, either. She remembered as a child picking grass and eating the white nutty part that came from the soil. Her mother had told her how dangerous that was – that if a cow had passed its water on the grass and little Florence had eaten it, she could develop a terrible disease which made her toenails drop out.

Dear Mother... dear timid little Mother with her constant warnings of doom and gloom. 'Never sit on the seat of a public lavatory, or get your feet wet, or let your head get cold. Never wash your hair at that certain time in a month; always breathe through your nose, but don't breathe at all if you're near a bad smell; eat your crusts to make your hair curl, and the skin off the rice pudding to give you pink cheeks.'

How had she married that terrible man with his thick bull neck and the thread veins in his eyes, when his daughter couldn't bear to be near to him? All that coarse flesh folded loosely like tyres – how had her little mother felt when he pressed her close to his side?

It was dark now, but Florence could see the water down below flashing again and again like the blade of a knife. There were dead dogs in there, and dead cats, their bodies hideously bloated and swollen, rotting and disintegrating just as her body would rot and disintegrate in the fullness of time. The stars were very bright; but there was one which looked as if it was caught in the branches of a tree; if she were one of the silly stupid women in the films she was forced to see night after night she would widen her eyes, run her fingers through her hair and start to warble a silly song. Then from over the hill behind her a man would appear. He would be tall and incredibly handsome – that went without saying – and he would pull her to her feet, in one graceful movement of course, and they would serenade the star together, cheeks welded close.

Daisy fell for that sort of tosh. Daisy believed that one day a man would come along and take one look at her and fall in love. Daisy believed in happy endings. Daisy was a romantic, but *she* wasn't. Not flamin' likely!

There wasn't a man in the world who could bamboozle Florence with sweet talk, a hard-luck story, or a little-boy-lost appeal. Men had tried; well, of course they had. A cinema usherette was easy meat for men on the prowl. Some nights she only had to sit down on the end seat at the back of the stalls to rest her feet and some pervert would be there, trying to put his hand on her knees, or up her skirt. Narrowing her eyes, Florence nodded to herself. Many a man had hastily moved to another seat when she'd dotted him one with the business end of her torch. And she wasn't saying where, either.

Florence was past the stage of coherence. She was exhausted, cold, hungry and thirsty. The cup of water the woman on London Road had given her had done no more than make her long for a proper drink. She closed her eyes. A cup of tea, so strong a fly could walk across it without sinking, and one of Daisy's mother's cream buns, the sponge so soft and the cream so sweet and laced with sugar it made you close your eyes in ecstasy. Or one of the vanilla slices Mrs Bell made – wafer-thin slices of puff pastry, glued together with custard, rich and vanilla tasting, topped with icing sticky-sweet to the tongue. Or Eccles cakes, brittle till you bit into them, with currants layered just beneath the surface, or parkin, moist with golden syrup and spicy with ginger. Or date and walnut loaf, cut thick and spread with butter. Was this how men lost in the desert felt when they saw a mirage?

Daisy would miss her and be suitably horrified when her friend's body was dragged from the pond. 'She warned me she was going to do it and I wouldn't believe her,' she would sob. But Daisy had another friend, someone Florence knew nothing about. She had gone to Blackpool for the day and taken her mother. On the train? Florence tried to imagine poor sick Mrs Bell struggling to the railway station, and failed. A charabanc? That would be more likely. Or maybe the *friend* had a car?

Florence stood up. She brushed the dry dirty grass from the back of her coat, the sudden movements making her sway and almost topple over. Her heart shifted with an emotion she couldn't define. She felt weak, she felt ill, she had no idea what to do or where to go. But hell's bells, she wasn't going to drown herself in that murky water down there lapping sluggishly against a mucky bank! She was at a point in her life where she felt so low that if she sat on a sheet of tissue-paper her legs would dangle; she was twenty-five years old, a *virgin*, if that wasn't too rude a word. She had legs that walked and arms that could hold a man tight, if she wanted to.

Florence lifted her arms to the sky. And she didn't want to! There wasn't a man alive worth any woman killing herself for. She would emigrate! To America, the land of the free; to Australia, to Canada. She'd had enough of showing morons to their seats in darkened cinemas, wearing a uniform she didn't suit, and a pill-box hat that made her look like Buttons in a Cinderella pantomime. She accepted that she was over-excited and confused, but she was *alive*! And suddenly and gloriously determined to stay that way.

The sun-scorched stubble crackled beneath her feet as she made her way back up the bank to the dirt road at the top of the hill. She had, at that moment, no clear conception of where she was going. All she wanted to do was to get as far away as she could from the pond. And, just as important, away from her father with his big hands with black hairs sprouting between the fingers, his florid face and his whisky breath. She was never going home again. Never, ever ever. Not even to get clean clothes, or her birth certificate from the wooden box on top of her father's tallboy where all the family documents were kept. Her mother had set great store on Florence always knowing where her birth certificate was kept. As if without it she could be crossed out, like a word on a sheet of paper.

It was no good, the hill was steeper than she thought, so

steep it was coming up towards her, hitting her smack between the eyes. But not before she had seen the outline of what looked like a wild woman coming towards her, falling over in her haste, picking herself up and lurching forward again.

'Florence!' Daisy reached her as she fell, knelt down on the dusty grass and pulled hard at her friend's shoulder to turn her the right way up. Then stared aghast at the tousled hair, the livid bruise on Florence's cheek, the swelling on her lip that had ballooned into a dark purple blister, and the eyes half-closed in cushions of swollen flesh.

'Daisy!' Opening her eyes, Florence stared up into Daisy's shocked face. 'I wasn't going to, you know.' She glanced back over her shoulder. 'I only came up here for a good think. I'd never have jumped in.'

'Waste of time if you had.' Daisy heaved Florence to a sitting position. 'The heatwave has dried it all up. There's just about enough water down there to brew a pot of tea.'

'How do you know that? Who told you?'

'A man I met putting his cat out on the way here.' Daisy was brisk, matter-of-fact. 'I shouted to him to follow me with a rope, and when I told him what it was for he said you'd be lucky if you got more than your knee-caps wet.'

The hard lump that had been in Florence's throat all day spilled out into hysteria. Shaking, laughing and crying at the same time, she clutched at Daisy. 'I can't go back home. I've made up my mind I'm never going back.' She touched her swollen face. 'He did this, Daisy. The humiliation of it made me sick to my soul.' Her words were staccato sharp as if she was tapping them out on a typewriter. 'I am not going back there. Never. Ever.'

'Then you must come home with me,' Daisy said at once.

The long hot day was ending. Over to the east storm clouds were gathering. The air was as thick and heavy as fog as they staggered down the slope, the tall fair woman leaning heavily on the shorter dark one. Clinging, without knowing who was clinging to whom.

Meeting Arnold, holding a hand to the stitch in his side and panting like a pair of bellows.

Daisy's tears came when she removed her mother's nightdress from the bed in readiness for Florence to climb in. Burying her face in the winceyette folds – Martha had always refused to wear anything thinner, even in summer – Daisy knelt down by the side of the bed and sobbed away some of the grief held tightly inside her all that long day.

Edna had gone back to her own house, hoping Daisy knew what she was letting herself in for, whispering that Florrie Livesey would be a hard one to shift once she got her feet under Daisy's table. All right Florrie saying she was never going back home, but where did she think she was going to live? Martha would never have allowed it, that much was certain. But if Martha had been alive there wouldn't have been the room, would there? Far better for Daisy to have come to their house as had been suggested, and let Florrie Livesey sort her own problems out. Look at that woman three doors up. Her mother-in-law had come for her tea and stopped fourteen years, only going back to her own house to collect her bits and pieces. No, Florrie should have been made to pull herself together and go back to her own house. Now Daisy was lumbered and would live to regret it.

Arnold watched his wife's mouth opening and shutting, able, by long practice, to let the sounds wash over him like waves on a distant shore. It would be a long while before he forgot the sight of those two lasses, leaning on each other and coming slowly towards him down the dirt road. If ever a lass needed a friend then it was Daisy that night. And Florrie Livesey looked as if she was all in till Daisy had bustled to and given her a basin of pobs glistening with butter, nutty sweet with brown sugar. It was the best thing out for Daisy having something to do, someone to care for. A giver, Daisy was. Not a taker. A right grand lass, and had been since a little whipper-snapper in a white dress at the Sunday School Field Day. Arnold nodded his head to show his wife he was still listening.

But that chap from London wasn't Daisy's sort. He'd not been able to get away fast enough once he'd handed Daisy over. Arnold nodded again, only to flinch at his wife's look of utter disgust. Maybe that was one time he should have *shaken* his head, he thought, setting his chair rocking in a way he knew annoyed her.

Florence's father had been and gone. Worried, he said, because she had run out like that and stopped out all day. But he knew she would be with Daisy, so now his mind could be at rest. He had looked sweaty and old, and frightened too, and when Daisy had told him about her mother his red-veined eyes had swum with tears.

'He always cries when he's drunk,' Florence had said, refusing to come out and speak to him. 'Bullies always have a sentimental streak in them.'

Florence was asleep in Martha's chair, wearing a pair of Daisy's pyjamas with the trousers at half-mast and her wrists sticking out from the jacket sleeves. She had agreed that maybe she *would* slip back for a few of her bits and pieces, and her birth certificate later on the next day when she was sure her father would be out. But Florence was adamant she would never speak to him again.

'No man hits me twice,' she kept saying.

Daisy was too tired, too numbed by all that had happened that day to explain that in her opinion Mr Livesey cared more than a little for his daughter. That from what Daisy had heard it could have been Florence's mother's fault for setting father and daughter against each other. But the day had gone on far too long for expounding theories. Daisy dried her eyes and went to tell Florence the bed was ready.

When Daisy got into her own bed and pulled the sheet over her face the darkness was filled with images that wouldn't go away. She dreamed at last, a terrible dream, where Sam appeared at Martha's funeral wearing a stove-pipe black hat with streamers, in the guise of an undertaker from Victorian times. When he took off his hat at the graveside there was no top to his head, and when he turned round Daisy saw that his eye-sockets were empty voids.

Afraid to sleep again, she padded through into her mother's room, sure that Florence would be awake, but Florence was sleeping the sleep of the just, mouth slightly open and a put-put snore coming from her lips.

Shivering in the chill left in the wake of the storm, Daisy crept downstairs and made herself a soothing cup of tea. On an impulse she reached to the back of the sideboard cupboard for the half bottle of brandy – strictly for medicinal purposes. Took it back to bed with her and slept like a log, to wake bleary-eyed with a headache that throbbed like a jungle tom-tom. Finding Florence in the kitchen scouring the bottom of the frying pan. Bringing it up like new.

The funeral was to be on the Friday.

'Not many people die in Wakes Week,' Mr Taylor the undertaker said. 'They seem to hang on till they get back from their holidays. There's no nonsense about an inquest, with your mother having been under the doctor.'

Edna's and Arnold's wreath was pink carnations in the form of a cross, and the five-day-old baby sent a posy of rosebuds which Daisy held in her hands and wept over. Sam sent a note to Daisy along with two pound notes, asking her to buy flowers and inscribe a suitable card. It came too late but Daisy showed it to Florence.

'That's from the friend I went to Blackpool with. I kept telling you how impersonal our friendship is. Read that. He even signs himself "Yours sincerely".'

Florence looked up from arranging biscuits on a blue plate. 'Well, he would, wouldn't he? That type of man is far too clever to commit himself to paper. Divorce evidence, or breach of promise. You know the sort of thing.'

'No, I *don't* know the sort of thing!' Daisy put down the knife she was using to slice ham off the bone. 'Look. I'm sorry I didn't tell you about it. But there wasn't anything *to* tell, and I didn't want to look a fool when he didn't come back.' She blushed. 'But he did come back, and here we are making my mother's funeral tea, and she might still be alive if I

106

hadn't made her go to Blackpool when she wasn't fit.' The doubts that had plagued Daisy surfaced with a rush of emotion. 'Was it the excitement? She was like a child getting herself ready. She went upstairs twice just to make sure she had everything.' Daisy began to cry. 'She stuffed her handbag so full it's a wonder she could lift it. Then the ride in that car . . . she was sitting bolt upright on the back seat between those two children with her eyes sparkling and an arm round the little girl. . . .'

'And she was happy.' Florence got a clean handkerchief from the dresser drawer and passed it to Daisy. 'That's what you have to remember and hang on to. That she died having a good day out.'

'Because of Sam.'

Florence's sympathy receded a little. 'I still can't understand why you never talked about him.'

'Because you would have *diminished* him.' Daisy was too upset to choose her words more carefully. 'You would have dismissed him as a rotter or a cad, or even a potential rapist, and you know it.' A loud sob filled Daisy's eyes with tears again. 'And that I couldn't have borne. Because he was kind. Married to someone else, but kind to *me*.'

'Do you love him?' Florence wanted to know, stopping clattering cups and saucers on to a tray.

Daisy flinched as if Florence had suddenly mouthed an obscenity. Her mother would never have come straight out with a question like that. It was personal, and highly offensive somehow.

For a full half-minute they stared at each other across the kitchen table cluttered with food for Martha's funeral spread. Both women were in deepest mourning, wearing black skirts and blouses, without a touch of colour.

'Mourning went out with Queen Victoria,' Florence had said.

'Grey or navy always does quite as well,' Daisy had said, but somehow they had borrowed, made do, and when the funeral car came for them they would emerge from the house like two black crows, determined not to show disrespect to the dead.

Daisy tried to answer Florence's question with honesty. She needed to talk about Sam so much the need was a physical ache inside her. But the past few days hadn't seemed to be the time and she was never sure when Florence was laughing at her.

'If thinking about him all the time,' she said at last, 'if seeing his face when I close my eyes, if crying about my mother then stopping and realizing with shame I am crying about him, well yes, I love him. But he won't come back. He is scared of involvement. He had told me we wouldn't be meeting again before ... before my mother died that day.'

'What was he like?'

'I thought Clark Gable at first. Then when I saw him the second time, when he was worried and concerned about the mess his own life was in, I saw he was more like Frederic March.'

'As Doctor Jekyll, or Mr Hyde?' Florence asked the question with a polite curiosity.

'Oh, you're hopeless.' Daisy took up her knife again. 'You're not normal, do you know that?'

'Do you mean I'm a lesbian?' Florence looked interested in the shocking idea. 'I suppose I may have more masculine than feminine genes, but no, I'm sure I'm quite normal, whatever normal is.'

'How do you know?' They had never talked like this before and it was Daisy's turn to be interested now.

'Because I was once in love with a married man.' Florence marched through into the living room carrying the plate of biscuits. 'But when I realized he would never leave his wife I saw him off.' She came back looking fierce. 'I expect your Sam is having a terrible time with his wife? Did he tell you she doesn't understand him?'

Daisy shook her head. 'But she doesn't. How can she? She should be helping him to get through his exams instead of gallivanting off to France with another man.'

'Exams? Exams he should have passed when he'd just left school?'

'Engineering exams to help him get a better job. That's why he's living alone in one room over a garage.'

'Leaving his wife to look after the children? She *deserves* a filthy weekend in Paris,' FLorence said. 'Good luck to her, I say.'

'You know *nothing* about it!' Daisy attacked a tomato. 'You pass opinions without knowing what you're talking about.' The knife slipped and she nicked her finger end. 'Now you know why I didn't tell you anything. You'd spoil the romance between Romeo and Juliet if you had the chance.'

'Always did think they were a couple of pie-cans,' Florence said, and when Edna came in without knocking she caught them giggling helplessly and rather hysterically over the funeral spread.

The shop opened as usual on the Monday. The baker came in with calamine lotion whitening the top of his bald head where the sun had got at it in Southport, and Edna served in the shop wearing her funeral black, asking who did that Florrie Livesey think she was getting in the way and when was she going back home where she belonged?

At half-past one Florence went to work and came back at half-past two with her cards in her handbag, saying she had got the sack and been given a week's wages in lieu of her notice. Insisting that Daisy took every penny of it for her keep.

At half-past three Edna marched into the bakehouse where Daisy was putting the finishing touches to a tray of mixed fancies, tore off her apron and told Daisy she wasn't going to work alongside Florrie Livesey, not even for the sake of her dear dead sister, with whom she'd never had a cross word. 'Told me I should be using tongs for putting the barm-cakes into the bags,' she said. 'As if my fingers were mucky! Who does she think she is? Tell me that! Who does she think she is?'

The machine mixing the dough for the last batch of bread had jammed and after it was whirring again Daisy ran up the street to her aunt's house to find Edna crying into a pile of nappies she was wringing in the kitchen sink, the sleeves of the black dress rolled up revealing arms as thin as twigs.

'You're tired out.' Daisy closed the kitchen door against the sound of the baby screaming its head off upstairs. 'Come on, leave those to soak and sit down for a minute. Florence can manage for a little while. It's the quiet time just now.'

'I'm not coming back,' Edna sobbed. 'I'm not kow-towing to that madam.' She started to get up from her chair, resisting half-heartedly when Daisy forcibly pushed her back. 'It's too much trying to look after our Betty, bless her, *and* serving in the shop. He's a colicky baby and had us all awake in the night. I'm fifty-four,' she told Daisy in between sobs. 'I can't be doing with all this upset. I'm still getting hot flushes, you know. I'm one of those women who never come out of the change once they've gone into it. I can feel my heart all of a flutter today, and when I think of Martha lying dead up in the cemetery and know I'm never going to see her again. . . . And that madam taking her place. . . .'

Daisy pulled her chair closer and took both her aunt's red hands in her own. 'Florence isn't going to take anyone's place, Auntie. She's unsettled at the moment, and she's company for me.' She glanced round at the normally tidy room, festooned now with nappies steaming round the fire, with two feeding bottles on the sideboard and a large tin of Cow and Gate on the mantelpiece. 'Of *course* it's too much for you. Anyone with only half an eye can see that.' She jiggled her aunt's hands up and down. 'So why don't you stay with Betty till she's over her fortnight lying in? You'll be paid just the same. My mother would have insisted on that.'

Edna's sobs began afresh. 'Oh, aye, she would have insisted on fair play, would my sister. Never a cross word between us all these years. She used to push me out in my pram when she was no more than a young lass, did your mother. Pure gold, that's what she was.'

'Then that's settled then.' Daisy leaned forward and kissed her aunt's cheek. 'We're all bound to be upset; it's only natural. The baby coming and my mother dying all in one week.'

'The Lord giveth and the Lord taketh away,' Edna said at once, beginning to roll her sleeves down again. 'I'll come back now till you can set someone else on. It's time that madam was going to her work anyway and you can't manage on your own. It'll be bread most of them want today with all their money gone and no pay till Friday. I know this lot round here.'

'Florence isn't going to work tonight.' Daisy saw her auntie's face drop a mile. 'She's got the sack, so there won't be any need for me to set anyone else on. . . .' Her voice trailed away.

'So?' Edna rolled back the sleeves and marched into the kitchen. 'So that's the way the wind blows, is it?' Even her back looked affronted. 'And I won't be coming back at all if it's a bit of plain speaking you want.' She twisted a nappy round till it resembled a rope. 'We had a talk the other day, me and our Betty, bless her. And she wants to go back to work to save for their deposit on a house, and I said I would look after the baby, if it wasn't for you needing me at the shop. But you *don't need me* – that much is obvious.' Another nappy, another vicious twist. 'So I hope you know what you've let yourself in for, because you'll live to rue the day you opened your door to that madam. And when she's taken you over, don't you come running to me because I have other fish to fry!'

Daisy put a hand to her hot forehead to find it streaked with flour. Knowing her aunt of old, she knew there was nothing she could say or do now that umbrage had been determinedly taken. Pity overwhelmed her for the spare little woman taking out her feelings on the towelling nappies, a pity mixed with exasperation. But the shop would be filling up with customers buying in for their teas; the last batch of bread and barm-cakes would be coming hot and brown from the fire-oven, and Florence hadn't got the hang of the till as yet.

'We'll talk about all this another time,' she said, but Edna turned on the tap to full throttle, splashing water into the sink for the second rinse, and pretended not to hear. Daisy walked back down the lobby to the sounds of the baby screaming from upstairs, and our Betty, bless her, calling down for her mother.

Chapter Five

The letter from the hospital came at the end of a dismal and disappointing August, with summer sliding away into a wetter autumn. They were very sorry, the letter said, it was very remiss of them, but they had come across an envelope containing a few of Mrs Martha Bell's effects. Would Miss Bell like them sent on, or would she prefer to pick up the small envelope personally?

By that time Edna was 'speaking' again. She came into the shop instead of walking past with head averted, pushing the pram, but by that time Daisy told herself she didn't care one way or the other.

'I can't be bothered with such pettiness,' she said. 'Is this to be it, for the rest of our lives?' she asked Florence one evening as they sat together in the living room over the inevitable fire. 'Do you realize what boring lives we lead? Some days I feel I can't bear the sight of another meat and potato pie. I count pies instead of sheep when I can't sleep. Do you know that?'

'There aren't any as good for miles around.' Florence had the bakehouse cat on her lap and was stroking it contentedly with a long thin hand. 'People come from the other side of the town for a box of your fancies.'

'Oh, my God!' Daisy raised dark eyebrows ceilingwards as if searching for the patience to tide her over to Florence's next remark. 'Well, if this is all it's going to be till we grow old and grey, then heaven help us.'

'It's not *that* bad, surely?' Florence leaned her head back against one of Martha's embroidered antimacassars and sighed with contentment. She had entered into helping to run the shop with verve and enthusiasm, standing behind the counter wielding the tongs which had annoyed Edna so much, wearing a clean Acdo-soaked overall each day, with her hair pushed up into an equally white mob cap. She had stopped talking about spinsters and their pension rights, which she had once told Daisy should be on a parity with widows', and her subscription to the newly-formed National Spinsters' Pension Association had lapsed. No longer did she burn to march in protest to Hyde Park waving a banner, and Daisy had decided she wasn't finding this new complacent Florence half as much fun.

'Do you know what that awful commercial traveller trying to make us order new baking tins called us yesterday?' In her disgruntled mood Daisy's sense of humour had totally deserted her. 'The Dolly Sisters! They must be forty years old at least! And he wasn't trying to be funny either. Just because I didn't give him an order for his flamin' tins.'

'Well, you must admit those in the bakehouse must have been around since Adam was a lad.' Florence's eyes sharpened with what Daisy privately called her 'hygienic' expression. 'Why are they never given a proper wash? It's disgusting.'

'To scour them would ruin them.' Daisy wondered how many times Florence would have to be told this before she believed it. 'They've formed a proper surface which even hot water would ruin. Allow me to know better, Florence.'

Daisy was wearing her round-rimmed glasses. She had been reading her library book at the same time as rolling up her fringe in pipe cleaners, hoping it would comb out with the same bounce and curl as Claudette Colbert's the next day. 'Why I try to look glamorous, I don't know. There's no Red Shadow going to come in for a box of fancies, take one look at me and carry me off to his tent in the desert. So why do I bother? Answer me that.'

Florence pushed the cat off her lap and began her own nightly preparations. Taking the Kirby grips out of her French pleat she allowed her barley-pale hair to fall unfettered round her shoulders, as fine and silky as a child's.

Reminding Daisy of Dorothy's hair; reminding her yet again of Sam. She took off her glasses quickly, as if he had suddenly materialized in a whiff of ectoplasm and caught her wearing them. She stored them away in the peeling case, and closed her book.

'Are you happy, Florence? I don't mean deliriously happy. Just day-to-day happy. Tell me honestly.'

'That's easy.' Florence began to massage Pond's Vanishing Cream into her long thin hands, working it well into the cuticles. 'I ask myself every day what would have become of me if you hadn't taken me in that night. I would never have gone back to live at home.'

'Well, you didn't have to.' Daisy's voice was sharp as she accepted that only her mother dying so conveniently on that very day had made it possible for Florence to move in straight away. 'But are you happy only because you were so miserable *before*? That's a mere matter of comparison. Like the feeling when you stop banging your head against a wall.'

Florence was storing the Kirby grips all facing the same way in an old Oxo tin. 'When you can go to the pictures again you'll feel better, though why you don't go now is beyond me. You keeping away isn't going to bring your mother back. Who decided three months would be a respectful time to keep away? Who made the rules? Six months for deep mourning, another six for wearing mauve or a decent navy-blue. On the day you wear a yellow jumper, will that free you from the obligation of ever thinking about your mother again? I went to *my* mother's funeral in a bright red hat.'

'And it didn't suit you neither,' Daisy said at once, sounding so much like Martha that Florence laughed out loud. 'Let's go to Blackpool on Sunday,' Daisy said, leaning forward. 'On a day excursion. We can pick the ... the things up from the hospital and have a blow on the front, and still be back in plenty of time for the oven if I bank it down carefully enough. It won't bother me,' she said quickly, reading Florence's doubtful expression. 'In fact, I would *like* to go again. Because if I don't go soon I may never want to go at all.'

'On account of your mother, or on account of Sam?'

Daisy was silent. If she saw the place, the very spot where he had tried so carefully to explain to her that he valued her friendship and nothing more, maybe the acceptance that it was all over would be easier. But friends wrote letters, didn't they? She had answered his note, thanking him for the money, not mentioning that it hadn't arrived on time. She had bought flowers the following Sunday at the shop across from the cemetery gates, filled a stone sarsaparilla jar from one of the stand taps and stood the jar on the newly-laid stone. 'From Sam', she had written on a card, that being as suitable a message as she could think of. 'And Jimmy and Dorothy' she had added, hoping the children had not *dwelled* on what had happened that day. Then she had written to Sam telling him what she had done, but although her heart skipped a beat whenever the postman called, he had not written back.

'I never give Sam a thought,' she lied. 'That's over and done with. So what about catching the early train on Sunday? We'll give chapel a miss for once.'

The train had just chugged its way beyond Wrea Green when Florence spotted a small dark finger rising up from the meadow flats.

'The Tower!' she announced, and everyone in the compartment smiled and craned their necks for a better look.

'Aye, it's still there,' an elderly man in the corner seat said with satisfaction. 'I were there at the stone-laying ceremony in 1891, and I were there in Whit week in 1894 when it opened. They reckon rain is worth a guinea a drop to the Tower Company. It fetches everybody in off the sands.'

116

Just outside Central Station the train stopped for almost five minutes. Florence jumped up from her seat and stuck her head out of the window to see, above the red signal lights, the marvels of the Tower in close-up, its ironwork impressive and detailed.

'Three years to build; more than one poor bugger falling to his death and five hundred and eighteen feet up into t'sky.' The man in the corner knew his facts and was determined to show off his knowledge. 'It has yon Eiffel Tower in Paris beaten to a frazzle.'

'I reckon he's a shareholder,' Florence said as they walked out of the station. 'Oh no! It's starting to rain. I knew we should have brought umbrellas.'

'We'll take a taxi.' Daisy wanted to get it over with. 'Hang the expense; there are no pockets in shrouds.'

She gave the name of the hospital to the driver and as they were driven through the closed shopping centre, past shuttered theatres and vast forecourts of newly-built garages, she saw how the Virginia creeper cloaking the red Accrington brick of the houses was already turning a dull coppery shade.

'It's very quiet today.' Florence always chatted to taxi drivers and bus conductors. It enriched the mind, she had often told Daisy, finding out about other people's lives.

'Aye, it's always quiet of a Sunday.' The driver had an angry boil on the back of his neck. 'But wait till the Illuminations come on. You won't be able to put a pin between the crowds then. Lodging houses are booked solid already.'

'Marshmallow ointment,' Florence told him, as Daisy paid the fare outside the hospital. 'Cut a hole in a piece of lint, then get your wife to put it on your neck and press, then apply the ointment. It won't even leave a scar.'

'You a nurse?' The man jerked his head towards the hospital main doors. 'Going on duty then?'

'Nightingale's her middle name. Come on, Florence,' Daisy said, and the mild joke got her through the swing doors and up to the reception desk. It was stupid feeling like this, but the last time she had been here Sam had been with her, the sun had been shining and it hadn't properly dawned on her that her little mother was dead. Whereas now. . . .

In the Almoner's office she signed for the buff envelope and put it in her bag. They walked back to the front, glad that the rain had stopped, but expecting it to begin again at any minute. It was there in the wind; it beaded their coats like hoar frost and brought the colour back to Daisy's cheeks.

They got vaguely lost in a labyrinth of little streets lined with lodging houses, with dining tables pushed close to the windows and peeling park benches outside. The air had an autumnal tinge to it, but back on the front they crossed the road to the promenade and walked on the almost deserted beach. Far out on the horizon a faded sun struggled to get through the mist, revealing long stretches of grey-green sea before hiding them again. With their backs to a breakwater, a family of late summer visitors sat huddled in coats and hats, sipping beakers of tea from a huge flask.

Daisy opened the envelope handed to her at the hospital and drew out a string of crystal beads, a seed-pearl brooch set in a rolled gold bar, and a hatpin with a mother-of-pearl head on it as big as a grape.

'My mother's jewellery.' The sight of it made her want to weep. 'That's it. The lot. Imagine working hard all your life long and ending up with as little as this.' She pushed the envelope deep into her handbag. 'Well, that's it. That's what we came for. The effects have been claimed by the next of kin of the deceased. Now. What shall we do now?'

'Go up the Tower,' Florence said at once. 'I've never been, but I'll try anything once. It'll blow your cobwebs away and warm your cockles, if that's possible at one and the same time.' Anything, she was thinking, to take that look of utter desolation from Daisy's face. Even though standing on the piano stool was enough to turn Florence dizzy. What were friends *for*, for goodness' sake?

It cost ninepence each to go in, and Florence paid with a flourish.

When the doors slid to with a silky whoosh she looked round for something to cling on to. Through the windows she saw the blurred skeleton of the Tower rushing downwards, taking her stomach with it, so she closed her eyes, opening them again when the jerk the lift gave as it stopped threw her off balance. Gratefully she stepped out into the enclosed gallery suspended seemingly, she decided, in the sky itself.

It was bitterly cold up there, so she wrapped the long trailing duster-coat closer round her angular body. Beneath the brim of her atrocious hat her pale face looked pinched and mean. 'It is a far far better thing I do . . .' she muttered, and turned her head away from the sight of Daisy rushing from one viewpoint to the next. The wind wailed and moaned, and Florence was sure the Tower itself was swaying to and fro. She wondered if she was going to be sick; summoned all her self-control and looked round, telling herself she might as well get her money's worth.

The tiny gift shops were closed and the custodian, a man with a large flat face, nodded to her, then went on reading a newspaper folded to the racing pages.

On legs turned into lettuce leaves Florence forced herself to walk to a window and look down. Down, down, down to a world of a few minute figures like ants scurrying about at the edge of a sea throwing up patterns of white lace. A boat bobbed about in the distance, a black fly thrashing around, drowning in a rippling sea. The wind rose to a crescendo, and oh Lord, the whole Tower was leaning forward to topple into the sea at any minute. Her breakfast of hastily eaten bacon sandwiches rose to her throat with a salty acid taste.

Florence gave up being a martyr and turned to totter back to the comparative safety of the lift.

In a moment Daisy was beside her, holding her arm, but worse was to come. The lift fell like a stone dropped down a well-shaft, and two shades greener than her hat Florence emerged to walk unsteadily out of the pagoda, out of the Eastern Temple, along the back of a high-ceilinged gallery glittered by chandeliers into the balcony of the Tower Ballroom.

'Fancy a dance?' Daisy, flushed and exhilarated, pointed down to the couples waltzing gravely, some of them wearing outdoor coats and hats. 'A nice old-fashioned waltz, with lots of twirls?'

'Aw, give over, Daisy.' Florence sat down on a red plush seat. 'If I never do that again it'll be too soon.'

'Did it really upset your stomach?'

'What stomach?' Florence held a handkerchief to her mouth. 'Lead me to some fresh air. Ground-level fresh air, and don't listen to any more of my good ideas.'

'And you in that hat n'all.' Daisy tweaked the flap at one side of the helmet-type hat. 'Amy Johnson would be ashamed of you.'

By the time they had walked along the front to the North Pier and turned back Florence declared she was made over again. Well enough to think longingly of a pot of tea and a hot toasted teacake. 'See, there's a place over there,' she said.

'A pity you didn't look out at the other side, over the town.' Daisy poured water from a plated jug into the teapot. 'You could see all the way back over the Fylde to the Pennines, even on a day like this. It's the view we get in reverse from the tank on Revidge on our Sunday walks.'

'I accept your word for it.' Florence shuddered. 'I'm definitely not going back up there to check.'

'I once took Sam up on to the tank. One cold rainy night last winter.' Daisy was glad she could mention Sam now and again, especially when she could see Florence was in no mood to turn nasty.

'That selfish rotter?' Florence said at once.

'My hat blew off.' Daisy's face was dreamy.

'Which one?' Florence was not going to listen to any sob stuff about Mr Samuel Barnet. You could have written her opinion of him on the back of a twopenny stamp in just one word – and not a nice one either. She had Sam's measure, and he wasn't good enough for Daisy. Let him keep away, please God, and get on with passing his exams, while his wife brought his children up all on her own. What did he think he was going to do when he'd passed the flamin' things, anyway? Walk into a job paying a thousand a year? Good grief, in these days of depression, there were B.Sc.s sweeping the streets. She'd heard that one so often it must be true.

'Which hat?' Daisy was smiling to herself. 'My dark green one, the one with the turned-back brim that almost matched my winter coat. Why do you ask?'

'So losing it was one of life's little bonuses,' Florence said, dead-pan.

As Daisy's laugh rang out, two youths sitting at a table across the centre aisle turned round quickly, then just as quickly turned back and went on with their conversation.

'We don't *appeal* to them,' Daisy whispered. 'I thought Blackpool was supposed to be a place for clicking? They're obviously on holiday, you can see them cursing the weather and wondering what to do next.'

'We're old enough to be their *mothers*,' Florence exaggerated, pretending to take Daisy seriously. 'But if we weren't, bags me the one without the spots.'

We look like what we are, Daisy told herself morosely. What we will be some day. Two unmarried friends – Miss Bell in her black, and Miss Livesey in her coat like a tent. Thousands like them all over the country, cast in the same mould. Women living on the stories of their sweethearts being killed in the war; women with mothers and fathers to care for, and women who couldn't get a man, as Martha would undoubtedly have said.

For such a little precious time Sam had made her feel beautiful. She had felt *passion* when he kissed her; she had gloried in merely walking along by his side, and because he had made her feel beautiful, the beauty had been there. She had seen it reflected in the fluted mirror over the fireplace. Her eyes had shone and her hair had curled round her face just the way she wanted it to. He had told her she reminded him of Olivia De Havilland, and she had believed him. Olivia De Havilland gazing up at Errol Flynn as he raised a quizzical eyebrow before sweeping her into his arms, devouring her with kisses before leaping off a balcony and swinging from a chandelier with a sword in his hand to fight off seven men single-handed.

Now all that was over and she might as well admit it. She was an *unclaimed blessing*, as she had told Sam, making him shout with laughter and lift her off her feet in the street.

'I once had an affair with a married man,' she would say in years to come. Just as Florence had said on the day of the funeral. She stared across the table at the familiar sight of her friend pulling on the lace gloves, adjusting the neat frill at her bony wrists.

'Have you ever slept with a man?'

She asked the question in a kind of desperation as they walked out into a day turned cloudy and grey. A gust of wind whipped an empty cigarette packet round her ankles.

'Don't talk filthy.' Florence laughed and held the folds of her coat more closely round her. 'Where to now? Home?'

She linked her arm in Daisy's as they moved into the labyrinth of streets behind the café, and Daisy wished she wouldn't. It made them look... oh, dear God, she didn't know *what* it made them look like, but it irritated her. What was wrong with her? There was a singing in her veins that would not be stilled; she felt as frantic as she imagined a butterfly would, held captive in the palm of a hand.

What was *wrong* with her? There was a man striding along across the street and she thought he looked like Sam, then admitted that every tall dark man reminded her of Sam. For a little while she fantasized that it had been him; that he had come to find her, telling her that his wife wanted to divorce him.

'I love you,' he would say in his beautiful voice. 'I thought I could go away and forget you, but I was wrong. You are there before me, every waking moment. I see your face before I sleep and wake to find you with me still. Come live with me and be my love, Daisybell.' Only Sam had ever said her name like that.

'There's a house across the street with a FOR SALE notice in the window,' Florence was saying. 'How would you fancy being a landlady, Daisy?'

She was joking. Daisy knew she was joking, but on a sudden whim she brushed Florence's arm away and crossed the street to stare up at the three-storeyed house, with a framed plate alongside the door: HAVENREST. MRS ENTWISTLE, CHORLEY.

'That's to show families from Chorley they will be welcome here,' she said. 'My father told me that was common practice when these houses were built.' She looked up at the dignified frontage. 'It showed Chorley visitors that if they stayed here with Mrs Entwistle from their home town they wouldn't be diddled. No charging for the cruet, a shilling a week, or anything like that. And look. This house is at the centre of the terrace, so it has a flattish gable in place of the normal eaves. My father used to spend most of the holiday week wandering about, leaving me mother to traipse round the shops. He used to take me with him and point things out to me.'

'A bit of a scholar, your father.' Florence stared up at the house. 'I guessed the books in your bookcase had once belonged to him. Philosophy, architecture, Victorian social history. I do admire self-taught men.'

'He was also a natural mechanic.' Daisy bit her lip, remembering the day when her beloved father had been called to the mill to tend the engine, and been carried back broken and bleeding to die in his bed. 'He could have been anything, given the chance.'

'He had an untutored intelligence,' Florence said, unable to hear any confidence without going one better. 'How many budding intellectuals lurk beneath the flat caps of our working classes? Think of the amateur botanists who leave the mills behind at the weekends and go out with haversacks on their backs.'

'He used to do that, too. He brought plants back, little shoots of wild flowers, to press in scrap-books with mother's flat-iron to act as a weight. She used to get so flamin' mad. Especially when she needed the iron to press her potted meat in a basin.'

'There's a woman come out of the next door,' Florence said, rolling her eyes in the appropriate direction and speaking from the corner of her mouth. 'She's been watching us from the window.'

'She's coming out to speak to us. Thinks we're interested in buying this house, or looking for a place to stay.'

'She's a NO VACANCIES, love. By gum, but she's never been short of a butty, has she?' Florence turned to smile at the stout woman advancing towards them, changing her accent with a speed that would have done a seasoned trouper proud. 'Good afternoon. Quite a change in the weather, isn't there? We've had a disappointing back end, haven't we?'

The woman's fat cheeks creased into a smile. 'I'm BALMORAL next door. Mrs MacDougal. I can show you round this place if you like.' She lowered her voice. 'Poor soul. Died at her post just when the season started back in June. Frying bacon when she should have been lying in hospital in an oxygen tent. Emphysema.' With a podgy hand she made the movements of smoking a cigarette. 'Couldn't give it up, not that I blamed her with what she'd had to put up with. Passed over with a fag stuck in her face.' She patted the pocket of her apron. 'I've got the key if you'd like to see inside.'

'We have a train to catch, I'm afraid,' Florence said quickly.

'Yes, please,' Daisy said. 'That's if you can spare the time.'

Deliberately avoiding looking at Florence's face, Daisy followed Mrs MacDougal into the house, into a hall dominated by a large antlered coatstand. The walls were painted a hideous mustard shade with brown stipples blurring into each other. Mrs MacDougal opened a brown door on the left with a flourish.

'The lounge,' she announced. 'You'd never find lounges in the houses up nearer the centre. These houses further north are far superior. Purpose-built this road was. Built to last. Like me.' Laughing, she patted a barrel-tight stomach. 'A piano,' she told them, pointing to an upright monstrosity. 'Mrs Entwistle's visitors liked a bit of a sing-song when the weather got them down.'

Daisy glanced round the room, wrinkling her nose at the smell which suggested the possibility of mice. A threadbare carpet, flanked by stained boards, a fireplace with a drunken fan of crêpe paper in the grate, assorted chairs with frayed covers, and a settee with the springs clearly defined through velvet cushions with the nap rubbed off them.

'Very nice,' she said insincerely.

The dining room was better, although the hectically patterned carpet vied for attention with the vividly flocked walls, and a flight of plaster birds soared on outspread wings across the wall where the clear marks of a boarded-up fireplace were only partly hidden by a table pushed close against it.

'Mrs Entwistle used to seat forty at high season.' Mrs MacDougal caught the look of disbelief which passed between Daisy and Florence. 'Needs must, Miss, with the season being so short, and with these tables pushed together and a couple of card tables, she managed fine.'

'May we see the kitchen, please?' Florence seemed to have found her voice, but Mrs MacDougal had decided that the shorter prettier one was the one that mattered. She hadn't taken to Florence at all. She turned eagerly to Daisy.

'This way, Miss...?'

'Miss Bell.' Daisy nodded towards Florence. 'And this is my friend, Miss Livesey.'

'This way, Miss Bell. And call me Mrs Mac. Everybody does, though there's not a drop of Scottish blood in my veins. It's me husband who comes from the land of the heather.'

'He helps you to run the business?' Florence was a bit put out at being ignored. 'The Scot has never been afraid of hard work.'

'Then my Angus must be an exception to the rule,' Mrs

Mac said at once. 'He's that lazy he'd scorch his trousers sooner than shift back from the fire. The kitchen,' she said, opening a door into a room so much smaller than Daisy had anticipated she felt her mouth drop open with surprise.

'It has to be the bedrooms,' Mrs Mac said, reading Daisy's expression. 'If you haven't got the bedrooms then you can't make it pay.'

'How many visitors stay here? At the busiest time?' Daisy stared at the shelves piled with crockery, each shelf hung with pans dangling from hooks on the underside.

'Eight bedrooms, four on each floor – say twenty-two guests. Two cots on the landing, and the put-you-up in the lounge. When the Illuminations begin I'll have one lad sleeping on a board across the bath, and his mate on a deckchair in the cupboard under the stairs.' Mrs Mac was unrepentant. 'Anyroad, who wants big bedrooms? They're not used to them where they come from, it's more comfortable with a place that's home from home.'

'They would be frightened away with more impressive surroundings. I can understand that.' Florence had been quiet for long enough. 'And I can also understand that seeing their landlady visibly involved must be reassuring.'

Mrs Mac's sparse eyebrows shot almost to her frizzy hairline. Lah-de-dah, they said silently. Who does Miss Livesey think she is? Talking like she's swallowed an 'apenny book. 'Well, I'm homely meself,' she said. 'And that's what they want. A home from home, like I said. Bedrooms now. Lead on, MacDuff.'

Purpose-built indeed. Daisy's eyes grew rounder as they opened first one door then another into what seemed like a warren of tiny rooms, each one furnished with a double bed, a marble-topped wash-hand-stand, and a single wardrobe, with the two marginally bigger bedrooms at the front of the house squeezing in a single bed and a cot at the foot of the bed.

'The bathroom.' Mrs Mac threw open the door of a narrow room with a pedestal bath in chipped white enamel, closed it quickly and inclined her chin to a closed door on the right. 'The W C,' she said unnecessarily, pointing to the two letters on the door. 'There are chambers in all the rooms, but we don't encourage their use with the cost of labour being what it is. I'm giving my girl this summer fifteen shillings a week and her keep, and she still feels she's badly done to, though back at home she's an out-of-work weaver.'

'Disgraceful!' Florence declared in a ringing tone, causing Mrs Mac to dart her a suspicious look.

'There's four more bedrooms up there.' She nodded towards a shorter flight of uncarpeted stairs. 'Mrs Entwistle kept her regulars up there, but there's only two left. Mr Schofield works for the post office, so he'll be out.' Without warning she lifted her head and called out; 'Anybody at home? Mr Penny? Yoo-hoo!'

The door at the top of the stairs opened almost at once to reveal a man with brushed-back brown hair, wearing a speckled tweed jacket and with the fingers of his right hand curved round the stem of a pipe. In his left hand he held a book, and by the absent-minded way he blinked down at them Daisy guessed he had been reading a passage he was loth to leave. Herbert Marshall, she thought at once. In *Trouble in Paradise*, an upper-class story of sophisticated jewel thieves, with Miriam Hopkins looking ravishing. A gentleman.

Cultured, Florence thought. A man of letters, maybe? More at home, she would have thought, in a book-lined study with a dog at his feet. Pedigree of course.

An unlikely pair, Joshua Penny told himself. The least likely of any of the potential buyers shown round by the indefatigable Mrs Mac. The younger one recently widowed? The other with a vague likeness to Edith Sitwell. Her sister-in-law? What a dreadful hat she was wearing. It reminded him of something, though he couldn't for the life of him think what.

'Good afternoon, ladies. I go with the house, I'm afraid.'

What an urbane smile. Florence was sorry when he nodded politely and closed his door firmly behind him. She would have liked to ask him the title of the book he was reading, or at least apologize for disturbing him so rudely.

'Very sad.' Mrs Mac went down the stairs crabwise, clinging firmly to the banister. 'All my family have rheumatism,' she explained proudly, as if it was an achievement of which to be justly proud. 'They wheeled my mother out in a Bath-chair with it for the last three years of her life. All her fingernails and toenails rotted off. With the acid.'

'I hope you don't go the same way.' Daisy exchanged a wicked glance with Florence.

Mrs Mac had at last reached the bottom stair. 'Well, if I do, yon husband of mine wouldn't push me out in a Bath-chair. Too idle to blow the skin off his rice pudding, that one is.'

'What was very sad about Mr Penny?' Outside again, Florence lifted her hooded eyelids. 'He looked quite cheerful to me.'

'Gassed. In the last war.' Mrs Mac led the way back to BALMORAL next door. 'Lungs shot, I gather. Then his wife, dead of the consumption, choking to death on her own spit, weighing no more than a pullet. He brought her here for the air, but it was too late, poor soul. He's a teacher in a school at Preston. He *travels*. Every day. There and back. Well,' she said, reaching her own front door, 'I'll have to get on. If you want to see the house again I can give you an address to write to. Mrs Entwistle's son. Never spent a penny on her when she was alive, but he's holding his hand out now for the money. Just goes to show, doesn't it?'

'Is she *real*?' Daisy and Florence couldn't walk straight for laughing. '*Travels*. To Preston. There and back. Oh, Florence, you'd have thought she was talking about Outer Mongolia!'

'That awful house! Poor Mrs Entwistle sure had no eye for colour. Heaven knows what lurked in the WC. Mrs Mac didn't even open the door!'

'I'm sure I could smell bugs.'

'And worse.'

'But the hairy tweedy man on the top floor was nice.'

'You mean the intrepid traveller?'

'Marco Polo.'

'Oh, stop it, Daisy. If we don't hurry we'll miss the train.'

'And the flamin' oven will have gone out.'

They caught the train with a minute to spare, but in spite of rushing into the bakehouse still wearing her coat and hat, Daisy found the fire had sunk to a pile of grey ashes, and with the rain lashing down outside, the bakehouse was as cold and unwelcoming as a coffin-strewed tomb.

Chapter Six

Daisy was finding it hard to rationalize her thinking. She was at a crossroads in her life, she told herself dramatically. There was some point in *everyone's* life when they stood irresolute, wondering which direction to take. Martha dying had removed the valid reason for keeping the shop going, she knew. Daisy did not feel like running up a flag over the bakehouse because the pies and the fancies had a reputation for being the best for miles around. Even keeping the recipes secret seemed a childish thing to do. A pinch of pepper here, a sprinkling of sage in the pork-meat; what did it matter if she wrote the whole lot down on a blackboard and set it up in the shop?

The baker was retiring at Christmas, and the two boys would be off as soon as they finished their apprenticeships. There would be dozens of applicants, maybe hundreds, then the whole cycle of training and adjustment would begin again.

'I could run a smallish place like that boarding-house at Blackpool with one hand tied behind my back,' Daisy said one evening after a particularly hectic day. 'Would you come in with me if I was daft enough, or wise enough to sell up here?'

'Whither thou goest . . .' Florence said at once. 'I'll tell you exactly what to do. It never fails.'

'Toss a coin? Take the best out of three?'

'Two columns.' Florence jumped up to take a writing pad

from the sideboard drawer. She ruled a steady line down the centre of a page and licked the point of a pencil. 'Now! Let's have the FOR.'

'No bakehouse fire to keep going. That one's easy.'

'But you'd have to get up early to fry sixty-four sausages and four pounds of bacon.'

'You've forgotten the eggs.' Daisy grinned. 'Number two on the FOR list. I'd enjoy doing that place up.'

'There are two unattached men in the attic.' Florence rolled her eyes.

'We never saw Mr Schofield. He could be bald and bandy.'

'Beggars can't be choosers, Miss Bell.'

'We could wing those plaster birds in full flight.'

'And find out what lurked behind the door marked WC.'

'I've just remembered.' Daisy got up and walked to the glass-fronted bookcase set in the alcove at the side of the fireplace. 'My father had a book on Lancashire houses. I'm sure he did. That kind of thing fascinated him. Here it is!' Daisy took out a thick book with a stained and mottled leather cover, its pages yellowed with age. She flipped them over, gave an exclamation of triumph and sat down again, balancing the heavy book on her knees. 'Here we are! Seaside Dwelling Houses, and three whole pages on Blackpool. Where's me glasses? In the eighteen-eighties a house just off the front would be assessed at between seventy and ninety pounds. Some further back and closer to the centre sold for as little as eighteen to twenty-five pounds.'

'Back in the eighties,' Florence reminded her. 'More than fifty years ago.'

'Mrs Mac was right about this, though.' Daisy turned a page. 'In 1893 the Borough Surveyor said that a Blackpool dwelling house needed ten or twelve bedrooms on a plot more suitable for three or four if the tenant was to pay his way.' Her glasses slipped down her nose and she pushed them back with an impatient hand. 'That was because the builders were able to dominate the Building Plans Committee. Some of the houses had no more than eleven feet at the back. Fancy trying to dry bed-linen in a space like that.'

'My mother remembered the landladies spreading their sheets out on the sands to dry.' Florence leaned forward, catching some of Daisy's excitement.

'Mrs Mac was right again. Mill workers wanted to spend their holiday in houses as much like their own as possible. Small rooms and cramped terraces. Women could make a reasonable living by lodging-house keeping until well after the war. Especially if they took in regulars. And *owner-occupiers* were a rarity. Still are I expect.' Daisy took off her glasses and closed the book. 'That's another thing my father taught me. "Never rent. Always buy." I can still hear him saying it. Rent is money poured down a drain. See something in the long run for your money, even if you have to wait twenty or thirty years. Give me that pad.' She stretched out a hand. 'I'm going to write a letter to Mrs Mac for forwarding to sad Mrs Entwistle's son who never came to see her.'

'Waiting, greedily, with hand outstretched for the money from his mother's house.'

'Exactly.' Daisy put her glasses on again. 'And I can beat him down from strength if I'm quoted a good price for this place. Which I will be.'

'You're a female tycoon!' Florence laughed out loud. 'Joan Crawford in a black dress with white collar and cuffs, and a clean pair of white gloves in her handbag, setting off to do business with a captain of industry.'

'I bet he sings in the chapel choir and cheats at snakes and ladders.' Daisy tore the first leaf out of the writing pad and wrote her address at the top of the next.

Mrs MacDougal wasn't too surprised to receive the letter from Daisy. She had shown a lot of people over the house next door, realizing the majority of them were there out of curiosity, sometimes merely for a nice look round on a day when it wasn't fit to go on the sands. But little Miss Bell was a different kettle of fish. There had been a genuine interest in her expression as she had looked around the rooms. Probably come into some money, a nice little legacy from a distant relative. The one she was in mourning for, poor thing. Mrs Mac filled in the appropriate address on the enclosed envelope and told her husband to go out and catch the dinner-time collection. That was if he could summon the strength to shift himself and totter bravely down the street.

'You're no' in the least bit funny, woman.' Angus MacDougal peeled himself from a kitchen chair with the reluctance of a sticking-plaster left on a cut finger for too long. 'Sticks and stones may hurt me bones, but your words they canna wound me.'

'I wasn't trying to be funny,' Mrs Mac said truthfully, going back to stacking the plates away in racks running round three walls of the tiny kitchen, feeling a headache coming on, wondering whether it was the onset of a migraine or possibly the first symptom of a brain tumour.

Mrs Entwistle's son lived up in Glasgow and hadn't spoken to his mother for twenty years since running away from home to join the navy. He was a small man with smooth fawn hair, large waxy ears, and a gargoyle smile which not many people saw as he used it very rarely. He had lived alone for the past five years, having left his wife when he discovered he disliked her with the same intensity as he had loathed his mother. Now he begrudged her every penny he was forced to contribute to her upkeep, seeing no reason why he should be her meal ticket for life. Working as a ledger clerk in the office of a large iron foundry gave him dyspepsia and made him bitingly sarcastic with the three young men beneath him. He had fallen out with the milkman, the boy who delivered the papers, and the neighbours on both sides of his tiny terraced cottage. He wanted to be left alone, that was all. When the letter arrived from a Miss Bell down in Lancashire he read it in distasteful astonishment.

Dear Mr Entwistle,
You don't know me, and why should you, but I was shown

133

over your property in Blackpool the other week by a Mrs MacDougal to whom you had entrusted the key.

First I must say how sorry I was to hear about your mother dying. I lost my own mother recently and so I can guess how you must be feeling. May she rest in peace.

Secondly, I would like to know a little more about your property. Details like how much are you thinking of asking for it? Would the price include the furniture and fittings? Here, without hurting your feelings, I must point out that most of them would have to be renewed. Also I would like to see any records kept of the weekly income and expenditure, and your dear mother's address book of her regular visitors. And any tradesmen's bills, of course.

I have no idea where you live, but perhaps you could arrange to meet me at the property in the near future. A Sunday would suit me best. I need a second and more thorough viewing of the property before I even consider taking the most important step in my life. I am sure you will understand my necessary caution.

I hope you are well, Mr Entwistle, and that we are able to meet soon.

Yours very sincerely,
Daisy Mary Bell (Miss)

Mr Entwistle was livid. How *dare* Mrs MacDougal invade his hard-won privacy like this? She had clear instructions to send anything on to the solicitor down in Blackpool, and yet here she had sent him a letter of such a personal nature one could be mistaken in thinking that the writer was actually acquainted with him. May his mother rest in peace, indeed! She didn't deserve to rest in peace, not after the way she had treated him. How she had treated her only son was becoming a bit vague after so long, but Mr Entwistle remembered the blistering rows and the way he had, in desperation, stolen the gas money as a thin, unhappy boy of sixteen, and caught the night train to Liverpool. Just for a brief moment he was that boy, huddled in the corner of a compartment, hungry and terrified, knowing only one thing – that he was never going to speak to her again.

Holding the letter between a finger and thumb as if it would contaminate him, he pushed it into an envelope, and sat down to compose a letter to the solicitor.

Dear Sir,
I received the enclosed today. Will you deal with it as you consider suitable.

> Yours faithfully,
> Bernard Entwistle

Sealing the letter, he put it in his pocket, tied his handkerchief in a knot to remind him to buy a stamp the next day, and went to boil an egg for his tea. A neat ugly little man without a friend in the world, shelled in his own solitude, telling himself for so long that he preferred it that way that now he believed it. Implicitly.

Mr Harmer of Harmer and Warton read Daisy's letter with a smile and passed it over to his secretary Miss Browne, spelt with an 'e' as she was in the habit of saying. Flipping over the pages of his desk diary, he ran his finger down the lined pages.

'Suggest the Sunday of the seventeenth,' he said. 'At around half-past eleven at the house. The property,' he amended. 'That should give me time to be back for my roast dinner at half-past one. I've a feeling our Miss Bell's intentions could be serious. She writes like a woman who has already made up her mind.' He picked up Bernard Entwistle's brief note. 'File this one-liner. Our Mr E. would communicate by Morse code if he could. A man of few words, Miss Browne.'

'I suppose it's the done thing to meet the solicitor instead of the owner,' Daisy said on the evening of the 16th. 'I'd have felt more comfortable meeting Mrs Entwistle's son. I wonder why he didn't answer my letter himself?'

'Probably a monk in some closed order, under a vow of silence.' Florence was ironing her best crêpe-de-chine blouse to look her smartest the next day. 'That's why his mother was sad.'

'Or married above his station.' Daisy looked up from whitening her shoes with a block of Blanco. 'To a wife who could never lift up her head again if her friends found out that her mother-in-law was a landlady.'

'The lowest of the low,' Florence said.

'I haven't committed myself.' Daisy looked suddenly vulnerable. 'Even though the price the man told us we'd get for this place almost sent me into a coma. Would you have guessed we were sitting on a little gold mine? That's what the man kept saying it was – a little gold mine.'

'There are *two* houses,' Florence reminded her. 'This one and the next door with the bakehouse down below and the storage place upstairs. Plus the fact that the custom is already there. Plus the mill right across the street, plus the fact that folks can't eat fish and chips *every* day and that your pies make a nice change, plus the fact that . . .'

The loud knocking at the shop door stopped her in mid-flow. Up-ending the flat-iron on to its asbestos stand, she glanced at the clock set squarely in the middle of the mantelpiece.

'Who on earth? At this time of night?'

It was coming up to half-past ten. It had been a dank and dismal day, and now it was a dank and dismal dark night. Before Florence had lifted the flap of the shop counter to pass through, the knocking began again. Loud, insistent, as if whoever was on the other side of the door was frantic with impatience.

'Ask who it is, first.' Daisy was right behind her.

But as if she had known, Florence drew back the bolt at the top, turned the key and opened the door wide – letting in the huge bull-like man with staring eyes and blood pouring from a cut on his forehead.

'I think I've killed her!' Matthew Livesey stumbled into the darkened shop, swaying where he stood, bloodshot eyes protruding with fear, smelling of Saturday-night drink, hatless, coatless, shirt black-wet with rain. 'You have to come, lass. It's either you or the doctor.' To Daisy's horror and disgust he dropped down to his knees and clutched at Florence's legs. 'An' if the doctor sees her he'll send for the police. An' if the police come then I'm a goner.'

Florence stood frozen for a long moment. Daisy moved first.

'I'll go and get our coats,' she said, 'and the first-aid box from the bakehouse.'

When she came back Florence was standing by the counter staring wide-eyed at the spectacle of her father sprawled on the floor, sobbing like a child, beating his fists on the oilcloth, moaning and retching, his mouth held loosely open as a thin stream of evil-smelling vomit spread like an obscene puddle.

The woman wasn't dead, but blood was pouring from a wound on the crown of her head. She lay on her side on the rug by the fender, her legs drawn up, almost to her chin. Steeling herself to touch her, Daisy turned her over, feeling the bile rise in her own throat at the sight of the woman's face battered almost to a pulp, with swollen lips drawn back into a grotesque snarl, and one eye no more than a slit in a mound of bruised flesh.

'Water,' she ordered. 'And cloths. If we get rid of the worst of the blood we'll be able to see. Stop that!' Her voice rose to a shout as Matthew Livesey began the low animal moaning again. 'Go and stick your head underneath the cold tap in the kitchen and stop that row! Do you hear me? STOP IT!'

As Daisy soaked the blood away from the tangled hair, the woman opened her eyes. Whether she was dark or fair Daisy had no idea, but the wound was gaping, the edges apart like smiling lips.

'It will have to be stitched.' Sitting back on her heels she

137

spoke with a firmness she was far from feeling. 'The hair will have to be shaved and it will need stitching.' Her voice softened as she spoke directly to Florence. 'Can you hold the cloth like this while I run and get Doctor Marsden?'

Florence backed away, a hand held to her mouth. 'I'm sorry, Daisy. I'm sorry... sorry... but I can't....' She looked frail and ill, all the animation of less than fifteen minutes ago wiped from her face as if it had never been. 'If she dies... oh, God!'

Daisy kicked aside a broken gin bottle with jagged edges lying on the rug. She handed the cloth to Florence, and showed her how to press it over the gaping ugly wound to stem the flow of blood, now mercifully reduced to a trickle.

'If she dies...' Florence said again, 'what will happen?'

'Your father will be tried for murder. Or manslaughter, as it's obvious she has been fighting too. Now hold that still. Are you listening? Wake up, Florence. It's happened and we have to make the best of it we can.'

Then she ran down the street, as she had run not all that long ago, to fetch the good Doctor Marsden from his well-earned rest.

It was the anger that had made her speak so harshly and cruelly, Daisy told herself, swaying with the movement of the train on her way to Blackpool the next morning.

It was the sight of Florence, lately so happy, reduced once again, in the space of a few minutes, to the state she had been in on the day she had contemplated suicide. Florence needed affection, Daisy realized, as a plant needed water, not as a reward but because her life was intolerable without it. Underneath that tall, drooping exterior, that know-all confidence, was an insecurity so near the surface of her emotions that Daisy feared for her. Thinking that no one loved her made it impossible for Florence to love herself. Misery had a bad effect on Florence, Daisy told herself, changing trains at Preston without really knowing what she was doing. Misery *diminished* Florence into a feeble and unhappy creature. No wonder she hated men in general and her father in particular when he was the reason for it all.

By the time Daisy had got back with the resigned doctor in tow, the broken bottle had disappeared. The cushions on the sofa had been put back in place, and the standard lamp up-ended in its corner. By then Mr Livesey, his black curly hair plastered to his head, was sitting hunched and silent, his big hands hanging loosely between his knees.

The woman – Daisy had to think of her as that, never having heard her name – had come round and told the doctor that she had fallen heavily, tripped and caught her head on the steel fender. No, she wasn't going to press charges, how could she, when it had been nothing more than a drop too much to drink, and a scuffle getting a bit out of hand?

'You must go and keep the appointment,' Florence had said about three o'clock that morning when the woman had been stitched up at the infirmary and kept in overnight, and Mr Livesey was snoring his head off in bed. 'It's too late to let anyone know anyway, but I'll have to stay here. He's going to be so sick and sorry for himself when he comes to there's no knowing what he'll do.' Something of the old Florence had shone from her eyes. 'And don't go all romantic and tell me it's on account of love. Because if you do I'll be sick. Love? Give me an honest dollop of hatred any old day.'

Almost pushing Daisy out of the door into a dark and deserted street she had said sadly: 'You're my best friend.'

'And you are mine,' Daisy remembered saying, wanting to put her arms round the tall drooping figure and not knowing how to. 'We'll work something out, you'll see.'

But would they? Daisy got out of the train at Blackpool Central Station and walked out into the forecourt. Florence had cast herself into the role of a dutiful daughter, and for her mother's sake would play herself into a permanent decline. Daisy could feel it in her bones.

*

The minute Daisy stepped into the brown hall of the three-storeyed house she knew that the feeling she had about it was still there. It *needed* her, this neglected, shabby dwelling, as the solicitor insisted on calling it. And oh, dear God, how she wanted to be needed at this moment. She was so tired, her mouth seemed to be having difficulty in stretching itself round the words.

Mr Harmer of Harmer and Warton had brought a large manilla envelope with all the details. He sat with Daisy in the brown lounge with its brown threadbare carpet and its beef-tea-coloured oilcloth surround, and talked to her in a measured legal voice, interspersed by little apologetic coughs. Cecil Parker, Daisy thought, unable as ever to meet anyone for the first time without casting them in a film. In *A Cuckoo in the Nest*. With a capacity to be either amiable or sinister.

'My client,' Mr Harmer was saying in Cecil Parker's silky voice, 'wishes to remain anonymous throughout any transaction. It would be better if you did not approach him directly again. His desire is to keep well out of any negotiations.' The long upper lip quivered. 'A most unusual condition, Miss Bell.'

'Guilt,' Daisy said at once. 'Because he never came to see his mother. I bet he's just sitting there up in Scotland, being anonymous with his hands outstretched for the money.'

'I *beg* your pardon?'

Mr Harmer liked this little Miss Bell. As honest as the day is long, he decided, his shrewd glance taking in Daisy's straight brown gaze and the tilt of her determined chin. Young though, to be considering a venture like this on her own. There should be a man somewhere in the background. A father, or an uncle. He glanced at her ringless left hand. Happily married to a wife who only breathed in and out when he did, it was inconceivable to Mr Harmer that any woman could stand on her own two feet without falling flat on her face. For one thing he wasn't at all sure how this bonny little woman would fare with the bank or with any of the monetary side of things without a man to guide her, advise her, stand in as security and nay, dammit, see her through the whole transaction.

'I'm sorry, I ought not to have said that.' Daisy looked as helpless as nature, in Mr Harmer's opinion, had intended her to be.

'That's all right, my dear.' Mr Harmer relaxed visibly. Now he could ask her the personal questions her attitude had precluded him from doing hitherto.

'I had a bad night,' she was saying. 'I only slept for an hour, if that.'

'Worried, my dear.' Mr Harmer, without moving an inch, patted her hand in a fatherly fashion.

'Oh, not about the house,' Daisy corrected him swiftly. 'Once my mind is made up, things will go forward. No, I was worried about my friend.'

'Your fiancé? You mean he isn't sure about you taking such an important step?'

'There is no fiancé.' Daisy sat bolt upright, a blush creeping up and staining her cheeks. 'I am doing this on my own. At least I may have to. Now it's not certain that my friend will be able to come in with me. For domestic reasons,' she added, seeing Florence standing on her father's doorstep only hours before, her long features ennobled by a shaft of moonlight.

'Did you hear what the doctor said about my father never really having got over my mother's death?' she had asked Daisy. 'He was trying to tell me in the nicest way he could that I had been so wrapped up in my own grief that I had shut him out. I *forced* him to drink,' Florence had intoned, presenting the flat planes of her face to the dark sky. 'He brought that woman here because he couldn't bear the loneliness. Oh God, I can see it all now.'

'My friend has a parent she feels is going to need her care,' Daisy told Mr Harmer. 'He ... he wasn't at all well last night. That is why she hasn't come with me today.'

'Ah, yes.' With two daughters happily married off, and an

141

elder one already filling her days ministering to his semi-invalid wife, Mr Harmer understood perfectly. 'Her soul will be enriched by her decision, my dear. God will reward her. If not here on earth, then in His heavenly kingdom.'

'That's a lot of sentimental tosh!' Daisy was too tired, too overwrought to be polite. The sleepless night and the silent brooding on the train journey had drained away her hard-fought-for control. Getting up from her low brown chair she began to pace up and down on the shabby brown carpet, her face drawn and pale beneath her shiny black straw hat.

'My friend's sacrifice would be an intolerable waste of a bright spirit,' she told an astonished Mr Harmer. 'She will turn out exactly as I myself would have turned out if. . . .' She walked over to the window, swallowing to get rid of the lump in her throat, trying to check the flow of words and finding to her shame that it was too late. 'If my mother hadn't died suddenly. Setting me free.' She wheeled round, causing Mr Harmer to shrink back in his seat. 'Oh, I loved my mother, and for as long as she lived I would have looked after her. But she *possessed* me, you see.' The lump in Daisy's throat dissolved into the threat of tears. 'I spent my whole life trying to please my mother, Mr Harmer. I was the good little girl she always wanted me to be, and I went on still trying to be that same little girl who always wanted to please.'

'Miss Bell. . . .' The solicitor put up a hand, as embarrassed as if Daisy had said: 'Excuse me while I loosen my stays.' Emotion in his own home was nipped in the bud long before it had a chance to flower. Emotion was for unbalanced females, and, let's face it, for neurotic spinsters like this one pulsating before him with tears in her eyes.

'And if I *did* please her. . . .' It would have taken more than a raised hand to stop Daisy now. 'Never once did she tell me so. I used to *ache* for my mother to praise me, Mr Harmer, just for any small thing, but she never did. And do you know why?'

'I really don't. . . .'

'Because praising me would have weakened her position,

142

which was to *dominate* me.' Daisy's voice rose, so that the man passing the lounge door at that moment stopped transfixed. 'I was unthanked. Taken for granted. Just as my friend will be. But it will be all the harder for her because she has a great and enormous *rage* inside her. It has nearly destroyed her once and it will destroy her again.'

All at once Daisy walked back to her chair, sat down, straightened her hat, held out her hand for the manilla envelope, and apologized.

'Thank you for listening to me, Mr Harmer. You have a kind face and that set me off. Being a legal man you must be used to hearing people's problems.' Daisy smiled a smile of such sweetness that the solicitor blinked.

'Well, I can't say I ever....'

'It was either blurting all that out or bursting, and that's only the half of it.'

'I really must....'

'Oh, I've finished, Mr Harmer. Thank you for meeting me and showing me round again.' Daisy clutched the envelope to her chest. 'I'll study this and let you know, and if there are any takers for the shop then I'll have a better idea of where I stand. How soon will you need to know my decision?'

Mr Harmer fingered his top lip, stroking it as if remembering the moustache once sprouting there when he was a captain in the Army Pay Corps. Two houses and a shop to sell. Hm... m... Hm... m... This could turn out to be a cash sale. One he could easily negotiate himself without bringing in a shark of an agent. Mr Entwistle had given him permission to execute proceedings any way he thought fit, just as long as he wasn't involved in any way. Hm... Hm... m.... That would mean he could quote his own terms.

'A month,' he said at last. 'Give or take a week or so. My client doesn't seem to be in any particular hurry.' He got up from the low chair and held out his hand. 'We will meet again, Miss Bell, and you know where I am should you need any further advice.'

At the front door he shook hands again before planting a

black bowler hat squarely on his head. 'Goodbye, Miss Bell. Hm ... Hm ... Goodbye.'

There was a smell of Sunday dinner coming from Mrs Mac's lodgings next door. Sitting at the table in the window, a party of four holidaymakers plied knives and forks with obvious enthusiasm. Daisy realized that she hadn't eaten a thing since the boiled ham tea shared with Florence the day before. But she wasn't hungry, she told herself, setting off to walk to the station to catch the next train back. She had more on her mind than her stomach, for goodness' sake. Decisions to make, big decisions, possibly the biggest she would ever make in the whole of her life.

'Miss Bell! Miss Bell?'

At the sound of her name being called, Daisy stopped, turned round and saw the pipe man from the upstairs room hurrying along the pavement towards her; looking more like Herbert Marshall than ever, she decided, with his nice kind face crumpled with anxiety and a teacloth clutched in his hand.

'Joshua Penny. I go with the house. Remember?' He hesitated, unnerved by the close-up of Daisy's tear-stained cheeks. 'Oh, look. I think it's a bit much that chap sort of dismissing you like this, and most places are closed, it being Sunday you know.' He stared down at the teacloth in a baffled kind of way. 'So I was wondering. Would you like to come back inside and have a cup of tea, at least. You can have a proper look at the kitchen at the same time. Sort of kill two birds with one stone. There won't be a train for a couple of hours. I know that line pretty well.'

The intrepid traveller, Daisy remembered, responding to kindness the way she always did. 'I'd like that very much,' she said.

Joshua Penny helped her off with her black coat and hung it on the antler coatstand in the hall. Daisy refused to part with her hat because she had gone to bed without her usual helmet of steel curlers, so felt her hair was best tucked away out of sight.

144

In the kitchen Daisy sat at one end of a table watching Mr Penny making heavy weather of brewing a pot of tea. No warming the pot first, no measuring the tea out carefully, just a sloshing of boiling water on tea-leaves he'd sprinkled in like salt.

'I have to tell you I heard most of what you said in there.' He poured the tea without letting it stand for as much as a single minute, then handed Daisy a cup of a white milky drink, tasting of steam and nothing else. 'I was passing the door when you were up to the bit about your friend, and I meant to move on but I couldn't take another step. I was *riveted*,' he admitted. 'I'm glad you had a bit of a cry. You *were* crying, weren't you?'

To Daisy's everlasting shame her eyes filled with tears again. What a peculiar man this Mr Penny was turning out to be. Admitting he'd been eavesdropping and dying to know what came next! A habit Daisy had indulged in many times.

'I don't really know why I am crying.' She took a sip of the tea and shuddered. 'I cried a bit on the day of my mother's funeral, but not much, and only once briefly on the day she died. But it's all in here.' She tapped the front of her black silk blouse. 'And now my friend might not be coming here with me, and as you heard, *not* coming with me could destroy her.' The tears began to roll unchecked. 'I am so sorry. I'm making such a fool of myself today. I'd have been better stopping at home. I really would.'

'Wrong.' Mr Penny was drinking the tea as if he relished every sip. 'I expect Mrs Mac told you about me?'

Daisy nodded. The consumptive wife who shrank to the size of a pullet, she remembered.

'I nursed my wife for almost two years. Taught during the day and took over as soon as I got home. Hardly any sleep, no proper meals, no tears, not even as I stood by her graveside. Then about six weeks later when I was buying a pound of potatoes from the greengrocer, he asked me how I was managing on my own. Sliding the potatoes into my carrier-bag and asking just a straightforward question in an ordinary voice. I only knew him as a greengrocer, Miss Bell. He wasn't a friend or anything, but there and then I began to cry. Can you imagine? A man holding out a paper bag to receive a few potatoes, shaking with sobs, with his eyes and his nose running, and the poor chap wishing the ground would open and swallow me up.'

'Oh, I can just see it,' Daisy said at once, because she really could. 'I'm so sorry for you, Mr Penny.'

'And I am sorry for *you*, Miss Bell.' Joshua got up and took a basin of eggs down from a shelf. 'So now we've established how sorry we are for each other, shall we have something to eat as a consolation? An omelette, perhaps? I'm a dab hand with those.'

But he wasn't. Daisy watched in horror as he broke the eggs into a basin, put far too much butter into a frying pan too large for omelettes, whipped the eggs furiously as if they were intended for a fatless sponge, then tipped them into the pan on top of the butter which by now was burned almost to toffee.

'This is a shocking omelette, Mr Penny,' she told him, cutting through the leathery pancake no thicker than a decent sheet of blotting-paper. 'You're helping me to make up my mind, you know.'

'I am?'

'At least with me to cook for you there'll be less chance of you ending up with chronic indigestion,' Daisy said, swallowing valiantly. 'If I hadn't seen you make this with me own eyes, I could be forgiven for thinking I was eating a corn plaster!'

'He only laughed when I said that,' Daisy told Florence that same evening. 'He's a nice man, is Mr Joshua Penny. Quite old, about forty-eight or nine, I should think. He reminded me strongly of my father. My father smoked a pipe, you know, puffing away in that chair you're sitting in now, his head wreathed in smoke.'

'Was Mr Schofield there?'

'Out again.' Daisy lowered her voice to a respectable level. 'How is your father? I hardly dare ask.'

'I must get back,' Florence said. 'It's terrible. He has spent the whole day wallowing in remorse, and remorse is such a wasted emotion, Daisy. He keeps on begging my forgiveness, calling on my mother to beg *her* forgiveness, and praying to God to pardon him from all his sins. He says Jesus appeared at the foot of his bed in the night and asked him to renounce all his wicked ways. I can't see Jesus setting foot in our house, somehow. The doctor came again and said my father needs a week in bed to recover from what he called nervous exhaustion. Doctors always say that when they're flummoxed. Nervous exhaustion! A glass of gin would set him on his feet again, but apparently Jesus made him promise never to touch the stuff again. I give him a week before he's on the booze again.'

'And . . . and the woman?'

'Discharged herself and gone back to her husband, can you believe it? The poor mutt has taken her in. With thousands of spinsters at loose in the country looking out for a man, and only half of them qualifying for a pension at the end of their long working lives. Frustrated neurotics like thee and me.'

'And a merry Christmas, to you, too,' Daisy said. 'Don't you want to know what I've decided to do about the house? Though I think I'll see what Uncle Arnold says before I make up my mind properly. I trust his judgement. I always have.'

'I'd get him on his own,' Florence advised. 'You don't want your Auntie Edna putting her spoke in. She'd put the kybosh on things right away if she knew you were consulting him. She could emasculate Tarzan, that woman.'

Florence walked hunch-shouldered from the room, a Kirby grip loosening itself from the French pleat to drop with a tinkle on the oilcloth surround by the door. 'But you'll take the house. Some things are written in the stars. With me or without me, whatever your uncle says, you'll take it. An' you know you will.'

Arnold spent many happy hours with Daisy during the next few weeks.

'All things being equal I would have liked nothing better

than an office job,' he told her when she remarked on the neatness of his writing and his quickness at working out columns of figures. 'But things weren't equal, were they, chuck? The war saw to that. Aye, there were more than bodies buried in Flanders mud. Ambitions as well. Chances lost, opportunities never taken up. Nay, a white-collar job was out for me by the time all that lot was over.'

'But don't you feel resentful? Bitter?'

'An' where would that get me, lass?' He opened the flap of Mr Harmer's manilla envelope, spilling its contents over the table. 'Right, now. Where was we last time?' He showed Daisy a closely written page of figures. 'This is the way I see it, lass. If you can up the Cronshawes a hundred pounds or so for the business, it will give you a bit to play with for solicitor's fees and the like.' He tapped the paper with a soil-ingrained finger. 'They can afford it. Their chip-shop's a little gold mine. They wouldn't be setting their daughter up in the confectionery business if they didn't know when they were on to a good thing.'

'I don't want to fleece them.'

'*Fleece* them?' Arnold clamped his lips together and moved his head from side to side. Tough on the outside this beloved niece of his, but with a heart as soft as marshmallow. 'Why do you think they asked for first refusal even before they knew you'd decided to sell? There might be a slump, but one thing always does well if you give value for money, and that's food. Folks can do without clothes and furniture, but food's a necessity. Go 'bout shoes and you get segs on your feet; go 'bout food and you die.'

He could feel the warmth spreading through his chest as Daisy listened to him, her bright eyes on his face, drinking in every word he said. It made him feel like a man again, to be taken for his proper worth. Not sneered at by his wife, a sneer often mirrored on his daughter's face. There were days when he felt like shouting his head off at both of them, asserting his authority, but what authority was left to a man out of a job for over two years, a man who still had an instinct to throw himself flat on the ground, or run for the nearest bolt-hole when a rocket whooshed into the sky on Bonfire Night? Nay, best let them get on with it, the pair of them, and leave him to his allotment and his dominoes down at the pub on a Friday.

'You'll be having it properly surveyed and valued, lass?'

'Mr Harmer is seeing to that, but they're good solid houses, Uncle Arnold. Not jerry-built like some they're throwing up further back from the promenade. I wish you could go with me one Sunday and give me your honest opinion.'

He had to pretend to have a coughing fit to hide his pleasure, but Daisy recognized it for what it was. 'It won't cost you anything,' she said carefully. 'We'll put it down to business expenses.'

'I'll come, and I'll pay my own way.' Arnold stood up to go. 'If I can't scrape up the train fare to Blackpool then it's time I threw the flippin' sponge in. Would next Sunday suit you, lass?'

'You're sure Auntie Edna won't mind?' Daisy followed him to the door. 'She won't feel left out or anything? I'd ask her to come as well, but she's not on my side about all this.'

Arnold unlatched the back door. 'Leave it to me, chuck. You might not believe it, but I know how to handle your Auntie Edna.'

'Well, what did you think of it?' Edna was feeding the baby from a bottle when Arnold got back from Blackpool, his cheek-bones flushed where the sun and wind had caught them. 'I hope you didn't encourage that young madam to do something she'll be sorry for. How she can even think of selling the shop our Martha worked her fingers to the bone for, I don't know.' The baby gulped the milk too quickly so Edna up-ended him and gave him a good thump. 'It's obvious the Cronshawes recognize they're quids in buying the shop for their daughter. Fat chance of you ever doing anything like that for our Betty, bless her.' She glared at him. 'An'

149

before I forget. I found another lot of flamin' green tomatoes at the back of the sideboard drawer where you'd hidden them to ripen off. If you fetch any more down from that allotment I'll chuck them to the back of the fire.'

'You could always make them into chutney.' Arnold sat down and unlaced his boots. 'It's a good house, but it wants a lot doing to it. Daisy is going to have to offer special rates for Christmas and Easter to attract the custom she's going to need.' He eased his feet into a pair of shabby carpet slippers. 'We found out today that the winter weekend trade is catching on fast. So there's money about in spite of the slump. And in the winter Daisy can take in regulars at reduced rates. There's two living in already.'

Edna had lost the thread of what he was saying, but she wasn't going to let on. She got up to put the baby in his pram, parked like a nuisance between the settee and the sideboard. 'Is it true that Florrie Livesey's going in with Daisy? Her father's living with that common woman again. She went back to her husband for a while, but he soon threw her out.'

'You wouldn't like to think Daisy was going in for all this on her own, would you?' Arnold reached up to the mantelpiece for his tobacco pouch, then realized his baccy money had gone towards his day out. 'She's only a girl in spite of everything.'

Edna's better nature struggled with itself and for once won. 'No, I wouldn't like to think of her going away on her own. For our Martha's sake I'd like her to be happy. God knows that was all Martha ever wanted for her. And if you're pining for a smoke there's an ounce of Tam-O-Shanter in the drawer behind those flamin' green tomatoes. I managed it with cutting down on the Co-op order, so if food's a bit short you'll know why.'

Arnold gave the pram handle a little jig as he took the tobacco out of the drawer. 'He's going off, love,' he said, remembering to keep his voice low.

PART TWO

Chapter One

Almost the last thing Daisy did before she left the shop and the bakehouse to begin her new life was to send a printed card to Sam. She wrote a gay little note on the back:

'Guess what? Can you see me as a Blackpool landlady?'

On the front the card bore the letters 'Shangri-La', a name dreamed up by Daisy who had resumed her picture-going by a visit to *Lost Horizon* with the gentlemanly Ronald Colman as the hero of a Tibetan Utopia. The address, with 'Proprietress Miss Daisy Bell' in the bottom right-hand corner, was flanked on the left by 'Breakfast and Evening Meal. Wash basins in all Bedrooms.'

It wasn't the same as a letter, she told herself. Not like running after him, as Martha would have said. Just a courtesy gesture to an old friend, in fact.

She gave him time to reply. She fantasized about him sending her a telegram wishing her well, or a Good Luck card, or better still giving her the best thrill of all by writing to book a nice holiday break for himself and the children.

But nothing came, and at the end of a traumatic fortnight spent training Ada Cronshawe, now a triumphant Ada Davison, and her new husband into the ways of counter selling, wholesale buying of flour, currants and fresh supplies of pork-meat and daily deliveries of cream for the famous fancies, Daisy was forced to accept that Sam had crossed her from his memory. So why then couldn't she be sensible and do the same? Why was he still there in the forefront of her thoughts before she slept at night, and there again when she opened her eyes each morning at the insistent ringing of her alarm clock? Why wouldn't he just *go away* and leave her in peace?

Florence went to say goodbye to her father, who was still in a state of holiness, and his equally sanctimonious lady friend, but when Matthew suggested they went down on their knees on the very spot where the broken gin bottle had lain to ask the Lord to shower His blessings on her new venture, she flatly refused.

'The Lord helps those who help themselves,' she said, leaving the pair of them to their devotions, hardly raising an eyebrow when Matthew swore the only drop he was ever going to touch again was Communion wine.

Edna was being decent about it all now that Daisy had given her and Arnold a firm invitation to spend Easter at Shangri-La. 'On the house, of course,' Daisy had promised, and Betty, bless her, whispered a heartfelt thank you to her cousin for giving her the chance of a few days alone with Cyril and the baby. Not that she meant it nasty, not after what her mother did for them, but it would be nice all the same.

At least twenty of the shop's regular customers had promised to come for their holidays, making firm bookings, and the good Doctor Marsden and his wife had sent a set of ecru antimacassars in drawn-threadwork which Daisy had already allocated in her mind for the backs of the new chairs she was determined to buy for the brown lounge of Shangri-La.

When the day came she went into the bakehouse for the last time. The new baker, with flour in his eyebrows, gave her a powdery handshake and one of the apprentices turned round from sliding a tray of loaves into the proving oven and grinned. Daisy patted the shiny black door of the fire-oven, stopped herself just in time from reaching up to adjust the damper, stepped out into the yard and walked through the door where Sam had once cupped her face in his hands and told her she was lovely. She was going now to a house where he had never been; where no memories lingered. She was free of him at last.

They were travelling in the furniture van, parked in the exact spot where, on a brilliant summer's day, the Rolls-Royce had stood at the kerb, gleaming with polish, with the Spirit of Ecstasy poised spread-winged on the bonnet.

'All set, love?' The driver, a scrawny little man, told Florence to hutch up. Daisy climbed in and they were off.

The driver's mate had helped to load the van with the few pieces of furniture Daisy had decided to take with her, had clutched his back, sworn he'd done it in and walking like a bent paper-clip, had gone off home to lie on a board.

'I'll manage, never fear.' The driver coughed and wheezed, thumping his chest with a closed fist. 'Breaks up the phlegm,' he explained.

After a few miles of listening to him hawking and rasping in his throat, Daisy uttered to Florence in a whisper she knew would be drowned by the noisy engine of the shabby little van: 'If he doesn't spit it out I'll go crazy!'

'If he *does*, I certainly will,' Florence said, speaking equally softly and smiling at him, as he clenched his fist to begin the thumping and hawking process again.

By a fluke of nature the day was more like spring; the Blackpool sky so wide and blue it reminded Daisy of a drawing in a child's reading book, the clouds as white and stuffed as fat feather pillows. Climbing down from the van she lifted her head to sniff the salt and shrimps smell she had associated with Blackpool since her childhood. It was a day for walking on the promenade with a headscarf tied under her chin, not for watching helplessly as the puny driver struggled to unload a single mattress from the van.

'He's got a terrible chesty cold,' she told Mrs Mac, who had appeared on the pavement the minute the van drew up at the kerb.

'And T B,' Mrs Mac said at once. 'His lungs are shot, that's

155

obvious. I hope he didn't breathe on you on the way.'

'Coughed in my face the whole time,' Florence said cheerfully. 'Where is the nearest sanatorium I can book into when I start spitting blood?'

Mrs Mac ignored her. 'No good asking my husband, not with his hernia. He can't move an inch without his truss, and Mr Penny's at work, of course. Ee, my goodness, that mattress'll flatten him if he doesn't watch out.'

With a swift exchange of glances, Daisy and Florence moved into action, spreading arms that didn't seem long enough round one end of the unwieldy mattress and tottering backwards across the pavement. Daisy's hat was knocked off, and Florence felt her hair coming down, but they managed to negotiate the front steps before setting their end down with a thud.

'What on earth?'

Two red faces turned as one in the direction of the voice. A man of slightly more than average height, his straight black hair plastered to his head with brilliantine, was coming out of Shangri-La wearing a camel-hair coat and a disbelieving expression on his neatly sculptured features.

Cary Grant, Daisy's mind registered at once, even to the cigarette held loosely in his left hand. She put a hand up to her unruly hair and bent down to retrieve her hat, thinking that if the vision stood still in a shop window as a dummy nobody would know the difference, so perfect was he in every detail from his polished shoes to his patent-leather hair.

'Miss Bell, I take it?' The vision held out a hand to Florence.

'*I'm* Miss Bell.' Daisy put out the hand holding the hat and blushed.

'Looks like you're having a spot of trouble.' Taking off the splendid coat, he handed it to Mrs Mac and tossed the cigarette away. 'Bobbie Schofield at your service,' he said, taking one end of the mattress and negotiating the steps as nimbly as a mountain goat. 'Up a bit with your end, old fruit. That's the ticket!'

*

'No, we're *not* going out for fish and chips.' Daisy stood in the middle of the kitchen late that afternoon, surrounded by cartons and boxes and things with nowhere to go. 'This is the first meal in this establishment and I won't sink so low!' She looked round wildly, trying to remember where she had packed the perishable food. 'Mr Penny will be back from work soon and he's going to sit down in the dining-room with Mr Schofield in a civilized manner and eat a decently-cooked tea. Ah, here it is!' She pounced on a carton of greengrocery. 'I knew there wouldn't be time to do any food shopping today, so I brought a few things with me. I'll make potato pancakes, with boiled beetroot and a nice slice of ham. And somewhere . . . somewhere there's a box of Eccles cakes. They'll have to do for pudding just for today.'

There was a gleam in her eye that wouldn't be denied. Florence could see already that Daisy was going to be in her element. The house might be in a turmoil of unpacked cases, books spilling everywhere, even down the stairs, no beds made up for them to sleep in tonight, and God knew where the knives and forks were kept underneath all this. But there were two hungry men to feed and come hell or high water Daisy would cook them a meal.

'They've been fending for themselves for several months now, for heaven's sake! One more day isn't going to make any difference!' Florence was really put out. The sight of Daisy wearing a blue scarf tied like a turban calmly gathering her ingredients together sent a prickle of irritation up her spine.

'All the more reason they should know what properly cooked food can taste like.' Daisy pounced with joy on a bag of plain flour. 'Now, if I can find the onions. . . .'

'Food!' Florence clenched her fists. 'You're obsessed with food!'

'Well, of course I am. It's my job, and always has been.' Daisy turned round in surprise. 'There's no need to be shirty about it.'

157

'I am *not* being shirty!' Florence made a last attempt to latch on to her slipping control, and failed. 'I just don't think now is the time to do your Mrs Beeton act, that's all.'

Her legs ached, and there was a low grinding pain in the pit of her stomach. She could feel her poorly time coming on and knew it was going to be bad this month. If they had remembered to bring the Indian brandy she had no idea where it was. She had no idea where *anything* was, and if Daisy didn't stop being so sweetly reasonable she might just clock her one. The force of Florence's rage took her by surprise.

'You were just the same at Guide camp,' she said coldly and clearly. 'Insisting on cooking flamin' rabbit pie when sausages and bacon would have done just as well. Standing there under a tarpaulin in a wet field rolling pastry to show off. Everybody was laughing at you, if you must know.'

'How many years ago was that?' Daisy was genuinely astonished. 'They ate the pie, anyroad. *And* enjoyed it, if I remember rightly.'

'Making you the heroine of the hour once again.'

'The what?'

'The flamin' heroine. Like one of your flamin' film stars. Who are you being now? Janet Gaynor?' With that she turned on her heel and lurched from the kitchen, holding a hand to her head.

Daisy heard her feet pounding on the stairs, then the slam of a door. It was a good job they were alone in the house, she muttered, following on with the potato-peeler still clutched in a hand. Imagine the visitors come for a nice holiday, sitting in the lounge or the dining-room, and hearing the staff quarrelling at the tops of their voices in the kitchen! She hurried along the landing to find that Florence had locked herself in a bedroom, turning a key that Daisy had thought was rusted into its lock.

'Florence?' She tapped on the door and waited, head inclined, listening for the sound of sobbing. She rattled the door knob. 'Florence? Come on out, or at least let me in so we can talk.'

158

'So you can use your charm on *me*?' There was such a wealth of bitterness in Florence's voice that Daisy recoiled.

'What is that supposed to mean?'

Silence. Daisy rattled the door again, then walked slowly back along the landing and down the stairs. So that was it! Mr Schofield. Pausing briefly by the mirror in the hall Daisy stared at the reflection of an ordinary round face with a halo of sausage curls, cheeks too pink for beauty, and brown eyes ringed with tiredness. Charm? Was that what Florence thought she had?

Yet *she* was the one Mr Schofield had flirted with. Not Florence. He had taken off his jacket, rolled up his shirt-sleeves and made endless journeys into the house with chairs, the back end of a dressing-table, joking with the driver, teasing Daisy. 'Now, Miss Bell, where shall we put this chair? Chippendale, I presume? Back a bit, Horace.' Winking at Daisy. 'Nasty cough you've got there, Horace.' And Daisy had just had to stop what she was doing and laugh, because whatever the driver's real name was, Horace fitted him perfectly. Mr Schofield was a bit of a gas, no doubt about that.

'Why aren't you at work?' she'd asked him, as he staggered upstairs, long legs bowed beneath the weight of a heavy mahogany bedside table.

'A bad back,' he'd told her, and after one startled moment her laugh had rung out again, the infectious laugh that Sam had once thought embraced all the sorrows of the world.

Mr Schofield went dancing every single night. He had more cups to prove his expertise at the tango than you could buy on a pot market, he'd said, and sure enough, when he'd invited her into his room for what he called a look-see, there they were on shelves all round the walls, big cups and little ones, all engraved with his name, Robert Schofield. Tango 1932. Quick-step 1933. Waltz, modern and old-fashioned, 1935.

'What happened to 1934?' she asked him, and he twirled imaginary ends of his five-a-side moustache.

'The year of me back,' he said solemnly, but not before she

saw a shadow pass across his face.

Where was Florence when all this was going on? Daisy reached up and took three eggs down from the bowl on a shelf by the gas cooker, and like the re-run of a film remembered Mr Penny doing the same the day he had made the leathery omelette.

Florence had been busily unpacking their joint collection of books, she recalled. Stacking them at the sides of the stairs and moaning about the lack of shelves. Florence, dusty and untidy, pushing the fine wispy hair from her face, with a streak of dirt down her long nose, hearing their laughter and tightening her mouth into a hard straight line.

Daisy rummaged in a carton and came up with the bottle of olive oil she had hoped to find there. She decided to grate a little cheese into the potatoes and onions to give them a bit of taste. She would have to have a nice long talk to Florence, but not now . . . not just now.

Charm. The very word tasted bad on Florence's tongue. What or who was it decided that some people had it in abundance, while others lacked it completely? Daisy wasn't beautiful, not in the conventional sense of the word, she didn't even have a way with men; she wasn't coy, heaven forbid, or flirtatious. She didn't play the helpless female, or flutter her eyelashes, or do any of the things Florence despised. Yet men took to her straight away. Why? Because she made them laugh? Because they knew she wasn't waiting for them to fall in love with her? Florence stared out of the window at a narrow yard flanked by a sandy strip of uncultivated garden. Was it because Daisy *liked* men, while Florence mistrusted them, found them on the whole to be like overgrown schoolboys, especially the twirpish Mr Schofield who obviously thought he was God's gift to unattached females?

Florence ran a finger down the pane of glass and grimaced at the grime it revealed. The grinding pain low down in her back was spreading round to her front. Angular, tall, long-necked, aggressive and filled at times with this undefined anger, she saw herself so clearly she wondered if she *could* just possibly be one of those unnatural women? But her furtive enjoyment of *The Well of Loneliness* had left her filled with pity, but with no sense at all of reader identification.

She had told Daisy of an affair with a married man. Florence pressed her forehead against the window, adding to the dirty streak already there. A few burning glances, hands held across a pot of tea in a café in Preston; a suggestion that she would meet him one afternoon in a dingy hotel room and Florence had heard the music of love fade away. No, if she couldn't have love that was pure and clean and undefiled, she would do without it.

Love from a gentle man, in both senses of the word. Gentle but strong, cultured, maybe not a scholar but a man fond of books, of music, of country walks in the rain. Not good-looking in a conventional way, but nicely spoken. A man something like Daisy's dead father. Florence sighed as the rage inside her began to subside. She could hardly remember him, but every time Daisy spoke about him, she *identified*.

Yet he had married Daisy's mother. That little woman with the razor-sharp tongue whose idea of culture was a night out at the Palace Theatre watching a variety show, with a hot potato from the cart on the Boulevard afterwards. Daisy's mother had admired Frank Randle, the music-hall comedian of overpowering vulgarity, and George Formby of the toothy grin and the ukelele, with the *double entendre* in his songs. It didn't make sense.

At the sound of voices down in the hall Florence opened the door and moved out to the landing, looked down over the banisters and saw Daisy greeting Mr Penny, home from his teaching job at Preston, the man Daisy had confessed reminded her of her father.

'No, I insist,' Daisy was saying. 'Your tea will be ready at six o'clock. If you can climb over all those books on the stairs, just go up and wash your hands and come down when you're ready. Mr Schofield will be back and I'm going to put you together, unless you would like to eat at separate tables. You've got the dining room to yourselves, so you can choose.'

'But on your first day!' The kind Mr Penny was objecting in his nice refined voice. 'I never expected . . . I really didn't.' As he lowered his voice, Florence leaned dangerously over the banister rail. 'You're sure you wouldn't like to sit down yourself while I make you an omelette? My speciality, as you know.'

As Florence began to walk slowly down towards them, Daisy's distinctive laugh rang out, as uninhibited and chuckly as a child's.

So that when Joshua Penny turned and saw Florence the merriment in his own eyes died away at the sight of the horse-faced woman with a streak of dirt down her long nose, glaring at them as if she had caught them out in some indiscretion.

'You remember my friend, Miss Livesey?' Daisy's voice was brittle with enforced gaiety. 'From that first day? You *remember*?'

'I can't think why he should.' Florence tripped over an *Atlas of the World* and almost fell, recovering herself enough to stalk past a bewildered Joshua with his hand outstretched in greeting. On into the kitchen, slamming the door behind her with a bang that seemed to shake the house to its foundations.

'She's tired.' Daisy spoke into the awkward silence. 'And not very well.'

'Understandable,' Joshua said politely. 'Moving day can be very trying.'

'We've got to get this straight. Right now.'

Daisy sat down at the kitchen table opposite a sulky Florence, viewing her with difficulty over the top of a big carton piled high with pans. 'I don't know what's got into you, but whatever it is you keep it between us from now on. To involve the boarders in petty squabbles is *wrong*.'

162

Impatiently she pushed the carton to one side, dislodging a milk pan which clattered noisily to the floor, setting her teeth on edge. 'The customer is always your first concern, just as it was when you were serving in the shop. That nice Mr Penny must be wondering what on earth is going on.' She lowered her voice. 'We *need* him. Can't you see that? We need him and we need Mr Schofield, and we're going to go on needing them until we can have this place ready for visitors. So . . . we've got to treat them right, *feed* them right, and make them happy and comfortable.'

'And kow-tow to them, you mean.' Florence sniffed. 'Demean ourselves, you mean.'

'Yes! A thousand times yes! And if you can't see that. . . .' Daisy hesitated, but went on firmly. 'You ought never to have agreed to come in with me.'

'Are you dismissing me, Miss Bell?'

Daisy ignored the break in Florence's voice. 'Don't talk *daft.*' She stretched out a hand across the cardboard carton. 'Aw, come on, Florence. You've known me for a long, long time. Can you really see me playing the big I AM? Wielding the whip while you scurry round to do my bidding? You're my *friend.* My partner, and if I go under in this, then you go with me. If I lose all me money in this venture then we'll have to unbutton the top two buttons on our blouses, get ourselves black stockings with clocks up the backs and go on the streets.'

There was a slight, only a very slight hesitation, but Daisy saw Florence's dusty nose begin to quiver.

'Or seduce Mr Penny and Mr Schofield.' The wide pale eyes sparkled with the relief of held-back tears.

'Bags me Mr Penny,' Florence said. 'I don't think I'm Mr Schofield's type.'

'Then I suppose *I'd* better start learning to tango.'

Daisy got up and moved over to the cooker. To let Florence get her bit of a cry over and done with in peace.

The potato pancakes went down a treat. Daisy had grated

potatoes and onions into a basin, added flour and salt, and mixed them with the eggs into a soft paste. She had heated the pan with no more than a dash of olive oil and dropped the mixture in, a tablespoonful at a time, turned them when brown underneath and Florence, with her face washed and her hair neatly pleated, had borne them into the dining room with all the aplomb of a Lyons' Corner House Nippy.

Mr Schofield had gone off dancing with his patent-leather pumps in a brown paper bag, and Mr Penny had gone to his room to get on with marking exercise books, once his offers of help had been firmly rejected.

Now, at almost midnight, with Florence tucked up in bed with a hot-water bottle and a dose of the Indian brandy, mercifully discovered at the bottom of a carton, Daisy was alone downstairs in the depressingly brown lounge. Bodily exhausted, but mentally as alert as if spiders crawled round and round in her mind.

Florence's outburst had depressed her more than she realized. There had even been a small 'do' about the dark and dismal WC on the first landing. Sharing that and the bathroom with two men had upset Florence's sense of what was right and proper.

'Suppose I have to go in the night and one of the men happen to be in? Suppose they *see* me in my dressing-gown? And know where I'm going?'

'I bet even Greta Garbo has to go to the lavatory sometimes,' Daisy had said. And your precious Shakespeare. I bet even he....'

'You can be very vulgar at times,' Florence had said, trailing listlessly upstairs with her stone hot-water bottle underneath her arm.

So what was it going to be like when Daisy reminded Florence that once the visitors arrived they might have to share a room on the top landing? With no privacy, and little time to indulge in its niceties, anyway.

Daisy closed her eyes to shut out the fawn-coloured walls, and tried to see them papered in an apricot shade, with maybe the faintest white fleck in it. . . .

Good heavens, there were some Blackpool landladies who slept on camp beds in the kitchen, putting their husbands out with the cat to sleep as best they could in the backyard shed, according to Mrs Mac who had popped in for an hour earlier on.

'Wish I could do that with mine. He's about as much good as a concrete cushion,' she'd said. 'Your friend's a bad colour, isn't she?'

'She'll be all right tomorrow,' Daisy had said, with meaning, and Mrs Mac's eyes had lit up.

'I had a neighbour suffered like that every month. She had to have everything taken away before she was forty, poor soul.'

Daisy leaned her head back and closed her eyes. The plumber recommended by Mrs Mac was coming tomorrow – well, today – and she was praying his estimate would be reasonable enough to include a downstairs toilet to fit in the long cupboard underneath the stairs. There was an outside porch, glassed-in at the back of the kitchen, where the Ewbank, the clothes-horse and the card table could go at a pinch. Wash basins in each of the bedrooms, that was priority. No queues on the landing, or visitors peering through a slit in their doors ready for a quick dash into the bathroom the second they heard the click of the lock.

'He's in there, bloody *shaving*!' she remembered one man shouting to his wife on a long-ago holiday with her mother and father.

'What does the silly pie-can *think* he's doing? Filling his Pools in?' Martha had said, fuming herself at the sight of Daisy's father sitting on the edge of the bed with a towel round his neck, patiently waiting his turn.

Her father would have liked this house, Daisy knew that. It had character; it had an Edwardian grandeur about it and, built on the periphery of the district around the North Station, it had 'class'.

There would be no sub-dividing the bedrooms, even

though she knew it was done. No visitors sleeping in the lounge, even at the height of the season. And definitely no extra charge for use of the cruet or the sauce bottle.

The visitors would be Daisy's own sort of folks. Respectable working-class, with lives that revolved round work, home, family and church or chapel. She could just see them arriving with their carrier-bags and roped-up cases, eyes shining at the thought of a week by the sea. A whole year of saving week by week for a chance to walk on the front breathing in the ozone with its medicinal properties, paddling in the sea, dancing in the Tower Ballroom, listening to Toni's orchestra on the North Pier. Relaxing in deckchairs, riding the trams along the promenade, walking in Stanley Park, strolling round the Pleasure Beach eating sticky candy-floss. Watching the chunky animals forever circling the Noah's Ark, then coming back here to this house, faces and arms burned brick-red by the sun and wind, to have a wash in the privacy of their own bedrooms before coming down to a meal that would make them sigh and pat well-filled stomachs.

And making firm bookings for next year's holiday before they left for home and another whole year of working in factories and mills.

They would have to pay just a little bit extra maybe, but Daisy knew her fellow Lancastrians. They wouldn't mind spending what they'd got, but by gum they would see to it that they never *wasted* it. Give them good value for their hard-saved brass, and back they'd come. Again and again.

She was half-way up the stairs, deciding to go curlerless to bed for once, when she heard the chug of a motorbike engine in the street; heard it slow down, then stop.

'Mrs Mac's son,' she thought, the one his mother said came to see her when he felt like it, and only then when he wanted to scrounge something. She remembered too the pride in Mrs Mac's eyes when she'd talked about her wayward son, and knew that in some ways Mrs Mac was very like Martha, her little mother who would have choked rather than allow a word of praise pass her lips.

Daisy went on climbing the stairs, smiling to herself. Outside Florence's bedroom door she hesitated briefly, remembered the lateness of the hour and Florence's dislike of being seen in bed, and passed on.

She was opening her own door when the knock came, followed by a single ring at the bell. There was a dimmed light bulb on the landing and instinctively she glanced up at the two closed doors on the upper landing. The men were obviously in bed and asleep, but a quick cry for help would soon bring them running down to her rescue. Martha had often said that a knock at the door after midnight always spelt trouble. As Daisy went quickly back downstairs she felt apprehension stir like a cold finger tracing the length of her spine.

Drawing the bolt, she opened the door a fraction. 'Yes. Who is it?'

'Daisy! Thank God!'

At first she didn't recognize him. The street lamp had been lowered for the night and the man standing there was a dark bulk of leather coat, his hair hidden by a flying helmet with ear-flaps. A pair of goggles swung from his hand, and his face shone eerily with a pale green tinge to it. Daisy blinked and looked past him at the motorbike and sidecar drawn up at the kerb.

'Daisy? Don't you know me?'

As he spoke her name again she felt the prickly waves of shock spring in her armpits. She had thought about him every single day, and yet he was the last man on earth she expected to see.

'Sam?' She swayed towards him, feeling as if she might faint, but recovered herself enough to open the door wide. 'Come in. Please come in.'

Snatching off the leather helmet he pushed it at her along with the driving goggles. 'You take these. I'll go and get the boy.'

'The boy?' Daisy knew she was beginning to sound like a backward parrot, but there was nothing she could do about it, and Sam wasn't listening anyway. He was out there in the dark silent street lifting his son from the sidecar and carrying him tenderly into the house. 'In here. Bring him in here.' Leading the way into the lounge Daisy moved to switch on the standard lamp, leaving the centre light off. Moving a cushion, she stood at the head of the brown sofa. 'Put him down on here.'

'He stinks like the devil.' Sam lowered Jimmy on to the sofa. 'He was sick twice on the way and I tried to clean him up, but I've not made much of a job of it. No, he's not ill. Just whacked. I borrowed the bike from a pal of mine and that sidecar is normally used for his painting tackle. I think the smell must have lingered and turned Jimmy's stomach. He's asleep now, thank God. Dead to the world. As you see.'

Daisy saw all right. Jimmy was so fast asleep every vestige of healthy colour had drained from his face. He looked like she imagined he would look if he lay in a coma, scarcely breathing, arms and legs in exactly the position in which Sam had placed them. A sour smell came from him, and when Daisy saw that his woollen scarf was stiff with dried vomit she eased it gently from his neck.

'I'll go and get the case.' Cumbersome in the heavy leather coat and leggings Sam walked stiffly from the room, leaving Daisy staring down at the small boy, a hand pressed to her mouth as if she still could scarcely believe the evidence of her eyes.

Forcing herself to do something, *anything*, she went into the hall and took her warm winter coat from its peg on the antler stand.

'There,' she whispered, tucking it round Jimmy. 'There, love. I'll light the gas fire.'

'He'd sleep on a clothes-line.' Sam came back with a suitcase and set it down by the door. 'We went to the shop in Blackburn first. I'd forgotten you'd moved. They gave me your address. I think I got them out of bed.'

'I sent you a card,' Daisy said foolishly. 'Telling you I was moving in here today. With Florence.'

'Florence?'

He wasn't listening to her – he never really listened. 'My *friend*,' Daisy said. 'She's upstairs in bed.'

Sam was drawing off his black leather gauntlet gloves. He dropped them on to a chair and ran his fingers through his hair, springing it back to life again.

'Damn and blast!' He spread oil-grained fingers wide. 'Still, never mind, it's clean muck. The bike conked out three miles out of Preston. I thought I'd never get it going again, but I was determined to get here somehow, and when I'd found the trouble we had a clear run. The policeman I spoke to in Talbot Square asking for directions to this address gave me a suspicious look and for one horrible moment I thought he was going to take me in for questioning, especially when he saw Jimmy lolling in the back. Is there somewhere I could wash my hands, love?'

Not a word had been said above a whisper; he hadn't touched Daisy, not even to take her hand. It was that single-mindedness again, she thought ruefully. There was yet another carton of books in the middle of the floor, three pictures propped against the arm of a chair, two rolled-up rugs by the far wall, and she could swear he hadn't noticed anything unusual.

The expression of despair clouding his handsome face touched her so deeply she had to restrain herself from going to him and putting her arms around him. She knew something awful had happened and that he would tell her when he was ready, and because she loved him so, she would wait.

'Upstairs,' she told him. 'On the first landing. The doors are marked. I'll go through in the kitchen and put the kettle on.'

Florence knew that something had awakened her, but Indian brandy always made her woozy, so she thought she must have imagined it. The griping pain in her lower abdomen had faded, and the stone bottle was growing cold so she moved it down to the bottom of the bed.

She had behaved badly. She could admit that now, and in the morning she wasn't going to let pride stand in the way of an apology. She turned on to her back, staring up into the darkness. It was just that she hated being *beholden*, and she was going to have to accept that independence wasn't a commodity she could afford for the time being. Daisy held the reins and more importantly the purse strings, and in spite of her genuine niceness there was a side to her that wasn't all sweetness and charm – that hateful word again – oh yes, Daisy was the boss, make no mistake about that.

Florence sighed so deeply that her breath fluttered the ribbon tie at the neck of her nightdress. It was the anger inside her that caught her unawares at times. A helpless rage against people and the way things were. She'd never be like Daisy, liking and trusting till she found out otherwise, then forgiving and understanding most of the time. But as Daisy had rightly said, kow-towing to people would be part of the job in this business.

She covered her face with an arm. Two strong-willed women in one house. Was it going to work? Would their long-standing friendship stand the strain? It had been fine in the little shop because there she knew what she had to do and did it well. Here there were so many things to do, so many decisions to be made, and Daisy would be the one to make them; she knew that already. Could she start behaving like a fluffy kitten when nature had fashioned her like a sleek and spitting Siamese? She doubted it.

Suddenly she sat up and swung long thin legs over the side of the bed. Dare she risk a quick dash along the landing without her dressing-gown which was as far as she knew at the bottom of an unpacked trunk of clothes? Needs must, she told herself, opening her bedroom door and stepping out on to the landing.

She reached the door marked WC at the exact moment a

tall dark man with staring eyes and a lean and haggard face opened it from the other side to a background noise of a lavatory cistern flushing. Not Mr Penny or yet Mr Schofield, but a man she had never seen in her life before.

When she screamed Sam gripped her by the arms to calm her, but at his touch she screamed louder than ever, bringing Mr Penny and Mr Schofield hurtling down the attic stairs in striped pyjamas, and Daisy at the double from below, her blue turban slipping over her forehead in her agitation.

From somewhere downstairs came the frightened wail of a child, and from God alone knew where, the Westminster clock loudly chimed the hour.

Chapter Two

'So that is friend Florence?'

A much cleaner Sam came into the kitchen after putting Jimmy into the bed made up for Daisy and staying with him till he slept again. 'I knew I had a devastating effect on women, but that's the first time one has thrown a fit at the sight of me. Is she highly strung, or something? She certainly took some calming down.'

'Sensitive,' Daisy said loyally. 'Reserved.' She poured tea from a brown pot. 'She'll be okay when she's got over the shock. She *feels* things more than most people do.'

Neurotic, Sam had decided straight away. Unappetizing, unfeminine and not his type. He dismissed Florence from his mind, and looked properly at Daisy for the first time since knocking at the door. He had been imagining her the way he saw her last. In the blue print dress with a string of beads like mint imperials round her neck. With soft curls blown round her face, her cheeks glowing from the sun and the brisk Blackpool breezes. The Daisy he had said goodbye to, dry-eyed and pale, he had preferred to forget. Now her hair was tucked away beneath some sort of scarf knotted above her forehead, and her eyes. . . .

'I never knew you wore glasses,' he said.

Immediately she snatched them off, pushing them deep into her apron pocket. 'Only for sustained reading,' she said stiffly, as if he'd made a personal insensitive remark about a physical deformity. 'I never wear them outside.' She sat down opposite to him. 'Talk, Sam,' she said. 'I know we're both half asleep, but you have to tell me why you've turned up like this with young Jimmy. It isn't a social call, is it, Sam?'

He saw now that her eyes were soft with the dreamy look of the slightly myopic, and he remembered in that instant the steely blue of his wife's eyes as she had confronted him in the room above Mr Evison's garage.

'I found out this morning – *yesterday* morning – that you are the only person in the whole world I can trust implicitly,' he said quietly. 'That you must believe, Daisy.'

Daisy ignored the sudden lift of her heart. 'No flarching, Sam. Just straight out with it, Sam. Please.' Her glance was direct and steady. 'You're in some kind of mess, aren't you?'

He stared down at the tea cooling in its cup with the unmatched saucer. 'A hell of a mess,' he admitted. 'It's Aileen. My wife.'

'Go on.'

'I'd just got back from taking the Evison children to their private schools in three different districts of north London, and I was more or less free for the day because I'd taken the boss and his wife to a business dinner and dance at the Dorchester the night before. I'd waited for them until half-past two, and for all his faults Mr Evison is no slave driver. I was going to work at my books all day.'

Daisy experienced a wave of tenderness and pity for him. Sam was floundering, unsure of himself, uncertain of what her reactions were going to be. Desperately wanting her to understand. 'Drink your tea,' she said softly.

'Take that scarf thing off your head,' he said, startling her into obeying him. 'How can I talk seriously to you when you sit there looking like Sabu, the elephant boy?' He stared up at the ceiling. 'It's Jimmy. His mother doesn't want him. She's divorcing me for desertion and going to live in Canada with the man she says she's going to marry. Taking Dorothy with her because this paragon of all the virtues, this man who is everything I'm not, according to her, prefers little girls with bows in their hair to wicked small boys with caterpillars in

173

their pockets.' His face darkened. 'He doesn't like Jimmy, so Aileen gave him to me.'

'*Gave* him? You mean handed him over, just like that? I can't believe it!'

'It's true enough.' Sam put a hand over his eyes for a second. 'Jimmy has, apparently, turned into a holy terror. The scourge of the Mixed Infants, threatened with expulsion, drummed out of the church choir, beastly to old ladies, foul-mouthed, disobedient, a sadist and a thief. And that's on one of his good days, according to his mother.'

'You're joking?'

'Nope. Dorothy is so terrified of him she cries if he as much as looks at her. He *tortures* her.'

'Tortures her?'

'Tied her to a tree on the common, ran off and said he'd forgotten which tree. Or so he said. Went off with his pals and it slipped his memory about rescuing her.'

'But that's just a boyish prank. *Surely, Sam?*'

'When his memory lapse stretched to two hours and a violent thunderstorm had scared Dorothy witless apart from soaking her to the skin?'

'Well, there's a reason, obviously.'

'Oh, yes, there's a reason. Aileen says he loathes this bloke she's set on marrying. Took his papers from his briefcase and set fire to them in the garden incinerator.'

'Oh, dear.'

'More than oh dear. They were the notes for an important conference this tycoon was organizing – the only copies – and Jimmy burned them the night before the conference was due to take place. Pranced round the fire brandishing a stick, like a dancer in some evil rite. Again according to his mother.' Sam nodded his head. 'I know what you're thinking and you're right. You don't have to be a psychiatrist to know the reason. In his childish way Jimmy has been behaving so badly he hoped to scare this bloke off. Hoped he would disappear and I would move back. We never meant it to be that way, but that was the way it turned out. Dorothy was

174

her mother's girl, and Jimmy was my boy. Divided, clean down the middle. Two camps, never a real family at all. But I hoped ... I thought that if we separated for a while, giving the kids a chance to grow, away from the everlasting rows and bickering, giving *me* a chance to pass my exams and get a better job – I hoped. . . .' His voice tailed away.

'You would get back together again?'

'Yes. No! Oh, God, I don't know *what* I thought. I don't know what I'm thinking now, if you want the honest truth. There'll be a divorce, and Aileen will marry again, and the paragon will adopt Dorothy and give her his name. . . .'

'You'd have a say in that, I'm sure, Sam.'

'But I'd agree if it would be better for her. I wouldn't want her growing up feeling the odd one out because her name was different. Anyway they'll be so far away she'll soon forget me. The paragon's father has a thriving firm in Ontario, something to do with storm windows. He's due to retire soon, so once his son takes over that's where they'll stay.'

'Is he *able* to take over? I mean, we don't have storm windows here, do we?'

'He has an engineering degree. So that qualifies him for anything, doesn't it? Paper qualifications, Daisy. Worth years of learning how to build a car engine from bloody scratch.' Sam tapped his forehead. 'You can have as much as you like up here, but if you can't write it down then what does it count for? I'll tell you, Daisy. Nothing!'

Daisy rubbed the back of her neck, trying unconsciously to rub the ache of exhaustion away. Her mind and her senses were alert and listening; it was just her body giving up on her, she told herself. Sam's voice was low, almost soporific; they were cocooned in an island of silence with the rest of the house sleeping around them.

'And your wife's mother? What does she have to say about all this?'

'Queenie?' Sam's mouth twisted. 'She's married a man half her age and they're running a pub together somewhere in Suffolk. Thrown herself into the role of chief barmaid with such abandon and verve, Aileen says there's a round of applause each time she pulls a pint. No room for a grandson there.'

'Poor little Jimmy.' Daisy's tired mind was refusing to accept the implications of it, but she realized she had known the score almost from the time Sam had carried the sleeping boy into the house. Sam had come to ask her to take care of his son. It was totally unbelievable, but it was true.

'And you can't have Jimmy living with you, Sam? Is that what you're trying to tell me? Is it?'

'How can I?' His voice rose, cracking with weariness. 'My living quarters are primitive, to say the least, even if Mr Evison would tolerate a child there anyway. Take the other night, for instance. I couldn't have left Jimmy alone in that room while I was up in town. There's only a rickety oil stove for heating for one thing.' His handsome face flushed. 'Besides, I'm in the last year of my correspondence course, and I'm going to get my Higher National Certificate if it's the last thing I do. I left school at fourteen, for God's sake, and book learning doesn't come easy. But I'm nearly there, Daisy! I can't stop now!'

He held out a hand across the table, and she gave him her own, closing her eyes as he traced the fine blue veins at her wrist, moving his thumb round and round. The remembered weakness flooded through her, accentuated by her weariness. *Passion*, she admitted shamelessly, the emotion she thought had passed her by, the emotion she had thought she would never experience. She was trembling when he came to her and pulled her up into his arms, and as he kissed her she melted into him, parting her lips as the kiss deepened. Olivia De Havilland kissing Errol Flynn.

'I love you,' she whispered. 'Do you love me, Sam?'

'You know I do.'

She wanted to draw back to look for the truth of it in his eyes, but he held her closer, tangling his fingers in her hair.

'I've brought you the most precious thing in my life. Into your safe-keeping, if you'll have him for just a little while,

176

Daisy. It's a big favour I ask, Daisy, an unfair advantage to take, but I'm at the end of the road, Daisybell, with no way to turn. And he *likes* you. He could be happy here with you. I wouldn't have brought him if I didn't know that.'

At last he held her away from him and she saw genuine tears in his eyes. The sight of them moved her so much she felt her own eyes fill.

'But you never wrote to me,' she had to say. 'All these months and not a word, Sam. Why?'

'I was trying to forget you,' he said at once. 'A part of me hoped that once I'd qualified Aileen and I might get together again.' He put a finger to her lips. 'No, don't say anything. I'm trying to be honest with you. I don't love Aileen, but I'm a better father than a husband and we'd have been a family again, and maybe... oh, I don't know, marriages are sometimes mended. For the sake of the children. But now....' He pulled her close again. 'I can't look any farther than the present – not even much farther than tomorrow.'

He was trying to tell her he wasn't going to ask her to marry him. Not just yet. He had been perfectly honest with her, and for her to ask him straight out would be unforgivable. Daisy sighed. Yet everything inside her craved the truth. She had always needed to get things *clear*, to know where she stood. She didn't want to make conditions or use moral blackmail. The subtleties of relationships with men were unknown quantities to her. She loved this man; he had said he loved her. He was asking her to take care of his child, so where did she stand? The practical side of her nature warred with the romantic. But her mother would have *needed* to know. As if Martha had suddenly materialized in a corner of the untidy kitchen, Daisy heard her chirrupy voice:

'Nay, lass. What kind of a tale is that? Have a bit of respect for yourself, for if you don't then nobody else is going to. I'm not suggesting you ask for it down in black and white, but is he going to marry you or isn't he? Or are you going to fetch up his lad till it suits him to take him away from you? He loves you, you say? Pull the other leg, lass. This one's got bells on. He's as much use to you as a chocolate fireguard would be, is that one. He'll break your heart as soon as look at you, that one will. Why should he choose you? Ask yourself that. Why *you*?'

'I have known your worth,' Sam was saying, 'from that first moment when I heard you laughing in your mother's shop. Pure gold, that's what you are, Daisybell. Pure solid gold.' Bending his head he kissed her again. 'Tell me you'll do it, Daisy. I'll come up as often as I can, I promise. There's nothing to stand in our way now.' A shadow crossed his face. 'Nothing at all.'

Too tired even to say goodnight – besides, there wasn't another bed made up – they gravitated rather than moved into the brown lounge and sat entwined on the wide ugly settee. Sam fell asleep almost at once, and Daisy tiptoed upstairs and brought a blanket down – brown again – and was tucking it gently round him when he stirred and pulled her down beside him.

'Don't leave me, Daisy, love,' he whispered, then at her involuntary start of dismay: 'I won't . . . don't be afraid. Just let me hold you. Like this. . . .' Almost at once he was asleep again, his head on her shoulder, and Martha's ghost materialized on the hideous brown and orange peg rug, wagging a telling finger.

'You daft 'aporth. See. I was right about him all along. Out for just one thing, like all men. Steal your virtue then leave you high and dry, spoiling you for a decent man. You silly, silly girl.'

But he wasn't, because he didn't. Daisy held him close and watched him sleeping, her mind in a turmoil of indecision and apprehension, until at long last she fell asleep herself just as a hazy dawn filtered through the brown curtains, and her body clock, conditioned to early rising, jerked her awake at half-past four in time to stoke the fire-oven. Till she remembered where she was and how, in the past few hours, her life had taken a turn she could never have envisaged, not in the wildest of her fantasies.

178

Florence came down before six, fully dressed and with her hair pinned up in its pleat, pale and composed and prepared to be servile and to keep her thoughts to herself.

'Well,' she said. 'Are you going to tell me what it's all about? Where is he?'

Daisy closed the kitchen door. 'Asleep. In the lounge.' She swallowed hard, hoping the hated blush wouldn't materialize, but she felt it warming her cheeks like a scald. 'He's going back to London this morning, but he's leaving... he's leaving his son with me.'

'He's what?' Florence forgot to be circumspect. 'For how long, am I allowed to ask?'

'Indefinitely.' Daisy avoided Florence's eyes. 'His wife has left him and taken the little girl with her, but she doesn't want Jimmy. So... I've said he can stay here.'

Florence stared hard at Daisy. At her crumpled skirt and tired puffed face. 'You've not been to bed, have you?' Realization dawned. 'You've been with him. All night! Haven't you?' She sat down heavily on a kitchen chair. 'You really have done it, haven't you? And I always thought you, of all people, had your head screwed on right.' Her eyes narrowed. 'You *didn't*, did you? You wouldn't be that stupid. Would you?'

'He has more respect for me.' The colour in Daisy's face deepened again. 'When he gets his divorce we'll be getting married. Oh yes we will,' she emphasized. 'So don't look at me like that.'

Florence flung out an arm in a dramatic gesture. 'And what about all this? The house? The lodgers? The money you've sunk into it? Everything? What is he going to do? Pass his flamin' exams, then come up here and sit in the corner peeling potatoes like Mr Mac next door, or stand at that sink washing up, with a towel tied round his middle? Or are you going to give all this up? Even before you've got started?'

And what about *me*, a voice inside her head was saying. Where do *I* come in all this? She pushed the ignoble thought aside. Daisy looked so crushed, so vulnerable, so *awful* with her hair as straight as a yard of pump-water; so much like an early Christian martyr resigned to being a lion's breakfast, Florence felt a sudden upsurge of exasperated affection.

'Let's have a cup of tea,' she said. 'Then I'll set the tables. You'll be cooking breakfast, that goes without saying.'

'Don't hate me, Florence.' Daisy's voice was very small. 'I couldn't bear it if you turned against me now.'

'Whither thou goest,' Florence said at once, about to qualify this when Sam opened the door. '*Excuse* me,' she said, managing to pass him without touching him.

'I'm going now, love.'

Sam rubbed a stubbly chin with a thumb. 'I've got to get back to take the boss into town this afternoon. I can shave when I get there.'

The kettle came to a noisy boil, and Daisy turned off the gas jet. He had done this once before. On the day her mother had died. Explained that he must leave and gone quickly, leaving her muddle-headed and bereft.

'I've been up and said goodbye to Jimmy. He knows what's going on. He's okay.' Sam reached into an inside pocket and took out his wallet. 'We agreed ten shillings a week, didn't we?' He put two pounds down on the table. 'I think you'll find all his things in the case. Aileen's pretty methodical.'

As if someone had nudged him, he came and put his arms round Daisy. 'I'm not going to say thank you, because there isn't a word adequate enough to express how I feel.' He traced her mouth with a finger. 'You've saved my life, Daisysbell. You're the best in the world. Do you know that?'

'*Excuse* me,' Florence said, coming into the kitchen for the knives and forks, then going out again, her back as rigid as an exclamation mark. From upstairs came the sound of a door banging closed and a man whistling.

'Mr Schofield,' Daisy said faintly. 'He works as a postman so he can go dancing in the afternoons.'

'Then I'll let you get on.' Sam nodded at the frying pan. 'Before I'm tempted to linger. I'll stop half-way down if I'm making good time.'

In the hall he kissed Daisy again, shrugged himself into the black leather coat, took the leather helmet down from its antler peg, hesitated, then pulled Daisy to him again.

'There's a lot more to say,' he whispered, 'and there hasn't been time, but I'll write. I'll write tonight. See you soon,' he added, opening the door to a tiny round man with a bald head ringed by a Friar Tuck fringe, and a boy with the aged crumpled features of a garden gnome.

'Mr Leadbetter.' The man's face widened into a smile. 'Your builder. Nowt like an early start, missus.' He stepped round Sam, followed by the boy carrying a bag of tools so obviously heavy it stooped his thin shoulders almost level with his prominent ears. 'Now, if you'll give me some idea, missus. . . .'

'I won't be a minute.' Flustered and unhappy, Daisy went out to the kerb and stood watching Sam straddle the motorbike, fasten the flying helmet beneath his chin and pull on the black leather gauntlet gloves. Her 'Goodbye, Sam' was lost in the sudden roar of the engine, but his eyes, behind the leather goggles, seemed to be signalling a message she failed to catch. With a roar that reverberated in her eardrums he was gone, bending over the handlebars of the hideous and noisy machine like a contender in the TT races on the Isle of Man.

Leaving Mr Leadbetter tut-tutting over the impossibility of turning the space under the stairs into a downstairs toilet and Florence scraping the burned bits off a slice of overdone toast in the kitchen, Daisy went upstairs to Jimmy.

'Well then,' she said, with a heartiness she was far from feeling. 'How about getting out of that bed and coming down to breakfast? A boiled egg,' she suggested, 'with toast soldiers. I expect you have toast soldiers down in London, don't you?'

'I *hate* eggs,' Jimmy said promptly, his eyes wide and wary above the blanket pulled up to his ears. 'Eggs come out of hens' bottoms. Yuk.' He made a vomiting sound, his eyes never leaving her face as he gauged her reaction.

'Well, toast and honey then.' Daisy remembered unpacking a jar, so that was all right.

'Yuk!' Again the graphically expressed disgust. 'Honey comes out of bees'....'

Daisy interrupted quickly. 'Well, I'm sure we'll find something.' She ruffled the dark tuft of hair which was all she could see now of Jimmy. 'Mr Penny's in the bathroom so you can wash your hands in the kitchen just for once.' She bent down to the case lying open on the floor. 'My goodness, this is a nice jersey. How about putting this on today?'

'Yuk....'

Daisy struggled to keep her voice even. What had she expected, for heaven's sake? That the little boy would throw his arms round her neck and tell her how happy he was to be dumped on her in the middle of the night, a strange woman he'd met once, almost a year ago? That he would trip merrily into the bathroom and wash and clean his teeth before coming down to eat his breakfast looking like Freddie Bartholomew in *Little Lord Fauntleroy*?

'I smoke,' came the announcement from the bed. 'Cigarettes.'

'Oh, really?' Florence said, appearing suddenly in the doorway. 'That's interesting. What brand?' She spoke quickly to Daisy. 'You'd better go downstairs. That builder says this house is falling to bits, and he seems to think that's so funny he's down there laughing his socks off. I don't know whether he's joking or not, but we can only hope he is.'

'Now then, young man,' Daisy heard her saying, as she flew downstairs to stem the builder's hilarity. 'Out of that bed!'

Mr Leadbetter thought that his every utterance was a scream and had the laugh to prove it. 'Haha, haw haw, haha.' Each burst of mirth only lasted for a second, but his obvious enjoyment had a profoundly depressing effect on Daisy.

'Jerry-built,' he announced, tapping a wall with a hammer. 'Haha, haw haw. See that crack in the ceiling, missus?

Subsidence, missus. Haha, haw haw. And that discoloration by the skirting board? Damp course faulty, if you want my opinion.' This last statement almost convulsed him so much that the ensuing laugh turned into a spluttering cough.

'Excuse me.' Florence pushed past them, giving Daisy the thumbs-up sign. 'Getting dressed,' she whispered to Daisy. 'And Mr Penny will be down any minute. He's in a hurry to catch his train.'

'Mr Leadbetter.' Daisy spoke firmly. 'While you're counting my blessings, could you go upstairs and look at the bathroom. And watch out for mildew. I've had four towels rotted since yesterday.'

'A joker, eh?' Mr Leadbetter winked at his apprentice, standing putty-coloured and shy behind him. 'Well, you're going to need a sense of humour before this lot's set to rights. Haha, haw, haw! Leave them tools down here, lad. And watch out you don't fall through the stairs, missus.'

'Dry rot?' Daisy suggested sweetly.

'All I will say, missus,' Mr Leadbetter replied dead-pan, 'is that if you've left owt on the landing it might be safer to go out and buy a new one than run up to fetch it. That's all I'm prepared to say.'

'Things will soon be running smoothly, Mr Penny.'

Daisy placed two perfectly poached eggs in front of her lodger, unaware that she was speaking on a note of rising hysteria. 'You must be thinking you've got a madhouse going on all around you.' She hesitated, feeling the hated blush warming her cheeks. 'It was just that my . . . my fiancé turned up unexpectedly. From down south. I'm going to look after his son for a while.'

'Nice little lad.' Mr Penny busied himself with his breakfast. 'I caught him hanging out of the landing window just before I came down. Not *too* far out,' he soothed. 'So your fiancé is a widower, like me?'

'No. Sam isn't a widower.' Daisy remembered the uninhibited curiosity of this man, and how she had recognized it as a trait she possessed herself. 'He's getting a divorce. It's just that it isn't convenient for Jimmy to be with his mother.'

'I see,' Mr Penny said, seeing nothing at all. 'I wouldn't take too much notice of Mr Leadbetter, Miss Bell. He used to do quite a lot of work for Mrs Entwistle, and he always makes it sound like it can't be done, and if it can, will take some considerable time.'

'Like four or five years, that's if the roof doesn't fall in first?'

Mr Penny laughed, dabbed his mouth with his napkin and stood up, draining his cup of tea. 'A nice breakfast, Miss Bell. Beats a banana and a cup of water any old day.'

Daisy followed him to the door. 'Is that *all* you've been having?'

'I survived. As you see.' He shrugged himself into a tweed overcoat, picked up a leather case and placed a brown trilby on his head. Opening the front door, he raised the hat an inch from his head and stepped out into the street. 'Till this evening, Miss Bell. There's a teachers' meeting, so I may be an hour or so late.'

'The meal will be ready when you are, Mr Penny,' Daisy said, going in, closing the door, then leaning against it for a minute.

What a funny man he was? Funny peculiar, not funny ha-ha. She felt as if she had known him all her life. Talking to him was like talking to an older brother. No need to be on the defensive, either. A *pal*, in spite of her mother always maintaining that there was no such thing as friendship between a man and a woman. She wondered if he taught boys or girls, and decided that either way he would be tolerant and wise.

'I'm not stopping here.' Jimmy was staring at a slice of toast when she went into the kitchen. 'I am going to run away.'

As Florence and Daisy exchanged a glance of dismay, he scraped his chair back and ran out into the hall, climbing the stairs two at a time, pushing past a chortling Mr Leadbetter gaily poking a floorboard with a giant-sized screwdriver.

'Jimmy?' Daisy followed the sobbing boy into the bedroom. She closed the door. 'That's right. Have a good cry. Here, have my handkerchief, it's not as hairy to the nose as that blanket.'

'I don't like you!' Jimmy wailed, snatching the handkerchief from her and scrubbing at his eyes. 'And I don't like it here, neither.'

Daisy carefully kept her distance. 'I agree with you, love. I don't much like me either. And *I* don't like it here one little bit. Not with everything cold and messy.' She dropped her voice to a whisper. 'You saw that man on the landing? He's just told me this house is dropping to bits before his very eyes.'

A gleam appeared between the swollen slits of Jimmy's eyelids. 'You mean *really* dropping to bits? Big holes in the floors and everything?'

'He says so.' Daisy sat down on the bed, still well away from him. 'So I might just have a good cry too. Have you finished with that handkerchief?' She accepted the sodden ball. 'So what I thought I'd do. . . . Yes, what I decided to do was to go out to the shops, and on the way back call in at the pet shop on the corner and buy myself a kitten. To cheer myself up. You know?'

'Or a puppy?'

'No, a kitten.' Daisy restrained herself from putting out a hand to touch the drooping bullet-shaped head. 'Do you remember coming to see me once when I lived in the pie shop?'

'No,' lied Jimmy.

'Oh, well, never mind. But we had a cat there. To catch the mice in the bakehouse. A ginger cat, striped like a tiger. When I came to live here we had to leave the cat behind.'

'Why?'

'Because cats get used to places, rather than people. And you know, that old cat didn't love anybody! He was so mean

185

he used to slink about just hating everybody. His eyes met in the middle. Like this.' As Jimmy forgot himself enough to steal a glance, Daisy crossed her eyes and bared her teeth, holding her breath when the corners of the small set mouth quivered briefly into the semblance of a reluctant smile. 'So I think I'll choose a kitten that is all furry and snuggly. One I can call something like Ethel.'

'That's not a right name for a kitten.'

'Or Kevin, maybe.'

'That's a *boy's* name. There's a boy in my class called Kevin. I *hate* him.'

Daisy got up and walked to the door. 'Of course, if you came with me to help me choose it, you could choose the name.' She hesitated, one hand on the door knob. 'But then if you're going to run away you'll have your packing to do, won't you?'

'I'm not *stopping* here, though.' Jimmy followed her on to the landing, tripping over what could only have been the faded pattern in the beef-tea-coloured oilcloth. 'My dad'll come and fetch me if I ask him. I can write letters you know.'

'I'll give you a stamp,' Daisy said. 'Now go down and talk to Florence for a minute. I've got to have a word with Mr Leadbetter.'

'I don't like Florence....' Jimmy's hoarse voice spiralled over his shoulder like a trail of grey smoke. 'I bet she's a witch. She looks like a witch. There are lots of witches about, you know.'

'Mr Leadbetter?' Daisy addressed the builder's right ear, the other one being pressed to the floorboards listening hopefully, she guessed, for the scurrying of the death-watch beetle. 'Could I have a word with you, please?'

With the ease of a man half his age, Mr Leadbetter peeled himself from the floor and stood up. 'I have to tell you, Miss Bell...' he began cheerfully, but Daisy held up her hand.

'I'm going to be straight with you, Mr Leadbetter, because that's the only way I know how to be.' She smiled, causing the builder to widen his eyes in surprise.

This lass was a proper bonny woman! Now why hadn't he seen that before? She was dressed like a rag-bag and her hair was crying out for a perm, but when her face lit up like that what a difference it made. Younger, too, than he'd thought. Nobbut a lass, really. He waited.

'I have only so much money to spend on the structural work in this house.' Daisy mentioned a figure. 'That much and no more, so we have to stick to priorities. Those are wash basins in all the bedrooms, a new bath, a new toilet, more working space beneath the cupboards in the kitchen, the whole house repapering and that ugly brown paint stripped from all the doors and repainted cream. A downstairs toilet built in, and the dining-room fireplace opened up so that a gas fire can be fitted. I believe you rewired the house for electricity not all that long ago, so I'm sure that's all right.' She paused to take a breath. 'I want it done as quickly as possible in order to have the hall and the lounge recarpeted in time for Easter visitors.' She smiled again, looking straight into his eyes exactly on a level with her own. 'So if you can give me your estimate, taking all that into consideration, maybe we can do business.'

She started for the stairs. 'I realize you'll have a lot of working out to do before you can give me a *detailed* estimate, and I appreciate your concern for the dry rot and the termites breeding merrily beneath the floorboards, but for the time being they'll just have to get on with their lives and let me get on with mine. Remember, I'm not going to try to cater for folks who can afford to go on a continental holiday or on a cruise; just for folks who work hard and need a week or a fortnight away from it all. To enjoy themselves in *comfort*, Mr Leadbetter, because that's what I'm determined to do for them. Feed them well and make them feel at home. An' I'm no novice at that either. I've been in the catering trade since I left school, so I know what I'm aiming for.' She put out a hand and let it rest lightly for a brief moment on the builder's jacket sleeve. 'Now! Do we understand each other, Mr

Leadbetter? I'd like to think we do.'

'You'll be lucky if you're ready to open by next Christmas, missus, with that lot on the agenda. You'll be lucky if you've enough money left for a chip butty by the time you've finished.'

'That was telling her,' he said to his apprentice. 'Now then, Mervyn, me lad, let's have a dekko at what passes for a toilet. I reckon this one was put in when Queen Victoria was just a twinkle in her dad's eye. Where's me pencil?'

'Behind your ear, Mr Leadbetter,' Mervyn said, with all the animation of a slug emerging from a rotten apple. 'Where you always keep it, Mr Leadbetter.'

'So that's the lowest figure you can quote me?' Daisy faced Mr Leadbetter at the end of a morning in which she'd shopped, cleaned, made a pan of chips for Jimmy which he hadn't eaten, and doubted the survival of the black and white kitten which was being cuddled, caressed, tickled, poked and prodded until it squealed for mercy. 'It's a lot more than I'd reckoned on.'

'You'd be paying for the labour, remember, missus.' The builder consulted a notebook with a hard grimy cover. 'These rooms have all been papered on top of paper. Layers and layers of it.' There and then he ripped off a strip of wallpaper, revealing another pattern underneath. He spoke jokingly to Florence, down on her knees by the lounge fireplace. 'More layers here, missus, than a Spanish onion. Take Mervyn the best part of a week to strip this one room. Ha-ha haw haw!'

'And I suppose by that you just mean the *top* layer?' Florence got to her feet, dwarfing the little man by at least six inches. 'But suppose *we* did the stripping and preparing ourselves? Leaving you with merely the papering? That would cut the cost considerably, wouldn't it?'

Daisy shot Florence a grateful glance. In her mind she was already busily calculating the number of rooms and the hours taken up when she should be making curtains, running up bedspreads, repairing what was fit to be repaired, cleaning up years of neglect, and laying acres of linoleum.

'Let me know when you've revised your estimate, Mr Leadbetter.'

She walked through to the kitchen in time to see the kitten daintily relieving itself beneath the table.

After dinner that night – lamb cutlets, with turnips and potatoes mashed together with butter, followed by steamed treacle sponge pudding and custard – Joshua Penny came into the lounge where Daisy and Florence were soaking the walls with water in readiness to strip away the accumulated layers of paper.

He had never, he thought, seen anyone look so tired and worn out as little Miss Bell did at that moment. Her friend, Miss Livesey, was wielding a large distemper brush, using it to sweep the water from a zinc bucket in wide arcs up and down the wall. Bending, then stretching up again, reaching the picture-rail without difficulty. In a way *enjoying* it, he could see.

'You ladies are going to do the decorating yourselves, then?' Moving a dust-sheet to one side, he sat down on the arm of the settee, then immediately got up again. 'Here, let me.' Smiling at Daisy, he took the brush from her. 'It's *all right*, Miss Bell. I was going to listen to a concert on my wireless, but I'd far rather be down here. One can get very tired of one's own company at times, even of Mozart's. If that isn't sacrilege bordering on heresy.'

'But it's not right.' Daisy hovered uncertainly behind him. 'You've been out working all day. No, we're not going to do the actual decorating. Just the stripping. It's cheaper that way,' she added, frank and honest as always.

'You are a musical man, Mr Penny?'

Joshua blinked at the change in Florence's accent. Not an hour before he had heard her chivvying the little lad into bed, saying that no, he *couldn't* have the kitten in his room, not until it was properly house-trained. He had peeped round the open bedroom door on the way down, however, and seen the pair of them fast asleep in bed. Jimmy holding the kitten close to him, as if he cradled a teddy bear. Somehow, the sight had moved him immeasurably.

'I love listening to music,' he said. 'But I don't play any instrument, I'm afraid. My wife used to play the piano, but I got rid of it when I gave the house up.' A shadow crossed his face. 'Do *you* play, Miss Livesey?'

'No, unfortunately.' Florence sloshed more water on to the wall. 'But, like you, I am a devotee. Opera,' she went on. 'My mother had a gramophone and we had the whole set of Pagliacci records. "On with the Motley" – the heartbreak of a clown. So poignant, don't you think?'

Joshua opened his mouth to reply, but Florence was well into her stride.

'I am a lover of the arts, Mr Penny. "If you tickle us, do we not laugh?" Shakespeare.'

'Ah, yes,' Joshua said, bewildered.

'Teaching is such a noble profession.' She was even using her brush more 'artistically', Daisy thought, suppressing a smile. What fun Florence was when she got into her cultural stride. 'I would have gone to college myself, but my mother's health made it necessary for me to choose my hours to suit her.'

'What *did* you do, Miss Livesey?'

Did Daisy detect an amused quiver in nice Mr Penny's voice? No, she decided, he was just being his polite and curious self. Fascinated. Wanting to *know*.

'Latterly, the cinema business. Since the onset of talking films,' Florence said in the clipped cut-glass accent. 'But Daisy here is the expert on that subject. She could tell you what the editor of *Picturegoer* had for his breakfast.'

'Really?' Joshua turned round, dripping water down his grey cardigan. 'Me, too. There are plenty of cinemas in Blackpool, Miss Bell. Do you like the Busby Berkeley routines? With all those dancing girls moving into kaleidoscopic patterns? Did you see his *Gold Digger* film?

About a group of girls in search of millionaire husbands? And Fred Astaire and Ginger Rogers in *Flying Down to Rio*? With the brilliant finale with chorus girls on the wings of flying aeroplanes? We must. . . .'

'I expect it's the sheer artistry that impresses you,' Florence interrupted quickly. 'The mathematical genius that goes into the formations. Are you on the science side, or the artistic, Mr Penny? No, don't tell me. Let me guess.'

'I teach backward children,' Joshua said. 'Mostly from deprived backgrounds. Undersized kids with rickets, or with impetigo on their chins.' His expression was serious and intense. 'A brother and sister, twins aged nine, with middle-aged faces on tiny stunted bodies. The father hasn't worked for five years apart from a temporary job with the post office at Christmas. Weekly income of twenty-nine shillings, and a rent of eight shillings to pay out of that. And *they* are well off compared to some. An adequate income according to the Ministry of Health. The father was a weaver, a good conscientious worker in plain weaving with a choice at the time of plain or fancy cloth. And not knowing any better he chose plain, because he had no way of knowing the way things were going to turn out.'

He *is* like my father, Daisy told herself, rubbing her aching arms and watching the way Mr Penny's face became animated when he talked about a subject close to his heart. She realized also that he was talking quickly, the way the lonely did, the words tripping over themselves. She felt a pang of pity for the kindly man and imagined him coming back night after night to the cold almost empty house, cooking himself a leathery omelette before shutting himself away in his attic room with his books and his wireless and gramophone. With only Mr Schofield to talk to, when that dapper man wasn't out practising his quick-step, or gliding across some well-sprung floor in tango rhythm.

'Little did we know,' Joshua was saying now, diligently watering the wall, 'what all those smiling students from the East were up to when they enrolled in our technical colleges.

The whole prosperity of Lancashire was based on the export of cheap cotton to Japan. Millions and millions of yards of the stuff, and now they are teaching their weavers *our* trade and the mills are closing down one by one. The father of my twins hasn't worked for five years. You tell me the answer, because I don't know it.'

'There are mill owners picking up cigarette ends out of the gutters,' Florence said. 'B.Sc.s sweeping the streets. And don't forget Gandhi in his loincloth. At one time the loins of every single Indian on that vast continent were girded with cheap fent woven in Lancashire.'

'I'll go and make a pot of tea,' Daisy said faintly, knowing when she was superfluous.

'"O brave new world" as Shakespeare said. . . .' Florence's dulcet tones followed her into the kitchen.

'Quite right,' Mr Penny replied, sounding as bewildered as he obviously felt.

When Daisy got back with the tea on a tray, Florence was still holding forth, but Mr Penny had exchanged his brush for a palette knife and was well on the way to stripping bare the wall at the window side of the fireplace. They worked for another hour, then he threw down the knife.

'Time for my nightly constitutional.' He addressed both girls, but looked at Daisy. 'The air on the sea-front takes your breath at this time of the year, but it'll bring the colour back into your cheeks.' A sudden shyness seemed to envelop him. 'Would you . . . ?'

'I'll get my coat,' Florence said at once. 'I've not put a foot over the doorstep all day.'

Daisy sat at the kitchen table, unscrewed the top from her fountain pen and began:

Dear Sam,
It has been a long day and I can't believe that you were here only this morning. So much seems to have happened, but the main thing is that Jimmy is fast asleep in bed. He's

bound to feel strange for a while, but I think I can start to believe that he will settle down eventually. So try not to worry about him too much. One of my lodgers is a teacher. He says he is friendly with the headmistress of a junior school not too far away – no big roads to cross – and he will go and see her at the weekend with a view to getting Jimmy into her school. He says it is a good school, a church school, which I hope pleases you. You and I never discussed religion, but I hope you feel it is important for Jimmy to have regular scripture lessons and know his catechism, even if he dismisses it all as nonsense when he is old enough to think for himself. He has been very good today, a bit quiet at times and that is only to be expected, but he will be all right, Sam. We are so busy I wish I had more time for him, but you can guess what it is like here. I am looking forward to hearing from you.

Yours,
Daisy

It was a *terrible* letter. Daisy just hoped he would understand and read between the lines, but that afternoon Florence had warned her about putting 'things' down in black and white.

'Remember you are the *other woman* in the case,' she had said. 'The judge might not agree about Sam's desertion being grounds enough, but adultery certainly is.'

Daisy had felt her blood freeze in her veins. 'I haven't committed. . . .' She couldn't bring herself to say the word. 'Sam would never put me in a position like that.'

Years of her mother's dire warnings surfaced. In her fevered imagination she saw herself as headlines in the *News of the World*: 'Love nest in Lancashire'. 'Miss Daisy Bell, a Blackpool landlady, the woman named in a recent divorce case. . . .'

She saw the clerk of the court hold a pile of her letters aloft. Worse, she saw him take one out and read it aloud, lingering over the 'purple passages' with the judge leaning forward, his wig slipping to reveal a bald and shining pate.

She thought of famous mistresses: Anna Neagle in *Nell Gwyn*, Greta Garbo in *Camille*. Her mind ran riot. Sam was a married man; there was no getting away from that. Suppose his wife had hired a private detective to follow him up north? Suppose when they had lain together on the settee all through the night, the detective had been out there in the street, wearing a shabby raincoat with the collar turned up, peering through the chink in the curtains, making notes in a little notebook?

'Your good name gone for ever,' Florence had said.

'Oh, you silly, silly girl,' her mother's ghost had echoed.

As a tripper down the primrose path, Daisy decided, she'd never even have the guts to step off the grass verge.

She slid the letter into an envelope and copied the address down from the slip of paper Sam had given her. She decided not to post it until she heard from Sam, which would be the day after tomorrow, she calculated, if he wrote straight away, as he had promised. She would take her cue from his letter, then make him promise to burn hers the minute he'd read them. That way she could write a proper letter and tell him what was in her heart. How she loved him and missed him already; how she had wanted him to make love to her in the night, though she had known it was wrong and would almost certainly have given her a baby. She knew about men taking precautions of course. She wasn't *that* naïve, but she didn't think Sam was the kind of man to carry 'things' around in his pocket. Like a boy at a Sunday School Field Day who had once blown one up like a balloon in a corner of the field, sending a ring of giggling girls screaming for safety.

At the very thought she blushed a bright and stinging scarlet. Even though there was no one to see.

Blackpool in February was dead. The Christmas and New Year visitors had gone back home and across from the wide stretch of promenade the stalls and shops were shuttered, buffered against the Atlantic gales. The smell of frying and sugary candy-floss had been whisked away by the cold bracing air. It tasted now of seaweed and salty sea, Florence decided, striding along by Mr Penny's side, without having to modify her steps to his. In the darkness the incoming tide battered its waves against the sea wall and sent glistening showers of spray over the railings, beading their coats and dampening the scarves wrapped tightly round their necks.

Florence felt gloriously and wonderfully alive. At one with the elements, she told herself. Now and again she glanced sideways at the man walking beside her, shoulders hunched into the collar of his tweed overcoat. She was going to enjoy getting to know this man better. How marvellous to meet a man with a soul twinned to your own, far removed from the furtive cinema-goers she had known with their wandering hands and common ways.

Mr Penny had been *humouring* Daisy when he talked about his fondness for Hollywood musicals. She was sure of that. For all her friend's untutored intelligence, Daisy was more than a bit *naïve*, one had to admit that. Two men huddled in raincoats walking a windswept dog passed them, leaning into the wind.

'Daisy's heart rules her head, I'm afraid,' she said. 'That child is the last thing she needs to be burdened with just now.'

'How long has she known Jimmy's father?' The howling wind almost tore his words away.

'A whirlwind romance, Mr Penny. Straight from a film in which everybody sings a love song at the drop of a hat. Preferably in Paris, in spring.' They crossed the road and as he took her arm she bent her knees slightly to make herself roughly the same height. 'Old Mrs Bell used to keep Daisy's feet on the ground, but she died, alas, in tragic circumstances and Mr Barnet was there at the time to console, so you see....'

'What *kind* of tragic circumstances?'

They walked back past the shuttered stalls which, on that sunny July day, had been piled with tiers of Blackpool rock 'lettered all through'. Florence told him how Martha had died in a deckchair with the sun shining. *In front of* Sam's children, though they hadn't seemed to notice, from what Daisy had said, which surprised her as young Jimmy took all in without saying much.

Florence marvelled at the way Mr Penny listened intently, inclining his head to catch her every word.

'Very traumatic,' she said, and he agreed.

'Poor little Miss Bell,' he said.

Florence bent her knees until she was walking almost bandy-legged. *Life* has written those lines on his face, she told herself. A mere glimmer of light shone from the Tower. Flattered beyond words at his interest in what she was saying, Florence told about the day she had taken Daisy up in the lift. 'To cheer her up.'

'Kind of you,' Joshua said. 'Have you been friends for long, Miss Livesey?'

'All our lives.' Florence clutched at her hat. 'That was the day we first saw the house,' she explained. 'It came at just the right time for Daisy. Her being at a crossroads in her life. "Men at some time *are* masters of their fates,"' she quoted as they turned away from the front into the web of dark and deserted streets.

'Shakespeare?' said Joshua, quickening his pace as they came closer to Shangri-La, wondering if Florence had some terrible affliction that caused her to walk bow-legged like that.

When Daisy went upstairs to take the kitten from Jimmy's bed to make it perform on the cindered tray by the back door, she found them both asleep. The kitten purring on each exhaled breath, Jimmy muttering and twitching, his cheeks flushed bright red.

Holding her breath, Daisy smoothed the tangled hair back from the rounded forehead, only to draw her hand back in horror. Jimmy's skin burned, and she saw now that his lips were cracked and dry with a yellow scum at the corners.

'Jimmy?' She sat down on the bed and took his hand. It lay horny and hot in her own. 'Jimmy, love?' Daisy tried to conceal the panic in her voice. 'What is it, pet? Open your eyes. You *can* open them, can't you?'

'My throat hurts.' Jimmy's eyes glittered at her from between swollen eyelids. 'My throat's got a knife in it, Mummy.'

He couldn't *see* her! Oh, dear God! Since putting him to bed something had struck him blind! Daisy was so shocked she found it was a real physical effort to stand up and walk to the door. He hadn't eaten, apart from a bite of toast that morning, not really *finished* his meals all day. Not even the chips smothered in tomato sauce. She had put it down to Sam going away and leaving him with virtual strangers. She had consoled herself with the thought that it was perfectly understandable, that in a few days he would adjust. Children were very adaptable; she remembered her mother saying that. Give them love and three meals a day and they'll survive.

Downstairs she stood in the hall, irresolute, the enormity of her responsibility hitting her with the force of a flat-handed slap. Back home she could have opened the front door and run out into the street, not even stopping to put her coat on. She could have rung Doctor Marsden's bell, and he would have come straight away.

'Children can be up one minute and down the next,' she remembered him saying more than once, smiling at her from the foot of her bed during one of her frequent bilious attacks. 'Let me know how she is in the morning. If it's going to turn to measles the spots will be out by then. Look for them first inside her mouth.'

Spots! Daisy ran back up the stairs. Measles! There was nothing to measles. Every child got measles. It was part of childhood. Nothing to worry about. Vaguely she recalled having to lie in bed with the curtains drawn all day to keep the light from her eyes in case she went blind. Her blood froze. Jimmy had been walking around all day with measle eyes, letting the light in and destroying his precious sight. Her blood froze harder. Or maybe the kitten had some terrible disease and had passed it on to Jimmy already? Rabies? But then, wouldn't Jimmy have lockjaw? He was tossing his head from side to side now on the pillow and moaning.

'Mummy? I'm a good boy, Mummy.'

'You're the best boy in the world.' Daisy pulled the blankets up round his chin.

'My head hurts, Mummy. . . .'

Meningitis! Daisy remembered a girl in the next street to the pie shop dying of it. Martha had insisted they show respect and call at the house with a sultana cake to cut at, because she knew there'd be no baking done for the next few days.

The dead girl – her name was Phyllis – was the same age as Daisy, seven, a member of the Junior Sunday School and a Brownie in the Pixie Patrol with Daisy.

'Here we come the merry Pixies. Helping people when in fixes.'

She lay in her coffin in the front parlour, wearing her Brownie uniform, with the badges sewn down a sleeve proving she could light a fire, clean a room and write a letter. Her hands had been neatly folded on her chest. *Pot* hands, Daisy remembered, cold and hard looking. Someone had combed Phyllis's hair and fastened it to one side with a tortoiseshell slide in a style she didn't suit. Phyllis had always worn her hair brushed straight back, held in place with an Alice band from Woolworth's, and now the strange flat style and the pot hands had turned her into a terrifying monster.

Jimmy's hands were scrabbling at the turned-down sheet. He rambled in a peculiar high voice, thin with fever.

Daisy turned an anguished face to the door to see Florence and Mr Penny standing there, scarf-wrapped and red-nosed, glowing from their long walk.

'I found him like this,' she said piteously.

Mrs Mac said you'd have thought a man with plenty up top like Mr Penny would have known where the nearest doctor lived. It wasn't far, she told them, so he should be back soon, even though the new doctor was so young she doubted if he'd even started shaving.

Mrs Mac wasn't going to pry because now wasn't the time, but she felt sure the man on the motorbike that had woken them all up at gone midnight was this little lad's father. She hadn't made up her mind about the mother, but if it was the long-nosed Miss Livesey, then he must have put a bucket over her head before he ravished her.

'If this new doctor comes up with the right diagnosis, then it's nobbut beginner's luck,' she told Daisy. 'He'd give you a bottle of stomach medicine for your bunions, this young chap would.'

She was like a death's head at the feast, but she was kind. 'Typical of her ilk,' Florence whispered to Mr Penny when he came back with the doctor in tow.

A pink young man, his diagnosis was swift and definite. 'Scarlet fever,' he pronounced, showing Daisy the red rash now emerging. He rolled up his stethoscope and stored it away in a brand-new bag with his initials tooled in gold on the side. 'This year isn't a bad year for it, whereas last year's epidemic was a stinker. I'll go back to the surgery and telephone for the ambulance.'

'Does he *have* to go into hospital, Doctor?' Out on the landing Daisy lowered her voice. 'He only arrived up here yesterday. From London. To put him in hospital now would be a bad thing. I'm quite prepared to nurse him here.'

The doctor fingered his smooth chin. 'Well, I don't know, Miss . . . ?'

'Bell.' Daisy's expression dared Florence to stick her oar in. 'If he would be in any danger, then of course he must go, but we can manage.' She nodded towards the bedroom. 'I can have a fire lit. There aren't any other children in the house. The district nurse would come and keep an eye on him, wouldn't she?'

'Total isolation, Miss Bell.' The doctor started down the stairs. 'I have to report it, of course, and they'll send someone round from the Health Department, but there's no rule against a child being nursed at home – if the conditions are strictly adhered to.'

'You'll call in again tomorrow?'

'In the morning.' He was very earnest, very sincere. 'They are sleeping two to a bed at the hospital, so I'm not insisting on admission.' His shrewd glance took in the purple shadows like bruises beneath Daisy's eyes. 'He will need his own crockery and books. His pyjamas boiled, and the room stoved when he's better. He won't feel like swallowing much more than milk puddings and egg custards for a while.' A glance at his watch. 'He's a sturdy little chap. You mustn't worry overmuch.'

Daisy followed him to the door. 'His father lives down south.' She blushed. 'Shall I send him a telegram? I'm the boy's guardian you see, and I feel responsible. I'm sure he would come up right away if you feel it's necessary.'

'Not at the moment.' The doctor turned up his collar. The situation was none of his business, unusual though it seemed, to say the least. But the boy was obviously clean and cared for, and from the anxious faces grouped at the foot of the stairs there'd be no shortage of willing helpers. Head lice up at the hospital was driving the Sister of the fever ward crazy. Two of her best nurses were allocated to the diphtheria wing of the hospital, where young patients were dying every day. He stepped out into the wind and the rain. If the child had turned out to be a diphtheria case, that would have been another matter. A child could choke on its own spittle without immediate life-saving surgery. He was very concerned, very keen to do the right thing.

'Have *you* had scarlet fever, Miss Bell?'

'Yes, I have. Me mother nursed me at home.' Daisy smiled her reassurance. She was feeling unaccountably light-headed. What was scarlet fever compared to inflammation of the brain, or leprosy, just to mention two of the dire possibilities she'd imagined. 'I'll sleep in his room on a camp bed.'

'Don't neglect yourself entirely, Miss Bell.'

The doctor did a little embarrassed shuffle with his feet before striding off into the black wet night, his fair hair bared to the driving rain.

'You must send for Sam.' Florence was adamant. 'You must send him a telegram first thing in the morning. Or better still, go out to a phone box and ring his boss. If he lives in a house with a Rolls-Royce in the garage, there's bound to be a telephone.'

After helping to put up the camp bed in Jimmy's room, Mr Penny had gone tactfully to bed. Mrs Mac had gone back next door, telling Daisy that scarlet fever was responsible for more children growing up with rheumaticky hearts than she'd had hot dinners. Mr Schofield, oblivious to the drama, had come in through the front door and soft-shoe-shuffled his way upstairs, whistling 'Cheek to Cheek' between his teeth.

'No!'

Daisy looked white and worn, but Florence hardened her heart. 'What do you mean, no?'

'I'm not going to tell Sam anything just yet. Not unless Jimmy gets worse.'

'Why?' Florence clapped a hand to her forehead. 'Oh, don't tell me. You don't want lover-boy to worry. Is that it? You don't want that noble brow furrowed with even the teeniest wrinkle of anxiety. You are looking forward to playing Florence Nightingale, then he'll think how wonderful you are, how marvellous, and how he must be the luckiest man in the world to have met someone like you. You want him to be in your everlasting debt, don't you?'

'I just want to spare him being hurt more than he's been hurt already.' Daisy's pale face gentled into love. 'He's so troubled. You can't begin to know how upset he is. He can't risk losing his job by asking for time off just now.' To Florence's dismay, Daisy groped up the sleeve of her knitted cardigan for a handkerchief. 'If he loses that he loses the very roof over his head. Then where would he go?'

'Back to his wife?'

'Impossible. The house is in her name. She's the one with the money. Anyway, Sam says she had the locks changed.' Daisy dabbed at her eyes. 'Besides, Mr Evison isn't going to put up with Sam constantly asking for days off to come up here. He could replace Sam the same day. They have a lot of unemployment down there, in spite of what we're led to believe?'

Daisy looked so defeated Florence wanted to hit her. 'You're really gone on him, aren't you? So besotted you can't think straight. You're like a silly woman in a silly film, thinking with your heart instead of using your loaf. We've only just got here and started to get things organized the way we planned, and yet in that short time you've slept with him. . . .'

'Not in the way you mean!'

'You've slept with him, adopted his son, and decided to take it on yourself to shoulder all his problems.' Florence made for the door. 'It's a man's world all right. If he's lucky enough to have a job then *nothing* must stand in his way to keep that job. But if a woman has a job – just a little sideline say, like running a boarding-house – she has to cope with other people's problems at the same time.' Florence was on her soap-box now, oblivious to anything but the force of her own rhetoric. 'Let a woman, in spite of doing five jobs at the same time, turn out to be a *success*, he regards that success as a personal affront to *him*, a fluke, a stroke of luck. Or possibly because she's flaunted her femininity. *Slept* her way to the top, if you want it spelt out.'

Daisy let her go on. There was nothing left to say, anyway. Florence could best anybody when it came to using words as weapons. In spite of her distress Daisy recognized, not for the first time, that Florence had a brain as sharp as a newly-stropped razor. She should have stayed on at school, gone to college, not left at fourteen to look after her mother, forced to take a job with nothing to recommend it but the hours that fitted in with a semi-invalid's needs.

Florence would have made a marvellous teacher . . . Daisy began to fill a tray with things she knew she would need for the long night ahead of her. Florence had every right to be angry with what life had dished out to her. And since coming here, Florence seemed to have been angry all the time.

Balancing the tray on one hip and carrying a hot-water bottle underneath an arm, Daisy climbed the stairs and went into Jimmy's room.

Jimmy was half awake and half asleep, hot and feverish, turning his head from side to side on the pillow, muttering unintelligible nothings, glittering eyes showing like slits through pink puffy eyelids.

By the side of his bed Florence was busily wringing a flannel out in a bowl of cold water and laying it over his forehead. She was wearing the hideous horse-blanket dressing-gown, her hair hanging thin and wispy round her face.

'I can manage now.' Daisy took her nightdress from beneath the pillow on the camp bed. 'Thank you, Florence.'

Without turning round Florence dipped the flannel into the water and laid it over Jimmy's forehead again. 'Turn and turn about,' she said quietly. 'I'm staying with him tonight. You go and get some sleep. There's no point in both of us looking like something the cat brought in. Goodnight, Daisy.'

'But he's *my*. . . .' Daisy felt the stupid tears prick behind her eyelids again. 'You know what you said downstairs just now. And you were right. I'll send for Sam in the morning.'

'Goodnight, Daisy.' Florence tucked Jimmy in firmly. 'I'm sure he's starting to sweat. That means the fever is beginning to break. And he's sipped some water without bringing it back. *Goodnight*, Daisy!'

It was all too much. Florence's fury was far easier to take than her kindness. Lack of sleep had heightened Daisy's emotions. Tears ran down her face as she climbed into her own bed. She let them drip, tasting the sad saltiness of them as they ran past the corners of her mouth.

She was asleep almost before her head had touched the pillow.

Dear Sam. Very dear Sam,
I wrote to you two days ago, but I've torn it up. It was a terrible letter, not the way I was really feeling or anything. It's no good. Even if my name *is* dragged through the divorce courts and you name me as the other woman, with my picture in the *News of the World*, I just can't write to you as if you were my brother or just a platonic friend.

I can't tell you how much I am missing you already. So much has happened since you went away, and I promise you I am going to tell you the absolute truth. I thought there might be a letter from you, but I realize how busy you are, my darling. I'm sure there will be one on Monday, after the weekend.

I have to tell you that when I went up to see if Jimmy was asleep that first night he was running a temperature, so Mr Penny (one of the lodgers) went for the doctor who said that Jimmy has a fairly mild attack of scarlet fever. *Please* don't panic. He was poorly for two days but now his temperature has gone right down. His throat is sore, but he managed to eat some ice cream which Mrs Mac from next door got from the newsagent's shop on the corner of the next street. The newsagent makes his own from the very best ingredients. It's really more like frozen egg custard and will help to build Jimmy's strength up.

Honestly he is on the mend. So don't worry too much, and don't blame me too much for not sending for you, but the doctor said he wasn't seriously ill. So I took a chance, knowing how difficult it would be for you to get away again so soon.

I know you will feel like borrowing the motorbike again and driving up, and you know how much I would love to see you, but I have explained to Jimmy and he understands. He is being spoilt rotten with Florence and Mr Penny taking it in turns to read to him, and he has a kitten which he calls Montague, although I suspect he is a girl.

The doctor said Jimmy must have been feeling off-colour for at least a week before his throat turned really sore, so that was why he was so sick on the drive up, I suspect.

I *promise* you that he is all right. I refused to let him go into the fever hospital because can you imagine how awful it would have been for him on top of coming up here?

Things are pretty chaotic. Mr Leadbetter, the builder, is about to turn the water off, so we are going round filling buckets and bowls. He seems to find this hilarious! Do you remember him? He was the little man coming in as you went out the other morning. He brought Jimmy two Jaffa oranges and a yo-yo, which will have to be burned when he is better. They sent someone round from the Health Department, and the room will have to be stoved and all the things taken away to be treated with chemicals. The district nurse has been to show me how to give him blanket baths, and Jimmy is insisting that everything done to him has to be done to the kitten as well!

You told me you could trust me to the end of the world, so you have to believe me when I tell you that Jimmy is truly on the mend. He didn't know what to call me so I said he could call me Daisy, and Florence said he can call her by her first name, too, but we had to laugh when Jimmy wanted to know Mr Penny's name. It is Joshua! Mr Schofield is Bobbie. So you see how matey we all are! Jimmy is sitting up in bed with the door open and ordering us all about in a hoarse little voice. He knows he has us all on a string, I can tell you.

Dear Sam. This is the first love letter I have ever written, and I am not very good at it, I'm afraid. The words are in my heart, but they don't come out well in black and white. Talking about black and white, please destroy this letter when you've read it. I wouldn't like to do anything which could stop your divorce going the way you want it to, and you did say our relationship must be a secret for the time being. I have never been mixed up in anything like this before, and even now I don't know if I am doing the right thing in writing to you so openly. But I miss you so much. I felt very alone when Jimmy was poorly that first night. I confess I hadn't realized the responsibility. He is such a dear little boy. Mr Penny, I mean Joshua, is going to see a teacher friend of his this weekend, though I promise you Jimmy won't be going to school until he is quite, quite better. The air here will do him good and put the roses back in his cheeks.

God bless you, my darling. And write soon.

All my love,
Daisybell

(No one but you has ever said my name in quite that way.)

Dear Daisybell,

I am answering your letter straight away. I am sorry that Jimmy has been off colour, but he has great powers of resistance, young Jimmy, and he seems to be enjoying playing the invalid! No, I am not going to panic. I trust you completely and know you will always tell me the truth, the whole truth and nothing but the truth!

I think you know that I would come up at once if you told me you thought it necessary.

I went round to tell Aileen. I thought she ought to know about Jimmy being ill and that he was in good hands, but the house was closed up. I saw the next-door neighbour, but she couldn't tell me where Aileen has gone. She *did* tell me that Dorothy was just getting over a fever. I wonder if she meant scarlet fever? Trust Aileen not to let me know.

Give young Jimmy my love, and tell him I'll send him a book. On second thoughts I'll enclose a postal order and perhaps you can get one and tell him it's from me.

I agree with you about the need to be circumspect. My wife is the guilty party after all and I'm damned if I'll spend a night in a Brighton hotel with a tart just to provide her with the evidence. Let her work a few things out for herself.

I told her, of course, that Jimmy is staying with friends of mine. At a boarding-house by the sea, I said. Joshua, Bobbie, Florence and Daisy. She said she didn't know I *had* any friends! It's funny the way things turn out, isn't it?

What more can I say about you keeping him like that? I might tell you I was at my wits' end. I even think I prayed a little, and when I prayed yours was the face I saw. You have given me the chance to make something of my life. I made a mess of my last set of questions and no wonder.

Very dear Daisybell. Goodnight. Take the greatest care of your good self. You are unique. I think God threw away the mould when He made you.

Yours ever,
Sam

He had forgotten to enclose the postal order, but Daisy knew he would remember next time. She would buy the book herself and tell him it was from Sam. The first thing to do was to run upstairs and tell Jimmy that his dad had written to them.

Jimmy was sitting up in bed reading a comic. He looked washed-out and seemed to have lost weight from his face and neck, making him appear younger and more baby-like.

'I don't want a book,' he told Daisy. 'I want a Meccano set. The O outfit is only three shillings. My dad said I could have it. This week,' he added, narrowing his eyes in the hope that Daisy wouldn't guess he was lying. 'I bet he'd let me have the Number Ten set. That one makes cranes what really work.' The eyes almost disappeared in his attempt at sincerity. 'My dad said he'd buy me a watch from Woolworth's. I bet he'd buy me a bicycle with a three-speed if I asked him. I don't want a rotten book. I *hate* books,' he continued in the same low monotone, grumbling in earnest as Daisy smoothed his undersheet and plumped his pillows up. 'Sissies read books.'

Daisy's silence was making him mad. She always stayed quiet when he made one of his fusses. Not like his mother who would have yelled at him to stop moaning and asking for things he knew he couldn't have.

He tried again. 'I want a train set,' he whined, 'with wagons and coaches, and a Flying Scotsman that reverses when you wind it up. I've seen them in books.'

'I thought you never read books.'

Daisy was smiling at him, not cross at all. Jimmy knew with a sickly certainty that if she ruffled his hair he would bite her. He closed his eyes.

'I bit Montague,' he said faintly.

'Whereabouts?' Daisy was still smiling.

'On his ear.'

'Did it bleed?'

'Ears haven't got much blood in them, especially kittens' ears.'

'Fancy you knowing that!' Daisy marvelled.

'What's a *fancy-piece*, Daisy?'

There! He'd got her now. Jimmy held his breath. He had known it was a pretty bad word by the way his dad had reacted that morning when his mother had screamed it at him at the top of her voice.

'Well, if *you* can't look after him, why not take him to your fancy-piece?' she had shouted, her face going white the way it always did when she was in one of her tempers. 'Oh, yes, I know all about you taking her to the seaside in the Rolls. I even know her name – Daisy. Oh, my God! You didn't expect the kids to keep quiet about *that*, did you?' Then she had said something about never going out in the Rolls herself, not *once*. And yet his dad had given his *fancy-piece* a ride in it. That had really got her going. Jimmy had thought his dad was going to hit her. He remembered the cold feeling of fear in the pit of his stomach.

'My mum said you're a fancy-piece,' he said, miserable

with the hurting memory of the ugly scene.

Daisy felt sick. She could have been sick right then and there. Holding a hand to her mouth, she ran into the bathroom, locked the door and leaned over the wash basin, feeling the bile rise and burn her throat.

To hear a child say a thing like that! To know it must have been said in his hearing. Oh, dear God, how stupid could a person be? *Of course* those two children would have gone back and talked about her. About the ride in the Rolls, about the meal in a restaurant, and possibly about Martha dying in her deckchair, though what Sam's wife would have made of that she couldn't imagine. And yet in Sam's letter he had said....

The letter was in Daisy's apron pocket, so she took it out and read it again. Friends, he had told his wife. Friends who ran a boarding-house by the sea. Joshua, Bobbie, Florence and Daisy. Unwittingly, in her letter to Sam she had verified that.

Daisy put the letter back in her pocket, her mind a turmoil of worry and apprehension. Oh, dear God, she wasn't cut out for this kind of thing. Respectability meant too much to her. Be honest now. Respectability meant *everything* to her. Take that away and you might as well strip her stark naked and stand her at the top of the Town Hall steps!

She splashed her face with cold water. Her mother had been right. Going out with a married man brought trouble, real trouble, especially if a wife was looking for evidence of her husband's infidelity with another woman. Fear, ignorance and guilt fought for supremacy. Why, oh why couldn't love be like it was in the films? Holding hands in candle-lit restaurants, running along deserted beaches, leaning over the rail of an ocean liner – a pure unsullied heroine gazing into the eyes of the man she loves. And coming to a bad end if he happened to be married.

'Why didn't you tell me, before I fell in love with you?' Claudette Colbert in *Zaza*, stalking her boudoir in anguish in a frilly loose gown over her nightie, with her married lover (Herbert Marshall) frowning elegantly in the background.

'What is to become of *me*, now?' Claudette had cried, not a hair of her fringe out of place.

Daisy looked at herself in the mirror over the washbowl. Putting up a hand she touched her own straight fringe and winced.

Since moving into the house there hadn't been the time or the inclination to bother with curlers. She wasn't even sure where they were. Daisy forced herself to look hard at her celery-straight hair. The grey buttoned-up cardigan she wore looked as if it had been knitted on poker needles by a very old lady with trembling fingers, and the pom-poms on her down-at-heel slippers resembled a couple of cremated ferrets.

This unlovely apparition a breaker-up of marriages? The object of a married man's unbridled passion? A *fancy-piece*?

When she went back into Jimmy's room she was outwardly composed. Sitting down on the bed she spoke quietly.

'Jimmy? I want you to listen to me. Carefully. That wasn't a nice word you used just now. You must never say it about me again.'

'What word?' Jimmy was reading a six year-old *Film Annual*, totally engrossed in pictures of Lupino Lane being chased by a shock-headed lion. 'I think I'm ready for a drink of lemonade.'

'*Fancy-piece.* It's a very bad word.'

'As bad as bum?'

'Worse.' Daisy took the book from him. 'So I want you to promise you'll never say it again.'

'I might forget.' His eyes were calculating slits in his small white face.

'Then until you promise I'll take this with me.' Daisy stood up and closed the *Annual*. She walked to the door, taking it with her.

'You're a fancy-piece!'

'Right!' Daisy had had more than enough. Taking off a slipper and flexing the sole she marched back to the bed.

'Over!' she ordered, ignoring the howls of protest.

She had never had the slightest intention of hurting him – a bedroom slipper, she knew, produced the maximum noise with no damage at all, but if she had hammered red-hot nails into Jimmy's behind he couldn't have screamed any louder.

Within seconds three faces were framed in the doorway. Florence disbelieving, Joshua trying not to laugh and Mr Leadbetter looking as affronted as if Daisy had just been caught swinging a day-old baby round by the heels and bashing its head against a wall.

'He asked for it!' Red-faced but certainly not breathless from her exertions, Daisy faced them. 'He's been using foul language and he's not too ill to be punished.'

'What did you say bad enough to deserve that, lad?' Mr Leadbetter glared at Daisy.

Jimmy's tears stopped as suddenly as if a tap had been inserted in the side of his head and turned off. Upending himself, he allowed a left-over sob to creep up into his throat.

'I called her,' he said, eyeing Daisy with a new awareness she had never seen in his eyes before. For a full minute their eyes held hard. 'I called her. . . .' Jimmy said, while Daisy held her breath. 'I called her a bum,' he whispered at last.

'Oh, Jimmy. . . .' When Daisy held out her arms he hurled himself into them and as she held him close Daisy knew she had won some kind of a battle.

But the most important thing was that Jimmy knew it, too.

Chapter Three

Dear Sam,

I made up my mind not to tell you how disappointed I was when your plans for coming up this weekend fell through, and here I am telling you in the very first line of this letter! Still, Easter isn't very far away, and though I'll be run off my feet – four lots of visitors up to now – you'll be able to take Jimmy out to enjoy himself. Blackpool is coming to life already. The season seems to start earlier each year according to Mrs Mac and that's in spite of so many folks being out of work. They come for short breaks now that the charas and the trains run special rates. We Northerners have always set great store by our holidays. We work hard and play hard and though we won't *waste* money we're not afraid to spend what we've got.

Jimmy is getting used to school, and goes off *unwashed* if he can get away with it! Florence caught him wetting his toothbrush under the tap and spitting vigorously in the washbowl one morning, and how he can have a bath without washing his neck beats me, but he won't allow us in the bathroom with him. Sometimes I suspect he just fills the bath, swishes the water round with his hands, then lets it out again, but you know how innocent he can look even when he's just emerged after a twenty-minute soak looking like a miner straight from a pit. Mr Penny (Joshua) made me laugh the other day. He has a really dry wit when you get to know him better. Jimmy refused to stop sliding down the banister, so Joshua said: 'Don't try reasoning with him. Just remember you're a lot bigger than him!' It did put things into perspective, I admit.

The house is looking so nice. Florence chose lovely friezes for the dining room and lounge – lightning flashes in orange and electric blue – they really brighten up the walls, which have come out a bit paler than I expected. Everything seems to have cost more than I budgeted for. I replaced all the flock mattresses with Vi-springs, and the worn blankets with soft fleecy. They were half a crown each! No wonder I have to run past the bank in case the manager sees me!

Sorry about all the boring domestic details, but my head is filled with them these days. Will the house be finished in time? Did Mr Leadbetter mean it when he said his workmen will be here for the next two years, give or take the odd Bank Holiday? There are days when I'm sure they'll still be here when Jimmy has gone into long trousers!

Dear Sam, it's past midnight and everyone in the house is in bed but me. I am sitting in the kitchen with wood shavings littering the floor and a pile of sand by the door. Mr L. and his merry men have been finishing off the downstairs toilet. They were here until six o'clock and they're coming tomorrow – Sunday. Do I mean today? The days seem to be blurring into one session of hammering, with men all over the house drinking gallons of tea laced with pounds of sugar. All on double pay, as it's the weekend. Oh, help!

I hope there's a letter from you in the post, but I understand how busy you are with your final exams looming. Take care and God bless.

Yours,
Daisy

Slowly, Daisy climbed the stairs to the top floor. When the visitors began arriving Jimmy would have to give up his room and move in with her. She would put a camp bed up for him. It was either that or having to share with Florence, and Daisy knew which she preferred. Privacy and modesty was an obsession with Florence. She undressed beneath the brown dressing-gown. 'As if the sight of an inch of your bare flesh would send strong men wild,' Daisy had once teased, but Florence hadn't smiled.

'I could hear Bobbie turning over in bed!' she complained. 'So he must be able to hear me.'

'Probably kneels up on his bed with his ear to the wall, his tongue hanging out as he listens eagerly for the snap of your knicker elastic,' Daisy had said, only to be reminded that she could be very vulgar at times.

'Honest vulgarity,' Daisy muttered, as she undressed quickly. 'Most Lancashire folk have a bit of that in them. Hardly offensive, surely?'

In bed she curled herself up into a ball. 'Back to the womb,' Florence had told her. 'Proving you haven't freed yourself yet from the umbilical cord, even though your mother is dead.'

It was all right Florence thinking she knew it all, but no one knew *everything*. One thing Daisy knew for certain and that was that the letter she had written to Sam was a disgrace. Boring and unloving. She closed her eyes, willing a sleep that would not come. But how could she write what she wanted to, putting her feelings down in black and white? The very mention of the word 'divorce' still upset her. Three out of every hundred marriages ended in divorce these days, and the figure was rising all the time.

Look how quickly the country had got rid of the new King when he wanted to marry Mrs Simpson. The newspapers had printed the news about the friendship, as they called it, in even bigger letters than the news about the Jarrow marchers. What Daisy's mother had said about Mrs Simpson couldn't stand repetition. Florence had said Mr Baldwin should keep his mouth shut till he knew what he was talking about!

Florence said that Joshua Penny was one of nature's

gentlemen. Florence said that Bobbie Schofield had twinkle toes but nothing between the ears. Florence said that Mr Leadbetter's laugh wasn't a laugh but a nervous tic. Florence said that Jimmy was a victim of circumstance and would probably end up in Borstal. Florence said the Depression had merely weeded out the people too inefficient to find work. Florence said.... Florence said....

Daisy sighed. There were days when she wished her friend would, just for once, express a bit of self-doubt. Would stop and question her strong beliefs. Not be such a clever-clogs all the time.

'Bound in to saucy doubts and fears....' The quotation came unbidden into her tired mind. Shakespeare, she wondered? Florence wouldn't need to wonder. Florence would know!

The next Sunday Florence got off the Blackburn train, walked with her mannish loping stride down the slope and out into the Boulevard. Past Queen Victoria, regal on her plinth, down past the White Bull, across the road to Woolworth's, then along the street flanking the market square.

Now, on that Sunday morning, the visionaries and the cranks and buskers had taken over. In the shadow of the Victoria Buildings a man stood on an orange-box, shouting the odds at the top of his voice to a small crowd gathered round him. What would his subject be? Florence guessed either the Means Test, the Spanish Civil War, Hitler, Mussolini, the British Union of Fascists, Free Speech or Communism. One of those burning questions for sure. All of them controversial. She wished she had time to cross over and do a spot of heckling.

She thought she caught a glimpse of Strong Dick, the local escapologist, who delighted his audience by wriggling free of his ropes and chains while his mate went round with the hat, then she remembered that Thursday afternoon was Strong Dick's day for performing his act.

215

We are all bound and shackled in some way, she told herself, passing the school clinic, then St John's Church with a stream of worshippers coming out with hurried steps on their way home to a Sunday dinner of roast beef and Yorkshire pudding. If they were lucky. Glancing upwards at the reed and shuttle weather-vane, she reminded herself that the lovely old church had been consecrated at the time of the French Revolution. A pity that same spirit of revolution hadn't gripped folks up here, she told herself, but along with so many other things patriotism was a dying virtue. The Depression was making people apathetic.

Daisy was so *insular* minded, she told herself, turning into the familiar street at the side of the pie shop and beginning her climb away from the town centre. Daisy's horizons were set no further than her own front door, her mind cluttered with trivia. Wash-basin taps, wallpaper, curtaining by the yard, bleached twill sheets – oh, the mediocrity of it all!

And that man of Daisy's, with his crisp black hair and his craggy dimples, like the hero of some stupid romance. Daisy was so guileless, so *innocent*, in spite of having spent an entire night in the arms of her lover. Florence felt her neck grow hot. She unfastened her scarf.

Samuel Barnet was a cad. She felt it in her big bones. He was *using* Daisy, and one day he would go back to his wife. His sort *always* went back to their wives in spite of all that talk about divorce and separation.

The house Florence had been born in was the only one in the street with an unmopped front step. So cleanliness wasn't necessarily next to godliness, Florence told herself, raising her hand to the iron knocker set high on the shabby front door.

'I could swear I just saw Florrie Livesey walk past the house.' Straightening up from pawing over the flocks in the mattress of the bed she had shared with Arnold since their marriage, Edna pushed past their Betty, bless her, and made for the top of the stairs. But by the time she reached the front door and wrenched it open the street was empty and Florrie Livesey, if indeed it had been she, had vanished.

'There's summat up. I've got one of my prepositions,' Edna told Arnold. He was hammering leather toecaps on to a pair of shoes, the last held firmly between his bony knees. 'I'll be glad when Easter comes and I can see for myself. Daisy sounded right powfagged in her last letter. She's bitten off more than she can chew with that lodging-house. I could have told her so at the time, but would she listen? Not on your nelly. I reckon her brain's been a bit addled since our Martha passed on.'

'Daisy knows what she's doing.' Arnold spoke through a mouthful of tacks. 'We're going for a bit of a holiday, not to put the cat among the pigeons, so don't go putting your spoke in where it's not wanted.'

Edna shot him a withering glance. 'I'll speak my mind. I've never done nowt else, have I?'

'Never!' said Arnold as, totally unbidden, an image of Edna's grey permed head sticking up from the ground like a tent-peg appeared beneath the hammer he was wielding with quite unnecessary force.

'Before you go,' said Matthew Livesey, humbled and docile in his striped flannel shirt, 'I would like you to join Nora and me in a prayer.' To Florence's acute embarrassment he knelt down on the rug her mother had once pegged and clasped his huge hands together.

There was more grey in his hair than when Florence had last seen him, but his eyes were clear and bright and the puffiness had gone from his face, smoothing his features into a semblance of uncharacteristic passivity. Nora was growing the peroxide from her hair so that it sprouted mousily from the parting, ending in yellowed tips as though she had accidentally trailed it through a tin of paint. She too clasped her hands together and closed her eyes.

'I am the resurrection and the life, saith the Lord.' Matthew's voice was resonant and deep.

'I will *not* kneel down,' Florence told herself, lowering her head and closing her own eyes in an agony of embarrassment. 'I would feel a fool. I will *not* be made to pray when I don't feel like it. Oh, God, this is awful. I wish I'd never come. He doesn't need me, not now he's got religion and Nora. He is transformed, and it's a terrible thing. God knows why, but I almost prefer him ranting and raving with the drink inside him. This is *obscene*.'

'He hath exalted the humble and meek,' intoned Matthew. 'Seek ye the Lord,' said Matthew. 'Amen,' answered Nora.

Thinking they were finished, Florence raised her head to see them swaying together, eyes rolled up ceilingwards in a fervour of uncontrolled emotion.

'I've got a train to catch,' she whispered in desperation.

Bending her head, she stared down at her net gloves folded neatly on her knees. She tried to make her mind a blank, but that was something she had never been very good at. She distanced herself from the small back living room with its square table in the middle and the shiny horsehair sofa flanking the fireplace, with yesterday's ashes forcing the ash-pan out into the hearth.

Daisy would be in the kitchen now, flushed from the heat of the oven, basting the nice piece of topside she'd got from the butcher the day before. Putting the par-boiled potatoes round the joint, mashing the carrots with a knob of butter, and making the custard to go with the apple sponge pudding risen to a brown glossiness with the apples spiced with just a sprinkling of cinnamon underneath.

Sunday to Daisy meant a roast dinner. Chapel first, of course, but since moving to Blackpool there hadn't been time for regular worship. Florence had been twice to the evening service with Joshua Penny. Surprised to find he had a pleasant light baritone voice, but why surprised? Joshua was a musical man, after all. She had seen him sitting in the armchair in his room, listening to a concert on the wireless, head back, eyes closed, somehow disarmed and helpless in his enjoyment of the soaring music. Played so quietly with the sound turned low, because Joshua was first and foremost a considerate man.

Florence could remember every detail of what she liked to think of as her growing relationship with the softly-spoken cultured man who came and went from the house, offering help at times, and keeping out of the way at others. Again she saw herself working with him at stripping endless walls of endless layers of wallpaper. Again she walked with him along the promenade, feeling the touch of his hand on her arm as they crossed the street.

Joshua was a lonely man; she had sensed that from the very beginning. A *good* man. Look at the way he managed to curb Jimmy's boisterous ways when he could see that Daisy was at the end of her tether. Florence's mother had always maintained that if a man was good with children that said everything there was to know about him. Kindness, the quality that counted more than any other. Stubborn perhaps, and rude when he wanted to be, but that made him more of a man, tempered his gentleness with a touch of masculine superiority.

'I was made whiter than snow,' said Matthew.

'Let my voice cry unto Thee,' replied Nora.

I love him, Florence's heart cried. Oh, why didn't I realize that before? If ever a man cried out for a woman's love, a woman's touch, then that man was Joshua Penny. He *admired* her, she had sensed that. He tolerated Daisy, but he admired *her*. When they talked about music and literature, his brown eyes sparkled. When he moved she was conscious of his strength and his gentleness. The combination of the two qualities was irresistible. When she was with him she could forget her own height, the angular set of her body; he was not the kind of man, she was convinced, who set great store on feminine beauty. In one way he was totally unobservant, wrapped up in himself, she had to admit that. But not in a selfish way, never that. He had suffered greatly in the trenches during the war, she guessed that without him having said so. Losing his wife had deepened that sadness. He was crying in the dark, and the flame consuming *her* could warm *him*, comfort him. She was strong, both in body and spirit; she had no time for the dreamy defeated kind of woman. She could bring him to life again.

'For the sake of Thy dear Son, Jesus Christ,' said Matthew.

'Amen,' said Nora.

'I have a train to catch,' said Florence, as they got up from their knees.

'May God go with you,' her father said, genuinely touched by the rapt unseeing expression in his daughter's eyes.

'I think we may have saved another soul,' he told Nora, as the front door closed behind Florence. 'The light was on her. She has stopped seeing through a glass darkly.'

'Praise the Lord,' said Nora.

Edna missed seeing Florence walking back down the street because they were round the table eating their Sunday dinner. But if she had been standing on the front doorstep Florence would have looked straight through her. As if in a trance, she put one large foot in front of the other, her unbuttoned coat flowing tent-like round her, the net gloves for once pushed deep into a pocket, and the ugly green hat slightly askew on the head that looked just too small for the rest of her.

Joshua. Joshua. His name was a hymn singing in her veins. Her life had been a barren waste up to now. How could she have considered going on with it as it was? Kow-towing to stupid people because Daisy said she had to. *Tolerating* them because they were paying for the privilege of being cosseted? Unlessoned minds; women with red hands swollen with work, cloth-capped men with their brains in their trousers, unruly children bringing sand in on their shoes. She could *pity* them, but unlike Daisy she could not love them. She thought of Daisy, for ever striving to please, loving a man who was not worthy of her love, giving him her unquestioning loyalty because he was the first man who had looked upon her and told her she was beautiful.

Joshua was not a man to tolerate fools gladly; she knew that, too.

She was passing the pie shop when she saw the Rolls-Royce parked in the short street outside the mill. She was hesitating, unable to believe her eyes, when she saw Sam Barnet get out from the driving seat, holding the door open for a squat little man wearing a black overcoat and a black homburg hat. She stepped back into the shadow of the greengrocer's shop, her foot squelching on a rotten tomato. She saw Sam back the car smoothly up the short street, reverse into the traffic-free Sunday street, and drive on away from her, passing so close to where she stood she saw the sculptured line of his handsome profile and the way his black hair curled up over the back of his chauffeur's peaked cap.

'I have a train to catch,' she reminded herself, forcing herself to come out from her hiding-place and start walking towards the station. There would be an explanation for it, she told herself. Sam's boss had made an unexpected trip up north. Sam hadn't *known* he was coming, it had all been arranged so quickly he hadn't had time to tell Daisy. Florence quickened her steps. But to be less than twenty-five miles away – miles that could be covered in a car like that at the blink of an eyelid. But then it wasn't Sam's car. He was on *duty*. He couldn't expect his boss to give him hours off to see his son, even if that son was merely a handful of miles away. She was being ridiculous, jumping to conclusions, refusing to give Samuel Barnet the benefit of the doubt.

Florence caught the train with seconds to spare and sat by the window seat staring unseeing through the grimy window. It could be that when she got back to Blackpool the big car would be parked in the street outside the house with Sam already inside, grinning at the surprise and delight on Jimmy's face, holding Daisy close, bringing the colour back to her cheeks and the sparkle back to her eyes.

'And if you believe that, then you will believe anything,' Florence muttered aloud, drawing the net gloves from her pocket and smoothing them over her long hands, being

221

careful to get the seams of the fingers just so.

Joshua came into the kitchen just as Daisy was starting on the washing-up after a Sunday dinner which he declared could have graced the table at Buckingham Palace and not been bettered. Picking up a teacloth, he advanced towards the draining-board.

Daisy was shocked. 'No, thank you, Joshua. You're a guest in this house.' She almost said a *paying* guest, then snatched the word back in time, feeling it might sound indelicate.

Joshua took no notice. He picked up a dinner plate and began to wipe it, rubbing it with a circular movement, the cloth all screwed up; Daisy had noticed in films that the men always dried up that way. 'I thought I was a *friend*.' He pretended to sound hurt. 'Anyway, why don't we get this lot finished, then take Jimmy out for a walk? It's so warm outside it could almost be a summer's day.'

'A walk?' Daisy's face was a study. 'Do you know what I have to do this afternoon?' She pushed a wayward strand of hair behind an ear. 'You would never imagine, would you, that with thirty-four samples to choose from for curtain material for the lounge I could pick out the wrong shade? Would you have guessed that what looked like a pale shade of apricot in the shop could turn out to be bright blood-orange when you get it home? Have you noticed that the chairs I bought that were so comfortable to sit in in the furniture emporium have turned out to be so near to the ground that it would take an athlete at the peak of a year's intensive training to spring out of them?'

'A *walk*,' Joshua said, picking up the gravy-boat and shoving the whole of the cloth inside it to get it dry. 'Jimmy's in Bobbie's room beating him hands down at Ludo. Telling Bobbie to look through the window at something or other, then palming his own counters and moving them on. That lad could make a seasoned card-sharper on an old-time Mississippi river boat look like an old lady at a church whist drive.'

Daisy looked worried. 'He's so *furtive*, Joshua,' she

frowned. 'Not a nice word to describe a small boy, but that is what he is. Furtive and sly. He came home from school last week with half a dozen crayons on his head underneath his cap, and *swore* he had no idea how they'd got there.'

'A crooked card-sharper and a kleptomaniac.' Joshua picked up a knife that hadn't been washed and wiped it vigorously on the cloth. 'Come on, Daisy. The blood-orange curtains will still be there when we get back.'

'And in a hundred years it will all be the same,' Daisy said, savouring the feeling of being ordered about instead of making all the decisions herself.

'Poor Sam,' she said, as they stepped out into a day so golden it could have been high summer. 'He's spending the whole weekend slaving over his books. If he fails these coming exams I don't know what he'll do.'

'Has his divorce come through yet?'

Daisy glanced at him sharply. The word had such a worrying connotation in her own mind that to hear it spoken out so naturally startled her. She was getting paranoiac about it, she thought, catching herself looking over her shoulder in case a woman coming up close behind had overheard.

'We never discuss it in our letters,' she said stiffly. 'Putting things down in black and white, you see.'

'Of course.' Joshua accepted her explanation immediately. But then, that was the way he was, asking direct questions, then accepting your answer without further discussion. A *comfortable* sort of man to be with. She relaxed, matching her steps to his, glad she had left her handbag at home so that she could swing her arms a little.

It was such a lovely afternoon. The wind had that first spring softness in it, and along the Golden Mile the new posters advertising the coming attractions had a shiny look about them. Far to the north, towards The Gynn and Cleveleys, the hotels and big houses were washed in a soft peachy shade, the exact colour Daisy had had in mind for the lounge curtains. Turning their backs on them, they began to walk south.

Half-way towards the pier they smiled at each other and

223

coming to a decision climbed down one of the iron stairways to the beach. The tide had left pools of clear green water and soon Joshua's brown suede shoes were muddied and stained.

'Your shoes will be ruined.' Daisy was anxious, motherly.

'They're only shoes.' Joshua kicked at a pebble. 'It's hard to believe that soon this stretch of sands will be crowded, with cars streaming past on the promenade up there, isn't it?' He pointed ahead into the far distance. 'Just look at those two horse-riders way over there. They're making the most of having the beach to themselves, and who can blame them?'

Obediently Daisy looked, shading her eyes against the sun, but the fast-moving specks were out of her limited field of vision. 'Oh, yes,' she said, but Joshua wasn't fooled.

'Why don't you wear your glasses more often, Daisy? You miss so much and they suit you. No, I mean it, they really do. You look about twelve when you're wearing them, especially when they keep slipping down your nose and you push them back with a finger. And while I'm being personal, can I say how it also suits you to wear your hair straight instead of curled? There are auburn lights in it that don't show when it's all curled up like....'

'Claudette Colbert's?'

'What I had in mind was Greta Garbo's in *Anna Karenina*. A big bunch of frizz stuck over her forehead.' He seemed to walk deliberately through a shallow puddle, like a naughty boy. 'Did you see that one?'

Daisy sighed. 'Twice.' She stopped suddenly. 'Do you remember the moment when she stepped from the train in a cloud of steam, and Frederic March saw her for the first time....'

'And their eyes met, and in that instant they *knew*!'

'Even though she was married to another. It made no difference.'

'And from that moment on they were *doomed*.' Joshua had stopped too. For a long breathless moment they stood quite still, staring into each other's eyes. As lost in a spell of wonder as if they sat close together in red plush seats in the

224

warmth of a cinema. With Tolstoy's tragic story firing their imaginations so that the real world faded and dimmed. 'They say that Tolstoy understood the working of the human mind better than any other writer has done either before or since,' Joshua said softly.

'She was honour bound to a selfish man.' Daisy appeared to be talking to herself. 'Basil Rathbone, with his long cold face and his possessive love for his young son. He used the boy to punish his wife for her infidelity.'

'You knew from the very beginning that it would end tragically.'

'*I* knew when they showed the wheel-tapper crushed to death between two carriages of the shunting train.' Daisy's face was rapt. 'The end was *terrible* when you saw her face and guessed she was going to throw herself off the platform beneath those grinding wheels. . . .'

Suddenly she gave a small scream as her feet were sucked from beneath her by a wave of the rapidly incoming tide. Always quicker to move than to cry out in any crisis, Joshua's arms came round her, lifted her free of the swirling water, held her close against him before carrying her to safety.

Her hair smelled of summer flowers, and her body was small and soft. He could feel the swell of her breasts as he strained her to him. She was suddenly the ghost of an old pain, the first woman he had held in his arms since his wife had died. She was, in that moment, the comfort and kindness, the warmth he craved, the expression of the aching need in him. Dear God, a voice inside him said, I would like this dear, dear woman to bear my child.

With that totally unbidden thought, he felt the shameful tears fill his eyes.

'Now *my* shoes are ruined.' Daisy was laughing up at him.

Reluctantly Joshua set her down on the rippled sand. It was the laugh he had found himself listening for when he came into the house in the early evenings, a combination of music and the promise of a lasting happiness.

As they walked back to the house together Joshua looked

up at the wide arc of the sky. The Tower rose into it, wreathed now by cloud drifting in from the east. He shivered and dug his hands deep into his pockets.

When they met Florence walking plod-footed from the station Joshua nodded curtly and excusing himself, broke away from them to hurry into the house and up the stairs into the solitude of his quiet room.

On her journey back, Florence had decided not to tell Daisy about seeing Sam until they were alone. Out of consideration for Daisy's feelings of course. She was bound to be upset, and who was it who had said evil news rides post? Shakespeare *could* have said it, but she had a feeling it was Milton.

'I see you've been for a walk,' she said, and innocently Daisy explained that Joshua had insisted.

'Been for a paddle in the sea?' Florence stared at Daisy's shoes encrusted with wet sand. 'Best go and get those off.'

She was glad to see that Daisy's hair looked such a mess, and eyed her own neat hair-do with satisfaction as she took off her hat and fluffed up the front piece in front of the hall mirror. She restrained herself from running upstairs after Joshua to tell him about seeing Sam, knowing instinctively how interested and concerned he would be. Knowing equally that it would be just like him to advise her to keep the news to herself.

But Daisy *had* to know. There was a tiny bubble of excitement inside Florence at the thought of the telling. Samuel Barnet *deserved* to be shamed. And the sooner the better. He was getting between Daisy and her wits. It was as if she saw him surrounded in a white shining light like a knight of old, his character unblemished, his integrity intact. That wasn't real love, she told herself later as she sat inserting hooks into the top hems of curtains newly machine-hemmed by Daisy. Real love saw a loved one's faults and accepted them as part of him. Just as she had accepted Joshua's apparent rudeness when he had barely acknow-ledged her earlier. Joshua could be cool, indifferent and unthinkingly uncaring when he'd a mind. And she loved him for it.

Poor Daisy. Florence felt very close to her as they worked together through what was left of the afternoon. They were making curtains for the room Jimmy had been sleeping in.

'Why don't we move him into my room now? It's better he should get used to it before the busy time begins.' Daisy frowned. 'It's not ideal, but I just can't give him a room of his own. He'll be okay with that old screen in front of his bed.'

In the room on the top landing Florence shooed the kitten off the foot of a rather rickety camp bed. She plumped up a pillow. 'How many kids did you know who had a room to themselves? Not many at our school. Do you remember the Cleggs? They slept four to a bed!'

'And had the nits to prove it.'

Florence wrinkled her nose in disgust. She wasn't in the mood for talking about or even thinking of nits. From Joshua's room came the faint sound of music. Debussy, Florence guessed. Oh, yes, it would have to be Debussy. Soaring, sensual music. She imagined him listening to it as he sat in his chair with his head back and his eyes closed. When their relationship deepened she would sit with him, without speaking, without the need to say a word. And when the record finished Joshua would discuss with her the merits of the strings versus the wind instruments – her thoughts were wild and vague – he would teach her to understand.

'If music be the food of love, play on. . . .' Shakespeare never failed her.

She gazed limp-eyed into the middle distance. She would try to convey to Joshua the way she felt when the chapel choir lifted their voices in *The Messiah* or *The Crucifixion*. The way she felt at times her heart would burst when the congregation rose to join in the singing: 'Alleluia! Alleluia!'

'Are you feeling all right?' Daisy's voice seemed to be coming from a long way away. 'You look like Jimmy looks just before he's sick without bothering where.' She bit back what she was going to say, then said it anyway. 'I expect it's because you missed a meal out. You'd think your father would have offered you *something*, even if it was only a cream cracker and a cup of tea.'

Florence shot her a venomous look. She'd often suspected Daisy had no soul.

Now what have I said, Daisy wondered.

'They were too busy praying, and anyway I wouldn't have fancied anything,' Florence said, taking umbrage. At what, Daisy couldn't imagine.

Jimmy went to bed quite happily. He liked the idea of sleeping in Daisy's room, but he wasn't going to say so. It could be dead good sleeping behind the screen in the narrow little bed. Like being in a den.

Before his dad had gone to live in the other place, before all that, when his mum and dad slept together, they had sometimes let him climb in between them if he'd had a bad dream. It was hot and squashy, but he'd liked it a lot. His mother always smelled of talcum powder he'd often seen her shake down the front of her nightdress, and he liked her with her face all shiny with the cream she used for her wrinkles, not that he could see all that many.

Bogey men hadn't a chance of getting at him when he was sandwiched between them. Even if the wardrobe door was slightly open he could be certain a body wouldn't lollop out with a knife stuck in its back with the blade gone all the way in and just the handle showing.

The worst dream of all was the one he'd had the week he started going to school – the one where his dad was driving the motorbike with his mother sitting upright in the sidecar with her hair blowing, where they'd gone over the edge of a cliff into the sea. Daisy had sat on his bed and read him a story till he went to sleep again and told him that everybody had bad dreams sometimes.

'No, they *never* come true,' she had sworn, and had spit on her finger and drawn it across her throat. 'Make me into rabbit pie, should I ever tell a lie,' she'd said, and laughed that gurgly laugh she had so that you had to laugh too, even when you'd rather have carried on being cross.

'You're as daft as a brush,' he'd said, *furious* with her for making him smile.

'Yard or tooth?' she'd joked, and when he'd worked that out, and she'd tickled the soles of his feet, he'd ended up laughing so much she'd had to go down again and fetch him a drink of water.

'I saw someone we know on my way back to the station.'

'Who?' Daisy wanted to know, folding up a pair of finished curtains, taking off her glasses to rub her tired eyes.

'Someone *you* know very well,' Florence said, wearing her fierce face.

'Tell me then. It's too late for guessing games.' Daisy yawned and stretched, raising her arms high above her head. 'I think I could sleep on a clothes-line tonight. I hope Jimmy doesn't wake up when I go into the bedroom. He's taking things too quietly for my liking lately. You can never tell what's going on in a child's mind, can you? He hasn't mentioned his dad for ages. It's strange that. I know kids are adaptable, but not *that* much, surely? He's got such a tight little shut-in face, hasn't he? Probably worrying his little guts out secretly and totally unable to communicate with us. I remember having the most awful fears when I was small, you know, irrational fears from things grown-ups said. I remember coming home from school once and calling out for my mother the minute I got in through the door the way I always did. And she wasn't there, but my Auntie Edna was, and when I asked her where my mother was she said she had gone off with the coalman. For a *joke*, for heaven's sake, but I *believed* her! I saw my mother sitting up behind the horse on the cart with all the folded sacks and the coalman whipping that old horse to a frenzy as he made off with my mam....'

'*Daisy!*' Florence closed her eyes and put up a hand like a policeman directing the traffic. 'You're not listening to me! I said I saw someone you know. I could keep it to myself, but

229

for your own good I think you ought to know.'

'Who then?'

Now that the time for telling had come, Florence felt flushed and uncomfortable. Daisy looked so trusting sitting there, talking too much the way she always did when she was overtired. Telling her would be like kicking a defenceless puppy on its soft white underbelly.

'I saw Sam.'

Daisy felt waves of shock prick like a whole paper of pins in her armpits. Her face went cold and somehow stiff.

'He was driving the Rolls up the street from the mill. There was a man sitting in the back wearing a black homburg hat.'

'Mr Evison,' Daisy heard her voice say. 'Sam's boss.' Her chin lifted as her mind raced ahead. 'Oh, yes, Sam said in his letter that he might possibly have to come up north this weekend. Driving Mr Evison up on urgent business. He asked me not to mention it to Jimmy because he didn't think there would be any chance of him coming to Blackpool.'

Don't overdo it, she warned herself. Not too many explanations. Keep it casual. Florence is opening and closing her mouth like a fish. She does look funny, but I mustn't laugh, because if I laugh then I'll burst out crying, and she'll guess I had no idea.

'Well, you could have told *me*.' Florence was blustering. 'I got quite a turn when I saw him.' She began to unpin her hair. 'I'll go up now.'

'How was he looking?'

'Very well.' Florence stored the hairgrips away in their little box and stood up. She was nobody's fool, but if Daisy wanted to take up this attitude then what could you do but admire her? The Florence Liveseys of this world though were too sensitive and all-seeing not to realize the truth of it. Daisy's smile was like the smile on the face of the Mona Lisa. Enigmatic, giving nothing away. She was making no move to go to bed, buttoning and unbuttoning her cardigan with fingers that Florence was sure were trembling.

230

'Did he see you?'

'No.'

As Florence climbed the stairs she saw an unflattering picture of herself hiding in the greengrocer's shop doorway, eyes almost popping out of her head in astonishment. Rushing off to the station to catch her train, anticipating the look on Daisy's face when she dropped her bombshell.

Florence began to dislike herself just a little, but not for long. There was a rim of light showing beneath Joshua's door. The temptation to knock gently and call out a tender goodnight was almost overwhelming. She could smell the smoke from his pipe and imagined him sitting there puffing away and reading, huddled against the cold in the grey plaid dressing-gown she had once seen hanging behind the door. She stood with a hand raised, head inclined forward, barley-pale hair wisping round her face.

'Goodnight, Miss Nightingale. Mislaid your lamp?'

She whirled round to see Bobbie Schofield standing right behind her, returned from God only knew where at this time of night, dancing pumps beneath an arm, black patent hair flattened to his head as if glued there by flour paste. Grinning at her and fingering his loathsome five-a-side moustache. Why had she never realized before quite how common a little man he was?

'Goodnight.' Her glance was withering, her tone barely civil.

'Be like that then,' said Bobbie, chirpily cheerful, going into his own room and closing the door.

Daisy needed air. Taking her coat from the antler stand she opened the front door and stepped out into the street. The lodging-houses on either side were blurred to wraiths in the darkness, the street lamps dimmed, the air fresh and salt-tasting. When she reached the end of the street she could hear the sea pounding at full tide against the sea wall, and imagined it sending showers of spray across a gleaming wet promenade. The weather had changed in keeping with her

231

mood, and for a moment she was tempted to walk down to the front and stand by the railings letting the wind and the unquiet water take her thoughts and whirl them away.

Sam had been within a few miles of her all that day and she hadn't known. She had gone about her day not knowing, not even *feeling* that he was near. She was not doubting him; there would be a reason why he hadn't mentioned he was coming north in his letter. Business transactions were planned overnight, important journeys made at a moment's notice. Besides all that, Sam was not his own master. No, Sam must have been feeling as bad as she was feeling now at being so near and yet so far. Within the next few days there would be a letter telling of his frustration. . . .

She turned into a side street, thrusting her hands deep into her pockets.

Did she believe all that? Could she *really* believe it? At odd times, heart-stopping times like now, there would be a chink in the curtain of her reasoning, revealing glimpses of the truth.

She was going to lose Sam, Her beautiful Sam was as far removed from her as the stars in heaven. He wasn't hers at all. Yet when she was with him she was sure that he loved her. Most of the time anyway. She could listen to his voice for ever and the way he lingered over her name. Daisybell. It sounded like music the way Sam said it.

She turned into a parade of shops bolted and darkened for the night. She had thought they were spiritually close and yet he had been within a few miles of her that day and she hadn't sensed his nearness.

Why, oh why hadn't he told her he was coming north? She was just kidding herself pretending he wouldn't have known. And why did he have to have a wife who *hadn't* gone away, however Daisy brushed her suspicions aside. There were so many things unexplained, so many subjects taboo. Sam's wife spoilt everything by merely existing.

Death not divorce would be a better solution, death being more final, less messy. A cosy sort of death, nothing too painful or too distressing. Daisy wasn't *that* ruthless. Something instantaneous such as Sam's wife having walked around all her life with a clot of blood a hundredth of an inch from her heart – a clot which moved and stopped her heart beating after a happy day spent walking in the country with her lover. Perhaps even as she lay by her lover's side in bed so that Sam wouldn't be able to feel too grief-stricken about it. Definitely no last-minute reconciliation scene leaving Sam with a sense of guilt to torment him for the rest of his days.

Automatically Daisy about-faced and retraced her steps. She imagined Sam sending for her after the funeral. She saw herself getting off the train at Euston with Jimmy, seeing Sam waiting for her, little Dorothy holding his hand, a big black taffeta bow in her hair. 'I knew you would come,' Sam saying simply. 'You'll have to be their mother now, Daisybell.'

The boarding-house would have to be sold, of course. Mr Harmer would see to that. Then there was Florence. With a sudden flash of inspiration Daisy married her off to Bobbie Schofield. Daisy would lend Bobbie the money to start a dancing school – in a small way at first till he worked up a regular clientele. Florence would accept the late flowering of passion gratefully and have two brilliant children who won scholarships to grammar schools without even trying.

Daisy crossed the street totally unrepentant that she had wished Sam's wife dead and married her best friend off to the nearest man just to ensure her own happiness. Then as the rain began in earnest the fear gripped her once again. Sam was not for her. Her breath caught on a sob. Oh, dear dear God, then if Sam was not for her she was lost. The years to come would be hollow; without him all would be meaningless, there was no room for any other emotion but her love for him.

Sam had looked on her with love. His eyes had told her she was beautiful. With his long slim hands, a pianist's hands, a surgeon's hands, he had held her face still for his kiss. Because of her love for him she was a stranger to herself, a different kind of woman who had found the love she always hoped would be there, waiting just for her. A love as full of joy as a bright summer's day.

As terrible as the last dark hour at the ending of the world. . . .

'You all right, lass?' A policeman riding his bicycle wobbled to a stop at the kerb. 'Best get on home.' He peered into Daisy's face. 'There's nobody been bothering you, has there?' He fell into step with her, wheeling his bicycle with one hand. 'Tell me where you live and I'll see you home. We've heard there's a man exposing himself to young women – down Talbot Square way. Not a violent man by all accounts, but it's best to be warned, and I hope you don't mind me saying, but it's a bit late to be out on your own, isn't it? I've not seen you before. You don't look like. . . .'

'No, I'm not!' Daisy felt her face grow hot at the inference. 'I just felt like a walk, that's all.' She pointed across the street. 'I live over there.' Very dignified she was. 'Goodnight, Officer. Thank you for your concern.'

Before she closed the big front door she looked up at the night sky. There were cloud mirages now over to the north, huge black mountain ranges. A man lurched along the opposite pavement, keeling sideways, sodden with drink. Daisy saw the policeman approach him.

She felt better; blown about and weary, but better. When she reached the top landing she saw a rim of light beneath Joshua's door.

He would be fit for nothing in the morning, she worried, her mind already on the good cooked breakfast she would see he had before he left to catch his train.

The nightmare gripped Jimmy around three o'clock. Surfacing from it he lay quite still, feeling for the kitten curled up at the foot of his bed.

It was worse this time. His mother's mouth was wide open in a silent scream. The motorbike hung suspended before plunging into the water, but his father was laughing, his head

234

thrown back and his teeth white in the light from the moon. Jimmy sat bolt upright, stretched out a hand and touched the screen. Only half awake, he fought his way out of the bedclothes, whimpering, trying to determine where he was, struggling against a terrible drowsiness that threatened to plunge him back into the dream again.

'Jimmy?' Daisy's voice sounded very near. 'It's all right, love. Don't be frightened. I'm here.'

The relief brought the tears up from his chest and into his throat to spill out from his eyes and roll down his cheeks. Jimmy pushed the screen aside and padded over to Daisy's bed. Shivering, he stood by her pillow, clenching his hands into fists as he made out the shape of her head and the whiteness of her arms as she stretched them out to him. She was all soft warmth and comfort as she held him close, tucked him in beside her and mopped his face with a handkerchief that smelled of lavender water.

'There, there, little sweetheart. You've had a bad dream, that's all. It's all right now. Shush, hush up now. Daisy's got you, safe as a row of houses. That's right, turn over and sit on my knee. We're like spoons in a box now, you a teaspoon and me a great big tablespoon. Go back to sleep, sweetheart. The bad dream's all gone.'

His hair smelled of the green soft soap she had washed it with the night before. His little bottom against her stomach was hard like an apple, and when she put an arm round him his fingers curled into her hand. Because he had not wakened fully he was asleep with the suddenness of a stone dropping down a well. By the rhythmic sucking sound Daisy knew he had put a thumb into his mouth, indulging himself in a babyish habit he would never have admitted to during the day.

This was Sam's child. Some other woman had given birth to him, washed his nappies, rinsed his feeding bottles out in Milton, spooned mashed-up carrots into his mouth, held out her arms to him as he took his first steps. And rejected him when he became what she described as impossible.

235

And he *was* impossible. In the way *all* small boys were impossible. Daisy smiled into the thatch of hair, clean-smelling it was true, but slightly sticky because he had fought the last rinsing water, yelling that she was trying to drown him.

Jimmy, who could run along the top of the backyard wall with the deftness of a squirrel, but who always managed to fall down the last three stairs to land in the hall with a thump. Jimmy, who stepped out of his clothes and left them lying there; Jimmy, who could tell fibs to music, who stole crayons from school and used Florence's lipstick to write a rude word on a newly painted wall. Jimmy, who had asked why Florence had no bosoms sticking out the front of her blouses, just as Daisy was up-ending a steamed sponge pudding from its basin. Jimmy, who swore that he was the only boy in the school not allowed to stay up till midnight and take a bottle of fizzy lemonade to bed with him when he finally decided the time was right to go. Jimmy, who had eaten two packets of Bird's Jellies and denied it with indignation flaring his nostrils, and who had come downstairs only last week at a quarter to twelve to tell an exhausted Daisy that he was Pontius Pilate in a play and needed a costume plus real-looking beard to take with him to school the very next morning.

Daisy was truly her mother's daughter when it came to enjoying the company of children. With them she became a child herself, caring not a jot for losing her so-called dignity, the maternal streak in her obvious for anyone to see. Glamour she might dream of, passion she might crave, but at heart she was an earth mother who should, as Martha had realized on the very day she died, have been married to a good kind man who would have given her the babies she needed to fulfil her life.

'My little love....' Daisy's arm tightened round the sleeping child. 'My own little love,' she whispered, believing for the moment that it was true.

*

236

She awoke from long habit at just before five, turned over on her back as Jimmy stirred beside her.

'Go back to sleep, love,' she whispered. 'You don't need to get up for a long time yet.'

But Jimmy was in the mood for conversation. Making the child's swift transition from sleep to wakefulness, he flopped over on to his back to lie with his snub nose pointing to the ceiling, snug and cosy, loth to have her leave him.

'My dad told me you can balance a glass full of water on the radiator of Mr Evison's car, and it doesn't spill even when he's driving it fast,' he said as a hopeful opening gambit. 'My dad was in the desert in the war.'

'He never told me that,' Daisy marvelled. 'Your father wasn't even in the war.'

'My dad said some officers fighting in the desert raced some rotten Germans and caught them. 'Cos our side was driving a Rolls-Royce and not a rotten old car like the Germans.' The hoarse little voice deepened with enjoyable relish. 'A Rolls-Royce car goes faster than *anything* – faster than an aeroplane. My dad said they caught that rotten old German car and blew it up. Into little pieces. And the rotten old Germans as well, I bet. My dad says he's going to buy a car like that when he's rich. Are you rich, Daisy?'

'Not rich, no, but not poor, either. Somewhere in between. Why?'

'Have you got any jewels?'

'Not *real* jewels. You've seen my coral necklace. That's real. That came from the bottom of the sea.'

'The Queen's got a lot of jewels.'

'Yes, I suppose she has.'

'My mum's got two rings.'

Daisy got out of bed. 'Go back to sleep now. I'm going to take my clothes down to the bathroom and get dressed in there. Okay? *Okay*, Jimmy?'

'My mum's gone on her holidays.' Did the hoarse voice waver a little? 'I bet she comes back soon.'

Daisy sat down again on the side of the bed. 'I've got a

surprise to tell you. I was keeping it secret, but I'll tell you now. In two weeks' time your dad is coming to see us. In just less than fourteen days he'll be here.'

'Will he bring me lots of presents? D'you think he might bring me a bike? A boy in my class has a watch that goes. His dad got it from Woolworth's and it broke so he took it back and they gave him another one that went. Then he broke that one, so this boy's dad. . . .'

'Try to sleep. You'll be fit for nothing if you don't try.' Daisy tiptoed to the door. 'I'll give you a penny to take to school.' She made her escape.

Leaving Jimmy lying with hands folded on his chest pleasurably anticipating the differing ways he could spend the penny to its fullest advantage. Four giant gob-stoppers that changed colour as you sucked, two long liquorice pipes, a bar of chocolate, or maybe best of all *two* bags of sherbet to suck up through a Spanish straw. His brow furrowed into genuine anxiety. What about *sixteen* aniseed balls?

He snuggled down into the warm hollow left by Daisy's body and closed his eyes, as his legs and arms grew heavy with sleep. What about jelly babies? He could bite all their heads off, and save the black ones till the last.

One floor down Daisy bolted the bathroom door behind her and leaned against the new white porcelain wash basin. That dear little lad. That poor little love, fretting for his mother and father up there alone in the middle of her bed. How little we know of what goes on in the mind of a child. Sighing, she pulled her nightdress over her head and ran the water for a good wash-down.

Or there were always coconut mushrooms, Jimmy fretted on the very edge of sleep. But then they were dearer and you didn't get as many. . . . Or dolly mixtures, but he was getting to be a bit old for those. . . .

Chapter Four

Sam wasn't absolutely sure whether the woman he had seen
out of the corner of his eye as he opened the door of the Rolls
for Mr Evison was Daisy's peculiar friend or not. By the time
he had reversed the car into the main street she had vanished
into thin air.

If it *was* her, what was she doing in the town, for heaven's
sake? He tried to remember what Daisy had told him about
Florence, but it didn't amount to much. Apparently she had a
father living not all that far from the pie shop, an unsavoury
character from all accounts. A nut-case probably. Sam was
sure the lanky Florence wasn't quite right in the head. He
frowned, tapping his strong white teeth with a pencil. So, in
that case, she could have been visiting her old man. It was
feasible, he supposed.

To cover himself he wrote a letter to Daisy, telling her
what was more or less the truth, goddammit. He had
intended to work at his books all the weekend, just as he had
said, but urgent business had come up for Mr Evison and
they'd made a brief visit up north with no time to contact
her. It had been heart-breaking knowing how near he was to
Blackpool, but there was nothing he could do about it. He
knew she would understand.

That should simplify things, whether the fleeting vision of
the tall woman in the voluminous swagger coat had been
Florence or not. There was no point in upsetting the

apple-cart. Jimmy was better off where he was at the moment, time enough to fetch him back when things were right. If ever they were going to be. He had to treat Aileen like a piece of delicate china at the moment. One false move and they were back where they started.

He saw me after all, Florence thought, when Daisy showed her Sam's letter. He'd had no intention of saying he was up here if he could have got away with it. The conniving rotter. She wouldn't trust him as far as she could throw him, that dago with the teeth and dimples. She was going to say something nasty till she saw Daisy's trusting face.

'None so blind. . . .' she muttered as she turned away. If Shakespeare hadn't said that, he should have. It was just the kind of thing the Bard in his infinite wisdom *would* say. She would ask Joshua to look it up for her that evening. Dear Joshua; very dear Joshua. He had looked so weary these past few days, going up to his room after the meal to listen to his wireless and play his records. Teaching backward children must be so wearing. He had even snapped at Daisy when she tried to press a second helping of ginger steamed pudding on him. Not like Bobbie Schofield who must have hollow legs considering the amount of food he put away. How he managed to dance the light fandango every night stuffed like a Christmas turkey she couldn't imagine.

'What about,' Bobbie said one evening, polishing off a second helping of spotted dick pudding bristling with currants and shiny with custard, 'what about you two gorgeous creatures coming dancing with me?'

Daisy, coming in with the tea – both men preferred tea to coffee to round off their meal – almost dropped the tray.

'We can't dance,' she said at once, answering for both of them. 'There was never the chance, was there, Florence?'

'*I* can.' Florence stopped clearing the two tables. 'I used to go to that little place almost opposite the park on my night off, with Mona Hargreaves out of Ribble Street. Don't you remember, Daisy?'

'So you did.' Daisy tried to imagine Florence dancing, and failed. 'You go with Bobbie. There won't be the time when the visitors arrive next week.' She caught Joshua's eye and wondered if she was imagining the wink. 'I think it's a marvellous idea.'

'You must come too, Joshua.' Florence looked flushed and excited. 'The break would do you good. All work and no play, you know.' To Daisy's astonishment she wagged a teasing finger, smiling coquettishly. 'Oh, let's be devils. Just for once.'

Asking permission first, Joshua began the laborious process of lighting his pipe. 'Daisy's the one who needs a break. I'll stay with Jimmy.'

'Mrs Mac!' Clasping her hands together, Florence made for the door. 'She's always offering to come in and see to Jimmy. I'll go and ask her. Oh, what fun! What a lark!'

Daisy stared after the amazing sight of Florence skipping from the room like an Angela Brazil fourth-former, all girlish enthusiasm. Florence was *never* girlish, for heaven's sake. Florence had been born as sensible as a cross-over pinny. What was *wrong* with her?

'Do *you* want to go, Joshua?' Daisy passed him the big glass sugar-bowl. 'I mean Florence does seem to be taking it for granted.'

Joshua gave her an extraordinary look – a frivolous look. As if he were *drunk*, Daisy thought. 'Why not? Let's *all* be devils,' he said, thanked her for the meal and left the room.

'That's it then.' Bobbie glided after him on the balls of his small feet, swaying from the hips. Like Rudolph Valentino about to ooze into a tango, Daisy decided. What was *wrong* with them all? Had they gone mad or something?

She began to clatter cups and saucers together on the tray.

The ballroom reminded Daisy of a Hollywood scene in a film set in a baronial palace in Vienna. When they first went in she stood transfixed, unable to believe the evidence of her own eyes.

Tier upon tier of cream and gold curves rose to the lavish

frescoes of the vast ceiling, with the dazzling chandeliers suspended in glittering beauty. Because this was a special evening at the very beginning of the season the band was on stage, grouped round the enormous organ, saxophones wailing, clarinets droning. In front of the band a tiny bald man with a small tenor voice was crooning, 'You're lovely to look at . . .', with his eyes closed and his shoulders hunched as if he was trying to force the words up from a sore throat.

'I bet his mother's proud of him just the same,' Daisy whispered to Joshua, catching his eye.

'Those colours suit you,' he said, as if she hadn't spoken. 'What kind of stuff is your frock made of?'

'Macclesfield silk.' Daisy stared down at the panelled skirt of the dress she had made from a pattern in her mother's *Woman's Weekly* magazine. 'Now this is the colour I wanted for the lounge curtains!' She pointed to one of the peach-shaded stripes. 'I should have worn this when I went for the material.'

'Yes,' Joshua said, patting the pocket of his jacket as if searching for his pipe.

'Shall we dance, Florence?' Bobbie, svelte of waistline, spotted tie carefully matching spotted handkerchief, swept her on to the floor.

'Crowded in here, isn't it?' Joshua gloomed at the dancers trotting, side-stepping and twirling in foxtrot rhythm, swinging and turning at the corners, the more ambitious executing intricate twiddles when they found a space big enough. 'And this is nothing to what it will be when the season starts. They say you can end up dancing with a complete stranger unless you're zipped fast to your partner.'

'I take it you don't like dancing?'

'I've been told that dancing with me is no more than walking backwards to music.' Joshua leaned back against a pillar and folded his arms.

'I've *never* danced,' Daisy confided. 'Only with the yard brush when no one was looking.'

'You wish you hadn't come, don't you?' Joshua gave her a

peculiar thin-lipped smile. 'I'll take you back if you want to go.'

'No. I find it fascinating.' Daisy pointed to a crowd of girls at the end of the ballroom, opposite to the stage. 'A whole bed of wallflowers.' Her eyes glinted with mischief. 'Why don't you go and ask one of them to dance with you?' She narrowed her eyes, trying to get into clearer focus the sea of rouged faces, tightly-curled hair, and the flashes of cheap jewellery on the girls' flowered dresses. Glamour, she thought wryly. Partnerless they might be, but at least they've got glamour. She smothered a yawn as Joshua ignored her question with the contempt she had to admit it deserved. There was one thing to be said in favour of going out dancing, she told herself. It was going to make stopping in every night in the near future seem like one big laugh!

The whole of the floor seemed to be revolving in front of her as more and more couples began to dance. Girls danced with girls, elderly women with husbands as straight and erect as in the days of their soldiering. A child, kept from her bed far too late, jumped and skipped along on the perimeter of the floor, holding fast to her mother's hands. Joshua's head sank lower on to his chest.

All at once, through a gap in the whirlpool of motion, Daisy saw Florence gliding by, holding the regulation dancing-class three inches away from Bobbie Schofield's chest. Her head thrown back and her eyes closed, she surrendered herself with total abandon to the rhythm of the slow-slow, quick-quick-slow tempo. Florence was dancing, as she did everything else, with thoroughness and intensity, her long feet in their sensible shoes slithering along in perfect unison with her partner's black patent pumps. Her fawn shantung dress was cut cleverly but mistakenly on the cross, and outlined her angular figure in an unflattering way. As she passed by she opened her eyes for a moment, the large lids lifting to emit a pale blue gleam.

'*Your* turn next, Joshua,' she mouthed. 'Don't run away!'

Daisy blinked, then as if she'd imagined it, Florence closed

243

her eyes again and executed a perfect cornering. Daisy blinked again and almost wished she'd worn her glasses. Had *Florence* been drinking? What *on earth* was the matter with everybody? She looked at Joshua, squarely moribund by her side, and through another gap in the dancers saw Florence, wakened now from her trance, trilling the words of the song into Bobbie's oiled and sleeked-back hair.

'Shall we dance, Daisy?'

Square and broad-shouldered Joshua stood before her, fastening the middle button of his dark brown jacket. *Handsome*, she saw with a start of surprise. A fish out of water, and bad-tempered because of it, but definitely handsome with his brown eyes regarding her sombrely. She slid into the circle of his arms.

'I can't do . . .' she began, but he tightened his hold on her, moving slowly to the music which had changed now to a slow foxtrot, guiding her into the solid mass of dancers in the middle of the floor.

This wasn't dancing. This was merely leaning on each other to music, Daisy thought, bemused and unaccountably flustered by his nearness. For the first time she was acutely conscious of his strength and her own fragility. She was sure she could feel the hard beating of his heart; the hand holding hers pulled it up against his shoulder so that they swayed as if welded together.

'Do you come here often?' she teased.

'Don't talk!' Joshua jerked her even closer.

Daisy closed her eyes, the intimate contact of his body alarming her so that she lost step. She felt his cheek against her hair. On the band platform a girl vocalist crooned a Jerome Kern melody into the microphone, her voice a throaty replica of Alice Faye's. A sudden fancy took hold of Daisy. . . .

It wasn't Joshua she was dancing with. It was *Sam*. He had driven up from London to see her, and they were dancing alone on an empty floor as mysterious as a lake bathed in moonlight. The couples swirling round them had vanished into thin air, just like they did in a film, leaving Daisy and Sam to their enchantment. Her striped Macclesfield silk dress, with its inverted pleat at the back and its Peter Pan collar, had changed into a floating gown of white shimmering organza which billowed out as they danced; round and round they went, merged as one into an intoxicating dream, with a sobbing saxophone playing from a deeply shadowed background.

Joshua held her close against his heart. She was small and light. She was the woman he had never thought to find again. She was sweet and warm and funny; she worked so hard her exhaustion at times almost broke his heart. She was loyal, tender, vulnerable, filled with an optimism he felt at times to be misplaced.

And she was thinking at this very moment of another man.

With a suddenness that startled both of them, the band stopped playing. The dancers clapped, and section by section the lights came up again.

Florence bounded over to them, linking her arm in Joshua's as they walked off the floor; her face was a bold brick-red and her hair was wisping down from its pleat. She was so highly charged with excitement Daisy wouldn't have been at all surprised to see blue sparks shooting out of the top of her head. She seemed not to notice that both Joshua and Daisy wore the bemused expressions of sleep-walkers wakened cruelly from their respective trances.

'The next dance is mine,' Florence enthused, giving Joshua's arm a little squeeze. 'Oh, I do hope it's a waltz. One-two-three, one-two-three.' Her hands dangled floppily from her bony wrists as she waved them about. 'One-two-three, one-two-three. Oh, I *love* the waltz, don't you? So graceful, so romantic....'

'Unless they've changed the programme, the next dance will be the Military Two-Step.' Bobbie fingered the pencil-slim line of his moustache. 'There's a friend of mine who always expects me to dance this one with her. Will you excuse me, please?'

Eyes shining, teeth flashing, he greased his way across the floor to approach a thin girl wearing a dress the colour of a cow-clap, with black bands round the hem.

'She must be very rich,' Daisy whispered to Florence. 'A dress that colour must have cost a fortune.'

Florence wasn't listening. She was tapping her feet in time to the trumpets sounding the opening bars. *Pawing* the ground, Daisy thought unkindly. Dragging an obviously unwilling Joshua on to the floor and *stampeding* him into the dance.

A long sallow young man, who looked as if something nasty could have happened to him in the woodshed in his youth, smiled furtively at Daisy and asked her if she would care to? He jerked a narrow head towards the dance floor, pulsating with the pounding of feet. It made no difference, he said, that she had never danced the Military Two-Step in her life before. He just walked round the edge anyway.

And wasn't that the story of his life anyroad up, him having been out of work for three years, with barely the strength to blow the skin off his mother's rice pudding, never mind hurl his partner round a dance floor like an Apache gone clean out of his mind. The world was a terrible place, what with the Depression and the way things were going in Germany, he opined as they trundled dolefully round the perimeter of the floor. Still, if the war came, it would give the out-of-work something to do, not that *he* would be affected with his bad health, but being a Christian Scientist he was used to smiling through his pain. Shoes were his worst problem, he said, stopping walking for long enough to lift a foot and display a sole hanging loose like the tongue of a panting dog. You could get shoes for twopence a pair at church jumble sales and if they didn't quite fit, the agony wore off in a couple of weeks. Oh yes, he granted Daisy, he didn't *look* all that poor, but if she saw him in the daylight she'd see that his suit shone like polished glass. How had he got in? Oh, he never paid. The woman in the cash desk knew his sad background and always waved him through. Anyway, as soon as the season started he would be in great demand as a partner for the hordes of mill girls who descended on Blackpool, hoping to click with a presentable young man.

'You?' Daisy asked, hoping the surprise showed in her voice.

But he wasn't listening. A captive audience was all he needed apparently for the continuing monologue. I might as well be a plank of wood he's trundling round with him, Daisy thought, as Florence and Joshua pranced by, Florence tossing her head with each thump of her feet and Joshua, polite and aloof, holding their joined hands high for the twirly bit so that Florence didn't have to bend her head too much.

On the next circuit Daisy sent him an S O S with her eyes, a frantic signal to be rescued, which, to the obvious annoyance of Florence, he obeyed with alacrity.

'Excuse me,' he said to Daisy's partner, tapping him on the shoulder. 'Time to catch our tram, dear,' he said to Daisy. 'The twins will be waking for their bottles.'

'And my shift at the factory starts at eleven,' Daisy said. 'Yes, you're right. We must go now, dear.'

Devoid of all expression, Daisy's partner held out his arms to Florence. 'Care to?' he asked hopefully.

But Florence was stalking from the floor in the highest of dudgeons. '*You're* ready to go home, so we *all* go home,' she told Daisy, as Joshua wove his way through the Military Two-Steppers to tell Bobbie what was happening. 'You can be very selfish, you know. I was really enjoying myself.' She looked upset.

'You stay on with Florence,' Daisy suggested when Joshua came back to them. 'I'll go and relieve Mrs Mac. It's not fair to keep her up too late, anyway.'

'Let Florence stay with Bobbie,' Joshua said too quickly, taking Daisy's arm. 'I've got some marking to do.'

Florence shot Daisy a filthy look. 'We'll leave Bobbie to enjoy himself. He doesn't need us. I'm ready to go, anyway. Dancing the night away is all right for some, if that's what they want, I suppose.'

247

Daisy's eyes widened in surprise. But why should she feel surprise? The whole evening had had more than a touch of Alice in Wonderland unreality. The last thing she noticed as they left the ballroom was her former partner steering a girl backwards round the dance floor, a girl dressed in green, so tall, thin and flat she would have won first prize as a runner-bean at a fancy-dress ball.

Outside the air was fresh and clean, gusting breezily from the sea. Belisha beacons glowed like oranges against the night sky.

'Now *this* is more like it,' Joshua said, striding out. 'Dancing is all right for some. As you so rightly said, Florence.'

'Great minds think alike, Joshua.' Florence smiled at him, restored at once to good humour. For a reason Daisy wasn't prepared even to *try* to fathom.

Daisy was still wide awake when Bobbie Schofield let himself quietly into the house at well past midnight. The hours he kept had long since ceased to intrigue her. It was none of her business, anyway. He was neat and undemanding and kept his room as tidy as a ship's captain's cabin, which incidentally *reminded* her of a ship's cabin because of the tin trunk covered with a Spanish shawl in the window recess. Once, out of curiosity, dusting round the lid, she had tried to open it only to find that it was securely padlocked.

'Hope there isn't a head in it,' she'd told Florence, who in one of her now frequent humourless moods had explained that there would have been a distinct *smell* if there were.

Daisy sighed and turned her pillow over, thumping it into a more acceptable shape, but not too enthusiastically in case she woke Jimmy, snoring gently from his little camp bed.

She folded her arms across her chest and stared up into the darkness. Something was worrying her and she knew she would go on worrying until she realized what it could be. Was it her decision to try to manage without outside help till they saw how things went? Was the prospect of having to work like a galley slave once the visitors arrived sending Florence slightly potty? Martha had always said that Florence was unstable, like her mother before her. Could she have been right? Florence was *eccentric*, that was all. Artistic clever people were often eccentric. Look at Virginia Woolfe. And *she* didn't have the frustration of having to work as a domestic in a Blackpool boarding-house.

The worrying was well established by now. *Would* they be able to manage, just the two of them? Daisy's feverish mind ran through what would be a typical day's routine.

Full cooked breakfast for at least twelve people. Beds made or changed, wash basins cleaned, floors swept, lounge tidied and the fire lit, unless there was an unlikely heatwave, the dining room cleared after breakfast and check tablecloths changed for white damask. All that *after* they had cleared the breakfast things and washed up. Plus the daily shopping for fresh meat or fish and the preparation of the vegetables before the cooking of the wholesome meal she was determined to provide at the end of the day.

She glanced across at the outline of Jimmy's dark head on his pillow. Could two people, however hard they were willing to work, achieve all that? And what time was there going to be to spare for a child? Daisy sighed and closed her eyes, seeing Jimmy creeping in from school, snatching a bite to eat at the kitchen table, trying to talk to her and being ignored because she was busy basting the day's joint or rolling pastry for fruit pies. Being forbidden the lounge because it was for the visitors, missing his bedtime story because there just wasn't the time.

She would have to discuss all that with Sam when he came. And *where* was Sam going to sleep? All the rooms were booked for Easter, and Mrs Mac had warned her that folks turned up on the doorstep, and she daren't turn paying guests away if she could possibly squeeze them in. Florence had had enough to say about Auntie Edna and Uncle Arnold coming for nothing at such a busy time. Florence had seen the books and knew what a narrow line divided them from sinking or swimming. Everything had cost so much more than Daisy had budgeted for. Getting things on tick wasn't Daisy's style at all, and to be in the red at the bank was unthinkable.

'Never spend a penny unless you can cover it with another,' Martha had always said.

'I owe no man a farthing,' her father had boasted.

He would have thoroughly approved of Hills' recent policy. The big department store had given up their hire-purchasing trading because of the recurrent financial instability of the town's landladies.

'If you can't afford a thing, then do 'bout it,' her father would have said. He had never been what you could call a deeply religious man, but all at once Daisy remembered a prayer he had taught her, saying he said it himself when things got too much for him:

'Dear God, I am sailing the wide wide sea. Please guide my little ship for me.'

Desperate for a sleep that would not come, Daisy clasped her hands together and began to pray.

'Dear God, I am sailing. . . .'

As she repeated the comforting words her breathing grew deeper, her whole body relaxed, her forehead puckered into a frown, as she slid at last into an unconsciousness as profound as a coma.

Chapter Five

'What's yon little lad doing here?'

Edna, freshly permed for her holiday, the tight helmet of grey corrugated waves imprisoned in an invisible net, jerked her pointed chin at Jimmy as he ran past her in the hall en route for the kitchen and the biscuit tin.

'Eh up, our Daisy. I know who he is. He's the little lad belonging to yon London chap, isn't he?' Edna's monkey face expressed amazement, then sorrow. 'Nay, don't tell me you're still carrying on with him? He's not here as well, is he?'

'Come in here, Auntie.' Daisy opened the lounge door. 'There's something I want to say to you.'

Chunnering, Edna followed Daisy into the newly furbished room with its flame-coloured curtains and peach-shaded walls, its mock-leather chairs and sofa, and the large square carpet blooming with yellow roses. Refusing to sit down, she stood straight as a ruler, the room's shining splendour wasted on her.

'Now then, Edna.' Arnold in his tweed flat cap, hovered uncomfortably in the doorway, holding their bulging suitcase strapped with stout string.

As ever, Edna ignored him. 'Well, our Daisy?'

Daisy spoke brightly to hide the despised blush creeping up from her throat. 'Sam is arriving tomorrow. He was coming for the Easter weekend but he has to work, so he'll only be here for the one night, that's all.' She tried to keep the disappointment out of her voice and failed miserably. 'He's not his own boss, you know.'

'You've not told me what his lad's doing here.' Edna sat down on the nearest chair to take the weight off her feet which always swelled when she'd been travelling. 'From the way that child came busting in it seemed to me as if he's been *living* here. Has he been stopping with you?'

'Now then, Edna.' Small and cowed, but not quite beaten into submission, Arnold smiled at Daisy, his pale eyes almost watering with kindness plus shame at his wife's behaviour. 'What Daisy does is none of our business. She's a grown woman now.' He nodded round the room. 'Nay, but this is a gradely room, lass. A real bit of class. I bet there's not a room in the Savoy Hotel to compare with this.'

'Has he got divorced?' Edna refused to be side-tracked. 'Because if he hasn't it's about time somebody with your best interests at heart put the kybosh on things.' Edna went into a little rocking motion to give herself the impetus to rise from the low chair. 'I've kept saying I had a feeling something was going on. I reckon we've come none too soon. What you need is someone to talk straight to you, Daisy. Our Betty, bless her, hasn't a mean bone in her body, she's never had a dirty mind, but even she thought there was something fishy going on, reading between the lines of your last letter.'

'There's *nothing* fishy going on!' Daisy appealed to her uncle, but he was tracing the outline of a cabbage rose on the carpet with the toecap of a brown boot. 'Sam asked me to look after his son for a while and I said I would. It's as simple as that.'

'Has his wife died? Done away with herself on account of his philandering?' Edna's nose looked hard and sharp. 'What about the little lass? Have you got her here an' all?'

'No!' Daisy tried not to sound exasperated. 'She's with her mother. Look, I know it all sounds complicated, but it *is* my own business, Auntie Edna. I've gone twenty-one, and I know what I'm doing.' She walked towards the door. 'Now, if you'll come with me I'll show you to your room.'

252

She turned to face them, one hand on the door knob. 'I've given you my best room, right opposite the bathroom.' Her voice faltered. 'I want you to enjoy yourselves. I want you both to have the best time you've had in the whole of your lives. There wasn't much I could do to repay you both for all you did when me mother died, but I want this next week to be one you'll remember for a long time to come.'

She started for the foot of the stairs. 'You're my very first boarders, apart from the regulars on the top floor. See, Florence has ruled lines in this visitors' book here. I want you to sign your names, then before you go back home I'd like you to put something in this "comments" column. Something complimentary, I hope.'

'A home from home,' Arnold said, trying to keep the peace.

Edna said nothing.

'She thinks she's fobbed us off by telling us next to nowt.'

In their bedroom Edna busied herself opening and closing drawers and testing the mattress for bounce.

'Why isn't that little lad with his own mother? I've never heard nothing as daft in me whole life. What does our Daisy know about fetching little lads up? Is that chap going to marry her, or isn't he? She went nearly purple when I mentioned the word divorce. She'll shame us all yet, you mark my words.' Pulling back the green candlewick spread Edna fingered the top sheet. 'Bleached twill, but then I don't expect she could afford better. She's been spending money on this place like it grows on trees. I'll have a word with that foreign chap when he comes. With our Martha gone to her rest I'm the only one that can.'

'He's not a foreigner.' Arnold was patiently picking at a knot in the thick string holding the battered suitcase together. 'He's not from abroad.'

'London *is* abroad to folks like us.' Edna bent down to look under the bed for the chamber. 'They've got different morals down there. It's all taxis and nightclubs and drinking cocktails like water. They're a different breed from us.'

She ran a finger across the narrow mantelshelf to check for dust. 'Anyroad, what sort of a man would let his child be fetched up by a single woman, with his own wife still alive? I'll get to the bottom of this. You know what our Daisy's like. Easy meat for any man just out for one thing. Our Martha never gave her no freedom; she'd have stopped the wind blowing on her if she could have. Going to the pictures three times a week wasn't right. Daisy was bound to get wrong ideas the way they carry on in pictures.'

She walked to the door and clicked it shut. 'And another thing. Those two regulars Daisy mentioned are *men*! I bet you never cottoned on to that. There's been two men under the same roof as two single women. You know what they say about frustrated spinsters. Give them the opportunity and over the windmill go their caps. It'll be fur coats and no knickers next.'

Arnold rolled the string into a ball ready for using again. Seen in profile his wife's face had a squashed Minnie Mouse look to it.

'I'd leave well alone, lass,' he said, without much hope.

When Sam arrived the next day Edna and Arnold were in Woolworth's searching for take-home presents with a seaside slant to them for Betty, Cyril and the baby.

'Best to get this job out of the way early on, there's nothing worse than worrying all week what you're going to take back.' Edna stood by a counter, trying to decide between a set of false teeth fashioned in bright pink rock – Cyril liked a joke – or a humbug the size of a large pin-cushion.

Arnold said nothing.

'I'm sorry it's worked out this way, Daisybell.'

Sam stood in the hall of Shangri-La wearing a new raincoat with the collar turned up round his chin. He looked so handsome Daisy felt weak at the knees.

'The Evisons have decided to dump the kids on a relative for Easter and go off to Cornwall, so naturally they want me to drive them there.'

'I understand,' Daisy said, wondering for a brief disloyal moment if this was the way it was always going to be. Sam apologizing and her understanding. She ached for him to put his arms around her, but Florence was in the kitchen with the door half open, and Jimmy was coming slowly down the stairs, to eye his father with grave and unchildlike suspicion.

'Have you brought me a present, Dad?'

When Sam bent down to kiss him he turned his head away.

'Big boys don't kiss, do they?' Florence came into the hall. She looked bad-tempered. 'Hello, Sam. Did you have a good trip up here the other week?' She gave a small sarcastic laugh. 'A pity we didn't get the chance to have a word.'

Sam composed his face into an expression of baffled bewilderment. 'How do you mean, Florence? Were you there?' He turned to Daisy for the explanation which came at once.

'Florence saw you driving Mr Evison past the shop. She was on her way to the station after seeing her father.'

'Ah....' Sam visibly relaxed. So that was it. He'd boxed clever after all. By his own admission in the letter to Daisy that he'd been in Blackburn, he was in the clear. His sigh of relief was almost audible. 'I wish I'd seen you, Florence,' he said with deep insincerity. 'It would have been nice to have some first-hand news of Daisy and this little chap, but when I'm driving I concentrate on the road.' His eyes narrowed. 'How is your father? I hope you found him in good health.'

'Very well, thank you. Excuse me.' Florence turned on her heel and marched straight-backed into the kitchen.

The flarchy rotter. Of course he'd seen her. It was there on his handsome face, as plain as a pikestaff for anybody not totally blinkered to see. He'd likely been up north for a couple of days, avoiding making the short journey to Blackpool for reasons best known to himself. Devious, that was Mr Samuel Barnet. Underhand, deceitful, and slimy as a toad, playing some game best suited to himself. He was as unrufflable as a slab of concrete; he was an unmitigated swine. The sort of fella who would make the suave George Sanders look like Little Boy Blue.

With quite unnecessary force she topped and tailed a carrot, chopped it up viciously and hurled it into a waiting pan of salted water. '*I'd* best him,' she muttered darkly. 'By billyheck, I'd have his guts for garters, the two-timing cad.'

Daisy felt as if the smile she was smiling was painted on her face. What was wrong? The touching little scene she had rehearsed so often in her head wasn't being played right at all. In her fantasy she had opened the door to a beaming Sam who had swept her up into his arms with a joyful cry, kissing her feverishly, holding her tightly as if he never wanted to let her out of his sight ever again. In her dream Jimmy had rushed down the hall to fling himself into his father's arms, all the pent-up longing on his little face bringing tears to Sam's blue eyes. In her dream they had stood there entwined, a little family like the advertisement for Better Homes for Britons, united in happiness and devotion.

As it was, Sam appeared to be suffering from amnesia, as if he had stepped into the wrong house, not knowing where he was, or why exactly he was there at all.

The painted smile widened. 'It was meant to be, you coming today instead of over the holiday weekend,' she said too brightly. 'I won't have time to breathe after today. Auntie and Uncle are here already, and two more early visitors arrive at six o'clock coming straight on from work, then it's all action stations.' She touched the sleeve of the smart fawn raincoat. 'I've planned it so we can take Jimmy out this afternoon.' Glancing over her shoulder at the kitchen door through which penetrated the furious sound of chopping: 'Florence has been marvellous about it.' She ruffled Jimmy's hair. 'We're looking forward to it, aren't we, chuck?'

'Daisy says we can go in Fairyland.' Jimmy was still eyeing his father's small suitcase hopefully. 'It's open now for Easter, Dad. We've got a week and a day and a half off school. Daisy says we can go on the Pleasure Beach as well. On *everything*.'

'I don't remember saying *everything*.'

'You said we could go on the Giant Plunger.' Jimmy put his head on one side in what Daisy recognized as the familiar lie-telling position. 'A boy in my class has been on it more 'n a hundred times. His dad is a sailor. He brings presents every time he comes home. A case full.' Jimmy's eyes bulged with greed as Sam picked up the small case. 'You can open it down here if you want to, Dad.'

'If you'd like to come upstairs, Sam.' Daisy spoke in desperation. 'I'll show you where you're sleeping tonight.'

Florence had voiced strong disapproval about the arrangement. The room had been booked for a couple from Darwen arriving the very next day, which meant Sam would have to move out early in the morning for the sheets to be changed and the room got ready.

'Extra work all for one night,' Florence had grumbled. 'Why can't he sleep on a camp bed in the dining-room for one night? I can't see Joshua putting you to so much trouble. Joshua thinks of others before himself. Your precious Sam has nobody on his mind but his precious self.'

Daisy threw a bedroom door open with a flourish. 'I think you'll be all right in here.' Her voice was high, false, a landladyish tone to it. 'The mealtimes are on the notice here behind the door. If you'd like early-morning tea, just say so.'

Sam slung the case on to the bed and unbuttoned his coat. 'Vamoose,' he told Jimmy. 'Right now! This minute!' He held out a threepenny bit. 'Don't spend it all at once.'

With lip-curling disgust Jimmy stared down at the tiny coin in the palm of his rather grubby hand. His mind calculated to the last gob-stopper how many sweets he could get for it. The picture he'd cherished of his dad staggering up the road laden with presents faded and disappeared.

'Can't you make it sixpence?' he wanted to know.

'Out!' Sam pointed a finger at the door. 'Or I'll take it back and swap it for a penny.'

Jimmy went, clattering down the stairs to jump the last

four steps and trip over his shoelaces in his headlong flight to the door which he slammed to with a crash that seemed to shake the house to its foundations.

'*He* hasn't altered much.' Sam clicked open the case and took out a shirt. 'You looked tired, Daisybell.' He didn't turn round. 'You're all big-eyed and thinner. Jimmy must be hard work for you on top of everything else you've had to do. You've done a marvellous job on the house.'

'Sam?' Daisy walked towards the bed, her going to him as instinctive as breathing. 'Put your arms round me. Hold me, Sam.'

The need inside her was so great she began to shake. This man was the dream she dreamed; he was the answer to her longing to be cherished. As he turned, she lifted a hand and traced with a finger the smooth wing of his eyebrows, the slight stubble on his chin. His mouth . . . oh, dear God, Sam's mouth, the lips firm yet soft. Her fingers lingered, tracing its shape.

'Oh, Sam. . . .'

It would have been hard to say who was kissing whom, but the emotion in her caught Sam unawares. His hand slid down her back, jerking her close.

To Daisy the kiss was as erotic, as sensual as she imagined the act of love itself would be. Tender at first, then demanding. She pressed herself against him, passion running like quick-silver through her veins. No part of her held back. *Love*, she told herself. This then was love.

He was only human. 'Daisy. Oh, Daisybell.' His voice was hoarse. When he released her she swayed and would have fallen across the bed but for his arm supporting her. His face was flushed, the dark eyes hooded as he looked down at her. 'Have you missed me all that much, darling?'

'I love you,' she whispered. 'The loving you gets worse. I think about you all the time. Do you think about *me* all the time, Sam?'

'If I were free,' he said carefully, 'if things were different, I would marry you tomorrow. You're so full of love you scare me.' Putting her from him he straightened his tie. 'You should never love *anyone* that much, Daisy. People get hurt when they love too much.'

'*Can* a person love too much, Sam?' Her eyes were dazed, her face soft, her eyes gentle with adoration.

'Yes!' He took a cigarette from his silver case and busied himself lighting it, annoyed to find that his hand shook. 'Don't put me on a pedestal, Daisy. I'm not worth it.'

'I think you are.'

'No!' He looked round for an ashtray. 'I'm not a saint, not even a plaster one. Daisy....' He inhaled, drawing smoke deep into his lungs. 'I want to take Jimmy back with me in the morning.'

For a moment she was lost for words. 'But how can you?' She frowned. 'I thought you said you were working? I thought you said you were driving Mr Evison to Cornwall? Has he said you can take Jimmy with you?'

'Nope.' He was obviously ill at ease.

'Well, where would he go?'

He refused to meet her eyes. 'To Suffolk. With his mother and Dorothy. Queenie wants to see him.'

'Queenie?'

'She's his grandmother, for Pete's sake!'

'Why are you shouting, Sam?' Daisy glanced towards the door. 'I *know* she's his grandmother, and it's only natural that she would want to see her grandson.' She hesitated. 'It's just that I thought... with your... your wife going to Canada and everything it wouldn't be.... Is her boyfriend going with them to Suffolk?'

'Did *I* say he was going? Did I even *mention* him?' With his back turned to her and the cigarette dangling from his lips, Sam began taking things from his case.

'No. But I would've thought, with them living together and everything....'

'Did I *say* they were living together? In so many words? Have I *ever* said that?'

'You *implied*.' Daisy looked stricken. 'I don't mean to pry....'

'Well, *don't* then!'

'Daisy?' Florence's knock at the door had a touch of hysteria about it. 'Your aunt and uncle are back. Did you know they were coming back for a midday meal?'

'I'm coming.' Daisy took a deep breath. 'We'll talk about it later, Sam. I must go now.'

'Talk about what?' Sam's face was sullen. Two angry red spots burned on his cheek-bones. 'There's nothing *to* talk about as far as I'm concerned.'

'Daisy!' Florence sounded as if she was beginning to froth at the mouth.

'I'm coming.' Daisy opened the door, the smoothness of her face at variance with the turmoil inside her. What was wrong with Sam? Why couldn't he *tell* her instead of flying off the handle like that? She would understand. She was good at understanding, wasn't she? She was the calm one, the smoother of paths, the peacemaker. Always in control. Not like Florence here, doing her nut because there were going to be two extra for dinner.

Daisy ran down the stairs. But why, for God's sake, why couldn't her auntie and uncle have stopped out just for today? Bought fish and chips. Eaten cockles off the stall on the front. Got a couple of meat pies and eaten them on the beach, or sitting in a shelter. It was warm enough.

Edna put her head round the kitchen door. 'I'd like a word with that London chap when he comes down.'

Daisy's control snapped. 'If you say one word to him, Auntie. One *single* word about what's none of your business I'll ... I'll ... I won't be responsible!'

'Well!' Edna drew herself up to her full height of five feet and half an inch. 'I've never been spoken to like that in my life before.' Her lower lip wobbled. 'Our Betty, bless her, would cut out her tongue rather than cheek me like that.'

'I *warn* you.' Daisy stepped back and closed the door deliberately in Edna's outraged face. 'That's why their Betty, bless her, is what she is,' she muttered darkly to an equally astounded Florence. 'A *nothing*. A lump of nowt with no mind of her own. Give me that omelette pan, or can we make that fish pie go round? They said they were stopping out. So why did they have to come back?'

'What's up with you, Daisy?' Florence stared at Daisy in surprise. 'You've had a row with Sam, haven't you? I could hear him shouting as I came upstairs.' She looked virtuous and smug. 'But you shouldn't take it out on your guests. Your auntie is a guest, or isn't she? Wasn't that what you told me? Kow-tow to the visitors, no matter what?'

Daisy banged a pan down hard on the cooker. 'Don't *you* start. And if you must know I *am* a bit upset. Sam is taking Jimmy back with him.'

'For good?'

'For the Easter holidays.'

'Well, surely that will help? With him out of the way. It was only the other day you were worrying because you said he'd be neglected this week. I think it's the best thing that could happen.'

Daisy felt too defeated to argue. Florence was probably right. Jimmy going away for Easter was a good idea. But *something* was wrong. Now she was calming down she still felt that something was wrong. Her hand holding the chopping knife was stilled for a moment. Maybe Sam's wife was missing Jimmy after all. Maybe she was going to take him with her to Canada, and maybe Sam suspected this.

In spite of the fierce blast of heat when she opened the oven door Daisy felt suddenly cold. Suppose Jimmy never came back? Suppose his mother applied for and got custody of him? Sam really loved his son. It would break his heart.

It would be bad enough if Jimmy never came back *here* where he had been for such a brief time. . . . Never to watch him lunging round the house again, bumping into everything, shaking the floor as he jumped from chairs or the settee, no matter how many times he was told not to. Never to hear him coming in from school, banging the door back, dropping his hat and coat on the floor, making a dive for the biscuit tin and telling her terrible corny jokes through a mouthful of crumbs.

Suppose she never saw him again?

'Daisy?' Uncle Arnold's nice kind face peered round the door. 'I think you'd best come and have a word with your auntie. She's upstairs packing her bag to go back home.'

By the time they reached the Pleasure Beach that afternoon Daisy was almost back to her normal unflappable self. Almost, but not quite. Edna's feathers had been too badly ruffled for her to be smoothed over with a few soothing words.

'Very well, then,' she had said. 'You've made your own bed, now lie in it, but don't come running to me when you need a shoulder to cry on. You've changed, our Daisy, and not for the better. That Florrie Livesey's a bad influence on you. There's bad blood there somewhere. And as for that London chap, well, just keep him out of my way, that's all. He's far too good-looking for his own good. Handsome is as handsome does, remember that. Our Betty, bless her, didn't choose Cyril for his looks goodness knows, but at least she knows where she stands with him.'

'Look at me, for instance,' Arnold had said, trying as ever to make the peace. 'Ugly as sin, but lovely with it.'

The Pleasure Beach was crowded. Weasel-faced men and leathery-skinned women shouted at everyone who passed by. They held out balls for hurling at dummies, or rifles to be fired at bobbing targets.

Sam and Daisy, with Jimmy between them, stopped in front of the Ghost Train. Jimmy jumped up and down with excitement, his eyes wide as he heard the thunder of the cars along the tracks, the blood-curdling yells and the piercing screams. It was all far better than he had ever imagined. Noisier, brighter, golder. He pulled at Daisy's hand, urging her towards the Noah's Ark with its rocking motion and its animals passing two by two. He ran on ahead past the raucous rattle of the Big Dipper and the Grand National, turning round impatiently when she didn't follow as quickly as he needed her to.

In front of the Giant Plunger he tugged at his dad's sleeve. 'Please, Dad! Please!' He gripped Daisy's hand. 'You promised Daisy! Oh, let's go on here first!'

'Seems we've no choice.' Pushing his trilby to the back of his head with a finger, Sam grinned down at his son. 'Okay, laddo. Come on, Daisybell. Hold on tight!'

Daisy wished she'd been sitting next to Sam, but with Jimmy sandwiched between them the car slid into a dark tunnel, the wheels grinding horribly on the iron rails. She was sure the startlingly sudden ascent would jerk her head off, and closed her eyes, opening them wide at the unexpected emergence into bright daylight. For a brief moment she saw the whole of Blackpool spread below them, spring-green and beautiful. She tightened her hold on Jimmy as the car climbed even higher, swaying from side to side, creaking and groaning. Just in time she snatched the knitted beret from her head, remembering another time, another place when the wind had taken her hat and tossed it away.

'Hold on to the rail. I've got Jimmy. Hold on fast, Daisybell!'

Daisy answered him, but the wind took her words and devoured them. The car crested the summit of a long slope, giving a stomach-churning lurch before rushing at speed down an almost perpendicular incline. Jimmy screamed loudly, eyes and mouth wide open in terror. The car climbed yet another track, higher even than the last, wheezing and juddering as if it knew it would never make it. For a heart-stopping moment Daisy was sure it would slide backwards, crushing them to pulp at the bottom. Risking a quick glance at Jimmy, she saw that his small face had turned the colour of risen dough.

At the top of a slope she nerved herself to look down. This time she saw the fairground's white buildings and beyond them the biscuit-coloured hotels and guest-houses along the promenade. Before the car plunged down again she glimpsed a flash of green sea, then it was holding the rail till her knuckles whitened, feeling the breath torn from her body. By her side Jimmy buried his head in Sam's shoulder.

By the last clanking climb, followed by yet another violent rush towards the ground, Daisy had begun to wonder if the ride would ever end. A bearded fairground hand in charge of the massive brake winked at her as she climbed from the car.

Sam caught the admiring glance and thought, not for the first time, that happiness changed Daisy's whole appearance. It lifted her features into quite startling loveliness. Seen like this, with her cheeks flushed and her dark hair blown round her vivacious face, she was almost beautiful. The tenderness she had always been able to evoke in him surfaced. Pulling her to him he kissed her cold cheek.

'Want to go on again, Daisybell?'

'I'm going to be sick,' Jimmy said. And was.

Joshua walked briskly along the front towards Central Pier. He had needed to escape from the house for a while to avoid Florence's simpering glances. He had refused her coy invitation to join her in the kitchen for a cup of tea.

'Earl Grey, of course. I'm sure you've read that Queen Victoria drank a cup of Earl Grey tea every afternoon at four.'

Women built like Florence should never be coy, Joshua thought uncharitably. She wasn't to know that today was the anniversary of his wife's death, and because of this Joshua hated Easter. He supposed his refusal had been a bit abrupt, but Miss Florence Livesey really was a most peculiar woman. He wished he could like her more than he did. But Florence was one of those unfortunate beings who brought out the worst in other people. Born into the wrong environment somehow, out of step with the life ordained for her, Florence held frustration and anger tightly inside her, as if at any moment she would lose control.

Joshua stopped for a moment to stare at the sea. Miss Livesey, a born teacher. He nodded to himself. He had met and worked with more than one Florence in his career. Met them trudging determinedly down long school corridors, wearing skirts which looked as if they'd woven the material themselves, shedding pins from slipping buns of colourless hair, gawky, unfeminine, ink in their veins, never really leaving their sixth-form years where, oblivious to their unpopularity, they had revelled in timetables and the school curriculum. Brilliant academics, stern disciplinarians, stalwart headmistresses of girls' grammar schools. Poor, poor Florence, with her total inability to suffer fools with even a pinch of gladness.

He walked on. Oh, dear God, how he hated Easter. To most people it was a time of rebirth after the sorrow of Good Friday. Easter was daffodils in the parks, hot cross buns, the first hint of warmth in the air. 'Jesus Christ is Risen Today' sung in church. Bank Holiday Monday with women in new spring hats. Painted eggs, simnel cake, a promise of summer not all that far away.

Joshua walked a little slower, bitter memories surfacing, reminding him of how it might have been. He shook his head slowly from side to side. He wasn't the sort of man to dwell to no good purpose on what might have been. Or was he?

'That way madness lies. Let me shun that.' Shakespeare, as Florence would have added. What would become of her? He saw no future as a landlady for Florence.

He would have to leave Shangri-La. There was no future either for him there. Yet he dreaded having to find another room at the top of some boarding-house or small hotel. There was comfort and stability in the familiar, and he'd grown to love the view from his window of rows of chimney pots and grey slate roofs, wet with rain more often than not.

He coughed, feeling the raw pain deep inside his chest. The doctor at the field hospital behind the lines in France had told him that mustard gas left a man vulnerable to the cold and the damp for the rest of his life. The wind was growing chill now, but perversely he decided to walk the length of Central Pier. He needed to isolate himself from the milling crowds, where everywhere he looked he saw couples walking side by side. Two halves of the same one, he told himself. He cursed at his mood of uncharacteristic self-pity.

Inside the pier toll-gate he paid the entrance fee and set his face towards the open sea.

Daisy. He remembered the day down on the sands when he had held her close in his arms, lifting her free from the creeping wave. He could still remember the soft warm feel of her held against his heart. Why not face the fact that his life, since she came into it, had held a purpose, even the chance of a happiness he had thought was denied him? Why not admit that she had quickened his steps each evening as he walked from the station after hours spent teaching children simple things they would have forgotten by the very next day.

He had grown to anticipate the way she always came to greet him as he stepped into the hall, smiling, cheerful, in spite of her at times obvious exhaustion. Not a martyred bone in her body, that was Daisy. Patient, calm, but not passive, never that. Her temper could flare and recede just as quickly. A great speaker of her mind was Daisy. Vulnerable, too. Blushing so readily. He had seen the tenderness in her expression when she was with Jimmy. As if the boy was her own . . . Joshua frowned. Florence had mentioned something about Jimmy going back with his father; maybe that was what she had wanted to gossip about as they sipped their Earl Grey together?

He was nearing the end of the pier now. The weak sun was fading, but when he turned he saw that it had bathed the long parade of hotels and guest-houses on the promenade into a mute glory. By a quirk of the fading light the buildings seemed to be outlined in black crayon. The lacy tracings of the Tower, the Jacobean Town Hall spire, the distant cliffs at the north end with their mock-medieval castle, all standing out in relief against the deepening sky.

Daisy. . . . How beautiful she was, and what made her even more so was the fact that she had no idea. At some time in her life, Joshua guessed, she had been starved of admiration, making her far too susceptible to flattery. Maybe that was why. . . .

266

Joshua pulled up the collar of his jacket and thrust his hands deep into his pockets before turning and walking on. His pace had slackened now, but there was still something of the soldier's slogging rhythmic beat in the way his feet marched along the boards.

Jimmy, recovered now from his sickness, had enjoyed the sound of his footsteps drumming on the pier. Between the boards he could glimpse a swelling sea, dark and mysterious. He was the captain of a pirate ship sailing the seven seas on the look-out for cargo ships to pillage and plunder. There was a cutlass in his belt, blood-stained from his last fight, and a black patch over his left eye.

Daisy and his dad were talking boring stuff. They were leaning over the pier rail with their heads close together. He expected they'd get married soon, then he'd have two mothers like a boy in his class.

He walked with a rolling gait over to the opposite side and raised a telescope to his good eye.

'Ship ahoy!' he shouted to his men, pointing a finger to a ship on the horizon. Even at that distance he could tell it had a hold stuffed with gold and jewels. He smacked his lips at the thought of its crew blissfully unaware of the gory fate awaiting them. 'Slit their throats first, then ask questions later!' he ordered his men. He drew the cutlass from his belt, spitting on it before giving it a good sharpen on the ship's rail. A blunt knife wouldn't draw much blood.

'So how will Jimmy get back here at the end of the week?' Daisy removed a strand of hair from her eyes. 'Will you be able to bring him yourself?'

'Nope.' Sam looked uncomfortable. 'I expect someone will put him on the train to Preston in charge of the guard, if someone wouldn't mind meeting him there.'

By 'someone' he means me, Daisy thought. She imagined herself leaving a meal half-cooked, visitors waiting in the dining room, Florence revolting – in both senses of the word.

267

'I have to go to Preston. Just talk between yourselves till I get back.' Miss Bell, the perfect landlady, standing in the doorway of the dining room to make her announcement. 'I won't be more than a couple of hours.'

'We could make it Sunday, if that's easier for you.' Sam tried to light a cigarette and failed.

'*We?*'

He wouldn't meet her eyes. 'Aileen and me.' When Daisy tried to draw away he tightened the arm round her shoulders. 'My wife and I, for Pete's sake.'

'So you're seeing her again?'

'Well of *course* I'm seeing her when it's necessary. When the children are involved. What do you expect me to do? Post letters to her in a tree?'

'What about her boyfriend? Is *he* there when you call round at your wife's house?'

'*My* house as well. I used to live there. Surely you realize that?'

'*Is* he there?'

'Not at the moment.'

Daisy studied the angle of his jaw-line. In a moment I will be shouting at him, she told herself, in the very way I'm sure his wife used to shout at him. Furious with him for his assumption that I understand. When the truth is I *don't* understand.

'Where is he, then?'

'If you must know he's gone over to Canada. To see his father and to fix up a few things.'

'Such as a place for him and your wife to live in when they are married?'

'I don't know!'

'Well, you *should* know. Surely that's the kind of thing you should be asking. If the divorce has to go through.'

Sam turned to face her, his blue eyes cold. 'The divorce, the divorce. That's *my* province, surely?' He was struggling to keep his voice even. 'You're beginning to sound like Florence.'

'You don't *know* me really, do you, Sam?'

'Not when you're in this mood. No, I don't. This isn't the Spanish Inquisition. Or is it?'

'I think I have a right to know what's going on, Sam. Your letters don't tell me anything.'

'Black and white. Putting things down in black and bloody white. I thought *you* were the one who had decided on strict circumspection? Anyway, I can't write letters. You should have fallen in love with a bloody poet if you'd wanted hearts and flowers.'

'Stop swearing, please!'

'Then stop nagging. Either trust me or don't trust me. But stop nagging!'

They were rowing. Jimmy, fresh from the heady triumph of a glorious battle, with dead bodies strewn in blood-stained heaps all round him on the sloping deck of the sinking cargo ship, sighed with deep resignation.

Daisy and his dad. Going at it like his mum and dad used to do. Angry faces shouting horrible things. Looking as if they could be hitting each other any time now. Once his dad had swiped his mum so hard she had fallen over, then when his dad had knelt down just to see if she was hurt bad she'd hit him – wham! So that his dad rushed from the house yelling at her to go to hell, that he was never coming back.

Daisy. Her face was all screwed up as if she was going to cry, but she wouldn't cry. Jimmy felt sick again. Daisy shouted when she was angry, but he'd never seen her cry. If his dad made Daisy cry he couldn't bear it. He hadn't liked it when his mum cried, but when he'd tried to put his arms round her and tell her it didn't matter she had pushed him away and told him to get out of her sight. If Daisy did that he couldn't bear it.

Stumbling, falling over his trailing shoelaces, Jimmy ran as fast as he could away from them, making for the end of the pier, way in the far distance, to where the sea rose and fell against the iron struts.

269

*

'I didn't mean it, love.' Sam pulled Daisy close, wrapping her in his arms, tracing her mouth with soft kisses. 'I get so worried. I don't know what I'm saying.'

'I understand.' There, she was saying it again. Daisy stayed quite still, unable to resist as his mouth covered her own. 'It's the way I am, the way I've always been. Needing to know. Wanting the truth.' She put up a hand and touched the lock of black hair falling in true Clark Gable fashion over Sam's harassed forehead.

'And you *shall* know, Daisybell. Just as soon as things begin to sort themselves out. You're right. I'm not being fair to you, but have you ever thought I might be trying to spare you the sordid details?' He gazed out to sea. 'Breaking a marriage isn't easy, especially when kids are involved. It's mean and petty, horrible and nasty. It's being greedy when you thought you cared nothing for possessions; it's wanting to hurt someone else just as much as they're hurting you. It's a sense of failure that you've done it all wrong when every other couple seem to have got it right. It's wounded pride that's the worst of all.'

'And me being difficult doesn't help.' Daisy could see a nerve jumping in his cheek. The sight of it twitching away tore at her heartstrings. 'It's just that finding myself the "other woman" has landed me in a role I don't know how to play. I feel guilty on account of *not* feeling guilty. I've shut my mind to what you must going through, Sam, so in a way I'm selfish and greedy too. In fact, there are days when I don't like me at all.'

Sam half smiled at that, so that the elongated dimples in his cheeks came and went. Daisy smiled back and leaned her head on his shoulder. She had to accept him the way he was. That was what loving someone meant. Loving them the way they were, not the way you wished they could be. She had to trust Sam, as he said, not make things harder for him by demanding answers he wasn't in a position to give. He was suffering enough without her making his life even more

270

difficult. She could carry on nagging, as he called it. . . . And she could lose him.

Losing Sam was something she couldn't face. Without him she would be all alone again. Daisy Bell, the joky girl from the pie shop, always good for a laugh. A long way from being old, but not young either, far from beautiful, but not so ugly children ran away screaming when she passed by. *Daisybell*, as Sam called her. Liked by almost everybody, but loved by no one in particular. Till Sam. . . .

The path of true love never ran smooth. The many books she had read and the films she had seen all proved that. Lovers were meant to suffer before they walked hand in hand into the sunset with a full string orchestra playing in the background. Idly, Daisy lifted Sam's hand to look at his watch.

'Oh no!' She whirled round in dismay. 'I promised Florence I'd be back over an hour ago!' She looked round for Jimmy, narrowing her eyes to peer into the middle distance. 'Can *you* see him, Sam? He was there a little while ago, over by the rail. *Leaning* over.' She tried to subdue the panic in her voice. 'You don't think he's . . . ?'

'No, I don't. We would have heard the splash,' Sam said, being flippant to hide his own feeling of unease. 'He'll be waiting for us by the toll-gate. To punish us for not taking enough notice of him. I know my son. He can't bear to feel he's being ignored.'

Outside the pier entrance on the promenade Daisy clutched Sam's arm. She looked down at the strip of sand pitted with darker patches, the shallow pools left by the receding tide. The face of every passer-by took on a sinister expression as, for a moment, her vivid imagination ran in terrifying riot. Far out to sea a dank and creeping mist already shrouded the far outline of the pier.

'You don't suppose he went *that* way?'

'Right to the end of the pier?' Sam frowned and shook his head. 'I can't see him doing that, can you?'

'Too far and too scary for him.' Daisy ran back to the toll-

271

gate. 'I'll just ask. You never know....'

The man in the cubby-hole shrugged his shoulders. 'A little lad? In a school cap with a red badge? Nay, love, there's been little lads here all day, with the schools breaking up yesterday. An' most of them without paying if they can manage it.'

'Black hair,' Daisy said desperately. 'Wearing a navy-blue raincoat. This tall.' Placing a hand beneath her chin. 'In the last ten minutes.'

The man liked the look of Daisy. She reminded him of Janet Gaynor, his favourite film star, with her wide-set eyes and small determined chin, but small boys in school caps were the bane of his life, forever snidging through past his little window before charging off like rampaging maniacs down the pier. 'Sorry, love. If I had a pound note for every little lad passing through here I'd be a millionaire. They all look alike to me.'

'You go back to the house.' Sam was worried now, trying to hide it. 'I'll walk back along the pier. He may have gone to see if he can find anyone fishing from the jetty.'

Waiting for a tram to rock by before crossing the road, Daisy suppressed a shudder. What chance would a small boy have if he tripped over his shoelaces in front of one of those clanking monsters? Who would see a boy fall from the end of the jetty, leaving nothing but a ring of bubbles and a little round cap floating on the waves? She narrowed her eyes at a harmless old man going home for his tea. There were sick and evil men about, even in friendly Blackpool. What was it the policeman had said to her that time she had taken a late-night walk down to the front and back?

'There's a man been reported for exposing himself round Talbot Square way. We don't *think* he would harm anyone,' he had said.

But you never knew. You never knew....

The town was already filling up for the Easter holiday. Day trippers pouring from the excursion trains, men driving sports cars. Daisy glared so suspiciously at a young man at the wheel of a pale blue and chromium car drawn up politely to let her cross the road he almost stalled the engine.

'You're not my type, ducky,' he called out, flicking his cigarette away through the open window, but Daisy was running along the pavement towards the Tower, hearing the breath rasp in her throat, ignoring the agony of the stitch stabbing at her side.

Florence was just about fed up to her large back teeth. Daisy had said she would be back over an hour ago. A couple from Accrington had turned up on an earlier train, and there they were, sitting in the lounge, a stunned and captive audience for Daisy's moronic auntie. On one of her dashes from the kitchen to the dining room Florence had overheard Edna holding forth about their Betty, bless her, and the baby who had walked so early he'd been able to pass beneath the table without bumping his head.

Lancashire hotpot was the dish Daisy had chosen to cook and make her visitors feel thoroughly at home on their first evening. Florence had watched her prepare it that morning with sheep's kidney and thick neck chops – two per person – lashings of onions, minced and layered with sliced potatoes.

'A good stock with plenty of body in it,' Daisy had said, just as if she was giving a cookery demonstration for beginners. 'Poured over like this and cooked very slowly for at least three hours.'

Before she'd gone out with the flarchy rotter and his son she had given Florence strict instructions about the time the brown dish had to go in the oven, giving herself plenty of time when they came back, she explained, to remove the lid and brown the top layer of scalloped potatoes, crisping them at the edges to add colour and what Daisy called 'eye appeal'.

After all these weeks of preparation for the first Easter visitors it was almost inconceivable that Daisy would go gallivanting on the very day. Yet off she'd tootled, all starry-eyed, twiddling her fingers at Florence in an airy ta-ra. She was besotted. Out of her mind, off her chump, and all for a man who wouldn't recognize the truth for what it was if it stared him full in his handsome face.

Florence picked up a fork and prodded away at a large bowl of red pickled cabbage. Thank God Daisy hadn't left any instructions about *that*. Evenly shredded, glistening with vinegar, it looked in a blessed state of readiness. Not like the Prince of Wales pudding she'd had steaming away for ages in its basin covered with double-thickness greaseproof paper. Twice at least she'd topped up the water from a boiling kettle in a fever of anxiety in case the pan boiled dry. They were going to have marmalade sauce with it, as a change from custard, but Florence was damned if she was going to try to make it.

The time she had been allowed to make the gravy – and ended up carrying it out to the bin wrapped in newspaper like a parcel – had convinced her that it wasn't true anyone could do anything just as long as they put their mind to it. Concentrating as hard as a chess player within sight of winning the world championship wasn't going to turn Miss F. Livesey into a cook.

'Our Florence is the only girl I know who can make a lumpy cup of tea,' her father had once joked. *Had* her father ever joked? He must have, Florence supposed. She lifted the heavy kettle to give the Prince of Wales pudding water yet another top-up.

'Jimmy! Have you seen Jimmy?'

Breathless from her headlong dash, heedless of the Accrington couple sitting stunned into silence before Auntie Edna's continuing saga, Daisy burst into the kitchen. Causing Florence to jump as if she'd been suddenly shot in the back, bang the kettle down on its gas jet, scorch the wide cuff of her knitted jumper and, missing the edge of the stove, tip up the kettle sending a cascade of boiling water down over her feet.

Opening her mouth wide, Florence yelped like a wounded dog.

'Carron oil!' Edna said, coming into the kitchen to see what all the noise was about. 'Poured on straight from the bottle.'

'A clean pillow-case wrapped round to keep out the air,' Mrs Mac said, following Daisy into the house to see why she'd been dashing about the street like a bee in a bottle when she should be putting the finishing touches to her visitors' first meal.

'Get her stockings off!' Uncle Arnold gently pushed Florence down into a chair, knelt on the floor and decently averted his eyes as Daisy unfastened Florence's suspenders. 'I'll try not to hurt you, lass,' he said, tugging with his large clumsy hands at the lisle stockings in Florence's favourite gun-metal shade.

And at the same time peeling clean away the skin from Florence's long thin bony feet.

Jimmy was relieved to find that when the man shrouded in mist at the end of the jetty swung round it turned out to be Joshua. Safe, nice Joshua, with his empty pipe clutched between his teeth.

Yes, he was quite by himself, he lied. Daisy and his dad had gone off and left him, so he thought he would just walk along the pier and climb down on to the jetty. Maybe have a bit of a fish. He took a length of string from a sagging pocket and began to unroll it.

Joshua could tell that Jimmy had been crying. There were the tell-tale dirty smudges round his eyes where he'd rubbed at them with grubby fists. A left-over sob crept up and trembled Jimmy's lower lip as he busied himself picking at a knot in the string.

'A bloody knot,' he muttered.

Joshua ignored the swear-word. 'Best be getting back to the house, old son,' he said. 'I doubt if the fish will be biting today. Too foggy.'

'Fish don't bother about fog.' Jimmy's voice was scathing, but he obediently rolled the string back into its little ball and shoved it deep into his pocket.

'Did you go on the Pleasure Beach?' Joshua waited patiently for Jimmy to fall into step beside him.

'No.'

'Really? I was sure you told me you were going on the Pleasure Beach with Daisy and your dad. Wasn't it the Giant Plunger you were going to try first?'

'No. That's kid's stuff. Dead boring that Giant Plunger. It doesn't go fast enough for me.'

'I see.' Joshua was a man schooled in patience. 'So the three of you went for a walk instead?'

'No.'

'Is no the only word you can say?'

'No.'

Joshua put his hand inside his pocket and brought out a wrapped sweet. 'Would you like a caramel? A banana split?'

'Yes.'

'Yes what?'

A sigh, seemingly dredged up from Jimmy's trailing shoelaces. 'Yes please, Joshua.'

'That's better.'

Joshua handed over the toffee and they trudged on in silence.

The worst thing to do when questioning a difficult child was to let exasperation show. Joshua's years of training and experience had taught him that truth. Shake a child, or *demand* an answer and they clammed up tighter than a miser's purse. He glanced down at the small disconsolate figure plodding along by his side. Jimmy would tell him in his own good time. But where were Daisy and her Sam? Searching frantically for this young whipper-snapper, Joshua would take a bet on that.

They walked past the place where Sam had shouted angrily at Daisy, gripping her arm and twisting her round to glare at her. Jimmy averted his face. He bet anything if his dad had hit Daisy he would be sorry. He bet Daisy was good at thumping people when she got really mad.

Joshua phrased his question casually, as if it didn't really matter one way or another. 'Did you come on the pier all by yourself, old son?'

A trickle of yellow saliva oozed from a corner of Jimmy's mouth. 'Oh, yes,' he fibbed, 'I come on here most days. After school.'

'Better get you home,' Joshua said, knowing when even he was beaten.

The couple from Accrington said afterwards that it was better than a front row seat at the pictures. First the poor lass with the scalded feet was given a drink of brandy out of a cup. Then a tall dark man had rushed through the open door, yelling for someone called Jimmy. He had dashed upstairs, stamped along the landing, flung doors open. In a right state. You didn't have to be Sherlock Holmes to know that!

Then, another man had walked into the hall holding a little lad by the hand. A little lad with a mucky face who looked as if he'd been crying. Jimmy? Yes, obviously the same, because the girl who had dashed past the lounge in her hat and coat just before the accident, came into the hall and went down on her knees to hug the little lad.

'Jimmy! Oh, thank God you're safe! We were so *worried* about you.'

'Jimmy! You young devil!' This was the first man, the younger one with the film-star looks, flying back down the stairs to put a stop to the hugging and kissing by walloping the little lad hard on his backside.

There was such a commotion the ambulance man at the door, followed by his mate carrying a stretcher and a red blanket, had to knock three times before he could be heard.

'This is the patient?' Advancing on the little lad, who proved he wasn't by running upstairs screaming blue murder, followed by the good-looking man who they could see now must be the father.

The Accrington couple stood in the doorway to the lounge watching with reverence as Miss Livesey was carried past, lying prone on the stretcher with her eyes closed and her face as white as a sheet.

'I'll go with her, Daisy,' the second man whispered to the

277

girl in the hat and coat. 'She'll be all right.'

Which should have been the end of the interesting drama. But no. The peculiar woman with the daughter called Betty Blesser suddenly let out a piercing scream before rushing into the kitchen. To emerge triumphant and announce that in the nick of time she had saved the Prince of Wales from drying up!

No wonder nobody took the slightest notice of the policeman banging the iron knocker against the front door.

'A Mr Schofield live here? A Mr Robert Schofield?'

The fat woman in the flowered cross-over pinny from next door came to first. 'Mr Schofield goes dancing every afternoon in the Tower Ballroom with Reginald Dixon on the organ.'

The policeman coughed apologetically. 'I have a warrant to search his room. If I may be shown. . . .'

'I'll be with you in a minute, Officer.'

The hat-and-coat girl stepped forward and almost pushed them back into the lounge. She closed the door.

'I'm Miss Bell. Your landlady. Welcome to Shangri-La. I'm sorry about the little upset, but your meal won't be long. You've seen your room? Good. I know you're going to enjoy your stay with us. Please sit down and make yourselves comfortable.'

'Well! I've seen nowt as funny as that lot since your mother got her beads caught in the mangle and nearly throttled herself.' The man from Accrington nudged his wife and winked. 'I reckon we've come to a madhouse, love. If Boris Karloff came through that door with a dirty great bolt through his neck I wouldn't bat an eyelid.'

'It wasn't me mother's beads got caught in the mangle. It was her scarf, and I never thought it was funny then and I don't think it's funny now.'

'Aw heck.' Her husband sat down on the settee. 'Come on, lass. Smile and give your face a treat. We're on our holidays, think on.'

Chapter Six

Standing just inside the door of Bobbie's room, her unruffled expression betraying nothing of the turmoil raging away inside her, Daisy closed her ears to the sound of pan lids clattering as Edna reigned in triumphant control down in the kitchen.

She would keep calm, she would cope, and the lump in her throat wasn't the onset of hysteria. Daisy Bell wasn't the type to roll on the floor with the screaming ab-dabs anyway.

But surely Bobbie Schofield with his matching ties and hankies couldn't be the notorious flasher of Talbot Square? Flashers wore dirty raincoats, not double-breasted camel-hair, with the belt knotted instead of threaded through the buckle. Besides, if Bobbie was the flasher, why was the policeman searching his drawers so diligently, rooting amongst the neatly rolled socks and folded cravats? Daisy wouldn't have thought that *equipment* was necessary. She felt her cheeks grow warm.

Sam had come downstairs to see what all the noise was about. He was very sorry that Daisy was having such problems, especially on her first day on the job, as it were. He wished he hadn't to go back the next morning, especially so early, but at least he was taking Jimmy with him, which would help.

Mrs Mac had gone back reluctantly to get on with her own cooking. She predicted that Florence would be laid up for at least a month, as scalds were always worse than burns. She

279

might never walk again, of course. It was best to take things a day at a time.

The policeman had rolling eyes like Peter Lorre. Daisy wondered for a moment if he could be doing an impromptu imitation of the film star.

'That trunk, Miss Bell. Do you happen to know where your Mr S. keeps the key?'

No, she said, she didn't know. She respected her boarders' privacy. She blushed again, remembering the times she had lifted the padlock and wondered what on earth the shabby tin trunk could have inside.

Without warning, the policeman sidled towards the dressing-table and opened a round leather collar-stud box. With a buttery smile he held a key aloft.

'Always in the most obvious place, Miss Bell. Nothing surprises me any more. This will be the one, you will see.' His voice deepened, throbbing with melancholy as he lifted the lid. 'Aladdin's treasure. Come and see for yourself, Miss Bell. The loot of a typical kleptomaniac. One with an obsessive impulse to steal,' he explained, as if he suspected Daisy had never heard the word before. 'We've been getting reports about him for a long time now. The gift shops and Woolworth's have been his stamping ground in the winter, but come the summer he starts on the bazaars and stalls on the front.' He held up a cigarette lighter. 'This isn't new.' He flicked it into action. '*This* kind of thing he takes from houses, breaking in when the owners are in their beds. Never risking the upstairs rooms where the jewellery might be, or where he might find spare cash lying around on dressing-tables.' He held up a miniature heart-shaped photo-frame. 'Hasn't even bothered to take the photograph out. That's typical, too.'

'But these things aren't worth the pinching!' Daisy stared down in amazement at the motley collection of trinkets: hair-slides fastened to display cards, two or three sets of bicycle clips, glittering Woolworth's brooches, tie-pins, boxes of paper-clips, tiny bottles of April Violet scent, a sixpenny tin of Milk of Magnesia tablets, pocket cases of

Mannikin cigars, tins of Carter's Little Liver Pills, sixpenny boxes of Pond's face powder, threepenny sachets of Amami wet or dry shampoo, and at least a dozen packets of Foster Clark's Cream Custard neatly bound together with rubber bands.

'He prefers evaporated milk to custard,' she said, stunned.

The policeman rubbed his hands together. 'Got him at last,' he enthused. As if, Daisy thought, he'd caught Jack the Ripper, or that doctor over at Lancaster who'd killed his wife and chopped her up into little pieces.

'What will happen to him?' She jumped at the sound of the front door opening downstairs. 'Will he have to go to prison?' Inadvertently her eyes went to the mantelpiece crowded with silver dancing trophies. Nineteen thirty-four, the only year not represented by a trophy of some kind or other. 'Has he been to prison before?'

'Well, let's say he's not exactly a first offender, Miss,' the policeman said, his eyes rotating like catherine wheels. 'Will that be him coming up the stairs now?'

Daisy wanted to warn Bobbie. To tell him to turn and run and never come back. She wasn't like Florence, always on the side of the villains, making excuses for them, saying that any man who had survived the trenches in the war was bound to be an emotional mess. But all the same Daisy had grown fond of the chirpy little man with his patent leather hair, and his size seven feet twinkling in their shiny dancing pumps. There was the time he'd brought her a bunch of daffodils, mysteriously unwrapped. Pinched from the display outside the greengrocer's shop, no doubt. And the box of sugared almonds produced from the deep inside pocket of the camel-hair coat.

'Sweets for the sweet,' he'd said, handing them over with a little bow.

Whipped straight from the counter of the newsagent's shop on the corner, almost certainly!

'Tea for two. . . .' Daisy thought she had never seen anything as sad as the dapper little man rounding the bend of the stairs, whistling merrily through his teeth, executing a Fred Astaire lighter-than-air dance step as he reached the top landing.

'Something smells good, Daisy. Were you coming to find me? I'll be down in the jolliest of jiffs.'

'Bobbie....' Daisy held out a hand towards him. 'Oh, Bobbie....'

Behind her the pop-eyed policeman opened the lid of the trunk with a flourish. 'We meet again, Mr Schofield. You've led us a pretty dance this time.'

Daisy couldn't bear it. Bobbie's shame was her shame somehow. When he sank to the bed and buried his face in his hands she went to him and pressed his shoulder. 'Don't cry, Bobbie. We'll help you. Florence, Joshua and me. We're your good friends. You mustn't upset yourself like this. You can't help it. It's like being ill.

'It's not as if anything in that flamin' trunk is of the slightest use to him!' she shouted at the policeman. 'Can't you see it's *help* he needs, not prison?' She was talking like Florence, and meaning it, too.

'Are you going to come quietly?' Ignoring Daisy, the policeman moved towards the door. 'We don't want a repetition of last time, do we?'

'Last time? What did he do last time?' Daisy followed them down the stairs.

'Only broke a colleague's nose in four places trying to avoid arrest. That's all.'

'He must have had a big nose!' Daisy wanted to weep at the sight of her top-floor regular being escorted down the hall and out of the front door, his neat little head sunk low on his chest and his feet dragging instead of gliding across the floor.

'I wouldn't put it past him being one of them pansies as well.' Edna's voice was strong and assertive as she prodded the carrots bubbling away in a pan. 'I've decided to mash these with butter.'

She looked so important, so *chuffed* that things were going wrong. So filled with triumph at being in charge, Daisy wanted to hit her.

'Why on earth should you think Mr Schofield was a pansy?'

'Going out dancing and wearing a camel-hair coat, and wiggling when he walks? Of course he's one, and I'll tell you another thing. I wouldn't be surprised if that Florrie Livesey isn't tarred with the same brush. She's never had a man, has she?'

Serving the meal, Daisy marvelled at her own self-control. She insisted that Edna sat down with the rest to enjoy her food, and when Sam winked at her over his plate of hotpot she winked straight back.

Sam had faith in her. Sam believed she was all right. A lot more than all right, he had once said, holding her face for his kiss. Somehow, since that day, she had grown in confidence. Yes, with or without Florence, she would make a go of things. Sam's wink had told her he was proud of her.

No, she told Edna, she wouldn't dream of allowing her to help with the washing-up. They were here for a holiday, and they must hurry if they were going to be in time for the second-house pictures.

It never once occurred to her as she began on the piles of plates and pans that Sam might have come in from the lounge where he was playing Ludo with Jimmy and offered to help. Joshua would have walked in, picked up a teacloth and that would have been that. But Sam wasn't Joshua, was he? It would be a funny world if we were all made the same, as her mother would have said.

What on earth were they doing to Florence? In the two hours since she had been carried into Casualty nothing had happened. Nothing but the silence of the long wide corridor. Once a nurse had bustled out in a crackle of starched apron and Joshua had asked what he thought was a perfectly reasonable question, only to be quelled by a glance from the nurse's beady eyes.

'The doctor will be along. All in good time,' she said in a scathing tone which implied, Joshua thought, that he had been jumping up every five minutes and rushing into Casualty demanding to know how long Miss Livesey would be, for God's sake?

At the end of the first hour the ambulance man who had brought them into the hospital came through the swing doors leading by the arm an elderly man with a blood-stained bandage round his head. He showed no surprise at all at seeing Joshua still sitting there.

'Your lady friend won't be long,' he said on his way out. He winked and walked jauntily away down the bleak corridor.

Joshua took his pipe out of his pocket, stared at it with longing and put it back again. His lady friend? Nothing could be further from the truth.

Tucked up in bed at last, Florence watched Joshua walk towards her down the long ward. He turned to smile at a child sitting propped up by pillows and she was immediately struck by the nobility of his profile. A great pity filled her for the other patients with their scrawny little husbands sitting by their bedsides for the visiting hour.

'You should have gone home, Joshua.' She held out a hand to him, wishing she was wearing a decent bedjacket and not the hospital issue nightgown, with its high round neck and row of calico-covered buttons mangled out of shape by the laundry.

'It doesn't matter.' He stood awkwardly by the side of the bed, wanting his hand back and not knowing how to manage it without giving offence. 'I got used to waiting around in hospitals. You could say I'm an expert, I suppose.'

'Your dear wife.' Florence gripped his hand even tighter. 'Life can be very cruel to some. Both you and I have had more than our fair share of trouble, but we'll win through in the end.'

284

Joshua wished she wouldn't stare at him with those pale bulbous eyes. Florence had a way of making him feel sorry for her and angry at the same time. She took for granted an intimacy that didn't exist, which irritated, then made him feel guilty because he *was* irritated.

Florence tidied her hair with her free hand. 'The blistering of my feet looks terrible, but once they've gone the doctor says there'll hardly be a blemish. Daisy was quick off the mark with the carron oil.'

'She never panics.' Joshua freed his hand at last. 'She would have made a marvellous nurse. I thought so when Jimmy had scarlet fever. She has a way with her.'

'She's not *perfect*, Joshua.'

Florence was appalled at the sharpness in her voice, but she couldn't help it. His whole expression changed when he said Daisy's name. He was either very fond of her or, dear God, he *loved* her. Was in love with her. The truth hit her like a slap. Florence opened her mouth and drew in a deep breath. Beneath the bed-cage the pain in her feet blazed into life as if she felt again the agony of the boiling water cascading over them.

Oh, dear God, how could she have thought . . . how for one moment imagined that this lovely quiet man would look twice at *her*? She trembled with pity for herself, and anger with him that all he wanted to do was to walk away and leave her feeling bereft and suffering. He cared nothing for her. She knuckled a fist into her open mouth. It was strange how in one blinding moment she had accepted that. It had been there, she now realized, in the way he walked towards her bed down the length of the long ward. There had been no eager anticipation on his face, no fevered anxiety for her pain, no desperate hurry to reach her. Just a good kind man plodding patiently up a ward after sitting for hours doing what he saw as his duty. Doing it for Daisy.

All self-control slipped away from her as Florence felt a hatred so hot for Daisy it flooded her whole body with heat. In that moment she wished her ill. She would have stuck pins in if she'd had an effigy of her. The pain in her feet was making her feel sick.

'She'll marry Sam, you know.' Her tongue was running away with her, but there was nothing she could do about it. 'Even against her better judgement she'll marry him.'

'I don't think we should be discussing Daisy.' Joshua backed away from the bed. 'I'd better go now, Florence. They must be wondering what's happening. It's almost three hours since we came here.'

'She is very sexually immature,' Florence said in a loud carrying voice. 'Because she spent the night with Sam the last time he came up, she'll feel committed. Daisy believes in one man, one woman. Like in the Bible. She's as good as married to him already.'

Joshua moved to the foot of the bed, regarding her gravely over the top of the cradle covering her injured feet. 'Goodnight, Florence. You'll feel better tomorrow. I think we'll both forget that last indiscreet remark.' He started to walk away. '*I've* forgotten it already.'

'Oh no you haven't!' Florence shouted after him. 'You're as daft as all the rest, Joshua Penny! You can't see past the nose on your face, and that's not far, for God's sake. She's not your type, Joshua! She was born with a bloody wooden spoon in her hand. Can't you see that? She *cooks* her way into men's affections! She's got everything, and I've got *nothing!*'

Visitors sitting on their little hard chairs turned astonished faces in her direction. Patients raised weary heads from pillows, and a nurse came in at a forbidden run to draw the curtains round Florence's bed.

It was no use. The finely balanced control holding Florence's anger tight inside her had been fraying for a long time. Now it snapped. The frustrations of a lifetime surfaced. The years of tending her mother, the suppression of her desperate thirst for knowledge, the need to be loved, the *knowing* deep inside her that she had somehow been born out of time, out of place, rose up to confront her.

'Oh, God!' Throwing herself back on the bed Florence

covered her face with both arms. There was something else. The worst of all. The terrible thing she had buried so deep inside her that it had been blotted from her memory. 'Oh, no. . . .' she sobbed. 'Oh, no . . . no. . . .'

'Miss Livesey?' The nurse came back with the Sister, a pretty dark-haired young woman from the Welsh valleys.

Florence opened her eyes and looked into a face as pleasantly round as hers was unattractively long; at cheeks as freshly pink as her own were sallow, into eyes fringed with eyelashes like spider's legs. It wasn't fair. Hysterical now, she screamed her fury aloud.

'It's all right now. It's all right. *All right.*' Seemingly from nowhere a young doctor materialized. Florence felt the slight prick of a needle in her arm.

'You don't know,' she whimpered, as the drug began to take almost immediate effect. 'You don't know what my father did to me when I was a little girl.' Tears held back for over twenty years rolled down her cheeks. 'He said if I didn't tell anybody he'd never do it again, and I didn't tell anybody.' Her eyelids drooped. 'And he never did do it again.' She opened her eyes with an effort. 'But he might have. He *might* have . . . any day he might have . . . I was so frightened . . . always so afraid. Till I forgot about it. Forgot. . . .'

Walking back down the long corridor the young doctor, who had almost decided to go on and specialize in psychiatry, pursed his lips in a soundless whistle. Interesting that last-minute revelation. If it were true, which he doubted, the patient being an obvious hysteric, a thing like that, festering away inside her subconscious, could have coloured her attitude towards men all her life. It would take a very special man to penetrate beneath that loathing; that rare being, a *good* man he supposed, one who posed no threat physically. Sexually, he supposed.

If what she said was *true*, of course, which one doubted in a spinster of her obvious type. He wouldn't have believed before taking up medicine the fantasies some maiden ladies insisted on describing to him. One had to beware of them, in fact. Still, Miss Livesey was an interesting case. Not quite run of the mill. Cut out with jagged edges, as if with pinking scissors.

Proud of his perception, he walked on, serious and dedicated, muttering to himself like an earnest professor three times his own age. He would suggest to his superior that they kept her in for a few days.

'I wish I knew what was happening at the hospital.' Daisy perched uncomfortably on the arm of Sam's chair in the lounge, which still smelled of paint and wallpaper paste. She wanted him to say that he would go there on the tram and find out for her, while she sat in with Jimmy and got on with all the thousand and one things she had to do, but he didn't offer. He seemed to have distanced himself from what was going on all around them, as if already he was miles away leading his own life which – she had to face it – hardly touched hers at all.

'You know what they're like at hospitals.' He pulled her down on to his knee. 'I once knew a man who waited so long in Out-Patients he was completely cured when his turn came.' He kissed the small hollow at her throat. 'Time being the great healer, you see.'

Daisy smiled. 'Oh, Sam. You can always make me laugh. I wish you weren't going back in the morning. Everyone will be arriving and I won't even have time to say goodbye.'

He whispered something in her ear, half teasing, half serious. She couldn't be sure which. She drew away from him, staring at him with startled brown eyes.

'Oh, no. I couldn't do that.'

'Why not?'

'Because it would be wrong.'

'A mortal sin? You're not a Catholic kow-towing to the Pope, are you?'

'You know I'm not.'

Daisy sat bolt upright on his knee, struggling to make sense of her emotions. What he had whispered had excited her; she could feel her heart beating faster. With frustrated passion, she supposed. She bit her lips and frowned. She was a two-headed woman, that's what she was. One half of her wanting to sink back in Sam's arms and let him have his way with her, the other half telling her not to be so daft. Besides, he was still married. He was still *seeing* his wife, even if only to have shouting rows with her about the children, which was what he had implied as they talked together on the pier. So if she gave in to him and had a baby there'd be no hasty marriage arranged to cover her shame.

'I wouldn't give you a baby,' he said, as if reading her mind.

Daisy blushed. What a way to be talking like this, with the middle light switched on and her still wearing her pinny from the washing-up. For a moment she felt as if she was back on the Giant Plunger on the Pleasure Beach, going far too fast, with the earth dropping away from her. *Everything* was going too fast. In the last few hours Florence had gone into hospital and Bobbie had been taken into custody. The Easter visitors were arriving and in spite of her determination to manage she knew she would have to get extra help from somewhere.

Besides, where would the *romance* be in her creeping down to Sam's room with her Auntie Edna straining her ears from the next room, maybe even bursting in and catching them in *flagrante delicto* – Florence had said that was a polite way of putting it. For Daisy to take the initiative like that would be awful, brazen. You wouldn't catch Janet Gaynor or Deanna Durbin sneaking about in the middle of the night in their nighties, climbing into beds, even when invited. Besides, suppose Jimmy woke up with one of his nightmares and found her missing? And *worse*. Suppose he came to look for comfort and found her tucked up in bed with his father? Then went down to London and told his *mother*? Miss Bell would definitely be cited as co-respondent then.

The awful thing was she really wanted to. She shivered at the thought of lying close to Sam with their bare skins touching. She would belong to him properly then. It would make them seem almost married. It wasn't as if she wanted to marry him wearing a wreath and veil, anyway. Daisy had never thought anyone over twenty-five suited orange blossom. A nice blue two-piece would be much more in keeping at a wedding where the groom was marrying for the second time.

But why didn't he pull her down against him, instead of lighting a cigarette behind her back? Why didn't he *force* her to make up her wavering mind?

'If you come to me it must be because you want to,' he said cheerfully, blowing smoke up over her left shoulder. 'Sex isn't the all-important thing you have built it up to be in your mind. You have to grow up some time, Daisybell, there's nothing endearing about a thirty-year-old virgin.'

She whipped round. 'I'm not thirty *yet*! Do I *look* thirty, Sam?'

'Not a day over twenty-nine and a half.' As he grinned impudently Daisy was sure her heart turned over. 'Come here, sweetheart. You don't know yet when I'm teasing, do you?' He ground the cigarette out in the copper ashtray on its leather strap taped to the chair-arm. 'You look about *seventeen*, all worried and anxious about whether to give in and do what comes naturally.'

'Don't make a joke of it, Sam. What if I did have a baby?' Daisy said all in a rush, bemused by the way his eyes, seen at such close quarters, had little yellow flecks in their irises.

'You wouldn't. I'd look after you.' He bent his head and kissed her.

'What if somebody saw me?'

'They wouldn't if you timed it right.' He kissed her again, parting her lips with the tip of his tongue.

'What if you lost all respect for me?'

'I would respect you more.' His hand crept down to the fullness of her breast. 'Oh, Daisy, I *need* to. You don't know how much.'

His face burned against hers; she closed her eyes as he

290

fiddled with the tiny buttons down the front of her Viyella blouse, then pushed the strap of her brassiere down to cup his hand round her breast. When he kissed her throat, she arched her back and tangled her fingers in his dark hair.

'Sam . . . oh, Sam. . . .'

The opening of the front door brought her to her feet in seconds. Struggling to fasten the tiny buttons, breathing quickly, embarrassment flooding her entire body, she heard the click of Sam's lighter as he lit a cigarette.

'It's okay, love. They've gone on through into the kitchen.' He adjusted the band on her skirt for her. 'Don't look so *stricken*.'

Joshua couldn't bear to look at Daisy. Her hair was mussed up, her eyes heavy, and her mouth still bore the almost visible imprint of Sam Barnet's kisses. There was a button undone down the front of her blouse, but he switched his mind away from the implication of that.

'Florence is okay.' To avoid looking at her, he ran himself a glass of water and stood with his back to her drinking it. 'Her feet aren't as badly scalded as they thought at first, but she's had a shock and for that reason they'll be keeping her in for a couple of days.'

I should have gone to the hospital, Daisy thought. Somehow I should have found the time. Surreptitiously she fastened the odd button. It wasn't that she didn't *care* what was happening to Florence, far from it. She stared at Joshua's broad back. It was just that with Sam around she seemed to become another person. A totally selfish person with no sense of loyalty or duty, no principles, no sense of right or wrong, unable even to *think* straight. Capable of *anything*.

'I hope they gave her something for the pain,' she said. 'Florence is so highly strung, pain demoralizes her.'

'She's *all right*.' There was such an edge of irritation to Joshua's voice that Daisy immediately put the wrong interpretation on it.

'You must be starving hungry, Joshua. If you'd like to go

through into the dining room, I'll bring something in a few minutes.'

'No!'

'Joshua!' Daisy blinked. What was wrong with him? The way he'd just banged that glass down on the draining-board showed him to be in a filthy mood.

'I don't want anything, thank you.'

'But you *must* have something. A slice of apple pie and a nice wedge of Lancashire cheese?'

'I am not hungry.'

The slow, barely controlled delivery of his words convinced Daisy that he was more angry than she had ever believed Joshua could be. When he turned round at last she saw the coldness in his eyes.

'You think I should have gone with Florence to the hospital. That's it, isn't it?' She shook her head slowly from side to side. 'Oh, Joshua ... I can't ... I can't be all things to all men. Isn't that what they say? I thought something dreadful had happened to Jimmy till you walked in with him; I was late, my visitors were waiting, and Florence was cross with me because I'd left her to cope with the meal. I *should* have gone with her to the hospital. It's just that *you* were there and I knew that you would look after her.'

'Good old Joshua!' There was such a wealth of bitterness in his voice that she flinched.

'I've gone down in your estimation, haven't I?'

Joshua folded his arms, averting his eyes from the red mark on her neck. Let her believe that failing to take Florence to the hospital was the cause of his anger if she wanted to. Let her think anything, but let him get to hell out of the house before he took her in his arms and shook her, or slapped her face. Or kissed her.

'I'm glad you found Jimmy, Joshua.' Daisy struggled to make things right between them. 'Sam and I were worried to death about him running off like that.' The despised blush betrayed her again. 'We were talking, and Jimmy must have got bored.'

'So bored that he wandered alone to the very end of the pier, to the far end of the jetty, a little lad on his own. Crying his heart out.'

'Crying?' Daisy put a hand to her mouth. 'Why should he be crying?'

'I should imagine you and Sam know the answer to that.'

Joshua walked towards the door. He could no longer stand there watching the changing expressions on Daisy's face. Now she was looking bewildered and contrite. Before, when she had first come into the kitchen, she had looked dazed, as if she wasn't quite sure what was going on around her. He ached to hold her in his arms and yet he needed to humiliate her. He was no longer in control of his own emotions.

'Bobbie's been arrested,' she said from behind him.

'*What* did you say?' He turned round and closed the door. 'Bobbie's been *arrested*?'

'For stealing from shops; for breaking into houses late at night on his way back from the dancing. The stuff was hidden in a trunk in his room.'

'I'm going for a bit of a blow. Coming with me, Daisybell?' Sam put his head round the door. 'So you're back, Joshua. Hope the damage wasn't too bad, but Florence is one tough lady. She's not going to let a scalded foot upset her too much.'

'Two scalded feet.'

Sam looked from Joshua's set face to Daisy's flushed one.

'Look here, old chap, I haven't had the chance to thank you for finding Jimmy and bringing him back, but he's old enough to know better than to run off like that. Used to make a habit of it at one time, running away, but I thought he'd grown out of it.' He did a little shuffle with his own two feet as if he couldn't wait to get away himself. 'Coming, Daisybell? Joshua will stay with Jimmy for half an hour or so, won't you, old chap?'

'I can't come with you,' Daisy said.

'Sorry, but I have to go out,' Joshua said. 'Right away. Sorry.'

'What's the matter with *him*?' Sam asked. 'Sure you won't come with me, Daisybell?'

Mrs Mac said she had bumped into that nice Mr Penny haring off one way down the street, and that young lad's father haring off in the other direction. Sitting down heavily on a kitchen chair, she said that her ankles came up like balloons about this time, and that what with all the upset, everything she'd eaten for her tea was talking back at her.

'It's bad news about Miss Livesey,' she said. 'You don't have to tell me. I can recognize bad news at less than spitting distance. Your Mr Penny had a face on him as long as a wet weekend. Scalds can take bad ways.'

'Florence is going to be fine,' Daisy said quickly, 'but it's not good about Mr Schofield. That policeman had come to arrest him.'

'What for?' All sorts of interesting possibilities occurred. Mrs Mac's nostrils dilated like an animal scenting the unknown. 'Don't tell me he's the Talbot Square flasher?'

'No, but it's bad enough,' Daisy said, knowing that to try to keep the news from Mrs Mac would be impossible. Wanting her to hear the truth before it was made worse by exaggeration.

'It's all that dancing.' Mrs Mac's neck was so non-existent her face seemed to rise from her high-necked blouse as from an Elizabethan ruff. 'He was bound to meet the wrong type at all those dances. But he was clean, you have to say that for him. Mrs Entwistle used to say it was a shame to send his towels to the laundry – there wasn't a mark on them.'

'I ought to go to the police station to find out what's happening to him.' Daisy wished Sam had stayed behind instead of striding off like that for a bit of a blow on the front. He didn't like unpleasantness, she didn't need to be told that, but going out had made him seem uncaring and unkind. 'But I can't leave the house, not with the visitors due back from the pictures and Jimmy to think about.' She sat down at the table, lacing her fingers together. 'It's all going wrong for me, Mrs

Mac, an' I thought I had it organized so well that nothing could spoil it.' Her expression was as serene as ever, but her eyes pleaded for reassurance. 'I don't know what to do, Mrs Mac. I'm going to *try* to manage on me own, but will I be able to? Do *you* think I can?'

'With every room filled? Just one pair of hands to cook and clean and fetch the shopping and see to the beds?'

Little Miss Bell was so put down, so out of her depth, Mrs Mac forgot all her jealous annoyance at the sight of the obviously new copper-bottomed pans hanging in a row, starting at the smallest one and working up to one big enough to boil a pig's head in. Besides, little Miss Bell was one thing, that long-nosed friend of hers was another. Not a finger would she have lifted to help *her*.

'I read in the paper there could be over seventy thousand vehicles coming into the town over the weekend,' she said, giving herself time to think. 'And it'll get worse when they open the Talbot Road Bus Station. We'll be sleeping them four to a bed. They make out there's no money about but it's like I always say where the unemployed are concerned. Show me a picture of one of them in the paper without a fag stuck to his bottom lip, and I'll show you one of my old man setting off with a smile on his face to do an honest day's work. It was the same in the miners' strike. They always managed to find the necessary twopence for five Woodbines or half a pint of beer. Yes, I think I *do* know of a girl who could help out temporary-like. She's got a slate or two missing, they say, but she's clean and willing. Her mother comes in and does the morning's rough at San Remo next door to me.'

'You mean she's. . . .' Daisy didn't know how to put it delicately. She felt she could be going slightly mad herself with her thoughts tangoing off in all directions. Some to the big piece of brisket she was going to stuff and roll for the special welcome dinner she had in mind for Saturday night, fried plaice being the only possible thing with tomorrow being Good Friday. Worried thoughts about Florence lying alone in the hospital with her blistered toes pointing to the ceiling. Sympathetic thoughts with Bobbie down at the police station. Would they have him locked away in a cell without his braces and his packet of Balkan Sobranie cigarettes? She'd often wondered how he could afford to smoke those – now she suspected that he probably helped himself to them when the tobacconist's back was turned. And miserable thoughts about Sam leaving for London in the morning.

'She's fifteen, but she could pass for eleven,' Mrs Mac was saying. She got up and waddled her way down the hall. 'I'll send Angus round to see Winnie's mother now. The exercise'll shake his liver up a bit.' She picked up the unread evening paper from the hallstand and glanced at the headlines. 'I see the death toll from that earthquake in South America has risen to over a thousand,' she remarked pleasantly. 'And those triplets born to that woman of fifty in Italy aren't expected to live. You'd think she'd have made her husband sign the pledge, wouldn't you? He looks seventy if he's a day. I suppose it's all that highly-spiced food they eat.' She paused on the doorstep. 'Or is that India? Still, it's all foreign muck, isn't it?'

'Mrs Mac?' Daisy was determined to get a word in, even edgeways. 'Thank you.'

'She's nobbut a lass.' Mrs Mac handed Angus his muffler. 'She's going to wonder what's hit her when her visitors start arriving in the morning. She's been playing at it up to now.'

'She's spent plenty of brass on doing things up.' Slowly Angus wound the muffler round his neck. 'High living standards mean higher prices. I hope she isn't over-reaching herself. She's taking a lot for granted if you ask me. It's those holiday camps we've got to watch, though we can thank the Depression for keeping folks from travelling further afield, so what we've lost on the swings we've made up on the roundabouts.'

'Here endeth the first lesson,' Mrs Mac said, giving her husband a helpful shove to send him on his way. 'And no stopping off on your way back. I'll smell it on your breath if you do.'

'You're a hard woman, Mrs MacDougal.' Angus opened the front door with reluctance. 'There's a wind blowing fit to freeze the . . .' He hesitated, then saw his wife's face. 'The *ears* off a brass monkey.'

Joshua needed a drink. He had played the Good Samaritan three times that day, and he was fed up with the role. Hands in pockets, collar turned up against the now biting wind, he walked past the impressive Imperial Hotel which always reminded him of the Tuileries in Paris, past the Savoy with its bluish cupola, on to Uncle Tom's Cabin.

He wasn't surprised to find that the inn was crowded. It was the warmth and friendliness that drew people in from the biting wind sweeping across the Atlantic. And had done for years and years. Ever since the place had been an old wooden shanty on the crumbling edges of the cliffs.

He found a table by the door and from a white-jacketed waiter ordered a pint of beer. He was glad when it came, borne aloft on a tray over the heads of the crowded tables. He wasn't hungry, just filled with a terrible thirst. He stared without seeing her properly at a Florrie Ford-type woman singing a song about tripe and onions, accompanied by a man half her size playing a tinkling piano.

'Come on, luv. Join in!' A woman with a headscarf tied round her hat at the next table raised her glass to Joshua. 'Don't look so bothered, luv. It may never 'appen!'

'I don't know the words.' Joshua moved so that his back was towards her. Let her think what she liked. Community singing had always embarrassed him anyway, and he refused to be kind, thoughtful or considerate to *anyone* for what was left of his day.

'Bail?' the sergeant down at the police station had thundered at him. 'Look, sir, your best buddy he might be, but biting one constable's ear and winding another so he still can't straighten up properly just isn't cricket. Not cricket at all, sir.'

Bobbie Schofield a man of violence? It didn't make sense. Unless of course he *wanted* to be locked away. Fastidious to the point of obsession, to be branded as a common criminal would be bound to almost destroy someone like Bobbie.

Joshua beckoned to a passing waiter and ordered two double whiskies.

'*Two*, sir?' Twisting to avoid a customer, managing to hold a tray of drinks above his head without spilling a drop, the waiter rushed away, coming back within minutes to put the two glasses down on Joshua's tiny round table.

Joshua took out his pipe and busied himself with the familiar rigmarole of lighting it. They were singing a song now about feeling a glow just thinking of some girl and the way she was looking that night. Serious, worn faces, men with coal dust etched in the deep wrinkles grooving their cheeks; women with faces the colour of putty beneath knotted turbans or C & A hats. Singing about when they would be old and grey and when the world would be cold. As if it wasn't cold for most of them right now. Joshua downed one of the whiskies and marvelled at the energy in the North Country voices. God, how he loved this windswept coast and these hard-working folks who had inherited from their ancestors the gifts of frankness, straightforward honesty and open-hearted sincerity.

Blackpool brought out all those qualities. After scrimping and saving for a whole year, Mother could loll in a deckchair or soak her corns in the sea while Dad rolled up his trousers and got down to the serious business of building a sand castle for his kids, bigger and better than any of those going up around him. The young ones could dance their feet off, flirt, and maybe fall in love. Joshua had met his own wife at Blackpool. He picked up the second glass and downed half of that.

Daisy was a typical Lancashire lass. Optimistic, laughing off setbacks, determined to make a go of things. They were singing about romance now. One with no kisses. Joshua narrowed his eyes against the pall of smoke clouding the rather ugly room. Someone had switched off most of the clusters of electric lights, and the fat woman on the platform held out podgy dimpled hands beckoning everyone to join in. Joshua beckoned for two more double whiskies.

The spirits, drunk on an empty stomach, went straight to his head. How beautiful everyone looked, how enchanting in the half-light. Salt of the earth every one of them. Sentimental tears filled his eyes. When, for some unknown reason, the pianist started to play 'Jerusalem' Joshua had to restrain himself from putting his head down in the beer spills on his table and howling aloud. He drained his glass. Dear God – this land of dreaming spires, of mists and mellow fruitfulness. And is there honey still for tea? His close friend drowning in a sea of mud in Flanders Fields, his face the last part of him to disappear, eyes and mouth wide open in a last terrible plea for help. Joshua's wife coughing her life away, haemorrhaging over the nice clean sheets, the blood bright red and foamy, running a hopeless race. With death holding the stakes.

By the time Joshua stepped out of the inn to walk only slightly less than steadily along the cliff drive, he was more drunk than he had ever been in his life before. In the pearly darkness the Tower rose over the huge complex of the Derby Swimming Baths as if from the green slope of a hillside.

'Jerusalem, Jerusalem,' Joshua sang in his head. 'With no kisses,' he sang aloud, passing a couple of mill girls on their way back to their digs from the second-house pictures.

'He's well away,' one of them said, leaning giggling on her friend before walking on. Switching her mind back into the dream where she danced with Fred Astaire in a deserted bandstand, her hair swinging out round her shoulders in a perfectly smooth and shining pageboy bob.

When he got back to the house, Joshua told himself, he was going to go straight through to the kitchen, open the door and give Daisy a watered-down version of his visit to the police station to see Bobbie. No point in worrying her more than was necessary. He had trouble getting the word right. Necessary . . . too many s's surely?

Daisy had such a tender heart. A sickly smile wobbled his features into a rubbery grin. Daisy liked Bobbie. Joshua liked Bobbie. Dammit, even pernickety Florence liked Bobbie. *Everybody* liked Bobbie. Bumping into a lamp-post Joshua doffed his hat, swept the lamp a deep bow and apologized to it.

What a pity that nobody liked Florence – apart from Daisy. But then, Daisy would have put out her arms and embraced the whole world if she could. Daisy was pure gold. But not perfect. Oh, no, not perfect. Joshua admonished himself with a wagging finger. Too gullible. He managed the word on a rush. Too taken in by flattery, especially from the dimpled Lothario. That was because . . . Joshua frowned, trying to get his thoughts into some kind of coherence . . . that was because he guessed that Daisy hadn't been flattered much before Romeo Barnet came on the scene. Joshua grinned, pleased with the brilliance of his thinking.

'And good evening to *you*, sir.' Joshua raised his hat to Mrs Mac's little husband coming down the steps at the front of Shangri-La, followed by a young lass with bright red hair and the look about her of a very old pantomime babe. Joshua opened the door and stepped into the hall, forgetting to remove his hat.

Daisy *was* in the kitchen, just as he had known she would be. And *alone*. As he had never thought she would be. She was standing at the sink peeling what looked like a mountain of potatoes. Getting in front with herself, as he had heard her say more than once. Where then was Romeo? Joshua closed the door and leaned against it, needing the support.

'Wherefore art thou, Romeo?' a voice slurred in his head. He smiled an oily smile.

'I have been to see Bobbie,' he began, enunciating each syllable with great care. 'At the po-lice st-ation.'

Daisy turned round, the potato peeler still clutched in one hand.

300

'He is up before the magistrates in the morning, and it all depends on how he pleads.'

'Yes?' What was Joshua doing talking out of the side of his mouth like a gangster and wearing his hat in the house? His familiar features seemed to be all out of flunter somehow, as if he was looking at her through the wire mesh of a flour dredger.

'If he pleads not guilty he may be allowed out on bail. But if he pleads guilty he will be remanded in cust-custody till his case comes up.'

'For stealing a few things that don't amount to much? Kept locked up?' Daisy clattered the potato peeler on to the draining-board. 'I don't believe it!'

'He belted a policeman.' Joshua shook his head from side to side at the seriousness of it, then grinned.

'Hard?'

'Necess... necess....' Joshua gave up. 'Needing five stitches.'

'Oh, no!' Daisy's face crumpled. It was all there, written in her eyes. The worry of the day gone so badly wrong, the exhaustion, the hurt and the disappointment.

Joshua, in his whisky-induced sentimentality, couldn't bear it.

'My little love, my very dear love.'

In two strides he was with her, pulling her into his arms, straining her close. Kissing her. Taking possession of her with the kiss, their bodies fitting together, just as he had dreamed they would.

'Daisy... oh, Daisy....'

When the kiss was ended and before she could move or speak, he bent his head and kissed her astonished mouth again. Briefly. Then he let her go.

'I should not have done that,' he said clearly. 'But I am not sorry. I do *not* agolopize. I am glad I did.' As if remembering he was still wearing his brown trilby hat, he raised it politely, then replaced it on his head, pulling it down over his forehead as if saluting her. 'Goodnight to you, Daisy.'

'And goodnight to you, madam,' he said to Edna, emerging from the lounge with a tray of cups and saucers and a plate bearing a single Marie biscuit. 'If I may...?' Joshua took the biscuit and started up the stairs. 'I find I am a little hungry, after all.'

Edna bustled indignantly into the kitchen and clattered the tray down on the table.

'If I had a suspicious mind, I would think your nice Mr Penny has been drinking,' she said.

Joshua *had* been drinking. Daisy had known it the moment she had turned round from the sink to see him standing there, too serious, too straight, too dignified, with a terrible yearning look in his eyes.

It would be with drinking on an empty stomach, she decided. Forgiving him.

Chapter Seven

Daisy lay in her bed, twitching and bothered, trying to decide what to do. Thinking and dwelling on *passion*.

She had lived this moment so many times in her dreams and fantasies of how it would be when she surrendered herself to the man she loved, giving her *all*, that now there was no turning back she wondered why she felt such a sense of anti-climax.

For one thing, in her wild imaginings, she had always been lying in a wide bed wearing a satin nightgown cut on the cross, with a halter neckline to show off her bust. Or, alternatively, a pair of scarlet silk pyjamas with the jacket fastened down the side Russian-style. Her husband, her brand-new husband, had invariably been out on the balcony – there was *always* a balcony – wearing a striped heavy silk dressing-gown with maroon lapels and smoking a last cigarette. He would toss the cigarette over the balcony rail into some sweet-scented bush, then stride eagerly into the bedroom, taking off the dressing-gown to reveal white tailored pyjamas with his initials embroidered on the pocket.

And in the darkness with her hair spread on the pillow like a dark cloud she would give of herself freely and without restraint, surprising him by the depth of her passion.

'How beautiful you are,' he would murmur, his voice husky with desire.

Daisy stretched her eyes wide to ward off the feeling of drowsiness creeping over her. The truth being that she *wasn't*

303

beautiful, in spite of what Sam had whispered in her ear downstairs. She had a tiny waist, it was true, but below that her hips were too rounded. Let's face it, she was *pear-shaped*, she thought in a sudden and great distress. Besides that, Sam had never put his arms round her when she hadn't been wearing a brassiere. She always wore Kestos, the make that promised to give a woman 'line'. So what would Sam think if her unfettered bosoms weren't quite where he expected them to be when he drew her close in his arms?

She had at least remembered to leave off her customary layer of Pond's cream. A sticky face next to Sam's on the pillow wouldn't have done at all. Daisy ran a finger down the soft smoothness of her cheek, made the mistake of closing her eyes and felt the bed begin to sink beneath her. At once she sat up, swung her legs over the side and groped with her bare feet for her slippers.

She glanced over to where Jimmy lay humped in his own little bed, snoring with the rhythmic put-put she had grown used to hearing. If an army of soldiers marched through the bedroom she doubted if he would wake up. The house was as quiet as the grave. Before she ventured out on to the landing Daisy tried to place everyone in her mind's eye.

The Accrington couple who had kept her up so late while they played endless games of snakes and ladders, or Ludo from the box of games she had provided for rainy days. They would be lying tidily side by side on their new Vi-spring bed. Auntie Edna and Uncle Arnold next door to them, Edna with a pink net over the invisible one to preserve her holiday set, and Arnold in his shirt because he had never taken to pyjamas. Florence's room empty, and Bobbie's the same, with Joshua in his sleeping off the drink that had made him behave so out of character.

Daisy touched her mouth as if to feel the kiss again. Joshua was going to feel very embarrassed if he remembers it tomorrow. It was tomorrow *now* though, wasn't it?

'Must get my beauty sleep in,' Sam had announced in a loud voice. For the benefit, Daisy guessed, of the Accrington couple, who had carried on shaking the dice and climbing up ladders or slithering down snakes for a long time after Sam had given her that meaningful look and gone upstairs. 'Got an early start in the morning,' he had said.

Daisy stood up and slid her arms into the wide kimono sleeves of her dressing-gown. Her mouth felt dry and her heart was beginning to throb in loud thumping beats. If you loved someone, really loved them, what she was about to do wasn't wrong. In fact, it was more wrong *not* to. Withholding yourself was cold and calculating; being so frightened was unnatural. She could lose Sam through being afraid.

Daisy tiptoed to the door. If she lost Sam, she lost hope. The hope that some day, no matter how far in the distant future, they would be married. It had come to her quite recently how foolish they would be to rush things. They couldn't anyway till Sam got his divorce. There were his exams to pass, and his ambition of getting a good job to be realized. Quite apart from the fact that she was determined to get the boarding-house on its feet before she started having babies.

Half-way down the top landing stairs Daisy stopped and shivered. This was a fine time to be thinking about *babies*! Sam had said she would be all right, that he would see no harm came to her.

'The only safe method of contraception is total abstinence,' Florence had declared one day in ringing tones, shaming Daisy on the tram to Bispham with a woman sitting behind them with her ears flapping.

All she *really* wanted was for Sam to *hold* her. Daisy negotiated the last three stairs, being careful to avoid the one that creaked. She would tell him that. To be *held* and told how much she was loved, that was the great need in her. Not to feel so alone in what she was trying to achieve; to have someone share the burden and the worry with her, and the joy when things began to go right for her.

In a sliver of moonlight filtering through the big landing

305

window Daisy saw Sam's bedroom door slightly ajar, opened it quietly and slipped inside.

At that exact moment Joshua woke up with a start. There was a terrible taste in his mouth and the pain of a thumping headache spreading across his forehead. He swallowed and the saliva in his mouth tasted like acid. That would be because he had drunk too much and not eaten anything. Or had he eaten something? He put out a hand to feel for his watch on the bedside table and closed it over what felt like the remains of a biscuit. He sat up and groaned.

Oh, God! He remembered now. Daisy's fearsome auntie had been coming out of the lounge carrying a tray and he had taken a biscuit from a plate. He remembered her looking at him with her nose sharpening into suspicion. And before that... before that he had been in the kitchen with Daisy, kissing her. *Kissing* her! Joshua groaned a bit louder. That meant he'd blotted his copy book good and proper. Had she smacked his face? He made the headache worse by forcing himself to try to remember, but it was no use.

What he did have was a hazy recollection of Daisy struggling for a moment, then winding her arms round his neck and kissing him back with a great deal of enjoyment.

Joshua sighed and pulled the blankets over his head. He must have been even more drunk than he remembered.

'You're shaking, love.'

When Sam's arms came round her Daisy's immediate reaction was an overwhelming desire to push him away, to ask him, *plead* with him not to be so eager, so rough, so *impatient*. Not to kiss her like that with his mouth open, his tongue probing, and his face burning against hers.

'Wait!' she whispered. 'Sam, please! Listen to me!'

But Sam was obviously in no mood to listen to anything she had to say. Not when he was smothering her with his weight, suffocating her, *terrifying* her so that she had to bite on a fist to stop herself from screaming out loud.

306

It was like being *attacked*, not made love to. Sam had gone completely *berserk*. Daisy fought him off with all her strength. This was nothing like her fantasies where honeymooners gazed into each other's eyes as the strings of a full orchestra soared in the background. This was a Sam she didn't know; a Sam she had never suspected existed.

'No! You mustn't! Stop! I don't want you to!'

She had thought he was beyond hearing her strangulated cries, but as he rolled away from her she saw in the half-light the look of total disbelief on his face.

'You bitch! You cruel little....'

He pushed her so hard she rolled to her side of the double bed, shaking and trembling with the humiliation of it all.

'Sam, I'm sorry. I just wanted you to....' The shame engulfed her, bringing tears to her eyes.

'Wanted me to what?' He was out of bed now, lighting a cigarette and be hanged to the bloody notice on the door. 'You come into my bed in the middle of the night and you just want me to... what, Daisy? What sort of game is this supposed to be, for God's sake? What do you think I'm made of? Bloody stone?'

'I've got feelings too!' Daisy got out at her side to stand huddled and diminished, the anger in her keeping her from total collapse. 'I've never done anything like this before! An' I couldn't have, not like that. Not without....' Not without tenderness, she had been trying to say; not without loving kindness, not without *romance*. But he would never understand.

'Not without a wedding ring on your finger, Daisy?' His contempt was all the more terrible for having to be whispered. 'A common streetwalker has more heart than you, do you know that?'

A sudden sharp scream of terror propelled Daisy to the door almost without conscious volition. 'Jimmy! He's dreaming....' She was up the short flight of stairs and back in her room before Sam had time to realize what was happening.

For a brief moment he considered following her, then as the screams died away he shrugged and got back into bed to puff furiously at his cigarette, flicking the ash contemptuously over the side of the bed and on to the new pale grey carpet, which was an exact match to the grey self-repeating pattern in the wallpaper.

'It's all right, love. I'm here.' Daisy rocked Jimmy in her arms, stroking the hair away from his forehead, feeling him relax against her, already drifting back into sleep.

Shivering, she crept back into her own bed. 'Dear God,' she prayed, lying curled up in the foetal position. 'Is that the truth about me? That I'm no better than a common streetwalker?'

How *dare* Sam say a thing like that about her? She clutched the top sheet, holding it to her like a shield. 'If a girl works a man up,' her mother had told her once, 'she only deserves what she gets. She *asks* for what she gets, and you can't blame the man because they're made different. More like *animals*.'

Well, she had done it good and proper, getting into Sam's bed and working him up, then expecting him to switch off and have a nice cosy chat. Guilt fought for supremacy with the humiliation and shame.

But suppose she had? Suppose they had? And suppose that in spite of what Sam had promised she had become pregnant? Daisy's eyes grew rounder in the darkness as fear possessed her once again and her vivid imagination took over.

There she was with her whole life ruined, growing fatter with each passing month. Fainting in the kitchen as she struggled with heavy pans, watching herself being watched in disbelief by Florence and Mrs Mac and then her visitors. Having to sell the house at a loss. Writing to tell Sam and not getting any replies to her letters.

Or not telling anyone, and going on her own down some back street to lie on a filthy bed and let an old toothless hag do something unspeakable to her insides with a rusty knitting needle.

Oh, she had done the right thing in not letting him. The

terror that had given her the strength to push Sam away from her had returned with a vengeance, but this time as an all-pervading sense of mounting horror. Martha Bell had done a good job on her only daughter. Nice girls never did; it was the scum of the earth who gave in, and yet ironically it was the 'nice' girls who got caught, got into trouble and brought disgrace on their families. The deeply ingrained beliefs, the shame of what she had almost done held Daisy rigid in a grip of horror, before the relief that she had emerged unscathed brought her to her senses.

'Thank you, God,' she whispered, meaning it with all her heart.

But what of passion? What of the love that was 'fathom deep', the love that Florence's Shakespeare was always writing about? The giving of yourself to the man you loved in feverishly unbridled lust?

'Them's mucky thoughts, Daisy,' Martha's shadowy ghost intoned from the end of the bed where she stood in her flannel nightgown minus her teeth, a work-roughened hand placed over her outraged heart. 'If you weren't too old I'd make you go through to the scullery and wash your mouth out with soap and water.'

But what she had done, or *not* done had been cruel. Daisy knew that. There was a word for what Sam would think she was, and it wasn't a nice word. It would be a long time before he forgave her, if ever. Daisy sighed. The truth was she hadn't been herself since the day she set eyes on him. Sometimes it was as if she was looking down watching herself behaving like a mad woman, all dignity forgotten, all pride gone. The shameful truth was she hadn't stopped Sam from having his way with her because it would have been a *sin*. The only reason she had fought him off was because she was convinced he would have got her into trouble.

'Oh, God,' she whispered. 'I really *am* sailing on the wide wide sea. Please guide my little ship for me....'

The light touch on her shoulder brought her to a startled sitting position, every nerve in her body alive and quivering.

'Daisy? You're making a funny noise. Can I come in your bed?' Jimmy dived in without waiting for an answer. 'Lie down, Daisy. You was talking in your sleep and making a funny noise. Not *snoring*, Daisy. Just making this funny noise.'

After a demonstration to illustrate exactly what he meant, Jimmy snuggled himself into Daisy's back and fell immediately asleep again.

Young Winnie Whalley was ringing the door-bell to be let in before Daisy had drunk that first essential cup of tea. Daisy poured her a cup and wondered if the girl would last the morning. Winnie was painfully, terribly thin, with a small white pointed face beneath the shock of fiercely ginger hair, and spindle legs. If Florence could see what was replacing her, even temporarily, Daisy thought, she'd be doing cartwheels in spite of her scalded feet! Winnie was so thin, she could have been dropped through a telescope without blocking the view.

'Now, what I'd like you to do first,' Daisy said, marvelling that the new help had found the strength to lift the cup of tea to her lips, 'is to run a duster over the lounge and the dining room, then Ewbank the carpets, making as little noise as possible. Do you think you can manage that, Winnie?'

Winnie, who had obviously been well-primed, narrowed pink-lidded eyes into cunning slits. 'Me mam said you'd give me a cooked breakfast before you set me to work, Miss Bell.'

Daisy went on cutting the rinds off twenty-four bacon rashers. 'When you've cleaned the lounge and the dining room, Winnie.'

'I might faint,' Winnie warned, walking so slowly towards the door Daisy was sure she would keel over. 'I've got terrible anaemia.'

'Who hasn't?' Daisy said. 'A doctor once told me that if he bled me dry it wouldn't fill a good-sized thimble. I'm a fainter meself,' she lied, 'so if you hear a thud it's me gone over, but don't worry, I'm never out for more than ten minutes. What's *your* record?'

She saw Winnie trying to weigh her up; she could almost see the cunning little brain working overtime. If the child was genuinely ill, then the kindly Mrs Mac would surely never have recommended her?

'Oh, yes,' Daisy went on, 'the Bells have always been a bloodless lot. I once had an uncle who cut his throat without even staining the knife.'

A strange sound bubbled from Winnie's small mouth. For a startled moment Daisy thought she really was going to throw a fit, then realized that the thin tinny noise was Winnie laughing. Not really to Daisy's surprise, she picked up the Ewbank and trotted quite eagerly down the hall.

'I thought we'd get off early,' Sam said, coming into the kitchen with a yawning Jimmy in tow. 'That way we won't get involved with your visitors.' He still looked very angry, refusing to meet Daisy's eyes. 'There's a workmen's café near the station, so we'll have something there. I'm not sure of the train times anyway, so we're better checking as soon as possible.'

Winnie, sitting at the table, munching a bacon sandwich, couldn't take her eyes off Sam.

'This is Winnie,' Daisy said. 'She's come to help me till Florence is better.'

'Remember me to Florence,' Sam said insincerely, picking up his case. 'Come on, son.' He turned to Jimmy. 'That cat will be here when you come back. It's your own fault if he scratches you. You're squeezing him too hard.'

Daisy followed them into the hall. Sam couldn't go like this, not without a word, not without giving her just a minute to try to explain. She saw that his eyes held the over-bright propped-open look of someone who had slept badly.

'Sam?' she began, but he looked pointedly at Jimmy, remote from her as if they were strangers. 'Jimmy. Go and ask Winnie to give you one of her sandwiches,' she said. 'He can't go out without *anything*,' she told Sam. 'I don't expect you to like me much this morning,' she said quickly, when

311

Jimmy ran into the kitchen ignoring his father's shake of the head. 'I don't like myself all that much either, but you can't go like this, not when I don't know how long it will be before I see you again.'

'Leave it, Daisy!'

'I'm sorry, Sam.'

'What for?'

'For last night.'

'I said *leave it*, Daisy!'

'No, I won't leave it.' She was near to tears. 'I can't let you go without things being sorted out between us. It's not my way.' She touched his arm. 'I say what I mean, and you say what you mean, then we know where we stand.' She lowered her head, speaking softly. 'I played a rotten trick on you last night, but I didn't know I was going to. I came into your room thinking you would *listen* to me....' She raised her head. 'But you never gave me a chance. You tried to *rush* me into something I wasn't ready for, but I see now I didn't take a man's normal feelings into account.'

'A man's *what*? Oh, my God, Daisy. You're unique, did you know that? Bloody *unique!*'

'I don't see why.' She was genuinely puzzled. 'I can't see anything out of the ordinary about me.'

'Well, *I* can.' With a laugh that was half a groan Sam pulled her into his arms. 'You make me spitting mad, then you make me laugh. You stand on the doorstep at seven o'clock in the morning calmly discussing your reasons for climbing into my bed in your nightie in the middle of the night, and yet another time if I as much as look at you, you blush.' He wrapped his arms tighter round her. 'Oh, Daisybell, you're a two-headed woman, did you know that?'

'I'm a Gemini, the sign of the twins, that's why.' Daisy stared at him, feeling love for him well inside her. 'I'm glad you didn't spare me last night. I deserved your anger. I'll be sorted out in my own mind the next time we meet.'

'I wish you'd sort me out at the same time.' Sam put her from him, grinning. 'But remember I'm a different breed.

From the wicked south. Like you once told me, we even *think* differently down there. We don't always call a spade a spade where I come from.'

'What are you trying to tell me, Sam?'

He was looking at her with gently sad eyes. 'That I never wish to hurt you. Will that do for now?'

She saw that he was looking past her at Jimmy swaggering down the hall with a glistening greasy chin.

'Say goodbye to Daisy.' Sam trailed a finger down her cheek before picking up the cases. 'I'll be in touch,' he whispered. 'Very soon.'

Jimmy hesitated, came towards Daisy, changed his mind almost visibly and took the three steps down to the pavement in one mighty leap. Then came back and kissed her, a swift smack of his lips in the air, but a kiss all the same.

Daisy watched them walk together down the long street of tall houses. It seemed important somehow that she imprinted the memory of Jimmy's back view on her mind. His over-long raincoat – bought on the big side for him to grow into – his grey knee-socks already concertina-wrinkled round his ankles, his belt twisted and the collar of his coat half up and half down.

Standing there, with a million and one things still to do, she waited until they turned the corner. She had the strangest feeling, quickly subdued, that she would never see Jimmy again. Pushing the thought away before it could take hold, she went inside and closed the door. And immediately smelled tobacco smoke.

In the lounge, sitting swamped in one of the brown chairs, Winnie was smoking the butt-end of a cigarette from one of the overflowing ashtrays. Inhaling deeply, she lifted the white planes of her small face to the ceiling and blew smoke down her nose. For a moment she blinked her sparse eyelashes up and down as if overwhelmed at the achievement. Then did it again, with more confidence this time.

Edna told Daisy that she'd passed a very disturbed night what with somebody chasing up and down the landing and somebody else screaming blue murder. 'There's nothing like your own bed and your own lavatory seat,' she said wistfully, tucking into her egg and bacon. 'You don't seem to get the comfort away from home.'

One half of the Accrington couple wanted bacon crisp, the other half told Daisy just to *show* it the frying pan, the way you did with liver. Joshua came down, asked for tea and nothing else and went straight out. Daisy wondered if he remembered kissing her and thought how awful he looked with his eyes all bloodshot and his face a nasty putty colour. Edna offered to stay in the house that afternoon to welcome the visitors when they arrived, leaving Daisy free for a snatched hour in which she could make a quick dash to the hospital and back.

'I want very much to go and see Florence.' Daisy looked worried. 'But it's my job to be here. One family is coming from as far away as Kilmarnock. They're Mrs Mac's overflow. They'll expect me to be here to show them to their room.'

'The graveyards,' said Edna with a sniff, 'are *full* of indispensable people. Six feet under. But suit yourself. One of these days you might be glad of me.'

'I'm glad of you *now*, Auntie.' Realizing that she was, Daisy leaned forward and kissed Edna's cheek. 'Okay, I'll go. I'll show you what there is to do first.'

'No need for that, chuck.' Chuffed to bits by the unexpected caress, Edna actually smiled. 'I'm not just a pretty face, you know.'

By two o'clock that afternoon Daisy had rushed around so much her hands shook as she combed her hair and caught it back at one side with a tortoiseshell slide. Twelve people had booked in, with another four to arrive. She had staggered up the stairs with cases, thrown open bedroom doors, pointed out the bathroom and the *two* toilets, and served tea and biscuits in the lounge to the new arrivals.

314

The fish for the evening meal, fresh hake, so fresh the fins were still flapping according to the fishmonger, was in the wire-netted safe out at the back, and the batter was settling in the big earthenware dish, just waiting for that important last-minute stir to give it the all-important air bubbles. She was making a coconut pudding with milk, breadcrumbs, sugar and eggs, and to go with the bedtime drinks a big batch of Easter biscuits, with plenty of chopped candied peel and just the right amount of cinnamon essence to give them a nice tang.

The tall old house was full of people; they either went straight to their rooms to unpack, or dashed out for that first exciting walk along the promenade. Winnie had staved off one of her threatened fainting attacks by stuffing herself silly with anything going, including the uncooked scraps left over from the Easter biscuits and the scrapings of coconut mixing from the sides of the big earthenware bowl.

'She's a scream,' Daisy told Florence, sitting by the side of the high white bed at the end of the long ward. 'You have to laugh.'

'Why?'

Daisy looked flustered. 'What do you mean, why?'

'Why do you have to laugh?'

Daisy sighed. So Florence was going to be in one of her moods, was she? Lying on her back, with her eyes closed, the lids rounded over her slightly bulging eyes, she had already told Daisy that the blisters on her feet were bigger than blown-up balloons; that a young doctor kept trying to force her to talk about her childhood. As if some memory from when she was no more than a baby had nudged her arm, causing her to spill the boiling water all over her feet.

'He's an amateur Freud,' she said scathingly.

'Sam's gone back,' Daisy said, thinking to cheer Florence up a bit.

'The flarchy rotter,' Florence said without opening her eyes.

Daisy fidgeted on the little hard chair. This was to have

been her big day. The day she had worked towards since first deciding to sell the pie shop and move to Blackpool. With her moving graciously into the hall to greet each new arrival, assuring them of her best attention at all times, inviting them to sign the visitors' book and anticipating their cries of delight when they stepped inside the bedrooms with the gleaming new wash basins and bedspreads matching the curtains. She felt impatient with Florence, then immediately guilty.

'Joshua got tiddly last night,' she said, trying once again to make Florence smile. She had already decided not to tell about Bobbie being held in police custody. That would have been too upsetting. 'Yes, Joshua was so much under the influence he lurched into the house, keeping his hat on, staggered into the kitchen, swept me into his arms and kissed me! Passionately!'

'Then what?' Florence spoke so softly Daisy only just caught what she said.

'Then he raised his hat, bowed politely, apologized out of the side of his mouth like a gangster, and walked straight upstairs to bed.'

'I'd like you to go now, please, Daisy.'

Daisy looked swiftly round for a nurse. Florence had gone so white her face seemed to merge into the starched cotton of her pillow-slip. Could a person faint while lying flat in bed?

'Would you like a drink of water?' Daisy picked up the glass from Florence's bedside locker. 'Come on. Lift your head up and I'll help you.'

Snapping her eyes open Florence stared up into Daisy's round rosy face, not a foot from her own. Look at her, a little voice inside her head screamed. Look at that face with its wide-apart dark eyes, the mouth curved and smiling. Oh, dear God, *always* smiling. The straight nose and the thick shiny hair falling forward to curve on to Daisy's cheeks with their peach-blossom glow. Joshua kissed those lips, not because he was drunk, but because he *wanted* to. Drunk with longing, drunk with desire, drunk with the need of her....

316

'I'll look after you,' Daisy was saying in her low husky voice. 'You won't have to do a thing till you're better. Young Winnie will soon get into the swing of things. I've got her measure already.'

Deliberately Florence knocked Daisy's hand away so that the water spilled over the top turned-down sheet. 'You mean you have *charmed* her,' she said in a cold distinct voice. 'Just like you set yourself out to charm everyone you meet. You *force* people to like you. You *use* people. You get at them by mothering them, by making a fuss of them. But you're not doing it to me. Because I don't *want* to be looked after. I refuse to be patronized. I will accept your charity no longer!'

'What on earth is all that about?' Daisy snatched the towel from the rail behind Florence's locker and began dabbing the sopping sheet with it. 'I don't patronize you, Florence, and I certainly don't see you as an object of charity.' She stepped back in astonishment as Florence jerked the towel from her and tossed it on to the floor at the other side of the bed. 'I *need* you, love. I couldn't do what I've set out to do without you. I would never have gone in for this business without you as a partner.' She sat down again and tried to take Florence's hand in her own. 'You are my *friend*. My best friend. Remember?'

'*Joshua* is your friend,' Florence said in a high piercing voice. 'Bobbie is your friend. Jimmy is your friend. "Daisy is my good friend," he told me one day, and that was after you'd walloped him one for being cheeky.' The large pale eyes glittered with a terrible rage. 'I would say that Sam is your friend, but what you and he feel for each other is not friendship. Oh, no, what you and he feel for each other is *lust*. Purely and simply L-U-S-T! *Lust!*'

'Florence!' Daisy glanced round the ward, but perhaps Florence wasn't speaking as loudly as she seemed to be doing. The afternoon visitors went on talking to the patients propped up for their benefit. A nurse at the far end of the ward trundled a tea trolley through the doors, the rubber wheels squeaking on the shiny floor. 'I'll go and get you a cup

317

of tea,' she said quickly. 'You'll feel better for a cup of tea.'

'You do that,' Florence said clearly, 'and I will throw it at you.'

'Stop behaving like Jimmy on one of his bad days.' Daisy pulled the chair closer to the bed. 'Let me tell you about the visitors. Do you remember that very fair girl from the mill who used to come in the shop and tell us tall stories about what went on in the weaving sheds? Finishing off every sentence with "God's honour, kid". Well, she's just the same. Every time she opens her mouth. "God's honour, kid, it's lovely. I like you with your hair like that, Daisy. God's honour, kid. God's honour, kid, what a thing to happen to Florence! You remember Florence, don't you?" This to her husband. "You *know*, Florence Livesey, Daisy's friend." Whispering to me: "God's honour, kid, his memory's shocking. I don't think he'd recognize *me* if we didn't live in the same house."'

'The thing is, I'm not cut out for anything.' Florence's long thin hands were scrabbling at the wet sheet, pulling it up into pleats. 'I'm not trained for anything apart from flashing a torch along a row of cinema seats. I can't sew a hem without tying the cotton in knots. The scones I make turn out like biscuits. I hate knitting, even if I was any good at it. I bet I could burn a cup of tea if I put my mind to it. I have no physical attributes to speak of, and I loathe being nice to people I dislike.'

'Apart from all that you're lovely,' Daisy said. 'Oh, come on, Florence. If I tried to list *my* talents, a twopenny stamp would be too big to write them down on. We're in the same boat, you and me. Both of us could have gone on and furthered our education, but circumstances saw to it that we didn't. You might have been a teacher, and I might have been the secretary to a top tycoon, going off to the office with a clean white collar stitched into my smart navy dress and a spare pair of white gloves in my handbag. *You* could have married the Prince of Wales if he hadn't seen Mrs Simpson first.'

318

'I am neither use nor ornament,' Florence intoned.

'And a happy Easter to you too,' Daisy said, getting up to go. Bending over the bed she dropped a light kiss on Florence's forehead. 'Cheer up, love. It'll all be the same a hundred years from now.'

'Is that a cause for rejoicing?' Florence raised a languid hand to push a wayward strand of hair behind her ear. 'Give my love to Joshua.'

'He'll be coming to see you over the long weekend, I'm sure of it. He's very fond of you, you know.'

The look Florence gave her would have floored a lesser woman. Now what had she said? On the way out Daisy had a quick word with Sister, who told her that Miss Livesey wasn't making the progress they had hoped for, that shock sometimes had that effect.

'She'll be all right when I get her home,' Daisy told her, hurrying away down the long corridor, her mind already firmly fixed on the busy hours ahead. She had seen Florence in this mood before. In particular, on one July day when the streets shimmered in the heat and Daisy had left her little mother lying dead somewhere in this same hospital. Daisy would have a word with Joshua when he'd recovered from his embarrassment over his silly behaviour of the night before. Together they would coax Florence back into cheerfulness again. And Winnie would help. Winnie Whalley was a laugh a line if anyone was. And the extra money to pay her wages? Well, Daisy had a motto for that: 'Spend and God'll send.'

She only hoped He would cooperate!

Joshua wasn't going to mention his lapse. Daisy was relieved about that. She was flip-flapping a fillet of hake in and out of the batter when he came into the kitchen.

'I know, I know,' she said, too busy to look at him. 'It looks like an earthquake has just hit us, but it's what you call organized chaos. We know what we're doing, don't we, Winnie?'

'We're a good team, Mr Penny,' Winnie said, repeating what Daisy had kept telling her. 'We have some good laughs too, don't we, Miss Bell?'

'We do an' all.' Daisy made the time to turn round and wink at Joshua. 'Go through and make sure every table has a sauce bottle on it, Winnie, love, and put the high chair round the Birtwistles' table. They're letting the baby stop up for his meal.'

'Winnie has five younger brothers and sisters,' Daisy told Joshua. 'And I suspect she's half-starved. The mother has to do *two* jobs to keep them, would you believe it? Charring by day and working behind a bar at night. The next one down to Winnie, a fourteen-year-old girl, will be taking over from today. By the way, Florence sends you her love. I went to see her this afternoon and found her plumbing the depths. Poor Florence, she feels things keenly, always has.'

Joshua couldn't take his eyes off her. Daisy was the only person he had ever met who could do not two things at once but three, *and* keep up a running conversation at the same time. Not many yards away, gathered together in the lounge, what looked like enough people to fill a football stadium waited noisily to be called into the dining room. A man with a beer belly and a Friar Tuck fringe strummed on the piano, one small boy had his brother in an armlock on the rug, while sitting on the settee showing her blue directoire knickers, Daisy's auntie passed photographs round of a large bandy-legged baby.

'Is there anything I can do?' Joshua felt a sudden pang of tenderness choke him in the throat. It was impossible, surely, that one young woman, almost single-handed, could produce and serve a meal for the obviously ravenous horde whooping it up in the lounge. 'Till Florence comes back,' he went on. 'Just for this school holiday?' The noise outside rose to a crescendo. 'Daisy! Make *use* of me. *I'm* panicking even if you aren't.'

'You can sound the gong,' Daisy said. 'For the very first time. I will give you that honour, Joshua. But don't hit it too hard. There's a four-month-old baby asleep in the double room at the front. I'd like its parents to enjoy their meal in peace.'

How on earth had she managed it? How had she kept all this food piping hot till the very last minute? Had he ever tasted batter so crisp, feather-light and dry? Chips so evenly browned?

'Nowt to beat home-cooked fish and chips,' Joshua heard the man on the next table tell his wife. 'Beats all this foreign muck they'll be having in the posh hotels on the front. Rice – and I don't mean rice pudding – served on the same plate as the meat, mushroom vollyvarnts and horses doovers. You know the kind of thing. I met this chap on the pier while you were round the shops and he told me about it. And they're paying eight shillings a night, with meals charged on top of that! I reckon we've struck it lucky here. Eh up, lass, it looks like we're getting a proper pudding as well.' He licked his lips at the sight of the wedge of golden-tinged coconut sponge set in front of him by a gently perspiring Winnie, her red hair almost standing on end.

Faced when it was all over by the mountain of washing-up, Winnie clapped a dramatic hand to her forehead. 'We'll be at it till midnight, Miss Bell.' She reached for a towel. 'Good job we made time for a bite before we began.' She eyed the remains of the pudding with a gleam in her eye. 'That going beggin', Miss Bell? I'm that hungry I might faint.'

'If you do I will cover you up with a tablecloth and carry on,' Daisy told her. 'Finish the custard up at the same time. It was worth making it properly with plenty of eggs and full-cream milk. I just hope they could tell the difference.'

'Oh, I told one woman,' Winnie said, scraping her spoon diligently round the large pie-dish. 'None of your powdered muck for Miss Bell,' I said. 'Everything's made from bloody scratch in yon kitchen. The eggs in that custard were still warm from the hens' backsides.'

'You never said that?' Daisy's uninhibited laugh rang out. 'Oh, Winnie. I do love you!'

It had been said lightly, a spontaneous remark from a full

and thankful heart that the first meal had gone off so well. What Daisy wasn't prepared for was Winnie's reaction.

Laying her head down on the table by the side of the scraped-clean pie-dish Winnie burst into noisy tears. 'An' I love *you*, too,' she sobbed. 'I've never been so happy in my whole life as I've been today. You don't know what it's like at our house with the kids crying and the boys fighting, an' no carpets down an' me mam coming in from work in a flamin' temper on account of being tired, then going out again in time for the pub to open, with too much rouge on her face so she won't look so pale behind the bar. It's like being in a palace in this house. Everybody happy and laughing with being on their holidays, and you and me such a good team.' She raised a ravaged face. 'An' when your friend comes out of hospital you won't need me no more. You an' her'll be having all the good laughs we've had today an' I'll be back at home wiping noses and worse – oh, Miss Bell, three of me brothers are all under four 'an you've no idea how many bottoms they seem to have between them!'

'Oh, Winnie....' Wiping her hands on her apron, Daisy came and knelt down on the oilcloth beside Winnie's chair. 'It has been grand today, hasn't it? If I could afford to I'd keep you on like a flash.' She was rapidly doing little sums in her mind. 'As it is, Miss Livesey won't be up to much for a long while yet. She'll need looking after and feeding up – she looked awful when I saw her this afternoon – so there's no question of you leaving here just yet.'

'I hope they send her to a convalescent home.' Winnie's expression was fierce as she began on the drying-up. 'Me dad went to one of those before he died and he was there for four weeks.' She rubbed a plate round vigorously. 'But it didn't do him no good.'

'Tell me about him,' Daisy said. 'All the nice things you remember, then we'll soon get through this lot.'

'He was... he had lovely manners. Like what I mean is, he never spit in the fire.'

'I like the sound of him already,' said Daisy, watching the

colour slowly creeping back into Winnie's pale face.

'Winnie could have Bobbie's room,' Daisy told Joshua at a
quarter to midnight on Easter Monday. 'Do you really think
he'll be away for all that time?' She rubbed her eyes in an
attempt to stop her eyelids drooping. 'I can't thank you
enough for going to see him again. I'll go myself later on this
week, though Mrs Mac says I could have a full house again
with the weather turning so mild. You're sure Florence will
be all right to come back by taxi tomorrow? It was so good of
you to go to see her twice this weekend.' She smiled a tired
smile. 'You're a very nice man, Joshua Penny.'

'Somebody has to try to look after you.' His mouth
tightened. 'Do you still want me to go to Preston to meet
Jimmy on Sunday?'

'If you're sure, and if you don't mind. . . .'

'I don't mind and I'm sure.'

'Remember that time when we sat in here like this, that
first time we met, and you made me an omelette that could
have been used to replace a tile on the roof?'

'That bad?'

'Worse.'

'We coped, Bobbie and me.'

Joshua knew that Daisy was only half listening to him, that
her ears were straining to pick up the second the insensitive
pair in the lounge stopped shaking the dice and ended what
seemed to be a spirited game of Ludo. He wished he had the
right to tell her to go on up to bed, that he would see to the
lights and the fire. He knew that he ought to have told her of
his decision to move out of his room and find another place to
live. He worried about the look on Florence's face when
Daisy's name came up. It was a look he recognized very well
from his specialized training of years ago. A child in his
school had it – a sly expression compounded of spite and
envy, destructive wasteful emotions both of them.

The scalding of Florence's feet was, in his opinion, merely
the culmination to months of mental deterioration. Her

moods had swung from near hysterical gaiety to bleak depression. Florence was unstable, and if he tried to warn Daisy she would refuse to believe him. 'Florence has a great burning anger inside her.' He remembered Daisy saying something like that to the solicitor on that first day when he had lingered shamelessly outside the lounge door and eavesdropped.

No, he must move on before he became too involved. After all, he had no claim on Daisy, and though the prospect of never seeing her again appalled him, he must remind himself what one of his favourite ancient Chinese philosophers had once said: 'You can't lose what you never had.' True, matter-of-fact and sensible.

'I think Sam is seeing his wife again.' Daisy picked up a spoon from the table and began to run her finger along its length. She raised troubled eyes. 'I have to talk to someone, Joshua. There isn't anyone else as totally unbiased as you are. Florence is scared in case I marry Sam and cast her aside – as if I would. She's very conscious of the fact that she's forced by circumstances to *rely* on me for her livelihood and the roof over her head. At least that's the way she sees it. She can never ever see that I need her as much as she needs me. For someone as independent as Florence it must be agony to be reliant on someone else. It's enough to make her hate me.'

She looked so distressed that Joshua had to clench his hands to prevent himself from reaching out to her. 'Sam will have to meet his wife to discuss what happens to the children,' he said quickly. 'I don't believe his wife has lost all interest in Jimmy. They would need to talk about that.'

'It's more. We... we were, at least *I* had brought the subject up when Jimmy ran off on his own. Sam got very angry in the way people do when someone has touched on a problem they don't want mentioned. For a minute I thought he was going to hit me. Not that he would, not Sam.' She put a hand to her mouth in a familiar gesture. 'Oh, Joshua. Here I am, telling you my troubles. It must be upsetting for you listening to me going on and on about Sam and his wife wanting to be divorced. It must make you feel bitter to think that some husbands and wives can't live together when the wife you loved with all your heart had to die.'

Joshua stretched out a hand across the table. 'I'd be a very foolish man to go down that road, Daisy. What we have to do is just carry on. The scales usually balance eventually.'

'Florence wouldn't believe that.'

'Not even if her beloved Shakespeare had said it?'

'Did he?'

'I'm damned if I know.' Joshua stood up and smiled. 'There they go at last, the Ludo fanatics. I'd hide those games before your next lot of visitors arrive.'

'Thank you for listening to me, Joshua.'

'Any time.'

They walked up the stairs together, switching off lights as they went. Like a comfortably married couple at the end of a long hard day.

Chapter Eight

Florence sat within view of the doors, waiting for the taxi driver to walk through them and claim her. She had scorned the suggestion that she went home by ambulance.

'I can walk all right in these slippers,' she told a nurse, run off her legs by the rush of all the after-Easter admissions. 'It's not as if I scalded the *soles* of my feet. I can manage to walk to the taxi, and out of it into my house. Into my *friend's* house,' she added quickly.

'And you have your appointment for Out-Patients?'

'Engraven on my heart. Thank you.'

The nurse left Florence sitting there, the small case with her belongings by her side on the bench. A difficult patient. Acerbic and uncooperative. Typical frustrated spinster. Nurse Hornby smiled at the thought of the brand-new engagement ring – three small diamonds in their claw setting – in the top drawer of her dressing-table. What Miss Livesey needed was a man, though she'd probably run a mile if one spared her more than a second glance.

Florence stared straight ahead. Joshua had offered to come and take her home, but she had refused. The taxi driver appeared and she moved towards the doors with the gingerly steps of a fakir on a practice trot across a bed of hot coals. She wasn't surprised to see it was raining hard. The way she was feeling sunshine would have seemed like an insult.

'Nice to be going home,' the driver said, as he helped her into the back of the cab.

'For some,' said Florence bitterly. 'Drop me here,' she said suddenly when they reached the town centre, pointing to an arcade of shops with crowds of holidaymakers pushing their way into it to shelter from the rain.

'As you say, Missus,' the driver said, fed up to the back teeth with the weather and the way things always seemed to be taking a turn for the worst.

The letter came by the second post. When Daisy recognized Sam's writing on the envelope she took it at once up to her room to read it in private.

Dear Daisy,
There has been a change of plans. Aileen doesn't want Jimmy to come back north. She sees a great change in him, and can hardly believe he's the same boy. She thinks Dorothy must have been fretting for him on the quiet as they got on really well together in Suffolk. She wants me to thank you for looking after him so well, and will be writing to you herself. I know there are still some of his things with you, but he has plenty of clothes to be going on with, and I will collect the rest when I come up to see you. When this will be I can't say, but I'll be in touch and let you know the exact date.

I would feel guilty about all this, as I know you are very fond of Jimmy, but I can't help realizing how hard it would be for you to have a small boy about the house during your busy season. It wouldn't have been *fair* to leave him with you any longer on top of all you have to do.

I hope Florence's feet healed quickly. I should imagine she has great powers of resilience. She always reminds me somehow of those pioneer Englishwomen who braved storm and flood in new continents, always keeping up standards and flying the flag at all costs. I can't imagine blistered feet will get her down for long.

Do you know I never met your Mr Schofield? I wonder sometimes if he really existed?

327

Dear Daisybell, we have a lot to talk about when I see you again. I promise it will be soon. Just parcel Jimmy's few things up and tuck them out of your way. He seems to be worried about the cat, but Aileen won't budge on that one. They make her sneeze.

I will express my gratitude properly when I see you, but I think you know what it meant to me you accepting Jimmy the way you did. They don't grow them like you very often, Daisybell. You are unique. But then, I've said that before, haven't I?

See you soon.

Yours with love,
Sam

Daisy had left the door of her room half open so that Joshua saw her struggling to dismantle the camp bed.

'It's supposed to *fold*,' she told him. 'The legs come off, then you take these struts out and the whole thing goes flat.'

He jumped at once to the wrong conclusion. 'You're putting Jimmy in Bobbie's room? That's a good idea.' Getting down on his knees he busied himself with the flimsy bed. 'I'd start getting used to the notion that Bobbie won't be coming back here, Daisy. My guess is he'll get six months at least. He's got too much pride not to want to move on after he comes out.' He slid a strut out from the canvas and added it to the pile by his side on the carpet. 'He sends you his love, by the way, but he doesn't want to see you. Couldn't face you, he says.'

'That makes me feel terrible.' To her horror Daisy began to cry. 'Does Bobbie think I'm perfect? That I've never done a mean thing in my life? That I'm so sanctimonious I would be ashamed to be his friend? Is *that* the impression I give? That they don't grow them like me very often? That I am so *unique* I don't have feelings like other people? Is that what he thinks? Because that's the way Sam sees me.' She groped for her handkerchief in the pocket of her morning apron and found instead Sam's letter. 'Here, you might as well read this. There's nothing personal in it.'

The tears were running down her cheeks, but she didn't wipe them away.

'Oh, I know I'm stupid. There was something telling me all the time that Jimmy would have to go away sometime. I couldn't believe that any woman could just give her son away like that.' She accepted Joshua's proffered handkerchief. 'I'd even gone as far as thinking that when Sam and me were married Jimmy would be with us, and in time come to look on me as his mother.' She blew her nose and pushed the handkerchief and the letter back into her pocket.

'You know what's wrong with me, Joshua? I've seen too many films. Up to coming here I used to go three times a week. One week I'd be Joan Crawford, the next Greta Garbo, and the next one after that Barbara Stanwyck. And most times things turned out all right. But they're not going to this time, are they? Thank you for not laughing, Joshua. You're the best friend I've ever had. Do you know that? In spite of being a man.'

She started to fold one of Jimmy's grey school shirts, smoothing the collar and tucking in the sleeves. 'Florence is my friend too, but she's more critical of me than you are. She sees me straight on.'

'And I don't?'

Daisy rolled a striped tie round her fingers. 'You only see me at my *best*.' There was the faintest suspicion of a twinkle in her red-rimmed eyes. 'An' because you're so kind and understanding, I *am* at my best.' She thrust a hand inside a grey knee-sock. 'I'll mend this before I pack it up. Oh, it's all too complicated, but what I think I mean is this: in everybody's life they meet, say, two or three people, sometimes more if they're lucky, people they are *comfortable* with. Real true friends. People they could trust to the ends of the earth.' She examined the second sock carefully. 'I'm so charged with emotion this morning, I couldn't feel worse if I'd drunk three sherries straight down. There was a cloud sitting on my head, an' I couldn't peer my way through it, but it's going. At least it's lifting. It started to lift when I read that letter.'

329

'Sam's letter?' Joshua willed her to carry on.

'Yes, Sam's letter.' Daisy got up from the bed. 'I'd better go back to the kitchen before Winnie collapses under the strain of having to scrape three pounds of carrots.' She turned round at the door. 'Thanks for listening to me, Joshua. I'm always saying that, aren't I?' She hesitated. 'But don't get the wrong idea of me. I've done some flamin' foolish things in my life. Really stupid want-your-head-examining kind of things.'

'Haven't we all?' Joshua said, gathering the dismantled bed together. 'Now tell me where you want me to put this.'

By late afternoon the sky was purple, thick with storm clouds. If the café in the Arcade hadn't been so crowded, the waitresses run off their feet, one of them would have noticed the tall gaunt woman drinking endless cups of tea, shuffling to the Ladies, coming back to change tables and ordering yet another pot of tea. Florence had abandoned her case a long time ago. It had been kicked aside and pushed out of the way by holidaymakers hideous in their bedraggled rainwear, the women with permed hair frizzed by the rain, and the men with raindrops dripping from the nebs of their flat caps.

To Florence every face had a pinched and mean look about it. These people *smelled*. The odour rising from their damp clothing was turning her fastidious stomach. Blackpool itself was ugly; cheap and nasty, stripped of its so-called glamour by the rain cascading from a gun-metal sky. Coming out of the Arcade Florence turned right instead of left. She didn't *choose* to go home yet. There wasn't much left to her really, was there, but freedom of choice? Resolutely she turned her long-suffering face towards the front.

Eight million visitors the resort was reported to have had the year before, and Florence calculated that most of them that afternoon were seeking shelter from the rain along the Golden Mile. On a corner of Brunswick Street a patient queue waited outside a palmist's booth. Florence stopped on the pavement to read the caption:

'Madame Boranev can help you as she has helped others. She will give you sound advice. Come inside and consult her at once! Only one shilling a session.'

Florence joined the queue.

'You know what it's like,' Mrs Mac said, coming in unannounced through the back door to ask Daisy could she possibly lend her such a thing as a cup of arrowroot? 'They never tell you the exact time you're being discharged, then when they do you have to wait around for your take-home medicine. They'll be keeping your friend doped to the eyeballs for a while after a shock like that. Did she ever have St Vitus's Dance as a child? She always looked to me ready to start twitching.'

'Maybe I got the day wrong.' Daisy reached up into a cupboard for the packet of arrowroot. 'She wouldn't let *anyone* go and fetch her. She's so independent she'd run her own shroud up on the sewing machine if she knew exactly when she was going to die.'

'Wouldn't surprise me if she doesn't work *that* out for herself,' Mrs Mac said, pushing the packet behind the bib of her pinny to keep it dry on her way back next door. 'Not that I'm casting aspersions, but your friend has always struck me as being a mite too big for her boots. A round peg in a square hole, if you get my meaning.'

Florence emerged from the palmist's booth muttering to herself. 'A tall dark man? Marriage within the year, followed by two children? Dear God, it would be funny if it wasn't so hopelessly untrue.'

Because she couldn't help seeing the humour in it, she laughed aloud as she joined the queue outside the peep-show next door. Admission twopence for the privilege of seeing 'Colonel Barker and his Bride on a Strange Honeymoon'.

They were displayed down in a pit, the army officer and his bride, with the crowds moving slowly round the top, staring down at the two beds separated by a pedestrian crossing embellished by orange Belisha beacons.

'A crude attempt at sexual innuendo,' Florence told a girl in front of her with tinselly fair hair and two red rings of rouge high on her cheek-bones.

'Potty,' the girl told her friend, a large girl with a laugh like a rasp-throated seagull. 'Take no notice.'

In one of the beds the fat Colonel lay in his nightshirt; in the other a very young girl in a chiffon nightie, showing thighs blue with cold, a large Dalmatian dog by her side. Florence spotted a bottle of whisky under the bridegroom's bed.

'Fancy lying there doing nowt for twelve hours a day.' The fair-haired girl leaned dangerously over the flimsy railing. 'They say the Colonel's a woman.'

'That's why they lie there doing nowt then,' her bosom friend said. 'What a rotten two-pennorth!'

'Can't you see the awful tragedy in it all?' Florence rounded on them in anger. 'Misery acquaints a man with strange bed-fellows. Shakespeare saw it all!'

'She should be put away.'

'Probably an escaped loony.'

The bosom friends hurried away, into an arcade of slot machines, where for an outlay of threepence between them they won a fourpenny packet of Player's Weights, a twopenny bar of Nestlés chocolate and a pocket mirror. Making their day.

'The first thing I'm going to do when I see I'm on the way to making me pile is to have a telephone installed,' Daisy informed Mrs Mac when she returned the cup of arrowroot later that afternoon. 'I could have rung the hospital by now to find out about Florence, or she could have rung me to say what time to expect her. As it is I don't even know whether I've got the right day. I'd run out to the phone box at the end of the street but Winnie says it's not working.'

'Hoodlums from the caravan sites,' Mrs Mac said. 'Rampaging back from the pubs at closing time. Angus says the corporation should step in to have those caravans taken away. It's no wonder the owners of those sites can charge less than what we do. They've got far lower overheads. *Our* living is precarious enough as it is. Though you have to say one thing in favour of the Depression.'

'What's that?'

'Well, all those folks who had started fancying going down south and even abroad for their holidays have settled back for Blackpool. Angus says there's going to be another war, and if he's right it'll be like the last time all over again.' She eased her considerable bulk down on to a chair. 'Angus's mother had a lodging-house up by the station during the last war. She had servicemen billeted on her from the beginning. She got three and fourpence a day for each man, but being a good manager she fed them well on one and sixpence a day. Her sister down Bispham way wasn't so lucky. *She* had Belgian refugees plonked on her and only got ten shillings a *week* for them. But her other sister over in the Isle of Man came off worst. They stopped the steamers going over, you see.'

'Those two ladies in number four have asked for a tray of tea in their bedroom.' Winnie's face round the door was stiff with disapproval. 'Why can't they have it in the lounge with all the rest?'

'You should start off the way you mean to go on.' Mrs Mac waited until Winnie had left the kitchen, stoop-shouldered from the weight of two cups and saucers, a small teapot and a tiny milk-jug and sugar-basin. 'I don't stop my lot from coming in out of the rain, but I don't provide tea. You try putting it down as extras on their bills and see where that gets you.'

Daisy, who had every intention of starting as she meant to go on and no intention at all of charging for the odd cup of tea, believing firmly that hers was the way to make sure her visitors came back the next year, said nothing.

'Owt to do with the last war,' Mrs Mac continued, picking up the threads, 'and Angus can remember it clear as a bell.

Ask him to fetch four things from the shops and he'll forget two of them.'

'Does he really think there's going to be another war?' Daisy looked alarmed. 'The local paper is full of nothing else but the arrangements for the Coronation celebrations in May.'

'Angus's niece went over to Germany last summer.' Mrs Mac drew her chair closer in to the table and lowered her voice dramatically as if she suspected the house could be teeming with spies. 'She is half-cousin to one of those Hitler Youth, a German girl from Berlin. Not, I might add, related on Angus's side. No, there's nothing like that in *his* family – where was I? Oh, yes. This niece came back from Germany with tales of hundreds and thousands of young men and women marching, drilling and singing war songs, going away for weeks at a time to these summer camps. Living like *soldiers!* Disciplined soldiers, not hoodlums like those from our holiday camps, running the streets and breaking telephones just for the fun of it.' She got laboriously to her feet. 'Well, you've detained me for long enough, Miss Bell, interesting though I always find your conversation to be.' She sniffed appreciatively. 'Something smells good. What's on the menu for tonight?'

'Savoury meat roll with thick gravy, served with roasted potatoes and carrots chopped fine with butter, followed by treacle sponge pudding and custard. Florence's favourites,' Daisy said. 'Though I doubt if she's coming out today. I'll ask Winnie if she can stay on for an hour tonight and try and get to the hospital and back to find out for myself.'

'They won't let you in out of visiting hours,' Mrs Mac said, longing to ask Daisy whether she used short or flaky pastry for the savoury roll, but pride forbidding. 'The prisoners in Sing-Sing get more freedom than the patients do in that hospital. If your friend didn't go in with a nervous breakdown she'll be having one by the time she comes out. That's if her blisters haven't turned septic, which wouldn't surprise me. There's a Sister up there who wouldn't bat an eyelid if a patient's feet dropped off with gangrene, as long as the sheets on her bed were mitred proper at the corners.'

Is it any wonder I love you, Mrs Mac, Daisy thought, when you cheer me up so much?

Florence had no clear recollection of how she had got on to the pier, but there she was, sitting in a shelter facing a watery sun next to a couple who were fast asleep leaning on each other, with a tartan car rug tucked in round their legs and their mouths wide open snoring in rhythm together.

She was damp, but not too wet, though the dressings on her feet were showing wet-black through her stockings, and the soles of the flimsy house slippers felt like soggy cardboard. If she leaned forward round the corner of the shelter she could see the dancing going on now the rain had stopped. Women mainly, dancing together, wearing hats and coats or their best costumes and court shoes, their handbags looped neatly over the gloved hands on their partners' shoulders. Gliding and turning on the boards of the pier, just as if it were the sprung floor of a proper ballroom.

'Pathetic,' Florence muttered, leaning her head back and feeling the sun warm on her closed eyelids.

Had she dreamed it or had she really stood on the jetty at the far end of the pier looking down into the sea and trying to find the courage to jump in and put an end to it all? Moving back when the height made her head reel, feeling her stomach come up into her mouth the way it had when she stood with Daisy on the Tower platform on a similar rain-swept day not all that long ago. The way it had done just the same on a hot summer's day, when she had stared down into the Delph trying to nerve herself to throw herself in.

What came over her when these black dogs of depression settled on her shoulders? Because that was all they were. Moods. Dark satanic moods over which she had no control. 'Bound in shallows and in miseries' as the Bard had said. She never *really* intended to make an end of it all. Life, in spite of all its vicissitudes, was too precious to be thrown away. A great wodge of uncharacteristic sentimentality settled on her, filling her chest, swelling her heart, so that the music from the pier dance band, the sinking sun setting the frill-trimmed waves of the receding tide dancing, merged and mingled. Her pale eyes filled with tears.

A string of fairy lights came on, lending fresh enchantment. Florence squared her shoulders. Her life wasn't over because a man had refused to fall in love with her. Joshua Penny would be moving on. He had hinted as much to her once or twice. But the flarchy rotter wouldn't marry Daisy. He would go back to his wife, as all flarchy rotters did in the end.

Daisy would need her then. Florence felt herself being stared at by the couple under the tartan rug. Wanting the shelter to themselves, she guessed, but hard cheese on them. . . . Had she really at times hated Daisy so much, *envied* her so much that she wished her dead? It was all the fault somehow of that young doctor in the hospital, sitting on her bed late at night, using his psychology on her and trying to make her talk about her childhood. Hatred, fear, insecurity, *anger*, all bound up somehow in her childhood. Florence closed her eyes as the couple folded the rug and moved away, leaving her alone.

Why had she been in the habit of sleeping with her mother in those far off pre-school days? With her father banished to the back room? She had been too young to be able to know why, but she remembered her own bewilderment and the terror, and the look on her mother's face as she hugged the young Florence close to the clean washed smell of her flowered cotton pinny.

She remembered too a flight of dark narrow stairs – stumbling down them in her nightie, calling out for her mammy. She must have been very young to still be saying mammy. And after the comforting rocking in the chair by the fire, being laid to sleep on the horsehair sofa that pricked the backs of her legs. Waking to hear the dreadful shouting coming from upstairs, made all the more terrible because her mother, mild of voice and manner, never shouted.

The banishment of her father to the back room, and Florence taking his place in her mother's bed seemed to date from then, a situation that didn't change until she was eleven or twelve years old, when she moved back into her own room and her father went back with her mother to share her room, but not her bed.

How *dare* that young doctor try to intrude on her privacy? She had *refused* to remember. She didn't *want* to remember. More harm than good came from remembering. . . .

'Now I must go home,' Florence said aloud.

In the winter when she had finished being nice to the visitors for Daisy's sake, when she had changed their sheets, wiped round their wash basins, hung their face flannels up to dry, rushed from kitchen to dining room with endless meals, emptied ashtrays, smiled till her face cracked at badly behaved children who needed their bottoms smacking, in the winter, when things were slacker, she would find a job. Part-time possibly, so she could go to night school in the evenings. English literature and social history. Those would be her subjects. She might even go the whole hog and be a mature student studying for a very belated Matriculation Certificate.

The future was full of possibilities. It always had been if there hadn't always been something holding her back. She came out on to the promenade with her slow imperious shuffling walk. On the way back home she would call in at the café in the Arcade and retrieve her case. That was if it was still there. She didn't much care if it had disappeared, there wasn't anything in it of value. And if there had been, what were material things anyway?

Daisy would be so surprised to see her. 'You are *impossible*, Florence Livesey!' she would say. Then she would put the kettle on and sit Florence down and tut-tut over her ruined slippers, and the kitchen would be warm and smelling of baking and roasting, and in no time at all they would be drinking tea together. It would be just the two of them, the way it was meant to be.

Daisy was her friend. Daisy was her family. Joshua would move on and the flarchy rotter would go back to his wife. It had all been written somewhere in the mists of time.

Florence waited impatiently to cross the road. She made one attempt, then to be on the safe side stood back as a bus lumbered past. Looking right, then left, then right again, she let a powerful-looking car whizz by....

And misjudged entirely the speed of an oncoming two-seater, impudently tooting as it overtook a lumbering taxi.

Giving the young driver no chance at all to avoid her as she seemed to step right in front of him before disappearing beneath the wheels of his sports car with its souped-up engine, its fancy cigarette lighter and its leather steering wheel.

Chapter Nine

Purely by coincidence the young doctor was on duty in Casualty when they wheeled Florence in. She had stopped breathing in the ambulance on the way to the hospital but he went through the motions, listening through his stethoscope for a heartbeat he knew was silenced for ever.

He wasn't surprised. He had diagnosed Miss Livesey as an hysteric from the start. She had refused to talk to him. She had set those thin lips of hers into a straight line, even turned her head rudely away when he had tried to help her. A waste of what could have been a good and productive life, but this patient's life had been programmed for disaster since her childhood. The coroner's verdict would be clear-cut. 'While of unsound mind....'

'Ring for them to take her downstairs,' he told the nurse, as she drew up the sheet to cover Florence's face. 'Don't suppose she gave a thought to the poor devil driving the car.'

Joshua, on his way out to post a letter, pulled the door to behind him when he saw the two policemen getting out of their car.

He lived there, he told them quickly. If it was bad news about Mr Schofield he'd rather be there when Miss Bell was told. No, he wasn't a relative, just a very good friend. It *was* about Mr Schofield, wasn't it?

The kitchen was in its usual late-afternoon state of what

339

Daisy called organized chaos. She turned a flushed and smiling face as Joshua came in and closed the door behind him.

'There's no word from the hospital, Joshua.' Lifting a pan lid she prodded the contents with a fork. 'I'm going up there as soon as the clearing away is finished. I need to know what's going on.'

'Daisy?'

'Yes?' One swift glance at his face and she knew something was dreadfully wrong.

'It's Florence, love.' His eyes were filled with pain for her.

'She's coming home tomorrow. I know it will be tomorrow, Joshua.'

He forced himself to say the words: 'Florence won't be coming home tomorrow. She . . . oh, God, I can't think of any other way to tell you. She's dead, Daisy. There are two policemen in the hall waiting to tell you about it.'

'How can she be dead?' Daisy's voice came out as a loud angry wail. 'I've never heard of anything so daft in me whole life. She isn't even ill! Someone has lied. Got names mixed up or something. It happens. . . . It's not true! I won't believe it!' When he tried to take her in his arms she pushed him away with the flats of her hands. 'You're making me mad, Joshua! I haven't got time to talk to anybody. . . . Tell them to go away!'

Joshua gripped her by the shoulders, forcing her to look at him. And wanted to die himself when he saw the agonized bewilderment in her eyes. 'Florence came out of hospital late this morning. She must have walked about for hours, then this afternoon she walked straight out into the road in front of a car. Deliberately. Without looking, the driver said. He's a very young man apparently, badly shaken up. There was nothing he could do to avoid her.'

'I see.'

Winnie came through the door to see what was going on. Policemen meant trouble, she knew that much.

'Florence is dead, Winnie.' Daisy's voice was flat. 'I am

340

going upstairs for a little while. Keep your eye on the pans for me, please.'

She walked out of the kitchen, past the two policemen standing awkwardly in the hall, brushing past them as if they weren't there. It seemed to her that someone was weeping noisily, but it couldn't be her. She would never dream of making a noise like that.

Winnie stood there with her mouth open trying not to be glad. There was only one place for you if you were wicked enough to think evil thoughts like that. Hell, with its flaming Lake of Fire. She shuddered. Poor Miss Bell. Making that awful moaning sound, with the Margerisons from Bolton coming in through the front door and wondering what on earth was going on. Mr Penny had explained it nicely. He had talked to the policemen, too, and they had gone away after whispering together for a few seconds.

Winnie turned down a gas jet beneath a bubbling pan. She couldn't be expected to feel *heartbroken*, could she, when she'd never even met Miss Livesey? Mrs Mac had told Winnie's mother that Miss Livesey was a bit too lah-di-dah for her liking. Fancied herself too much. If she wasn't coming back, then her room would be free. The wicked thoughts were intruding again.

Miss Bell might ask for Winnie to live in. In this lovely house with its carpets and two inside toilets. Jessie was fourteen now and left school. Let *her* take over looking after the kids at home. She'd always had more patience with them, anyroad.

Winnie raised pious eyes ceilingwards. 'I'm not really rejoicing, God. Just finding it hard not to be a little bit glad. We're such a good team, me and Miss Bell. She says so every day. It would be a shame to split us up now.'

Be hanged to sensitivity. Joshua ran upstairs to find Daisy. If she was in trouble he had to be there. There was simply no way he could help himself. He found her behind the door in

Florence's room, sobbing quietly now into the blanket roughness of Florence's old brown dressing-gown. This time, when he pulled her into his arms, she came unresisting.

'She tried to do it once before, Joshua. Her father had shouted at her and disgusted her. He seemed to have the power to disgust her. But I thought she'd put all that behind her. She was happy most of the time. Not *all* the time, but then nobody's happy all the time, are they? She loathed housework, you see, even though she liked things to be clean and tidy. She was a *contradiction*, Joshua.'

'Not knowing what she wanted, but knowing it should be something better.' Joshua remembered Florence's face that first day in the hospital when she had talked about Daisy as if she hated her. 'And sometimes not being able to accept other people's happiness,' he said softly.

'But none of those things add up to being bad enough to make her want to take her own life.' Daisy raised a tear-stained face. 'She must have been desperately unhappy to do a terrible thing like that. I can't believe it. She drew back at the last minute the other time, Joshua, and I knew then that in spite of all her black moods Florence's common sense never really deserted her. I *knew* her!'

She was growing calmer by the minute. The frozen mask of shock had gone from her face. Joshua wondered why he had been afraid that she might collapse or have to be put to bed under sedation. So many things were going wrong for her.

She wiped her eyes and asked him did she look too awful? 'I'll just splash my eyes with cold water in the bathroom on the way down,' she said. 'Then I must go and rescue Winnie.' She laid a hand gently against his cheek. 'Thank you for being so kind to me, Joshua. I don't know what I'd do without you.'

'You *never* need to do without me,' he said at once, but she was already on her way down the first flight of stairs to bathe her tears away and get on with what she had to do.

But Daisy *didn't* know Florence. *Hadn't* known Florence.

Joshua went into his own room. He had seen the dark side of Daisy's friend that afternoon in the hospital, seen her face contorted with rage and envy. She had told him that Daisy had spent the night with Sam, then watched his face to test his reaction. Tormented by rage, frustration and pain, she had done that.

Joshua picked up a hairbrush and smoothed back the sides of his thick brown hair. He narrowed his eyes at his reflection.

'Oh, no, Daisy. You didn't know Florence. You might think you did, but you were wrong.' The brush was stilled in his hand. 'But *I* knew her. After that revealing outburst I knew her very well. She couldn't bear to think of you with a man.' He threw the brush down. 'And in your blessed innocence you never suspected the inference of that for a minute, did you, Daisy, love?'

Edna didn't bat as much as an eyelid when she heard. She told Arnold that Florrie Livesey was neurotical. Hadn't her mother been the same, scrubbing her flags till you felt you ought to step out in the road rather than walk on them? She was sweet on that lodger on the top floor, you know, the one in prison for stealing and thumping policemen. She'd gone dancing with him, and now she couldn't bear the shame. How did she know he'd been arrested? Well, of *course* she knew. It wasn't the sort of thing Daisy or that nice Mr Penny would keep to themselves when they visited her in hospital, now was it? It was all right for Arnold sticking up for her. He didn't see her walking the streets last summer with her nightie sticking out from beneath her coat. He didn't hear the mucky thoughts coming out of her mouth about her father, either. They were all the same, the Florrie Liveseys of this world. Sanctimonious on the outside, run a mile if they were involved in as much as a breath of scandal, yet underneath as depraved as the rest. Oh, yes, she'd had Miss Livesey weighed up right from the start. Bad blood would out in the end.

*

Arnold couldn't quite make it all out. He had *liked* Florence. He would never forget the day he had seen her staggering down the hill leaning on Daisy. Something had told him she had never meant to do away with herself. More a cry for help, he would have said. And he couldn't understand her choosing such a horrible way to end it all. Too messy and undignified for Florence. No, there was definitely something wrong somewhere, if only he could put a finger on it. He had a feeling Florence was being misunderstood right to the very end.

The boy driving the car lay on his bed at home going over and over it in his mind. He had been going too fast. He had pulled out to overtake. The woman had appeared out of the blue and there had been nothing he could do. It wasn't his fault. There weren't any actual witnesses, but his parents kept on reassuring him that it wasn't his fault. The woman had been seen behaving strangely, walking about with bandaged feet in over-large slippers in the pouring rain for hours. She had been in hospital, the police had said, and apparently there was more to come out. They more or less *told* him to try not to take it too much to heart. Someone commits suicide every minute of every day, they had said.

He put an arm across his face to hide the sting of tears behind his eyelids. So why wouldn't the look of horror on the poor woman's face in that split moment of sickening impact fade from his mind? Why was he convinced she had tried to step *back* when it was too late? And why didn't he go downstairs now and tell his father about it? Why was he so sure he would *never* tell anyone about it? Ever. Ever.

Because he wasn't *sure*. How could you be sure about a thing that had happened so quickly? And if you weren't sure, wasn't the best thing to keep quiet? For ever.

But what a thing to happen on his eighteenth birthday. There was such a mist in front of his eyes he could no longer see the bust of Molière he had won for French speaking at school last term on his tallboy by the far wall.

Dear Daisy,

Your letter really shocked me, but I have to say right away that I'm not surprised. Florence was *unstable*. The way she used to look at me at times gave me the creeps. I have to say this, because I know that you will be blaming yourself for not realizing just how unbalanced she was. I'm sure you'll be glad that Jimmy was well away before it happened. He keeps mentioning you, calling his mother Daisy when he forgets, but he's settled back at home as though he'd never been away. Kids are far more adaptable than we give them credit for.

Knowing you, I expect you will be coping. Perhaps you've asked your aunt to stay on with you for a while? She's hated my guts since she first set eyes on me, and who can blame her?

It's no good, Daisybell. There is so much more I would like to say to you and yet when I try to write it down it comes out like a school composition. I'm far better at writing technical reports. By the way, my last examination results were excellent. I have now got my Higher National Certificate in Mechanical Engineering, which means I can start looking round for a job that fits in with my qualifications.

This brings me to what I intended to say right at the beginning of this letter. I will be coming up to collect the rest of Jimmy's things and to see you in roughly two weeks' time. I can't tell you the exact date, but it will be over a weekend. We have a lot to talk about, Daisybell.

Yours,

Sam

P.S. Don't be too sad. I couldn't bear that.

'What hurts the most is the way everyone seems to have written Florence off. As though they were just waiting for her to jump off the end of the pier or step into the road without looking.'

Joshua knew Daisy was referring to something in the letter

345

she held in her hand. He had picked it up himself from the mat, noting the London postmark. 'Did Sam say why he didn't come to the funeral?'

'I never expected him to,' she said, so quickly he knew she was lying.

The funeral had been bleak and terrible, with Florence's father telling everyone that his daughter had merely gone through a door to live with Jesus, and Daisy so overwrought she felt overwhelmingly grateful for the feel of Joshua's arm around her. She had dried her eyes, gone back to cooking a dinner for thirteen, and agreed with Uncle Arnold, who had made the journey to Blackpool on his own, that life must go on.

'You're not one for chucking the towel in, lass,' he had said, then he had caught his train to be back in time for his tea, still shaking his grizzled head at the mystery of it all. It was like a jigsaw puzzle with one piece missing, he told himself. Everything slotting into place nice and easy, but not making a complete picture. He had carefully avoided getting into the same compartment as Florence's father. 'If he thinks he's going to convert me between here and where we change at Preston he's got another think coming,' he had muttered, lighting a Woodbine and hiding behind his copy of the *Daily Herald*.

'Sam is coming up in a couple of weeks, as a matter of fact.' Daisy walked behind Joshua to the front door. 'To collect the rest of Jimmy's things. And to see me, of course.'

'Of course.' Joshua picked up his case and opened the door. As he always did, he raised his hat to Daisy before walking quickly down the street to the station to catch his train. She had got into the habit of seeing him off in the mornings, handing him his brown trilby and reminding him to wear his scarf if the weather had turned unseasonable.

Winnie as usual missed nothing. 'If you have to get married, why don't you marry Mr Penny instead of that London chap? He's divorced, isn't he?'

'Who told you that?'

It was no use getting on her high horse with Winnie. Daisy accepted that Winnie had no finer feelings. If Winnie wanted to know then Winnie asked. She never took umbrage, never sulked. Since moving into Florence's room she had sung her way round the house, polished the gleaming new taps of the wash basins in the bedrooms, whipped pillow-cases on and off, frightened the lives out of sleeping holidaymakers as she clattered into their rooms with the early-morning tea, flinging the curtains back with a flourish, her red hair standing on end with enthusiasm.

'Mrs Chadwick in the front double wears *French* knickers, though she must be forty if she's a day! Talk about mutton dressed as lamb. That little fat man from Darwen hangs his hair on the bedpost when he goes to bed. That young girl in the small back room sleeps in a *brassiere*, would you believe it, not that I blame her with bosoms like hers. I don't know where they would end up if she didn't keep 'em jacked up.'

She paused for a moment in her brisk beating of the eggs which were to go to table scrambled that morning. 'Mrs Mac told me mam that your London chap is divorced. They're always pumping me to find out what's going on here.'

'Well, there's been plenty going on lately, hasn't there, love?' Daisy poured boiling water over a dish of Canary tomatoes to prepare them for skinning. 'I think most of those booking to come back in July must be making sure they don't miss the next instalment.'

Winnie took Daisy's every utterance quite literally. 'Oh, I think they like the food as well,' she comforted, frothing the eggs over the sides of the basin in her enthusiasm.

Work was Daisy's comfort and lifeline. Hard work and cooking. But it had always been so, she realized. No glamour, just a day-to-day slog, smiling at the visitors instead of the customers in the pie shop, getting up early, not to see to the boiler but to light the gas fire in the lounge, empty the ashtrays and open the window.

Word had got round, and most weeks she was fully

347

booked. Hopeful couples knocked at the door on spec, slept one night then wanted to stay on. Daisy developed her own style of cooking, based on her knowledge of what tired workers coming home hungry liked – big helpings of unpretentious meals, avoiding extravagant delicacies which they couldn't afford at home anyway. Which would have been immediately suspect in any case. Fish, fresh from Fleetwood, was on the menu at least twice a week. Fish pie, Joshua's favourite meal, was easy to prepare. Smoked cod, coley fillets, peeled prawns, mushrooms, potatoes and cheese, butter and milk. All the ingredients were ready to hand on the kitchen table when the door-bell rang.

It was the early-afternoon lull in a landlady's long and busy day. A spring-lit day, so warm that Winnie had gone off to see her mother wearing a knitted cardigan over a pink and white gingham dress. Daisy hadn't the heart to tell her that the high round neck of a woollen vest was showing, or that the Evening in Paris scent she had doused herself with was enough to strip the bark off a tree at three paces. Winnie was so happy these days, so *keen*, so exuberant, she almost gave off sparks as she dashed round the house.

'By gum, but yon lass is a worker,' the last departing visitor had said, and no fewer than three families had mentioned her in the visitors' book in the hall.

'Like being mentioned in dispatches,' Joshua had said, showing her the written comments, pleased as punch for her.

Joshua was biding his time. Daisy was in no way her normal ebullient self since Florence's death; her smile was there, but it had a frayed-at-the-edges look about it. She had stopped talking about Sam altogether. Once Joshua had mentioned his name and she had flinched away as though the very sound of it upset her. He was coming to see her, she had said, and on that visit Joshua pinned all his hopes and his fears. Much more sophisticated than Winnie in his thinking, he didn't exactly pray that Sam would drop off the nearest precipice, but he was ready metaphorically holding out the blanket of his love for Daisy if needed.

Daisy was wiping her hands on her apron as she opened the front door.

'Yes? Can I help you?' Her smile was warm, tinged with genuine regret as she pointed out the NO VACANCIES sign in the window. 'If you want a room for this week I'm sorry but I'm fully booked. Next week I could manage to fit you in . . .'

The woman was slim-built, taller than Daisy, smart without being a fashion-plate. Thin, by Daisy's yardstick, with white-blonde hair on which a powder-blue halo hat sat precariously. Her blue speckled tweed suit had a three-quarter coat and calf-length skirt, and the leather case she carried matched her gauntlet gloves and brown court shoes.

'Miss Bell? Miss *Daisy* Bell?' She seemed half amused by the supposition, but the little half smile did not touch her eyes. 'Do you think I could come inside? The wind's a lot fresher up here than it is down in London. I should have worn a top coat I suppose. I'm Aileen Barnet. Sam's wife.'

It was no good Daisy trying to control the blush. Blushing had always been her downfall. She felt it suffuse her face with colour as the shock sent pricking sensations down her spine.

'Please come in.'

Her voice, even to her own ears, sounded high-pitched. She led the way into the lounge, whipping off her apron as she went. Oh, dear God, it had happened, just the way her mother had prophesied it would right from the beginning. 'His wife will come up and smack your face,' she had said, 'because she'll find out about you. They always do.'

'Please sit down,' she said, sending up a fervent prayer of thanks that the house was empty of visitors for the time being with the weather being so unseasonable and everyone taking advantage. Then she sat down herself before her legs gave way beneath her.

'Thank you.' Aileen Barnet crossed slim ankles. 'Do you mind if I smoke?'

God alone knew why she was nervous, but she was. So *this* was the Daisy young Jimmy brought into the conversation so much. 'Daisy said that, Daisy did things this way. Daisy made chips better than shop chips, Daisy cut his hair, Daisy put *expression* in when she read to him.' Aileen lit a cigarette, narrowing her eyes against the upcurl of smoke. So *this* was the Daisy Sam had described as being a typical old maid. Homely, with glasses, motherly and kind.

'I must say you're not a bit like I expected you to be,' she said.

'Oh. Am I not? *Aren't I?*' Daisy's mind was racing ahead. If this were a film she would be in total command of the situation, smoking a cigarette like Sam's wife, flicking the ash .at the cream tiles of the new fireplace, cool as a cucumber, finding out how much this woman knew, telling her in a husky voice that the first thing they must do was to be *civilized* about the whole thing.

'No, you're not.' Aileen had come prepared to be pitying; now she felt anger building up inside her. Sam had lied to her. Lied by inference, but lied all the same. Daisy Bell was lovely. Even smelling of fish, and without make-up, there was a freshness about her, an *innocence* that was in no way a naïvety. Put her in a white bonnet with the strings blowing in the wind and she was the Ovaltine Girl from the advertisement. Beside her Aileen felt over made-up, over-dressed and, let's face it, bloody middle-aged.

'I'll go upstairs and get Jimmy's things.' Daisy was so agitated she hardly knew what she was saying or doing. 'How is he? I miss him a lot.' Oh, God, should she have said that? Oh, why hadn't Sam put her in the picture more so she would know what to talk about, how much to give away?

'When I thought I was going to Canada,' Aileen was saying in that plum-in-the-mouth accent so like Sam's, 'it seemed the best thing for him to stay in this country. Schooling and everything, you know. We can't thank you enough for fostering him for us at a difficult time.' She was staring straight at Daisy, stubbing out the cigarette, taking another from the packet with a black cat on the front.

'That's all right.' If Daisy didn't escape from the room her

350

expression would give the game away. *Fostering* Jimmy? When this pretty woman with the young-old face *thought* she was going to Canada? She ran upstairs so quickly she almost tripped and fell, and once in her room took the brown paper parcel with Jimmy's things in it from the top of her wardrobe to stand holding it to her, feeling her heart beating wildly. She would never forgive Sam for this. She put a hand over her mouth. If indeed he *knew* that his wife was here. The case Aileen had with her was empty – Daisy had kicked it aside accidentally as she left the room. So she really had come for Jimmy's things. Perhaps that was all? *Could* that be all?

All at once an upsurge of fury caught her unawares. What did she think she was? A cringing door-mat? Was she going to let Aileen Barnet go away without knowing whether Sam had sent her or not? Was she going to wait for the next non-committal letter, telling her nothing, promising a visit which would or would not materialize? She had always liked things clear, always wanted an honest and straightforward explanation for everything. Why had Sam sent his wife instead of coming himself? Did Sam even *know* that his wife was here? Well, there was only one way to find that out. Still clutching the parcel to her chest, she ran down the stairs.

'Are you going back to London straight away, Mrs Barnet?' Surely that was a harmless enough question.

'Oh, no. I haven't come from London. We're based in your home town all week. Sam left me there for a few days while he drives his boss and the mill bloke up to Scotland. The children are being looked after by a friend with two of her own, roughly the same age and at the same school, so it isn't much of a problem for her. She knows I'll do the same for her any time.'

It was hard to take in. And yet at the same time it was only the confirmation of what Daisy had vaguely suspected for a long time now. Aileen Barnet wasn't going to marry again and go to live in Canada. Somewhere along the line that affair had petered out. She and Sam were living together again. There wasn't going to be a divorce. Maybe there was *never* going to be a divorce. Sam would never write and tell her he had found a better job, never come up and insist she sell the boarding-house, or hand it over to Florence. How could he when Florence was dead? How could any of that happen when he had been lying to her all the time, *using* her, persuading her to go into his room in her nightie and climb into bed with him.

It was no good, she couldn't cope with it. Her thoughts spun out of control as the guilt flooded through her. How could she stay here in the same room as Sam's wife when she had got into bed with her husband in the middle of the night and almost let him have his way with her? She could have cried aloud with the shame of it all. She had no idea how her face mirrored her thoughts. Unaware that Sam's wife was reading her like an open book.

'You're not the first one, you know.' Aileen drew deeply on her cigarette. 'Not by a long chalk, oh dear me, no.' She cocked her neat little head to one side. 'Different though. Not Sam's usual type. He likes his women a bit younger usually. Younger and harder, not still damp behind the ears.'

'There was nothing....' Daisy had the overwhelming guilt still on her. It was choking her, forcing her to explain, not to let herself be seen as a... what was it Jimmy had said?... a fancy-piece. 'We never....' Her voice trailed away in distress.

'Really? That's not like Sam.' Aileen's arched and plucked eyebrows ascended almost to her fluffy hairline. 'Are you thinking you love him, Miss Bell? Did he promise to marry you when our divorce came through? Yes, I see he did.' She tut-tutted as if she found the whole thing mildly irritating. 'Two years ago one of his little paramours actually turned up on the doorstep with her case packed, ready to move in with him. She didn't bargain on seeing his wife open the door. Please do something with that cat. It's making me sneeze.'

It was Aileen's apparent lack of concern that did it. If she had cried or looked miserable Daisy would have held her tongue, but to see her sitting there puffing on her third cigarette, missing the ashtray more often than not . . . well, as Daisy's own mother would have said, it was more than flesh and blood could stand.

'Yes, Mrs Barnet, I *was* thinking I loved your husband. Notice I said *was* thinking, Mrs Barnet. I haven't had much experience in loving a man, but to my mind love is a bit like a plant – if it's not watered and fed it wilts and dies.' She lifted her chin and raised her voice. 'I've been that carried away I haven't known what I've been doing. Making excuses for him, *understanding* him, making a door-mat of meself just for the sake of a smile from him.' She put up a hand. 'No, don't speak yet. Let me finish. You've nothing to worry about. You're getting him back as good as new. Because you *are* having him back, aren't you?' She dashed a hand across her eyes. 'I can understand you having a bit of a fling yourself after what you've told me, but what about Jimmy? How could you do what you did? You didn't know where he was going, you had no idea what I was like. Suppose I'd been cruel to him? Would you have even cared?' Tears were pricking behind her eyes. 'Because *I* cared about him, Mrs Barnet. Would you like a proper laugh? I'd even gone as far as imagining that Sam and me might adopt him legally when we were married. Jimmy was *ill* while he was here, proper ill. He might have died. An' he needed you. He kept calling for you when the fever was on him. I can understand you playing the old tit-for-tat with Sam, but I'll never see how you could let your child go to a stranger like that.'

'You're a bit of a hypocrite, aren't you, Miss Bell?' Aileen ground out her cigarette. 'Telling me one minute how carried away you were yourself. You don't think you're the only woman to make a fool of herself over a man who wasn't worth it, do you?' She started to take another cigarette from the packet, then pushed it back into her handbag. 'I would have laid down and died for David.'

'David?'

'The bloke I was supposed to be going to Canada with. I loved him so much it was as though another person lived in

353

my skin. Jimmy was awful to him, and Jimmy can be hard work when he sets himself to be awkward. He got on my nerves so much I was making myself ill. David couldn't stand him, and to say that Jimmy couldn't stand David would be the understatement of the year.' She spread her hands wide. 'So I took him to his father, they'd always been as thick as thieves anyway, and the next I knew Sam had fostered him out with friends. Two maiden ladies with a lodging-house by the sea, he told me, just for the time being till he finished with his exams and could move out of that grotty room over Mr Evison's garage.' She took off her hat and placed it on the settee cushions beside her. 'Sam was biding his time, that's all. He suspected that David had no intention of marrying me and starting off with a ready-made family in Canada. It takes one to know one, Miss Bell.'

Daisy said nothing. She was staring at the wide black parting revealed when Aileen Barnet lowered her head. Like a dirty stripe at least an inch wide. It made Sam's wife more human somehow, vulnerable. More of an ally. More like a *friend*.

'Seems we've both been a couple of pie-cans,' she said at last.

'Pie-cans?' Aileen raised a bleak face.

'Lancashire for silly buggers,' Daisy said deliberately, wanting to shock a smile out of the unhappy woman now lighting yet another cigarette. 'Stay where you are and I'll bring you a cup of tea.'

'So that's that,' Daisy told Joshua later that evening after Winnie had gone to bed. She had spared him what she thought of as the sordid details, telling him that Sam wouldn't be coming up again, that his wife wasn't going to divorce him, and that when he found a better job, as she was sure he would, Sam and his wife were going to try and make a go of it.

She was very matter-of-fact as she spoke. Brisk, no nonsense, almost as if it had been a foregone conclusion. 'You know, I could have *liked* her, Joshua. Her hair needed touching up, but apart from that she was really quite pretty.'

'So now what are you going to do?' There was a singing in Joshua's head, but he wasn't going to listen to it, not yet. In spite of Daisy's flippancy he had known something was wrong the minute he came into the house, and known equally she would tell him about it at the first opportunity. He was her best friend now that Florence was dead; probably she had thought of him as that for a long time *before* Florence did what she did. He was Daisy's confidant, her sounding board. Good old Joshua, always there, forever reliable, a friend in need and a friend indeed. What more could he ask?

Suddenly he knew there was a lot more he could ask. His instinct should have warned him it was too soon, the wrong moment, but he was impetuous, eager, a man in love, and he had bided his time for too long.

'I could give up,' Daisy was saying, 'or I could carry on. I could tell myself that losing Sam, Florence dying – I could tell myself it was all too much for me to bear.' She tucked the wayward strand of hair behind an ear. 'Or I could put up a fight. I could remind myself that we are like animals, you know, the law of the jungle, kill or be killed. I could, for the time being, till the hurt goes away a little, live one day at a time, not looking to the future too much. The way I think you do, Joshua.' Her smile almost broke his heart. 'At least I've got your friendship to keep me going. You should be called Peter, really. You know, Peter, the rock.'

The long day had drained the strength from her, but with only that red-haired flighty child to help her he knew she would get up the next morning and carry on. Beds would be made, meals prepared with care, families would come and go, determined to enjoy themselves whether it rained, blew a gale or even snowed. From the lounge a loud burst of laughter reminded Joshua that they were far from alone.

'You could always marry me,' he said, timing it wrong, saying it clumsily, smiling when he should have looked serious. In his eagerness there was even the hint of a swagger in his voice.

'Yes, there's always that possibility.' Daisy laughed into

his eyes. 'I might consider it too if it wouldn't be too much like marrying me dad. Did I ever tell you how much you remind me of my father, Joshua? I think that's why I'm so fond of you.'

Joshua stepped back swiftly as if she'd hit out at him. 'Yes, boys have become fathers at fifteen,' he said stiffly, 'so I suppose that in a literal context I could be your father.' He raised a non-existent hat from his head in a mock salute. 'Goodnight, Daisy. Tomorrow is another day.'

The hurt was deep inside him as he slowly climbed the stairs to his room at the top of the tall house. It festered inside him as he pulled on his dressing-gown and sat in his chair listening to Chopin's *First Prelude* on his wireless with the sound turned low. He smoked his pipe till the air felt and smelled thick, but the music that night was of little comfort to his soul.

He woke to the sound of footsteps on the stairs and a frenzied knocking on a door. Out on the landing he bumped into Daisy struggling into a cotton kimono-type dressing-gown. She clutched at Joshua.

'It's the man in number four. He says he left the plug in his wash basin and the tap running.' She was already half-way down the stairs. 'Oh, no! Look at it! *Do* something, Joshua! Oh, my new carpets... they'll be ruined.'

'I can't tell you how sorry I am, Miss Bell.' The commercial traveller in number four slip-slapped his way towards them through the water soaking its way through the pile of the new landing carpet. 'I was so fast asleep, I didn't hear a sound.'

'The overflow must have been blocked.' His face grim, Joshua paddled out of the bedroom. 'Where's the fuse box?' He patted Daisy's arm as he sloshed his way to the top of the stairs. 'Don't panic now. Just leave it to me. We'll need candles and torches. I'll have to turn the electricity off at the master switch.'

'Candles and torches.... All right, Joshua.'

He could sense Daisy being determined to keep calm, but all the lights went out as they reached the hall together. 'What the 'ell's going on?' By the sound of things, Joshua realized, at least two of the men visitors had emerged from their rooms, ready and willing to help – he hoped. 'Good girl.' He took a torch from Daisy's outstretched hand and moved into the lounge.

'As I thought,' he muttered, shining the beam on a damp circular patch on the ceiling, dripping water down the light cord. 'It's not too bad in here,' he reassured Daisy. 'Bring me the washing-up bowl, love, then you'll need mops and buckets, and saucers for the candles. Don't say young Winnie's managing to sleep through all this?'

'She'd sleep through the Charge of the Light Brigade once she's got off.'

'Then let her be.' Joshua was half-way upstairs handing out candles to the men from number two and number three. 'Don't tell me the bloke responsible for this flood is back in bed?' He stared round in disbelief.

'He is, y'know.' Number two was using one of Daisy's good towels to mop up with, bending from the waist, sloshing it about in the water, twisting the Christy towel into a rope before squeezing the water into a chamber pot hastily snatched from the cupboard by the side of his bed. 'I've sent the missus back to bed; she's neither use nor ornament at the best of times, but would you credit that fella doing the same? Does he expect us to mop round him while he lies there like bloody King Canute?'

'Well, they say it takes all sorts.' Number three up-ended a candle into a saucer, letting the wax drip before he anchored the candle firmly. 'Right, gaffer. Let's be having me marching orders.'

'Just get as much water up as you can, as quick as you can.' Joshua's mind accepted that he was wearing his captain's hat once again as he issued orders, handed out jobs, urged and cajoled. Captain Penny of the East Lancashire Fusiliers, in charge of his men, liked and respected because he would not

357

ask them to do anything he would not willingly do himself.

In number four bedroom he glanced round at the tell-tale signs, the torch beam showing a waistcoat stained with yellow vomit over the back of a chair, an empty whisky bottle, an overflowing ashtray. His temper flared.

'Out of there, man!' Without ceremony Joshua whipped the blankets away. 'On your feet, there's work to be done.'

The man was a pitiful sight, but Joshua hardened his heart. He guessed how the poor devil felt, he could imagine the thousand demons pounding away in his head, but the careless blighter was *responsible* for this unholy mess! 'On your feet!' He waited none too patiently.

'I can't. If I bend over I'll be sick again. Oh, God, is it worth it? Is anything bloody worth it?'

One minute he was lying there, sick and sorry for himself; the next he was out of bed, gasping as his bare feet met the drenched carpet. Yet he had no firm recollection of the man standing there having touched him. Brown eyes blazed at him from a face as hard as granite.

'If you're sick use that.' Joshua thrust a bucket at him. 'But for now face up to things. We *know* it was an accident, but buckle to and help to put it right. At the double! D'you hear me?'

By four o'clock they had done what could be done. A shivering Daisy was ordered back to bed by Joshua. 'Do you want to be ill? Do you want to crack?' He steeled himself against her pleading expression. 'And change out of that nightgown. The hem's soaking.' His voice softened. 'I'll go down and make them a pot of tea, love. You can do your thanking later. They *wanted* to help.' He half smiled. 'All but your precious number four, though I soon had him sorted out.'

'They are my guests.' She was so tired the words came slurred.

Joshua shone the torch on to her feet, blue with cold and none too clean. Without giving himself time to think he scooped her up into his arms and carried her up to her room.

Kicking the door open he deposited her none too gently on her bed. 'Right! Are you going to take off that wet nightie, or do you want me to do it for you? That's what your dad would have done, isn't it, when you were a child? And if I remind you so much of him. . . .'

In the kitchen the four men leaned against whatever was handy and sipped hot sweet tea, as close as if they were life-long mates. Joshua had seen it happen many times in France. Catapult a group of strange men into a crisis and they end up closer than blood brothers. Number three passed round a battered packet of Woodbines, and it was like lifting a curtain on his memories. . . . Shadowed weary faces lit by flickering candleshine, the quiet murmur of voices, frozen hands held round steaming tin mugs.

Number two had been in the bloody battle of the Somme. Number three had lost an eye at Ypres. Only number four was too young to join in the reminiscing.

'The insurance?' Sitting down at the table, lingering behind when the other two had gone up to bed, he buried his face in his hands. 'Will Miss Bell be covered? It wasn't an act of God, was it?' He groaned. 'Nothing goes right for me. Not one bloody thing. I'm a walking disaster zone, that's me.'

'Want to talk about it?' Joshua sat down, facing him across the table. 'If you feel like talking I'm here, listening.'

It was an all-too-familiar story. Days of tramping the streets in first one town then another. Shopkeepers shaking their heads, some of them hardly sparing him the time of day. At the end of the week an empty order book and the threat of finding himself out of work yet again. A wife and two children at home. Behind with the rent on their new council house and behind with the payments on the three-piece suite and the clothing club. Cardboard in his shoes because it seemed a drink and a smoke was more of a necessity.

'The worst thing is knowing they're going to say no even before I open my case.' His voice breathed defeat.

'Is what you're trying to sell good quality? Value for money? Do you have faith in it?'

'Yes, oh yes. You won't get better writing paper nowhere.'

'Then let that faith *show*.' Joshua leaned forward. 'Have you heard of thought transference?'

'What's that? I wasn't much of a scholar, Sir. Book learning has always come hard to me.'

Joshua blinked at the 'Sir'. He drummed impatient fingers on Daisy's well-scrubbed table, weighing his words:

'I had a pal during the war who had managed to evade the school system almost entirely. He had a vocabulary of about ten words, nine of them filthy, but what he saw out there in France incensed him so much he came home determined to get his own back somehow. He talked his way into a job; he convinced his employer he knew more about timber than the poor bewildered chap had forgotten. He went to the public library of every town he visited and made lists of all the builders. By the force of his anger – because it was anger driving him on – he persuaded them they needed more wood than they would ever use. He didn't walk into their offices with his shoulders slumped, *knowing* they were going to say no. They'd been sitting on their fat behinds during the war while he'd been fighting that they might live, so he looked them straight in the eyes and....'

Joshua paused. This insignificant little tyke didn't look as if he'd ever stared his own mother straight in the eye, but he was taking it all in, nodding his head. 'I'm angry too.' He actually beat his puny chest. 'I wasn't in the war, but that wasn't my fault, and I deserve better. My *wife* deserves better.'

'Channel that anger in the right direction. Make it positive. Make it work for you.'

'You smug bastard.' Getting wearily into bed ten minutes later, Joshua closed his eyes. 'Playing God isn't a role you're much fitted for, *Captain* Penny! You're not making much of a success of your own life at the moment, are you?'

From along the landing he heard the muffled sound of coughing, fancied he heard Daisy turning over in bed.

He hoped she'd done as he told her and changed her wet nightgown; he told himself it was none of his business if she hadn't. He snuffed out his candle and reminded himself to go out and phone the joyful Mr Leadbetter before breakfast. And fell asleep with the sound of the west wind rattling his window frame, overwhelmed with weariness and the utter hopelessness of his love.

Chapter Ten

It took just two months for Daisy to realize that her infatuation for Sam was over.

It was unbelievable, *impossible* that during those long frustrated months of her loving she had looked in her mirror and seen a face with a dreamy abstracted expression gazing back at her. With lips half parted and eyes shining like the proverbial stars. All because of Sam.

Impossible to accept that she had actually prayed to God for a letter with a London postmark; trembled at his nearness, *wanted* him, with her body actually aching for the need of him. Walked by his side with the wind on her face, and not known that the wind was blowing. Remembered every single word he had said to her, storing even the mundane remarks away in her head like jewels in a box, giving them fresh meanings each time she took them out to mull over them. Read his horoscope before her own in the morning newspaper; seen his likeness round every corner, down every street.

Work had helped her get over him, of course. There was plenty of that. The NO VACANCIES sign had gone up again in the window of Shangri-La. Mrs Mac was genuinely amazed at the way little Miss Bell had coped with the routine of shopping, cooking and cleaning, with only Mrs Whalley's Winnie to help out. Mrs Mac was *pleased* for Daisy, of course, even though she was sure the reaction from her friend's suicide was bound to set in. And there was never a peep about that chap from London. Not as much as a word about him for weeks now. She told San Remo next door that Shangri-La's visitors got a bedtime drink with a homemade biscuit, all inclusive. San Remo sniffed and said that Shangri-La would learn to cut corners with the rest of them in the end, especially in the winter when the trade went dead.

Winnie was pleased that Daisy – they were on first-name terms by now – had gone out with Mr Penny for his nightly constitutional, leaving her to serve the bedtime tea and biscuits. She could have a crafty fag if she left the back door wide open, and a hefty slice of Daisy's richly moist slab cake. Not that she would be begrudged a crumb if she asked for it. Not being hungry all the time took a bit of getting used to; sleeping in a room of her own was taking even longer. Some nights she would lie awake on purpose, just for the novelty of being able to stretch her arms and legs out in bed as far as they would go without encountering a sister's backside, or sharp toenails.

Finishing the cigarette, she wrapped the stub up in a piece of newspaper and buried it deep in the pig bin outside the back door. No point in looking for trouble, even though Daisy had never actually *said* she didn't like Winnie smoking. A furtive fag tasted much better than one smoked openly, and anyroad the fag-end was the pig's problem now, not hers.

Joshua and Daisy walked towards the North Shore, through the alpine rock gardens with their artificial crags.

'Would you ever have imagined just after Florence died that you would be coping as well as you are?' Joshua turned to Daisy, walking serenely by his side, her hands thrust deep into the pockets of a long knitted cardigan.

'I couldn't have done it without you.' Her smile was warm and direct. 'You've been a pillar of strength, Joshua.'

'You won't *let* me do as much as I'd like to. I haven't done all that much.'

363

'You've *been there*, to hold my hand when things went wrong.' Her laugh was infectious. 'Like me trusting Winnie with the ledger, and her booking two honeymoon couples into the same room for the same week.'

'That could have been tricky, I admit.'

'Or the time a tap was left running in a wash basin and that commercial traveller didn't wake up till his bed was floating out of the door. The lights fused and everyone came out on the landing for a paddle at one o'clock in the morning. You were *marvellous* then, Joshua.'

'You'd have coped.' Joshua spoke so sharply that Daisy stared at him in surprise. 'You're what is called a tough cookie, as they say in American films.'

'I'd much rather be a fragile flower.'

Joshua pointed at an iron bench with its back towards the cliff drive. 'Let's sit here for a while. I want to talk to you.'

Daisy was quite content to sit quietly, waiting for Joshua to collect his thoughts. She knew him so well by now. Never an impetuous man, apart from that one time when he had drunk too much and kissed her passionately. She smiled at the memory. Joshua was a man of integrity. A true gentleman, as her mother would have said. Modest to a fault. It was only recently that she had picked up a letter from the mat addressed to Captain Penny, MC. He never used that form of address, he had said, taking the letter from her quickly. MCs were two a penny, he had said when she tried to talk to him about it, his eyes twinkling at the terrible pun.

It was a beautiful night, with a full moon sending silvered beams across the faintly murmuring sea far below. Such a perfect setting for what Joshua had to say, and he wasn't going to bungle it this time. Sitting close to her, filled with love for her, he reached for her hand. At once her fingers curled into his palm.

'How would it be if we got married?' he said.

Daisy stared at him for a while. 'I wish you hadn't said that, Joshua. I *love* you, but not in that way. I never want to

364

feel that way again.' She smiled. 'What I feel for you is the warmth of a loving friendship. I like you and admire you. I wish I had a quarter of your stability, your confidence, your belief in yourself.'

'Is that how you see me?' He sounded deflated, almost bitter, very sad.

'Yes, it is.' She hesitated. 'Since Sam I don't trust my own judgement. I feel *safe* now, you see. I'm no longer looking for admiration. I hate to even *think* about Sam. I am so angry with him for being the cause of me behaving so stupidly. He *humiliated* me, Joshua. He diminished me, and, maybe unfairly, I can't forgive him for that. It was self-inflicted, I know, but still I can't forgive him. I never want to hear from him or see him again. What I felt for Sam can't ever dissolve into friendship. I was weeping and laughing at the same time. I was either dizzy with happiness, or drowning in despair. I am never going to go through that again, Joshua.'

'And what about how I feel?' He was only human, so very much in love. 'I *want* you, Daisy. I want to touch you when you stand before me; when you laugh I want to hold you and be part of that laughter. I am a normal man, Daisy, and in spite of what you think, far from old enough to be your father!'

'Did I say that?'

'You did.'

She looked at him, at his strong profile, the firm set of his jaw, and knew in that moment how easy it would be to say yes and be married to this lovely man. Before Sam, she would have accepted his proposal without reservation, knowing that men like Joshua Penny didn't grow on trees. Her mother would have *adored* Joshua.

'I *do* love you.' She squeezed his hand. 'But not in the way a woman should love a man if they are going to....' The darkness hid her blush, but she could feel it warming her cheeks.

'Make love?' Joshua's voice was cold.

'Well, yes.'

'You mean I repel you physically?'

'Oh, no!' She turned to him in distress.

'But you had no objections to Sam. . . .'

Joshua wished the words unsaid, but it was too late. He had convinced himself he had forgotten Florence's hysterical betrayal of her friend's secret; he had closed his bedroom door quickly that night on the sight of Daisy creeping down the stairs in her nightgown. He had heard her come back when Jimmy cried out, and he had sworn that he would put both episodes firmly out of his mind.

'I *love* you, Daisy.' He tried to draw her to him and felt her stiffen before she jerked away. 'You've got me in such a turmoil I say the wrong thing. I'm *terrified* of you rejecting me. I vowed never to love again after my wife died. I would never risk such hurt, such pain. But I want you. You've shown me I can be happy again.' He pulled her down beside him when she tried to stand up. 'Daisy! Please listen to me. I want to marry you and *cherish* you. Can't you understand? I want you to bear our child.'

Daisy heard nothing more than the impassioned pleading in his voice. The words slid over her as she sat there feeling sick, choked with the shame of him finding out, of knowing about, of believing that she and Sam. . . .

'There was nothing! I didn't! We never. . . .' Ingrained guilt, the unbalanced sense of shame bred in her and carefully nurtured in her since childhood surfaced. If Joshua had accused her of murder she would have felt less ashamed, less embarrassed and humiliated. He probably thought now that she was – what was the phrase her mother had often used? – easy meat. If she were foolish enough to marry him he would throw it back in her face during their first tiff. Her mother had said men always did that. He would be jealous if she as much as joked with the coalman or asked the milkman in for a cup of tea. He would never *trust* her, never respect her no matter how much he tried to convince himself otherwise. She had heard it all so often it came out in her mind as pat as if she were reciting the Creed.

'Even if there was a . . .' she groped for the telling word
'. . . that kind of *spark* between us, Joshua, I wouldn't marry
you. You misjudge me, but that doesn't matter. I have only
myself to blame.'

'I blame you for *nothing!*' Joshua was growing more
exasperated by the minute. At himself for making such a hash
of things and at Daisy for thinking it mattered whether she
and Sam. . . . 'I *love* you,' was all he could say. 'For you as you
are.'

'Warts and all?' she asked coldly.

'Warts and all,' he said. 'No! That's not true. To me there
are no warts.' He rubbed his forehead with a clenched fist.
'What the hell are we talking about? I'm damned if I know.'

'I was refusing your proposal,' Daisy said stiffly, the shame
still on her.

'Then I would like to give you a month's notice to quit my
room.' Joshua took out his pipe and curved his hand round the
comfort of its rounded bowl. 'I had decided to go anyway.'

But not in anger like this, he thought, not with this stupid
misunderstanding between us. In a strangely paradoxical
way they were *too* honest with each other, too close, if that
were possible.

'I am only *human*,' he burst out, provoked by her silence. 'I
can't be with you every day, seeing you, living with you in
the same house. Not wanting you the way I do.'

'Then of course you must go,' Daisy said. She got up and
began to walk quickly away. 'Stay there and finish your pipe,
Joshua. I'd like to be by myself for a while.'

He made no attempt to follow her. What would have been
the use? Her temper was up. He could tell that by the way she
was wagging her bottom as she walked. Damn her! He knew
her so well, with an intimacy that went beyond friendship.
Far, far beyond that. Couldn't she see?

He puffed ferociously at his pipe, then knocked it out on
the iron bench. He walked without slackening speed all the
way along the promenade to South Shore, oblivious to the

wide sweep of the night-blue sky above him and the soft murmur of the sea on the sands below. He walked like a man with a purpose, who knew where he was going, when in reality the truth was he was going nowhere at all.

'Mr Penny has every right to move. To *better* himself,' Daisy told Winnie the day after Joshua had moved his belongings out of Shangri-La. 'That room of his is very cramped, you know, and the place he's going to is more of a *flat*. With his own kitchen and sitting room.'

The cat was scratching to be let in, and when Winnie opened the door he shot straight up the stairs making, they knew, for Joshua's empty room.

'It's half of a headmistress's house, isn't it?' Winnie was wearing her know-all expression. 'Mrs Mac told me mam he's been friendly with that teacher for years. They're much of an age, and of course they'll have a lot in common.' The end of a pink tongue protruded as she grated bread on to a board. 'Mrs Mac says she's not a bit like an old maid. Smart. You know. With a lovely slim figure. Mrs Mac knows the woman who does her washing. She says Miss Halliwell never wears a vest, not even in winter, and that all her nighties have lace on them. She gets them from Affleck and Brown's in Manchester.'

'Is there *anything* Mrs Mac doesn't know?' Daisy was flushed and unaccountably furious. 'Why do people always expect a hot meal when there's a heatwave going on outside?' Sliding a roasting tin of sizzling fat from the oven, she emptied a pan of par-boiled potatoes into it. 'They'd turn up their noses at a nice green salad and a plate of cold ham and hard-boiled eggs.'

'Bet you wish I'd told you that Miss Halliwell was boss-eyed and bandy-legged, don't you?' Winnie's expression was sly. 'But I cannot tell a lie.'

'Mr Penny came straight here to live the week after his wife's funeral,' Mrs Mac told Daisy. 'They had a little house, but he

368

wanted nothing from it. Gave a lot of good stuff to the Salvation Army by all accounts. He was proper poorly, Mrs Entwistle used to tell me, but he never missed a day off work.' She tapped her front. 'Chest. Lungs filled with mustard gas during the war. They're never the same; it can work its way through the system years afterwards. So it's nice he's got a little place of his own after all this time.' She fanned her hot face with her apron. 'This flamin' job of ours is three months' hard labour and nine months' solitary confinement. My ankles are up like balloons again with this heat. She's a nice lady,' she went on, 'this headmistress he's living with. I expect you met her when you had young Jimmy here? She was head of his school.'

'Of the Juniors, not the Infants. No, I never met her.' But I know she has lace on her knickers, Daisy thought, whipping a tin of evaporated milk into a half-set jelly to have with ice cream for dessert that day. 'I'm glad Mr Penny is settled,' she said firmly. 'I only wish I could say the same for Mr Schofield. I heard from him the other day to say he won't be coming back here when he comes out of prison. He's asked me to pack his things ready for collection. It's obvious he can't face coming back here.'

'It's a disease,' Mrs Mac said. 'So they *say*. Like drinking too much.' She got up to go. 'Not in my book it isn't. Light-fingered greediness. *Thieving*. Why don't they give it to them straight? The same with alcoholics. Weak-willed ninnies, that's all they are. They'll be making excuses for murderers next, saying it's all right to kill your mother if she never tucked you in and kissed you goodnight when you were a child. The same with adulterers. . . .' She was warming to her subject. 'They can always say no. I'd sit down if I were you,' she told Daisy. 'I'd say you were having a hot flush if I didn't know you were too young to be having an early change. I'm giving my lot pineapple chunks tonight, out of a tin. You'll live and learn. That's if you haven't worked yourself into an early grave through being over-conscientious.'

'And the best of luck to you, too,' Daisy said underneath

her breath. 'With a friend like you, dear Mrs Mac, I'll never want for an enemy, that's for sure.'

In August Daisy put Winnie's wages up to a pound a week, with her keep. The wash basins in the bedrooms and the separate tables in the dining room had lent 'tone' to Shangri-La. Most of her bookings now were from personal recommendation.

'Mrs Mac is talking about having wash basins put in her best bedrooms,' Winnie told Daisy with glee. 'She knows she'll have to do something if she wants to keep up with us. You're feeling all right, aren't you, Daisy?' Her thin pointed face was suddenly sharp with worry. 'Mrs Mac told me mam she thinks you're wearing yourself to a frazzle. She thinks you're pining for that chap from London.'

'Which one was that?' Daisy flipped a double sheet over to Winnie's side of the bed they were changing. 'We'll miss the laundry man if we don't look sharp. C'mon, love. Get your skates on.'

There were days, and this was one of them, when Daisy was so overworked, so rushed, she felt she would meet herself coming back if she wasn't careful. Winnie was a joy and a treasure, there was no doubt about that, but she never worked from her own initiative. Daisy knew she had to spell things out for her, sometimes *show* her how to do the simplest tasks, over and over again.

Could a person *die* of tiredness, she asked herself seriously as she carried the sheets down into the kitchen and folded them into the laundry basket. And now she had to find the time to give the stairs a good brush-down before doing the shopping. A woman to do the rough, that would be the answer, a good woman in a sacking pinny with arms on her like ham shanks. At times she'd been tempted to advertise, then caution stepped in. Everything had cost so much more than she and Uncle Arnold had reckoned on it doing, and the insurance for cleaning the carpets after the flood hadn't come through yet. Daisy ran upstairs with the dustpan and a stiff

370

handbrush. But for Joshua taking the whole thing in hand, she might not have been promised a penny. There was a tenacity to Joshua she'd never suspected.

There was half Blackpool's beach trodden into her stair carpet, lurking behind the stair-rods and settling in the corners. Oh dear God, but she was on her knees, figuratively as well as literally. Daisy blew a strand of hair out of her eyes and thought longingly of a dip in the sea.

There was still the shopping to do. She ran over in her mind the list for the day. The basic groceries were delivered twice a week, thank goodness for small mercies, but any landlady worth her salt knew the importance of carrying on a personal relationship with her butcher. Almost like a love affair really. She had planned on mince that day, but only freshly made from best stewing steak. Daisy knew she was good at chatting and laughing with the red-faced butcher, but supervising the way he fed the meat into the mincer at the same time. Not a lump of fat or gristle would go through if Daisy kept her eyes skinned. There was a determined jutting of her chin as she planned the menus for the next few days.

A nice piece of top-side, she thought, for a special treat for Sunday, and for Saturday brisket pressed into the big basin to have with salad and potato cakes as the weather had turned so warm. The sweat was running into her eyes and her back ached with nagging persistence. Reminding her of Florence and how she had suffered once a month.

Daisy rested for a moment. Florence, Bobbie, Jimmy and Joshua. And Sam. All gone from her, leaving her alone. With too much to do; far too much to do. Last night she had been exhausted past the point of sleep, tossed and turned for ages, then wakened up tired.

She was in what she privately called one of her 'bring on the violins' moods. Sorry for herself and sickening with it. Zasu Pitts, the tearful comedienne with her drooping jowls, Greta Garbo in *Camille*, dying beautifully and taking her time about it. Daisy lengthened her face into mock misery, rolling her eyes and groaning at the same time.

371

'Daisy! What's the matter?' Winnie's pointed mousy face was on a level with her own as she stared anxiously through the banister rails. 'You're not ill, are you?'

'Not ill.' Daisy's eyes were twinkling again. 'Just sick to my very soul with life and its vicissitudes.'

'Aw, them,' said Winnie. 'I never have no truck with them.'

'Wise,' said Daisy. 'Very wise.' She began brushing away at the carpet again. 'Ah well, KBO I suppose.'

'KBO?'

'Keep buggering on,' said Daisy, dead-pan.

At the end of August Daisy received a letter from Sam. There was no lifting of her heart when she recognized his writing on the envelope, no frantic urge to open it and read what he had to say over and over again. The anger in her had gone; the disbelief that she could ever have felt such agony of mind *remained*.

Sam wrote to tell her that he had found just the job he had hoped for, as assistant to the engineering manager of a large road transport company in North London. At a salary of £500 a year. He had underlined this, and Daisy could just imagine him saying it with an impudent grin and a lift of an eyebrow. He was back with Aileen, and it looked as though the bad times were behind them. At least he hoped so. Daisy turned over a page. The children were spending a couple of weeks in Suffolk with Queenie and having a whale of a time with the weather being so lovely. There was no way he could find adequate words to thank her for all her kindness. There was a corner of his heart kept specially for her, and he hoped she was able to find a little time to enjoy this wonderful sunshine. He remained, hers with affection, Sam.

Daisy put the letter at the back of her dressing-table drawer, behind her stockings, took it out again, tore it across and threw it away.

Joshua kept in touch with her too, but not by letter. He called round twice and found her in the kitchen both times, doing three things at once, as usual.

'You look well.' Daisy said it quietly, carrying on with what she was doing.

'You look tired,' he told her, refusing to sit down, standing stiff and serious by the door with his arms folded and his expression stern.

She wanted to weep. For some inexplicable reason she wanted to go to him and have him put his arms around her to feel his gentleness, and his strength. His presence made her feel so vulnerable she wished he would go and leave her alone. Yet when he went she never knew how the sound of a door closing could hurt so much.

It was only natural she should be missing him. He had been so dependable, so loyal a friend. He had talked to her each night after Winnie had gone to bed as she waited in the kitchen half asleep for the last of the visitors to go up to bed. At least, *she* had talked most of the time and he had listened. There was a great and comforting stillness about Joshua, a wisdom, a towering compassion. He had outward control, where she had none. He was free to be always himself, where she was still bound to the values set for her by her mother. Joshua controlled his own thoughts; hers had been taught and ingrained in her from a puritanical childhood.

Why was she seeing all this so clearly now? Daisy drooped over the big account ledger lying open before her on the kitchen table.

How could she have been so close to Joshua and not known how much she loved him? How could she have wasted all that tearing emotion, that *anguish* on Sam, who had never loved her at all?

'If there is ever anything I can do to help you. . . .' Joshua had said the second time he came. In the lounge one of the week's visitors was playing the piano badly. Two small boys, up far too late, were using the new brown settee as a trampoline, shrieking and bouncing with joy. Joshua raised his voice slightly. 'You know where I am if you need me.'

She would remember, Daisy told him. And if Winnie had not come into the kitchen at that moment she would have gone to him in utter humility, begging his forgiveness for hurting him with thoughtless, childish words on the night he had asked her to marry him.

How clever he was at knowing just the right moment to walk away. Smiling at Winnie and sketching the familiar salute at Daisy, he turned and left the house. In complete command of the situation, leaving her feeling empty and bereft. Knowing instinctively that she must give herself this time of waiting before she went to him.

As a late summer slid into a windy winter, Blackpool was lit up for a continuous six miles along the promenade by over three hundred and seventy-five thousand lamps. They were massed, looped and garlanded along and across the full width of the wide sea road. On a clear night the glow in the sky could be seen from the Isle of Man.

Shangri-La was bursting at the seams. Daisy had even found two 'regulars' for the vacant rooms on the top floor. One, a red-faced Irishman working on the last extension of the promenade, and the other an under-gardener at Stanley Park. They were both much-married men, hating the separation from their wives and families, but appreciating Daisy's cooking to such an extent she found their lavish praise almost an embarrassment.

She knew that after the Illuminations finished in October there was bound to be a lull before Christmas, and had already drafted an advertisement offering half board, good home cooking and constant hot water for reasonable terms.

And in the meantime the biggest spectacle of all was in full swing.

In the last week of the Illuminations Daisy wrote a brief note to Joshua asking him to meet her. Not at the house where they were likely to be disturbed, but by Central Pier, she suggested. At nine o'clock, which would be about the time he took his nightly constitutional.

Another thing her mother had taught her was that a girl never ran after a man. That it must be left to *him* to make the advances; that if she was foolish enough or fast enough to do the chasing, his respect for her would vanish.

'You are still trying to please your mother,' Florence had said. 'Even though she is dead.'

'I need to see you,' Daisy wrote defiantly. 'We must talk. There are things I have to say.'

The first thing she saw when she left the darkened streets behind and turned on to the promenade was the Tower, outlined in brilliant lights zipping up one side and down the other, its summit shining with glowing colours like the imperial crown. For a moment, a child again, Daisy held her breath in wonder. The crowded promenade was a seething mass of excited voices, moving along from one set piece to another, rapt faces glimpsed first in blazing light then in shadow.

A tram-car disguised as a Venetian gondola swayed its graceful way along the promenade. An outline of an aeroplane in twinkling diamond lights dipped its shining wings over the kiosks of Central Pier, where Joshua waited for her.

'Joshua?'

He looked different. That was the first thing she noticed. Hatless for one thing, his thick brown hair unruly from the wind. *Wilder* looking than she had ever seen him, the opposite of his usual quietly courteous self.

'Daisy.' He took her hands in his, trying to read her expression. 'Your letter had me worried. Is something wrong?'

She shook her head, trying hard not to smile, and failing. 'There is nothing wrong, Joshua. I just wanted to see you, that was all.'

'But why here?' He nodded at the tightly packed crowd,

375

snail-paced as if they moved on a slow conveyor belt. 'Why not at the house?'

'Because the house is filled with strangers; because Winnie is in the kitchen making bedtime drinks for the children, eating twice as many biscuits as she puts out on the plate. Because I haven't seen the Illuminations since I was a little girl, and I wanted to see them with you.'

They looked at each other for a long time, then walked on in silence, Daisy's hand tucked into his arm in a way that could have meant everything or nothing at all. From the top of the winking glittering Tower a searchlight swooped across the shadowy sea, over the town's grey houses and round and beyond over the wide flat countryside with its darkened fields and meadows.

Now it was Daisy's turn to be afraid. He was so unlike his usual self, so visibly anxious. When she moved her hand down his arm and squeezed his hand, there was no response, no answering pressure. She glanced at him and saw the way his eyes looked troubled and wary. In that moment the glory of the lights dimmed, the whole panorama turned tawdry and cheap. Even without her glasses she could faintly see the wire frames behind the elaborate set-pieces and blinking, winking, gaudy tableaux.

Her thoughts were unbearable. *She* had stopped loving Sam. Why then had she taken it for granted that *Joshua* would go on loving *her*? She had hurt him so much, loving Sam so *visibly*. How could Joshua be expected to believe that she had changed, stopped dreaming, faced reality? And grown up at last.

Could it be that he had fallen in love with the lace-trimmed Miss Halliwell whose house he shared? Was he wondering now how to let Daisy down easily, not wanting to hurt her because she was his friend? His *friend*, that was all.

Her heart filled with darkness. Her footsteps flagged.

The themes outlined in twinkling lights meant nothing to her now. Cinderella's glass coach had golden wheels, revolving perpetually, but going nowhere. Further on the

Babes in the Wood slept beneath scintillating emerald-hued trees, with fluttering red-breasted robins scattering red and yellow leaves which seemed to melt away even as they touched the ground.

As they walked along the sea-front shimmering canals flowed alongside them with Dutch girls in winged caps bowling sparkling hoops along the banks. Fairies, elves, and gnomes pranced and pirouetted among rainbow-coloured herbaceous borders, while further on towards the north riders in hunting pink urged horses over gates which appeared and disappeared out of the surrounding gloom.

It was beautiful and it was terrible. The whole of Blackpool, it seemed to Daisy, illuminated with brightly coloured lights, hundreds of thousands of them. The miles of concrete promenade, the three piers stretching jewelled fingers out into the invisible sea, and the Tower etched against the night sky by the lights zipping up one side of it and down the other.

She stopped walking, forcing Joshua to turn and face her.

'Joshua ... dear Joshua ... Listen to me. I have something to tell you.'

'You are back with Sam,' he said at once. 'He has left his wife again and is going to marry you. Your silence has told me, and I am too selfish to be glad for you. We have seen the lights together now, so shall we go home?'

Slowly and deliberately Daisy began to unbutton his brown tweed overcoat, opening it so she could get close to him, unbuttoning her own to get even closer.

'I love you,' she whispered as his arms came round her. 'I am about to do a shameless thing, Joshua Penny. Something that would make my mother revolve in her grave. I am going to ask you to marry me. I am *chasing* you, being forward, *asking* for you to lose your respect for me. I want to cook for you, bear your children for you. Come home again, Joshua.'

His mouth tasted of the wind and sea salt. Their first slow kisses were tender, sweet and brief, lips touching, parting slightly, lingering, a slow throb of mounting mutual desire.

Stepping back into the shadows Joshua tightened his arms round her. This time his mouth on hers was gentle at first, then deliberate, searing her with longing, so that when he let her go she clung to him, weak with want of him.

'No *spark*?' His eyes teased her. 'None of that feeling a woman should have for a man when she wants him to make love to her?'

'Oh, Joshua, I love you so much that beside the passion burning in me all the lights of the Illuminations are just a candle flame.' She laughed up at him. 'Will that do?'

'To be going on with,' said Joshua.